Marked "Personal"

Marked "Personal"

Anna Katharine Green

MINT EDITIONS

Marked "Personal" was first published in 1898.

This edition published by Mint Editions 2021.

ISBN 9781513280554 | E-ISBN 9781513285573

Published by Mint Editions®

 **MINT
EDITIONS**

minteditionbooks.com

Publishing Director: Jennifer Newens
Design & Production: Rachel Lopez Metzger
Project Manager: Micaela Clark
Typesetting: Westchester Publishing Services

Contents

PART I

A DRAMA WITHIN A DRAMA

I

The Statesman and the Student

On the evening of July 13, 1863, two men left their homes, one in Washington and one in Buffalo, under circumstances strangely similar.

Each had received a letter in the morning mail, which he had quickly destroyed. Each had given evidence of strong and increasing agitation during the rest of the day, and each had taken leave of his family with tokens of increased inward excitement, which the mere fact of his being summoned to New York on some unknown business did not seem to warrant, notwithstanding the fact that a dangerous riot was just at that time making a battle-ground of the metropolis, and threatening the safety of citizen and stranger.

Samuel White was at once a retired broker and an incipient statesman. His means were large—or so those who knew him best were wont to say—but he made no display of wealth, and lived in a quiet, unostentatious way which seemed contrary to an evidently ambitious and luxury-loving nature. But the times were troublous, and for one living in Washington, and involved more or less in the affairs of the nation, it was certainly more seemly to curb tastes which in a brighter era of our history might have merited a proper indulgence. Still his manner of life had invited gossip, and many frequenters of his home had been heard to say at this time, that they were sure that there was some hidden and imperative reason for the restraint he placed upon himself, other than the public one just alluded to.

He had an invalid wife, but she did not like seclusion or meagre and inadequate apartments any more than he did, nor was the character of his only child one which would develop best under cramped conditions. Why, then, did he allow his money to gather interest in a bank, (he who was no miser,) while those he loved lacked luxuries, and he himself that wide and public exercise of power which seemed native to his talents and disposition?

It was a question often mooted and never answered. It was a question which his wife once ventured to put to him, but was so met by a look of profound emotion on his part, that she recalled her words as soon as they were spoken, and, with a wife's loving anxiety to appear always trustful, covered up her confusion and his by a kiss, in which he felt no diminution of the perfect confidence she had always reposed in him. Yet there was a faint wavering in her wifely trust, though no one ever knew it, and when on the 12th of July she perceived this same look reappear in his face, and remain there all day, she was conscious of a great and unreasoning premonition of coming disaster, which was quite different from the feeling with which she had contemplated from time to time the possibility of his raising a regiment and entering the war in an active capacity. The dread which she had suffered then was the common shrinking of an affectionate heart from a separation which might end in death; but the terror which influenced her now was a nameless one, growing out of the discovery of something unknown in one she had hitherto thought she knew well—a something so unknown that she found herself unable to define her very fears, and so disturbing and suggestive in its character, that against her own will it caused her to take up the past and survey it again with changed heart and questioning eyes.

She had always known Samuel White. They had been reared in the same country town, and were playmates before they were lovers. When he went West to make his fortune, she had remained at home to plan for their union, and dream of their future happiness together; and when he returned (ah, how the old days came back as she thought of them!) she had not waited to hear whether the fortune had been made, before holding out her arms in a glad welcome to the wanderer. The fortune had been made, and she soon heard of it. But now that she forced her mind to dwell upon those hours, she remembered that there was something strange in their meeting, after all; that although he had manifested love for her, he had also manifested a reluctance to accept her affection, and that what to her inexperienced mind had seemed timidity, now showed to her riper judgment to have been a distinct shrinking from the solemn responsibilities of wedded life. Yet had he married her, and made her a good—nay, more, a devoted husband. No jealousy had ever found footing in her breast, though he possessed that species of good looks which irresistibly attract women and provoke their attention. She had been conscious of but one keen disappointment in the years that had since passed., In vain had she hoped that he would give his ambition wing, and let his talents have more scope. She would have so enjoyed his success. She would have found such solace for her own physical sufferings and disabilities in the excitement of watching him rise step by step up the political ladder. She was so sure he merited a lofty place in the nation's councils, even at this time of great men and tremendous issues. He had the breadth of character which fits large places. And he loved power, loved work. Why, then, had he shrunk from both, doing what he did in a secret and shame-faced way, utterly inconsistent with his general character? She had wondered often, and, as I have said before, had even questioned him once about it; but she had never weighed the matter as she did now, or sought as she did on this day of secret agitations, for a solution of the mystery which involved her peace of mind if it did not his.

They had been married eleven years, five of which had been spent in New York, and the remainder in Washington. In the former place he had been actively engaged in the brokerage business; but on removing to Washington he had given this up and gone into politics, but in such a quiet, almost clandestine way, that, while his influence was felt, his name was rarely heard, and his person seldom if ever seen outside of his own home or the private committee room. Lately, this shrinking from the public eye had grown upon him, and was the reason, doubtless, why he dallied with his opportunities of obtaining distinction as a soldier. She found it impossible to fix the time when she first saw a look of dread on his face; but the effects of the letter he received on the 13th of July were so great that she knew, from the moment of his receiving it, that the climax of his unknown trouble had been reached, and that she had but to stretch out her hand and take from him the slip of white paper which he held, to learn the cause of the many inconsistencies that had so long baffled her.

But she did not make a move toward him, though if she had been asked if she had done so, she would have said *yes;* and the next moment it was too late, for he had torn the letter into shreds and had walked away to the other end of the room. There he stood gazing helplessly into space till she came within sight of his dull eyes, when he stretched out his hand as if to beg her not to speak, and staggered quickly from the room. When she saw him an hour or so later, he had become more composed, and told her that he had received a letter necessitating an immediate departure to New York, and begged her to send for Stanhope, their son, as he wished to see him before he went. This demand staggered her, for Stanhope was several miles away, at a school in Georgetown; but presently remembering that there were great disturbances in New York, she endeavored to attribute his wish to say good-by to the lad, to a natural anxiety as to the result of his visit in a city so mob-ridden. But her heart told her that no fear of this kind would affect a man of so much nerve as he possessed; and moved to speak, if only to hide her own doubts of his intentions, she asked him if his business would detain him long.

His answer should have reassured her, but it did not, nor did his manner through the remainder of the day. Though she saw him but a few minutes at a time, he being for the most part busy at his desk, she perceived, through all his efforts at naturalness, a strained anxiety and an almost unbearable grief, that at last drove her to fall at his feet and cry out in anguish:

"What is the matter, Samuel? What is taking you away so suddenly? Public business, or some personal affair that should be known to me as well as to you?"

For a moment he did not answer; then he said in a way to prevent further questions on her part:

"My business in New York is personal. If it were well for you to know its nature, I should not withhold my confidence from you." Then, as he encountered her hurt look, he sweetened his words with an embrace that was so clinging and passionate she was startled. "Remember," he added impressively, "that I have always loved you;" and walked away before she could recover herself.

"I will wait till Stanhope comes," thought she. "He will find out what troubles his father, or at least why he takes a journey to New York just at this time."

But the coming of Stanhope only complicated matters. Instead of summoning the boy to his presence, Mr. White seemed to shrink from seeing his child, and remained at his desk till it was almost time to take the train. Then he came down to where he was, and placing the lad between his knees tried to talk, but failed, and recognizing his failure, bowed his head for a moment over the child, and then, putting him aside, rose hurriedly and grasped his hat to depart.

"I shall do what I have to do, to-morrow night," said he, in an odd, unnatural voice, to the mother who stood waiting with one hand held out as if to stay him. "The next day you will hear from me, and on the following I shall probably be home again,"

And so he was, but not in the way he had evidently expected.

Lemuel Phillips of Buffalo, who also on this day received a letter summoning him to New York, which he as instantly destroyed, and as instantly acted upon, was a very different man from the one whom we have just attempted to present to our reader. In place of being large and imposing, he was slight and meagre; yet there was an individuality in his finely cut features, that made him an interesting spectacle to thoughtful eyes, though whether the charm was that of heaven or hell it would have been difficult to decide even after much consideration. In age he was about forty; but, from a certain stoop his shoulders had acquired, he looked to those who followed him in the street like a man twenty years older. His alert eye, and sensitive, ever-working mouth never deceived those, however, who met him full in the face; nor were there any signs of failing strength in his quick, sliding walk—the walk some said of a man who felt himself followed and was always trying to escape. The looks he cast behind him at intervals favored this notion; and had he not been well known as a respectable citizen and honest man, he might have had some disagreeable experiences just from this very cause. As it was, he was simply denominated eccentric by his equals, and "queer" by the boys, who often imitated him behind his back.

He lived in an unpretentious house on the west side, and employed himself in study, though upon what topic few knew and fewer cared. For he too eschewed publicity, and cherished in his own bosom whatever ambitions he may have possessed. Though not without means, as his comfortable way of living plainly showed, and not without public spirit, as was evinced by certain charities secretly bestowed, he, like Mr. White of Washington, was never to be found in public places or where large numbers of men were to be seen together. He kept to his own fireside; and, to those persons who caught a glimpse of him there, was always something of a mystery; for even in his own house his restless eyes were ever flashing over his shoulder, as if he feared the intrusion of some unwelcome step across the door-sill. Was it a habit, this constant watchfulness? It might have been, and one of which he himself was unaware. Yet, from the fact that his little child, a tiny, fairy-like girl, had learned the trick of saying before she entered a room, "It is I, father!" I judge that his peculiarity was known and recognized both by himself and the members of his family. If so, this greeting of hers was a touching tribute to his weakness, the tone of the little one being ever one of reassurance.

He had lived in Buffalo three years. When he came there he was alone; afterward he sent to some unknown place for his child, who was then an infant in arms. He said that he had been a widower five months. Of his wife herself, or of the life he had led previous to coming to this city, he never spoke. Yet he always had the confidence of people, perhaps because his tastes were so studious, and his love for his child so manifestly sincere and engrossing.

Had people seen yet a little closer into his life, I doubt, however, if this confidence would have held good. A man who starts at every sound, and visibly shrinks from turning a corner, must harbor some secret terror in his soul; and when, as in this case, the terror grows to culmination in the hours of a single day, there is evidence certainly of some mystery in his past worthy of investigation.

The day that saw this feeling at its height was the 12th of July, 1863. For a month he had not been even his usual anxious and nervous self. His idiosyncrasies had become more pronounced, and if there had been any one near him who loved him well enough to note his manner there would have been found evidences of dread in it over and above those which had been habitual to him. On the night of the 12th he did not even retire, but sat up in his study sorting papers with a very trembling hand. When morning came, and with it the postman, he was so agitated he could hardly take the letter brought to him by the one faithful woman who cared for his wants; and when, having opened this letter, he read the solitary line it contained, the suppressed cry he gave would have frightened his little girl, had she been so unhappy as to have been awake at that hour.

As it was, the little thing saw that something was very wrong when she came bounding down to breakfast an hour later; and, being as yet too young to reason, she clambered up into her father's lap and commenced to give him a series of kisses which seemed absolutely to paralyze him.

Putting her down, he rushed into the kitchen where Abigail Simmons was at work, and taking the good woman by the arm he gasped forth:

"You have promised to be always kind to the child, you remember."

Startled, the woman turned about and looked at him.

"How you do flurry one!" she cried. "Of course I shall always be kind to the little pet."

"But if she should be left alone! If anything happened to me—"

"Are you sick?" she broke in. "Is anything the matter?"

"No; but I am going to New York," he returned, dropping his eyes. "I have never left her for a night alone since she came to me three years ago, and I dread some evil. May I rely on you to be a—a mother to her if I do not come back?"

"She is all I have to love in the world," said the good woman, simply, but with a very sharp look at him which happily he did not see.

"You relieve me," he rejoined, and was about going away when she stopped him.

"Is it the riots you are afraid of?" she asked.

He looked blankly at her. I doubt if he heard what she said.

"I should be afraid of them myself," she remarked; but she kept her eye on him, for all that, and continued to look in his direction long after he had left the room.

Could she have seen what went on in his study after his return to it, she would not have contented herself by gazing after him: she would have followed him back into the child's presence.

The little one was sitting at the breakfast-table when he went in, and was as merry as a healthy, happy-hearted child could be. Her blonde curls danced with the tossing of her little head, and her silvery voice filled the room with musical chatter. As he saw her sweet face, and caught the gleeful accents he so dearly loved, he seemed to shrink into himself, and, looking and listening, grew visibly older from moment to moment, till the child herself might have been startled had she turned her gay little head in his direction. But she was used to silence on her father's part, and never thought to look around: so the blithesome chatter went on at the table, while over the face of the old young man behind her, the gray shadow deepened as some fearful purpose formed itself in his mind, and lent its horror to the glance of his eye and the movements of his ever restless hands.

"Papa, deary, how do you spell 'fortunate'?" piped out the little one, holding up a big ripe pear which had been laid at her plate.

"F-o-r," he began, seeming to feel himself forced to speak, "t-u-" (he was crossing the room to his desk) "n-a-t-e," he finished, laying his hand on a little drawer at one side of the desk with a look such as may it never be our lot to see on a human face.

His tone, which he had tried to make natural, was so far from it that instinctively she looked around.

"Why don't you come to breakfast?" she asked, half petulantly. "I can't keep the pear much longer. Something in me makes me eat it up."

Instantly his hand fell from the drawer, and he stood still, trembling and not daring to meet her innocent brown eyes.

"Come!" she cried imperatively, and pointed to his chair like a little queen giving commands. "I want company. I don't like sitting all alone."

His lips, which had been shaking like one smitten with a chill, began to part again in a repetition of his former speech. "F-o-r," he muttered blankly, and reached out to the drawer again, this time opening it and taking out a small phial.

"I know how to spell that word now," she responded with superior calmness. "F-o-r-t-u—"

He was standing behind her now. His lips were of the color of clay, and his forehead was dripping with sweat

"Let me have your cup of milk," he whispered hoarsely.

She tossed back her head and looked at him wonderingly. He took the cup, held the phial over it, then gave a great shriek and tossed it far away from him to the other side of the room.

"I cannot," he cried out aloud, and staggered back to his desk, where he fell into his seat, giving vent to sobs he made no effort to restrain.

She was really frightened now, and got down from her own chair and stood gazing at him for a minute with big eyes and blanching cheeks, then she ran out to Abigail. Did she know how near the death-angel had been to her in those last few minutes? I think not, for in five minutes her listening father heard her voice laughing again in a merriment from which all trace of fear had departed.

II

31 Amity Street, July 14, 1863

It was seven o'clock in the evening. Though it was by no means dark, New York City had been subject on this day to so many outrages, that more than one house was already closed for the night. In the old street called Amity, this was especially noticeable. Wherever there were negroes there was alarm, and in this quarter there were at this time many negroes employed in the various old dwellings stretching between Sixth Avenue and Broadway.

There was one house, however, which if closed was brilliantly lighted. This was the occasion of much remark in the neighborhood, for till within a day or two the place had been empty, and, beyond the fact that a large negro had been seen fastening the shutters and lighting the gas, nothing was known of its occupants. It was one of those old houses common in this district, with low stoop, flanked by wrought-iron posts of quaintly forged work. A balcony ran along the front of the parlor windows, and over the door was a half-oval glazing, through which the hall light shone invitingly. Two dormer windows at the top completed the picture, which was common enough at that time, but which is fast disappearing from our ever changing and constantly remodeled streets.

But the curiosity which had been raised by this sudden occupancy of an empty house soon gave way to an alarm which made this and many other things forgotten. For the rumor had entered the street of a coming mob, and already in the far distance the ominous sound was heard of treading feet and clamoring voices, which, to those who have ever listened to the roar of maddened men, is so much worse than that of beasts, or of that element to which it is sometimes likened—an angry sea. But as yet the noise was distant, and the street quiet, almost unoccupied. So much the more distinctly were two men to be observed who at this moment appeared at the two ends of the block on which this house was situated. One was finely formed and handsome, with a blond mustache and melancholy eyes, which seemed fixed in an anxious stare, as he hurriedly walked along. The other was spare, and bent about the shoulders, but with an expression so baffling that it would have made his face remembered if any one had been there to see it. Both were unencumbered, and walked like persons driven by some other will than their own. In front of the house I have already mentioned, they stopped. Both had advanced with lifted eyes gazing straight before them, but not till they thus paused did they appear to see each other. Then the shock which passed through both was instantaneous. Each opened his lips to speak, and each closed them again without uttering a word. But they bowed like persons moved by some strong, sympathetic impulse, and, glancing hurriedly at the number of the house before which they stood, moved mechanically toward the door, the larger man giving place to the slighter.

Once on the stoop, they looked again at each other, and both stretched out their hands to the bell. But there was hesitancy in the mutual action, and both hands fell again. "You have changed," ventured the younger man in a low tone to his companion.

The other did not answer. He was trembling visibly. "I have not your courage," came finally from his lips.

His companion started and nervously jerked at the bell. "Let us have it over," said he; then, as he heard an advancing step within, whispered rapidly, "Have you made arrangements for secrecy? Have you a family?"

"Come in, sirs," invited an unctuous voice from behind. "You are from Washington, are you not, and you from Buffalo? All right, sirs, the gentleman is expecting you."

The door had opened, and in the gap stood the large, smiling, and excessively courteous negro, over whose identity the neighborhood had been speculating for the last twenty-four hours.

The two gentlemen, different as they were in both personal and mental characteristics, gave a similar start as they were thus addressed; and each, without paying further heed to the other, cast a peculiar and not easily explainable look at the sky, and at the street below them, like men who felt themselves parting forever with the world and all that there is in it.

If they heard the low rumbling of the approaching mob, they did not show it. Other fears were at work in their breasts; and not from without this house, but from within, sprang the cause of dread under which both seemed laboring.

After that one look—to all appearance one of farewell—they passed in, and the negro closed the door behind them.

He was a very affable, well-bred servant. Taking their hats from their unresisting hands, he ushered them into the large front room at the right.

"The gentleman will be here soon," he assured them, and softly withdrew.

The two men paused in the doorway and looked anxiously about them. Evidently the well-spread table upon which their eyes first fell was a surprise to them. Advancing involuntarily toward it, the larger man, whom we have already recognized as Mr. White, pointed to the chairs about it, and uttered in significant tones the one word:

"Three!"

The other, who was strangely like the Mr. Phillips of Buffalo, whom we know, gave a slight shudder and advanced in turn to the table, about which he began slowly to pace, eying as he did so the various articles of service with which it was loaded, with a fascinated gaze, that was not without its element of wonder.

"He intends that we shall eat with him," he finally observed.

"A course dinner," continued the other, with a significant gesture toward the cluster of glasses standing beside each plate.

"I am not hungry," protested the student, shrinking back. "This farce unnerves me. I had rather have found nothing in the room but two—"

He stopped, glanced again at the table, and darting forward, lifted the cover from a dish which stood directly in front of one of the plates. "I thought so," he continued, staggering back.

Mr. White, paling a trifle, lifted in his turn the cover from a similar dish standing in front of another plate, and after a short look gently replaced it.

"The man has been studying comedy in Paris," he remarked. Then, after a moment, "You see, there are but two covered dishes."

The other, with a wild look, stretched out his hand to the dish he had so boldly uncovered. A small pistol was lying on the bottom, cocked and ready for use.

"Let us have it over," he cried, clutching his weapon in frantic haste.

But his companion protested. "No," said be, "the line I received said eight o'clock. It yet lacks fifteen minutes to that hour." And he pointed to the clock which stood beating out the moments on the mantelshelf.

"Fifteen minutes? Fifteen eternities!" gasped the other. But he let the pistol fall back into the dish and moved back, while Mr. White quietly replaced the cover.

"We are certainly expected to dine," observed the latter, "but we can decline the honor." And a silence came over them which was both solemn and pregnant.

It was broken by the reentrance of the negro bearing some bottles of champagne. His imperturbable face and deferential manner seemed to irritate Mr. White beyond endurance.

"Did you set this table?" he asked, with harsh demand.

"I did, sir."

"All of it?"

"Certainly, sir."

Mr. White interrogated him no further. There was nothing but respect in the even tones of the negro, nothing but the mild surprise of the disciplined servant in the eyes that were neither withdrawn nor dropped before Mr. White's searching gaze.

"My master must be here very soon now," the man added, with a short glance at the clock, and again bowed himself out.

Mr. Phillips started from the fireplace where he had been standing during this short colloquy.

"You asked me," he said, addressing Mr. White in eager hurry, "if I had a family. I have one child—a daughter—young—merry—motherless. . . For her sake—"

The other's hand went up in protest. There could not be much speech between these men. But the next moment he was holding out a *carte de visite* which he had taken from his breast-pocket. "I have an invalid wife, and—this," he faltered, in an odd, muffled tone.

Mr. Phillips took the card from the other's hand and glanced at it.

"A boy!" he cried, almost as if startled. A lightning flash seemed to pass between the two; then Mr. White said, almost in a whisper:

"He is only ten, but I understand now: that is why I am so submissive."

Mr. Phillips's slight form shook, but he did not offer to return the picture. It seemed to charm him and hold his thoughts in check through all the excitement under which he was laboring.

"Noble! Beautiful!" he exclaimed, devouring the photograph in his hand with a growing wistfulness.

The father gave a sigh which seemed to rend his heart. "I do not know his equal," cried he, and took the picture from his companion's reluctant hand.

He did not venture to look at it himself, but put it back carefully over his heart. Mr. Phillips, watching him, seemed about to speak, when the noises, which had been rapidly increasing in the street without, rose to such a violent pitch that they were obliged at last to hear them, despite their absorption.

"What is that?" demanded Mr. Phillips, wonderingly, but with no especial interest.

He was answered by the negro, who at that moment entered.

"Do not be alarmed, gentlemen," he anxiously entreated. "There is a slight disturbance in the street, outside. Colored people are at a discount just now, and I think the mob has heard of me."

Amazed, in spite of his own profound preoccupation, at the ease and quiet assurance of the man who thus announced his own danger in the most correct and mellifluous English, Mr. White was about to ask if the mob did not mean mischief, when Mr. Phillips's voice rose in ringing tones:

"The mob! The rioters! Are they coming here?" And he glanced at the table in sudden hopefulness.

"They are in the street," answered the negro, with unwavering calmness. "But there are two dwelling-houses employing negroes between us and the corner, which means two short fights, or, if the police come up in time, two sufficiently long ones to enable you gentlemen—to—to finish your dinner."

The significance and suavity with which this latter clause was uttered brought the hue of anger to Mr. White's cheek, but it seemed to awake different emotions in the breast of Mr. Phillips, as was shown by the wondering question he put to the negro.

"Are you not afraid?" he asked. "These rioters, I hear, stop at nothing."

"I am only concerned about one thing," returned the man. "My master expected to come by the way of Sixth Avenue. If he does, he may fall into the crowd, and so not be able to keep his appointment."

The start given by Mr. Phillips at this, and the no less eloquent change of color on Mr. White's part, may have been observed by the speaker; but, if so, he gave no evidence of it in his manner.

"These windows had better remain barred," he suggested, pointing to the front of the house. "But, if you please, I will go up another flight and look out." And seeming to take it for granted that their agitated silence meant consent, he left the room and proceeded softly to the floor above.

Left alone, the two men stood for a moment without movement. Then Mr. White observed in a constrained tone:

"The tool is as much to be feared as the hand wielding it. This is no common serving-man. If he whom we dread fails to appear, there will still be a witness left."

"But the mob is shouting, 'Death to the negroes!' If a diversion occurs—we still have five minutes left—who knows what may happen to release us?"

There was the quick, ringing tone of hope in his voice. For the last minute he had been a different man.

Mr. White, who had shown but little change in manner, quietly shook his head.

"Would we not still be bound by our oath?"

The other, startled and shocked, drew slowly back with dilating eyes.

"Is that the way you look at it?" he asked. "If yonder man should be hurt—killed, say,—would you still—"

He stopped, trembling; the negro had slid again with velvety tread into the room.

"It looks bad," he gravely remarked. "Though it is too dark for me to see plainly, I can hear stones flying in all directions, and not a few groans and cries. Somebody is being hurt."

"And where are the rioters now?"

"In front of a gentleman's house lower down the block."

Here an unusually loud yell came through the uproar.

"They have battered in the door," commented the negro, imperturbably. "That will delay them a few minutes."

Neither of the gentlemen spoke; they were looking at the clock, it was on the verge of eight. Suddenly Mr. Phillips moved and excitedly remarked, with a side glance at the negro:

"If your master is not here at the hour he appointed I shall consider myself at liberty to leave the house."

"He will be here," was the quiet response, with the simple qualification added, "if he is alive."

"But," triumphantly began the other as the first stroke of the clock sounded, "it is already eight, and—"

His voice ceased, his forehead fell, and his whole frame suddenly collapsed. A short, sharp ringing at the door-bell had proclaimed that some one stood on the stoop outside.

"You see," observed the negro, with a deferential bow, "my master is a man of his word."

He went to open the door, and while he was gone the two men, without a glance at each other, mechanically approached the table and took their places behind the chairs evidently intended for them. To see them standing there, pale, absorbed, statue-like, the one with lifted head and determined aspect, the other with chin fallen on his breast in a gloomy despair he made no attempt to hide, one would not have dreamed that within a few rods of them a work of demolition was going on amid a rattling of musket shots, crashing stones, and demoniac yells.

And for them there was at this moment no outside tumult or overthrow. All the disturbance present was within their own breasts, and if death were near, its breath came not to them from the midst of the mob.

Had the rafters cracked over their heads they would scarcely have looked up.

The opening of the door behind them they did hear, however; at the sound, both men stretched out their hands to the covered dishes before them, but neither spoke and neither turned. A minute of silence followed, then a voice spoke in tones so unexpected that they both wheeled suddenly about, only to again confront the negro.

"I am sorry, gentlemen," said he, "but my master cannot get here. He has just sent a street urchin to say he is detained by the mob in which he has become entangled, and begs you to wait a few minutes till he can free himself. The dinner shall not suffer, gentlemen. I shall see to that myself."

"No doubt," screamed Phillips, angrily, "but one loses appetite after the hour is passed. I shall have to beg to be excused."

"It would not be safe for you to leave the house," remarked the negro, calmly. "Bullets fly about freely at such a time."

"Have you a weapon yourself?" asked Mr. White, suddenly, stepping up quickly to the table.

"Two," answered the negro, drawing his hands from behind his back.

"I see," remarked the other, quietly retreating again. "We had better wait for our host," he suggested to Mr. Phillips with a sigh.

The negro smiled; neither noted it. It might have been better if they had.

III

Passions Manifold

And now there arose from without such an infernal din, that if these three men had wished to talk they would have found it difficult. Drunk with success, the mob was on its way down the street, hooting and yelling, while crashing panes and women's shrieks marked its progress. In a few minutes more they would be in front. Suddenly there came a second ring at the door-bell. This time the negro paused before opening it.

"That is not my master's ring," he declared, and laid his ear against the panels of the door.

In an instant he started back. Thundering knocks were shaking the wood against which he leaned.

"Open!" came in harsh demand from without. "We see your lights! Let us have the negro and we won't stop."

A hundred voices took up the echo. "The nigger! The nigger! Let us have the nigger!"

The rioters were upon them. Mr. White and Mr. Phillips, standing side by side in the adjoining parlor, mingled their glances, and Mr. White reached up his hand toward the chandelier. But the negro, entering hurriedly, made him a motion and his hand fell back.

"Don't, gentlemen," he pleaded, coming very near and shouting to them, for the noise was deafening. "You are not afraid of the mob, nor am I. Wait a moment longer for my master, and if he does not come—" He paused, listened, and suddenly raised his hand again. "Hush!" he seemed to say and quickly passed again into the hall, this time toward the back of the house.

"What shall we do?" said Mr. Phillips appealingly to Mr. White, as they were left alone. "I had rather face those demons," he declared, pointing toward the front of the house which was already being assailed by stones and bullets, "than meet the man."

"We have no choice," shouted back Mr. White. "To be sure, if the mob forces its way in, we cannot help ourselves. But the house is strong, and I think I heard a volley just then, as if the militia were coming."

Mr. Phillips shook his head and looked eagerly at the door. The key was gone from the lock. "We might unbar the windows," he appeared to signify by the gesture he made.

Mr. White frowned. Mr. Phillips, dropping his head, moved timidly toward the front of the house. A splinter of wood flew to meet him; it came from one of the shutters that had just been crushed in.

"The nigger! the nigger!" rang through the gap, in startling distinctness.

Mr. Phillips, dizzy, maddened almost by conflicting fears, shrank back and peered wildly about. Suddenly he darted toward the table, and dashing aside the cover from the dish he had previously opened, he reached for the pistol within, hoarsely shrieking, "I will sell my life; I will not throw it away! Come, White, let us fight them with their own weapons!"

But a grasp of iron falling on his wrist made him look around. It was the negro who stood calmly over him, shaking his head, and holding before his eyes a slip of soiled paper on which some words seemed to have been hurriedly scrawled.

"From my master," shouted the man, between the clamorous blows that were now shaking the doors and windows alike.

Mr. Phillips stared, but could read nothing. Mr. White took the paper, and managed after a few minutes' study to make out these words:

"Hurt—dying—tell gentlemen to go.

D.

A flush, red as the blood which was being spilled so near them, swept up over Mr. White's pale face. He trembled, and for the moment looked weaker in his relief than he had during the worst moments of his late suspense.

"We are released, pardoned, told to go," he shrieked in Mr. Phillips's straining ear. "The man is dying, and it has opened his heart to pity."

The cry the other gave was shriller than any which came from without.

"Let us fly, then," he shrieked. "Life! Life! I shall know you again—see my little one—"

But the leap he gave toward the door was cut short. The consciousness of the pandemonium holding revel on the other side of it deterred him. There was no escape by that road. He looked helplessly at the negro.

This man, thus appealed to, bowed low with all of his old deference. Then, turning, he beckoned them both toward the rear.

"There is a ladder leaning against the further fence of the yard," he confided to them, as soon as they had reached a spot where their voices could be more readily heard. "I had it placed there for my own escape, but it is at your service."

Mr. White, putting his hand in his pocket, looked at the negro. "Where is the man who brought this scrawl?" he asked.

"Gone. He came by the back yard, and has gone by it."

"And your master—where is he?"

"Lying on the floor of a drinking saloon around the corner. He was just breathing his last when the man came away. A stone had hit his chest and broken in his ribs. Otherwise," the negro added, with an odd return to his former smooth and significant manner, "he would not have failed of entertaining you at dinner."

Mr. White, with a muttered oath, gave the man one rebuking stare and then seemed to forget him.

"Come!" he cried to Mr. Phillips, in the ringing tone of a great relief, and bounded down the half dozen steps he saw before him into the back yard.

Mr. Phillips, hastily passing the negro, followed joyfully; but, as he did so, a sudden cessation of the noises in front made him look back. It was an unfortunate glance; for, by means of two mirrors hanging on opposite walls, he caught an unexpected glimpse into a room they had not entered, and in that room he discerned a man whose countenance he knew, though he had not seen it before in twelve years.

It was that of their long-expected and redoubtable host, and so far from showing injury or death, wore not only the hue of health, but an expression of diabolical triumph as at the success of some well-planned game.

Paralyzed at this sudden shock given to his hopes, Lemuel Phillips paused. The negro, unsuspicious of what he had seen, thought that his agitation was occasioned by his fears of the mob, and hastened to explain that the police had shown themselves at the corner, and that the rioters were now flying toward Broadway. At which information, the spell of the other's terror was broken, and throwing back his head he burst into a loud laugh and cried:—.

"Then I will fly, too!" And dashing after Mr. White, he disappeared into the yard just as the lights went out in the house behind him.

For some reason he never told his companion what had been revealed to him by that one backward glance.

PART II

AN IMPERATIVE MANDATE

IV

A Gap in the Feast

On the afternoon of September 20, 1878, two men were taking down an awning in front of the Collegiate Church on Fifth Avenue. There had been a large wedding there in the morning. One of the foremost men in New York had been married to a young and beautiful girl, and the crowd which had attended the ceremony had been so great that the neighboring sidewalks had been blocked with people who had not been able to gain admittance to the church. All of these persons had disappeared. But in their stead was another crowd of hustling, jostling people, whose excited looks, turned toward the church entrance, betokened some new and unusual interest connected with the spot, to which the taking down of the awning seemed to give fresh spur.

From the words that were dropped here and there, we may learn what this interest was.

Such phrases as, "Killed!" "Not five hours married!" "A man with millions, who came near being run for governor last fall," showed that the wedding which had gone off with so much *éclat* that morning had been followed by a violent death, presumably that of the bridegroom.

A gentleman, young, dashing, and with an air of festivity about him, was passing in a carriage. Seeing the crowd, he leaned out with curiosity on his face, and hearing possibly some one or more of these phrases I have just quoted, he thrust his head forward in sudden agitation and asked the man nearest him what the matter was. The answer came back briefly, and with all the shock of unexpected news.

"Samuel White is dead, sir. Shot, as he was about to leave the house with his bride. Here is where they were married this morning."

The young man sank back in his carriage as if he had been shot himself. All traces of the wine he had been drinking passed from his face, and in the pallor which followed, could be read the signs of a great emotion. Leaning out again, he glanced rapidly up the street. Another crowd was collected before a house on the upper corner; and, seeing it, he seemed to have no further doubt of the truth of what he had heard. Calling to the coachman, who seemed himself dazed by what he had heard, he bade him drive on, and, as the carriage moved slowly ahead, dropped his face into his hands with a quick shudder, which as rapidly gave way to a wild impatience.

"You go too slow," he shouted through the front window to the bewildered man in front. "They are in trouble; they may need me; hurry up, and stop as near the house as you can."

The swish of the whip answered him. The carriage rolled on more rapidly, but a few minutes later came to a sudden stand. Jack Hollister looked impatiently out. They were not far from the curb, on which a policeman was standing.

"No use, sir," that person was saying. "Mr. White has been shot, and the house is closed to guests; you had better drive back."

"Wait, wait! I am a friend—an intimate of the family. Mr. White—the son, I mean—will want to see me. I will give you five dollars to get me in." And he hurriedly stepped from the carriage.

The policeman, after a brief survey of the young man, turned and confronted the crowd. "I am afraid it can't be done," said he, "but I will try."

In five minutes the five dollars were in his hand, and Mr. Hollister in the vestibule of Mr. White's house.

A detective confronted him.

"What is your business, sir?" he asked.

"I am a friend of the family. I want to see Mr. Stanhope White. Here is my card; let some one take it up."

The detective beckoned to a man who was waiting near.

"Is young Mr. White willing to see any one?"

The man, who was an old servant of the family, glanced at Mr. Hollister and started forward.

"I think he will see this gentleman," he declared, and opening the parlor door he ushered him in.

Mr. Hollister, who under a light, almost dilettante manner possessed sensibilities of the keenest nature, flushed as he crossed the threshold. Though the shutters were closed, sufficient light sifted through their cracks to make the place seem bright after the close darkness of the hall; and whether it was that the quick glance of the persons seated about disconcerted him, or whether the odor of the wedding flowers which pervaded the whole atmosphere brought too sudden a sense of the funeral blossoms which must soon take their places here on mantelpiece and table, he staggered for an instant before he sat down. But emotion was natural under the circumstances, and no one noticed it.

A man he knew sat near him. It was Dr. Forsyth, the family physician. Meeting his eyes, Jack rose hurriedly and seated himself beside him.

"What is this dreadful thing which has occurred?" he asked. "Mr. White shot? Who shot him? It is all a terrible mystery to me."

"And to every one," returned the other. "He was in his bed-room, making, as every one thought, his final preparations for leaving with his bride, when a pistol shot was heard. Mrs. White who was in the front room, and Stanhope who was on the floor above, both rushed at the sound, and found him lying on the floor, with the pistol smoking at his side."

"Then he killed himself. I thought—"

"Hush! It was an accident. He was probably putting the pistol into his bag, when by some careless handling it went off. The discharge passed through his heart. It is a startling end to a prosperous career."

"And—and—the bride?"

"Is prostrated, of course. Such a grand man! But the loss which the country must sustain is of the greater moment. He would have filled the governor's chair, had he lived."

Mr. Hollister was growing uneasy.

"Where is Stanhope?" he asked. "I thought it probable he would see me."

"I do not think he desires to see any one. I have been here an hour and a half—ever since the fatal affair occurred, indeed—and no one has been allowed to go up-stairs but Mrs. Hastings. It is very soon, you know, and even I feel myself more or less of an intruder."

But Stanhope did want to see his friend, and a few minutes later Jack found himself passing on tip-toe up-stairs, around the balustrade of which still clung the smilax wreaths which had been placed there in honor of the bride. The sickening odor of the great bouquets followed him.

At the head of the stairs he paused, to collect his courage possibly, and then hastily passed on in the butler's wake. As he did so, he heard a voice, and paused again. A door was opening before him, and from it was stepping a middle-aged lady, clad in the gorgeous attire of a wedding guest. She was speaking, and there was something in her tone—was it a secret complacence?—that caused the dark flush to reappear on Mr. Hollister's impressionable cheek.

"Do not give way, my dear child," she was saying with motherly impressiveness. "After I have seen your father, I will return. You must not be left alone at this terrible time."

The faint murmur which came in answer from behind the half-closed door was in feminine tones, and betrayed the fact that it was the bereaved wife she had been addressing. Mr. Hollister, placing himself close against the wall, let the mother go by without a word, though he knew her well. She, on her part, was so engaged in plucking up with careful hand her voluminous draperies, that she did not even see him. He heard her murmur some words about her carriage as she passed him, and that was all. The door at his side gently closed, and all was still again.

"Will you come up now, sir?" asked the butler from the stair above.

Mr. Hollister started, and hastily advanced. As he passed the door which had just shut, he cast a glance at it. What was in that glance? No common emotion, it is evident.

Stanhope was in his own room, and greeted Jack with eager warmth.

"I did not know what I wanted," said he; "it was you."

Jack, flattered as he always was by his friend's preference, shook the other's hand and endeavored to utter some well-meant phrases of condolence, but failed. There was that in Stanhope's manner which cut short such efforts. For emotion like this, Jack had no words. That the emotion was not the simple one of shock, or even of bereavement, did not make the moment any easier for Jack. Dropping his eyes from his friend's face, he waited for Stanhope to speak first.

Stanhope White had fulfilled the promise of his childhood. He possessed a face and figure calculated not only to arouse instant admiration, but to awaken likewise sentiments of the utmost confidence. No one surveying for the first time his handsome features could doubt for a moment that their attractiveness sprang largely from the earnest, candid, and generous nature that informed them. Men liked his straightforwardness of character, women his chivalrous deference to themselves, and children his gay laugh and brotherly tenderness. A conqueror from his birth, it had taken a wise mother's most careful attention to keep under the egotism which usually springs to meet an almost universal admiration.

But her efforts had been rewarded, and at twenty-five years of age Stanhope White was a man whose claims upon your attention lay deeper than any given by perfection of features, or the charms of address and bearing. In disposition he was cheerful, and it was a rare thing to see him without a smile upon his lips.

This was why Jack Hollister felt himself in the presence of a stranger on this fatal afternoon. To behold gloom upon that face was a revelation;

and, though nothing could rob it of its sweetness, there were strange lines about the mouth and eyes, which would have to be studied to make the face seem familiar again. Then the restlessness in his manner! What did it mean? Jack wished his friend would speak, and relieve him from a tension of feeling that unnerved him.

Finally he did. But the words were unexpected and somewhat startling.

"Jack, you are a lawyer, and have a keen eye and quick understanding when you wish to use them. I have something for you to do, if you feel like giving me any help at this time. Are you willing? It will require caution and self-control. Can you muster them? I am well-nigh powerless from the shock myself."

"If you need me, here I am," answered Jack, promptly, but with a slight inward shrinking he happily concealed. He could not imagine what Stanhope wanted, and hesitated to ask any questions even of himself.

Stanhope, with a sudden relief of manner, passed to the door and locked it; then he came back and sat down in front of Jack on the broad divan, upon which the latter had so often seen him lying outstretched in the delicious reverie born of youthful hopes and the curling wreaths of a cigar.

"Jack," he earnestly began. "there is something more terrible than death in this house."

Jack started, and a deep flush rose to his face and spread a haze over his eyes.

"What!" he stammered, "has—has—she—"

The grasp with which Stanhope seized his hand was painful.

"I mean," explained the latter, "that there is doubt here. The accident which robbed my father of his life—Was it an accident, Jack? To be sure of it, I would give the millions that have so unhappily fallen to me. Nay, more—I would give my life."

Jack, astounded and greatly disturbed, stared at his friend in a secret dismay which threw all his own thoughts into tumult.

"I do not understand," he protested; "I thought your father loved Miss Hast—What makes you think it was not an accident?" he demanded.

"I—cannot—tell you—Jack. That is why it is so difficult for me to get help. No one but you can give it to me, for every one else would insist upon my reasons."

More and more moved by some strong internal agitation, Jack rose, but as precipitately reseated himself.

"What can I do?" he asked. "Tell me, and I will make what endeavor I can."

"Go to the room. See him. See everything. Be my second self, and draw your own conclusions. They think—all think—that the pistol went off inadvertently. But what did he want of a pistol on a wedding tour; and if he had wanted it, was he, my father, the man to handle it carelessly?"

"No; no—and yet men in a state of agitation—"

"True, true! and he was agitated—has been agitated all day!"

"Have been known to meet with such accidents. I cannot conceive of it being anything else, Stanhope. With such a bride, such a son, such a position—a man would be mad—"

"Or secretly very wretched."

Jack, with his two hands gripping hard the arms of the chair in which he sat, stammered as he inquired:

"And was your father wretched?"

"I have never thought so," answered Stanhope. "But we never know what goes on in the hearts of those who are nearest to us."

Jack, shifting uneasily, dropped his own eyes.

"No," returned he. "But we usually see evidences."

"He was not himself, to-day."

"No?"

"Not since the ceremony."

"I did not observe,"

"No one observed it; but I know my father."

"And—and—"

"I cannot tell you any more. If you can tell me, sometime, that there is no doubt—you have no doubt—that my father was the victim of a mistake, you will make me the happiest man on earth. That is all I have to say now, except to pray that you will not desert me. Stay with me till this is all over. I am weak as a woman, and I want your support."

Jack looked embarrassed.

"We are not alone in the house," said he. "I saw Mrs. Hastings below. She does not like me. I had rather not remain here; it might prove disagreeable to her."

"I had forgotten Mrs. Hastings. I wish you would, too. Stay with me, Jack. We will not trouble the ladies."

"Well, we'll see," said Jack, turning away. Unlocking the door, he stood ready to go out. "Will it be necessary for me," he somewhat reluctantly asked, "to have any conversation with Mrs. White?"

"Mrs.— Oh, no, no. Do not disturb her, Jack; her grief is great enough without having her mind disturbed by any such suspicion as I have mentioned to you."

"Of course, of course. I will go down, then; and bear up, old fellow; everything now depends on you." The stern line taken by Stanhope's lip showed that he realized this only too well.

V

On the Scene

Jack did not like the duty which had been imposed upon him; but he was naturally loyal, and he had no thought of refusing to do anything which Stanhope might demand. There was hesitation, however, in his step as he descended the stairs, and he seemed to have the same difficulty in passing the door, at the foot, which he had shown in going up.

A *posse* of gentlemen were standing in the lower hall. As he reached the passageway leading to the rooms formerly occupied by Stanhope's father, he heard them coming slowly up. At the same moment the butler appeared on the back stairs, and, seeing Jack, said imploringly:

"It's the coroner and his jury, sir. They have been asking for Mr. Stanhope. Shall I fetch him?"

"I will do that," answered Jack, and immediately returned to the room above.

"It's too bad," he exclaimed, as his friend opened the door, "but the coroner is here, and I am afraid you will have to go down."

Stanhope, turning pale, glanced down at his clothes, which naturally were the same he had worn at the wedding. "What shall I have to say?" he asked, tearing away the faded rose which still clung to his buttonhole.

"Answer their questions, that is all. You are not called upon to utter any surmises, fears, or doubts. I do not think your suspicions are shared by any one in the house. Do not, then, be the one to awaken them."

"I will not. The honor and happiness of his young widow must be considered, as well as my own. Go on, Jack."

And they proceeded at once to the rooms below.

The body of Mr. White had been lifted from the floor, and now lay upon the bed. As they entered the room, the twelve men stood about it; but these soon drew back, leaving the fine figure and regular features of the deceased in full view. Stanhope could not control his feelings at the sight. Samuel White had been a good father, and the void made in his son's breast by his unhappy death was deep and never to be filled. At the sudden moan of grief he uttered, all the men present bowed their heads; but in a few minutes the necessities of the hour brought restraint, and such questions were put as were suggested by the appearance of the room, and the position in which the dead man had been found by his son, and such others as had entered immediately after.

From these appearances, and the other facts connected with the case, the conclusion of accident was so evident, that the jury saw small reason for delaying their verdict. It was, therefore, given upon the spot, to the immense relief of Stanhope, and, I do not hesitate to say, of Jack Hollister also. As the various figures, large, small, tall, short, fleshy, and angular, shuffled from the room, the latter drew a deep breath and seized Stanhope by the hand.

"Now, all will be easy," said he. "No suspicion will be raised by any questions *I* may ask. Go to your room. I want to chatter with Felix."

With a grateful look Stanhope prepared to obey; but, as he stepped into the hall, the door in front (the door of which I have already more than once spoken) opened softly, and he drew as suddenly back.

"Go with me," he said to Jack. "With these doubts in my mind I cannot risk an interview with Mrs. White. She might read my thoughts, and that would bring wretchedness."

Jack, with a searching look at his friend, did as he was bid. As they passed down the hall they heard the sound of eager breathing before them, and Jack espied the tip of a little boot projecting beyond the threshold. Summoning up his courage, which seemed rapidly on the wane, he at once addressed himself to Stanhope in some commonplace phrase; at which utterance the little boot quickly disappeared, and the door which had been held partly open softly closed, till the snapping of the lock announced that all danger from interruption in that quarter was, for the moment, safely over.

Stanhope gladly passed on his way up-stairs, and Jack went back to the rooms he had left.

The facts he had gleaned from the inquest were very simple. Mr. White and his bride had gone immediately from the church to her father's house, where a short reception had been held. Thence they had driven here, it being a notion of Mr. White to introduce her to her future home before proceeding on their journey south. Accordingly, upon reaching the house, he had taken her through the various apartments, till they reached the boudoir on the second floor, where he had left her to rest while he went to make the final preparations for their departure.

These took him to his bedroom, which was at the rear of the house on this same floor. To reach this room, one was obliged to go through a small study, where, in the days of his widowerhood, he had been accustomed to carry on his correspondence and receive such men as he did not wish to meet in the drawing-room. This latter room, or ante-chamber as it might be called, jutted out some few feet into the hall just beyond the main staircase, and, small as it was, contained two doors besides the one opening into the bedroom. One faced the front of the house, and formed the usual means of entrance for the members of the family; the other was at right angles to it, and led into a narrow, rear hall, connecting with a back staircase used chiefly by the servants. Adjoining this, and opposite to the door leading to the front, was the one opening into the bedroom, and in the middle of the floor, facing this latter, was the table at which his work was done, and where he was usually to be found seated when not in the library below. This fact of a rear entrance, noticed by Jack, seemed to have attracted no attention at the inquest; and the reason undoubtedly was that there had been no evidence connecting that back staircase with the shooting, which every circumstance, so far as known, showed to have been purely accidental.

As I have previously stated, this had taken place in the bedroom, whither Mr. White had gone almost immediately after leaving his bride. His trunk, which he had packed before the ceremony, stood ready strapped, on one side, and only the open bag resting on it proclaimed that his preparations for departure had not been quite complete. His form, outstretched on the floor at the foot of the trunk, was clad in the same garments he had worn to church; and from the fact given by Felix, who had entered the room behind Mrs. White and Stanhope, that the keys dangling from the bag were swinging slowly to and fro, it was evident that Mr. White's hand had been in contact with the bag when he fell. The jury, after surveying the situation, had drawn the conclusion that Mr. White had been putting the pistol into the bag, when it went off; but Jack asked himself, as he looked the same scene over in the company of the respectful Felix, if Mr. White could not have been taking it from the bag at that fatal moment, though the latter would look like intention, while the former pointed solely to inadvertence. That there should be a pistol at all in the case, and that it should be one which had never been seen before by any member of the family, might mean much and might mean little. What did mean much to Jack, though it had seemed to have had little weight with the hastily formed jury, was the fact that a man of so much experience as Mr. White should have endeavored to pack a weapon at full cock. Yet there might have been some obscure reason for even such a piece of carelessness as this, and till he knew that Stanhope had been right in his fears that his father had not been as happy on this day as the occasion seemed to warrant, he would believe that it was in his attempt to rectify this dangerous oversight that Mr. White had taken the pistol into his hand.

For it was dreadful, horrible to Jack Hollister to entertain the least suspicion of suicide on the part of Mr. White. It caused his cheeks to whiten, and the hair to rise on his forehead, merely to contemplate such a possibility; and had he not given his promise to Stanhope, he would have been ready to take the conclusions of the jury as his own, and have accepted without query the verdict which they had given of accidental death.

For Jack's instincts, if not his practices, were invariably noble and unselfish, and there were reasons—reasons which he shrank from remembering—why it would rouse nothing but wretchedness in him to find that his friend's suspicions were true. Yet there was no faltering in Jack, and after seeing for himself all that there was to see, he beckoned Felix from the room, and with a show of shallow curiosity, which hid the deep and real interest which he felt, ventured to ask where were the letters which Mr. White was said to have written before his marriage.

"Oh, sir, mailed long ago. The footman took them; I saw him go out of the basement door with them before the gentlemen went to church."

Jack wondered if the footman had read the addresses on those letters before he put them into the box.

"The poor young bride!" Jack now exclaimed with an effort known only to himself. "It is a sad ending to her hopes."

"It is, sir," acquiesced Felix, heartily. "I never saw a lady so overcome. When she came into the room and saw what had occurred" (this was what Jack wished to hear), "she gave one shriek and then cowered down as if some heavy weight had fallen on her head. But she has grit, sir, and the true spirit; for, when she saw that her husband was really dead, she grew quieter and put a constraint upon herself, so that we have been let do what we thought best, without any hindrance from her. Oh, she's a fine and beautiful lady, sir, and would have done Mr. White great credit! I hope she will stay as the missus here."

Jack with an easier feeling left the old servant to the duties that were pressing upon him, and went to the drawing-room to think. Open evidence there could never be that Mr. White had meditated the death that had overtaken him; but what could not the young wife tell if she chose to speak? That she suspected a deeper tragedy in this matter than was apparent to the outside world, seemed evident to him; and yet, as he remembered her at the altar, she had shown nothing but what he had then considered to be a chill self-possession, not unmixed with complacency.

"The face and figure of a proud woman," thought he, "conscious of wearing a fortune on her head in lace and diamonds. How I hated the sight! How much more I admired her at the reception, when there seemed to be some feeling in her heart, some tremor in the daintily gloved hand she stretched out to the friends who crowded about her." He had not been quite himself at that reception (he blushed as he thought of it), but his wits had not been so clouded that he could not recall the looks of the bridal couple as they stood at the end of the long room. There was a sweetness in her face which had both pleased and angered him at the time, and, now that he thought of it, he had detected her more than once steal short glances at her husband which had something deeper than curiosity in them. And that husband? Had he been quite natural? It was hard to tell. A man under such circumstances, even when going through them for the second time, is apt to show some loss of self-possession; and Mr. White, if he betrayed any feeling at all, did so by the extreme quietness of his manner rather than by any undue excitement. Yet the Mr. White of the bridal ceremony was not the Mr. White even of the evening before. Some change, subtle but deep, had passed over him; and it was on account of this change, perhaps, that Stanhope had drawn the conclusions he had confided to Jack.

But had it been a change great enough to warrant a belief of premeditated suicide on the part of this successful and highly honored man? No; not in Jack's judgment, at least. Such an intention in the heart of a man, at a moment acknowledged to be the happiest in life, would have plowed deep traces even in so composed and courageous a countenance as that of this great public leader. No man could have stood thus with a young and lovely bride at his side, and thought of death, without a shudder which would have affected his whole bearing and drawn the attention even of the gay throng which surrounded them. No: Stanhope had been mistaken; some petty anxiety, some secret hitch in his business interests or in his political aspirations, may have drawn a shadow over his spirits, but nothing serious, nothing breathing with life or death.

And yet something in the temper of his own mind, some latent instinct of heroism perhaps, told him that a great despair often brought great calmness; and that if Mr. White had received some heavy shock, affecting his whole present and future happiness, there might have come with it sufficient strength to steady his outer man, however much it may have broken his inner spirit.

Moved by doubts to which meditation gave no answer, Jack left the drawing-room to return to Stanhope. As he passed into the hall, a man who was standing at the front door made him a short bow. It was the footman of the establishment. Jack, with a sudden recollection of the letters which this man had mailed during the morning, paused and in his own good-humored, somewhat careless way addressed him. Peter, sensible of the honor, replied with great freedom, and in five minutes, after some very delicate manipulation, Jack was so happy as to learn that Peter had not read the names of the persons to whom Mr. White had written, for the very good reason that he could not read writing.

Had this been in Mr. White's mind when he summoned him, instead of Felix, to execute this little commission for him?

VI

The Bride

S tanhope welcomed his friend as eagerly as if hours instead of minutes had passed since he last saw him.

"Well?" he demanded, with a haggard inquiry in his eyes that made Jack's heart sink like lead into his bosom.

"I don't know what to say. I have learned nothing that would seem to give color to your doubts; and yet something in the air, some emanation from your own fears perhaps, has made me feel that it was well for us that the jury gave their verdict from such evidence as appeared to-day."

Stanhope sighed; the world was looking very dreary to him. The next minute he was opening the door; some one had knocked.

It was one of the maids of the house, as was shown by her neat print dress and white apron.

"O Mr. White—" she began impetuously, and as suddenly stopped. Jack's presence in the room was unexpected to her.

"What is it?" Stanhope kindly inquired.

She essayed to whisper. "The missus—Mrs. White—wishes very much to see you down-stairs, I was to be very particular to say it was important, and that she hoped you would come right away."

"Tell her I will do so," was the quick reply. But as soon as the girl was gone Stanhope turned in real distress to his friend.

"What am I to do?" he asked. "I cannot see her—that is, alone; yet such a request cannot be slighted. Will you go with me, Jack?"

"*I?*"

"Yes; you are intimate enough with us to warrant it. I shall take it for granted that it is in reference to some matters about the funeral she wishes to consult me."

"I—I am afraid she would consider it an intrusion." Jack endeavored to steady his voice, but I am afraid it was not a very successful effort. "I do not think I am on such terms of intimacy with her, as to make it possible for me to enter her presence just now without an invitation."

"You will go as my friend."

"Impossible, Stanhope."

"I do not see why."

Jack in sudden agitation grasped Stanhope by the hand. "I thought you knew my secret," said he. "I thought that was why you were troubled by these doubts—these fears—concerning your father. I have tried to control myself—to give you such help as I could, and to be your friend. But there are bounds to every man's effort. I cannot go down with you into Mrs. White's presence, because I love her—have always loved her, even before she became acquainted with your father."

"Jack!"

The word came thickly; Stanhope was certainly taken aback.

"I see you have never suspected it," Jack went on. "That strikes me as odd, for it has always seemed to me that I wore my heart upon my sleeve. But when a fellow sees such a rival as your father come between him and the girl he loves, he naturally puts a curb upon himself. I ought to put one upon myself now, but this tragedy has unnerved me. I am as weak as water, and not even for your sake could I trust myself."

"Do not say any more," broke in Stanhope. "I will go down alone." There was suppressed excitement in his voice, and the face he half turned from Jack looked strange and unnatural. But the latter, in his relief, did not notice it. He was mainly anxious about one point.

"This—this confession of mine," he said in some constraint, "will not weaken our friendship, will it, Stanhope? I have some sense of honor, I hope, and I shall never forget that she is your father's widow."

"I am sure not," rejoined Stanhope, with gravity, and yet with an odd touch of eagerness in his voice. "Do not think of it any more, Jack. We are in troublous waters, and must strike out with what courage we can." And he was gone from the room before Jack remembered that his friend had not once met his eye since the revelation of his wretched secret.

Stanhope walked rapidly down-stairs. Knocking at the door below, he heard a low "Come," and, entering, encountered the twilight gloom of a heavily darkened apartment.

"I am here," uttered a soft voice. "It is very good in you to come so soon. I would not have troubled you, but I have something to ask you before mamma returns; and she may be here any minute."

Stanhope, with a very troubled face, which happily it was too dark for her to see, advanced slowly toward the corner from which the voice seemed to issue. Though he was in his father's house, and in a room hallowed by memories of his mother, all seemed as strange to him as some new scene. As he moved forward, weird and beautiful objects started out of the darkness with faint gleams on their polished surfaces, while from the dim recesses about him rose odors of a spicy nature, that, mingling with the ever perceptible perfume of hot-house plants, gave a languorous weight to the atmosphere which seemed to transport him into foreign climes. A dull fire burned on the hearth, and it was from this alone that the room received any light.

"It is dark here," ventured Stanhope, stopping near the shadowy form of his father's wife.

The absence of light did not conceal her extreme agitation.

"Shall I not ring for candles, or are you willing I should light the gas?"

"Do you wish light?" sprang from lips he could not see, but of whose trembling he had no doubt "It seems to me as if light would kill me. I want darkness, Stanhope, if only to hide from my own eyes the sight of my own face."

"Mrs. White—" Was this his voice, so chill, so harsh, so metallic! Starting himself at the sound, he modulated his tones, till something like gentleness pervaded them. "You have something to ask, some questions to put concerning the preparations necessary for the funeral before us. Let me hear them, for it is my earnest desire to fulfill all your wishes."

A soft rustle came from the heap of cushions before him, but no words. Frowning slightly, perhaps to keep down the show of sympathy in which he did not dare indulge, he took a step nearer and waited. As he did so, a tongue of flame shot up from the smouldering coals in the fireplace, brightly illuminating for a moment his tall figure, and the regular beauty of his melancholy and earnest face; then the flame died down, and it was dark again. But a soft sigh had been uttered in that passing moment, and its faint, sweet echo seemed to be still lingering in the room.

"I feel," he now ventured to say, "that any speech must be painful to you at this time. We have met with a loss so sudden, so disastrous—" He paused and started back. She had sprung to her feet and was standing before him.

"Light the gas," she cried, "for *your* face I must see. There is something so strange in your voice. Do you—you too—think that he learned in some way of—"

"Hush!" interrupted Stanhope, with more sternness, perhaps, than he realized. "Let us not talk—let us not breathe—doubts—fears—suspicions. The jury have just given a verdict of accidental death. For God's sake—" He paused, choked; something deeper than grief held him by the throat.

"Ac—ci—dent—al death!" The broken words fell from quaking lips. "O Mr. White, if it only were so! But to you I must reveal my whole mind, for the horror is maddening me. He was not himself at the ceremony. He was not himself at the reception. He was not himself when we came here. He tried to be amiable, tried to show his consideration and care for me; but it was no use, and I was not deceived for a moment. But I never dreamed—I never thought he would—would—"

"Wait!" came shortly from his lips. "This moment is horrible enough without darkness." And he rapidly struck a match.

Instantly the young bride faltered back, and the head which had been lifted imploringly fell slowly till her chin rested on her breast. With the full blaze something of the horror went, but in its place came an embarrassment almost as painful.

"Oh, it is dreadful for me!" she murmured. "To be released in such a way is to rob the future of every hope."

He would have liked to answer her with compassion, with tenderness almost; but ghostly hands were waving between them, and he saw them plainer than he did her face. Yet her face was one worth looking at, especially in this moment of deep feeling; for the charm which it sometimes lacked, of feminine softness, was there in all its fascination, and features which were frequently called haughty were now informed by a spirit so gentle, so timorous even, that perhaps for the first time in her life was their full beauty made apparent. She was clad in the rich travelling costume in which she had come to the house, but she had swathed herself in a long black shawl—obtained who knows where—and above this sweep of darkness, her pale face, with its dusky locks, rose in its tragic intentness, till it seemed to be the only thing in the room.

"I had rather you had not uttered your fears," he declared slowly, feeling her presence too oppressive to be borne. "You have no real ground for them, and to have such a consciousness between us makes this sorrow unendurable to us both."

"But I must speak. I cannot be alone with such a horror. Talk to me, Mr. White; do not leave me all alone with my fears and my remorse. There is no one but you who can help me; no one who could understand—"

He was pointing upward.

"Ah!" she exclaimed, "you do not wish my confidence; you had rather not listen to my words. You are sure, then, that he did know what—

what I tried so hard to keep from him—and that it was this which drove him to suicide on his wedding-day, almost at the foot of the altar."

"Flora" (she was younger than he), "I only know that by a cruel fatality I have lost a father and you a husband. Beyond that let us cease all inquiry, since inquiry promises to bring us nothing but wretchedness." Two gleams of sudden whiteness started from the straight blackness which enveloped her. They were her hands, which she threw up wildly over her head, then dropped before her with the moan, "True! true! One could never forget the echo of that pistol shot, or the sudden sight of blood!"

He shuddered as only a man can shudder. A stern change passed over him, and he looked at her searchingly for the first time.

"A moment ago," said he, "I prayed you to drop a veil upon the past, and let appearances stand for facts; but I feel now that I can no more rest than you, with this hideous doubt preying like a canker upon our hearts. Let us attack it, then, and see if we cannot destroy it. It will take courage; but you have that, have you not?" She seemed to breathe a faint "Yes," but her attitude contradicted this assurance. Surveying her downcast face, her shrinking form, he grew troubled, and again somewhat embarrassed, yet he went on, though with much gentleness:

"You say my father was not himself to-day. Was he himself yesterday?"

She shrank in bitter humiliation—this proud, almost commanding woman. "Yes," she answered, but so low that he was forced to gather her meaning from the movement of her lips.

"He was like himself at the breakfast-table," Stanhope declared; "but at half-past eleven, when we started for the church, he was not himself, though I did not thoroughly realize it then. Now, what could have happened in that interval? Did you send him any message, any word?"

"No; what could I have sent him? You told me—" Stanhope did not need to raise his hand to stop her; her own heart stopped her—or was it the look of icy reserve which had crept into his face? "I meant to be his true wife," she brokenly murmured. "Before I left the doors of my father's house I had taken an oath to see no other face than his in my thoughts or in my dreams. I went to him clean-hearted, and—and then I found a bridegroom cold as stone, and so absorbed in miserable thought that he did not hear the clergyman when he asked him if he would take me for his wife—did not hear him, and did not answer, though Dr. De— thought he did, and went on with the ceremony as if all were well. It makes me feel," she softly whispered. "as if I had not been married to him. Yet must I bear his name."

Did she expect any reply to this? any flash of comprehension on his part which might ease the maddening pain that was so fiercely gnawing at her heart? If so, she was disappointed, for Stanhope had missed these final words, this latent appeal. He was thinking of his own sensations at the altar as the bridal couple turned and he caught his father's eye. It had flashed from his bride to him, his son, and the look, short as it was, had told Stanhope such a tale of disappointment and despair, that the church, the bridal couple, and all about him had swum before his eyes as if he had been struck with a vertigo. It was this memory, and the memory of its probable cause, which had turned his grief into gall and wormwood. Not anything he had really done, but what his father had thought he had done.

She, watching him, saw not what was in his mind, but in her own. Visions of things which should have been forgotten, scenes innocent in themselves, but which yet brought a thrill which should have had no place in her breast on this day of mourning, would recur to her memory. A widow before the day was over which had made her a wife, she saw not the figure of her husband lying so near her in still and awful majesty, but the young face of his son as it had appeared to her in the memorable hour when she saw him for the first time. Happy, fatal hour, which it was both bliss and torture to remember. How it had overturned all her views of life, and made the marriage she contemplated seem a sin when it was too late to withdraw from it! The struggle all came back as she stood there staring with wild eyes upon the man who, wittingly or unwittingly, had provoked it. All her shame, her longing, her secret hesitations and vain opposition to the steady pressure urging her forward, rushed upon her recollection in a flood, till her thoughts broke upon one memory, and were swamped there in a chaos of fear and darkness.

It was not a far memory—it dated back only some twenty hours; but it seemed now as if it had always been a part of her. As she felt herself possessed by it, she tried to think what had been said and done. Had she stopped Stanhope as he was leaving her presence with his father, or had he stepped back to her side of his own accord? It was all done so quickly, she could not remember now which had been the first to make this move, and she did not dare to ask the troubled man before her. But she thought she had breathed his name, and that it was in response to this he had recrossed the threshold of the parlor. However that was, what she had said had been nothing—and yet it had been everything. The passion, the terror that was welling up in her at that moment would have outlet; and, driven as she was into marriage, she felt bound to know if her fate were as irrevocable as it seemed. So she had said what? Not that she loved him! Oh, no; even she could not have said that. But she asked—yes, that was it—asked if she should keep her word to his father; if she should go on with a marriage in which she had no heart? And when he looked his astonishment—noble, loyal soul that he was—she had cried out, not loud—oh, no, not loud—but fervently, for she meant every word she uttered, that she did not see her way clear before her, that she threw herself upon his mercy, and would do just what he bade her. And he had bidden her; had bidden her keep her word and make his father happy, and she had obeyed him, and this was the result—a dead husband lying in the other room, and before her this statue of frozen manhood trying to be patient with her and to show her no hate.

As she reached this point in her thoughts a look of shrinking came into her face.

"Could your father have overheard what we said?" she asked.

Stanhope recoiled, but soon regained his assurance.

"No," he declared. "When I joined him in the carriage he was quite natural, and spoke tenderly, proudly of you, like one who felt his happiness unassailable."

"Ah!" she exclaimed, with an involuntary gesture of pain, which, however, soon gave way to an impulsive rush of hope. "Then perhaps we have mistaken his trouble, or—or exaggerated it. If so, may we not hope that the pistol did go off unexpectedly, and that we have only his loss to deplore?"

She looked so eager, he had not the heart to gainsay her; but with the memory of the look he had received from his father at the altar, he could not himself obtain much comfort from any such supposition.

"You have the right to hope that," said he. Did she notice that he had said *you*, while she had said *we?* I have no doubt she did, for there was great intelligence in the wide low brow, now frowning in its pain and perplexity, above the searching eyes with which she regarded him. But her tones as she answered showed that she meant to gather comfort from his words, whether he would have her do so or not.

"Then I will take that right," she cried. "I will hope, I will believe that I am in no wise accountable for what has happened. How could I live if I did not? How could I live?"

He shook his head: what other answer had he for such questions, and his eyes turned imploringly toward the door. Seeing this, her lips quivered, and a cry, involuntary as her grief, broke impetuously from them.

"You wish to go!" she exclaimed. "My fears and my perplexities weary you. Well, you are wise. My mother will be coming soon, and it is only folly for us to talk, since speech brings but little comfort. If you could have told me of some other trouble he had, or if I could have seen that you believed what those men said—that it was all accident and a stroke of Providence—then I might have felt justified in having asked for this interview. But now another regret has been added to those that went before, and that is that I have disturbed you in your grief by any plaint of mine."

Instantly his manner altered. "Do not say that," he protested, all eagerness now. "I am happy to be of service to you; I desire to show you my respect. We are members of one family, remember; and, though I may soon go away myself, this is your home and must always remain so."

For a moment the bitterness in her soul seemed to choke her. Then a look of self-scorn rose in her eyes and breathed in her voice as she cried:

"Yes, this is now my home. I married its splendors, and it is meet that I should enjoy them."

Hurt so that he showed it, Stanhope hesitated, opened his lips, and hesitated again. "I would rather think," he ventured at last, "that this house would be dear to you because it was the abode of a husband who in his lifetime devotedly loved you."

Was it a rebuke? She felt so and accepted it Bursting into tears, she exclaimed, "Oh, you are good—good and strong and noble! Go from me now, I pray; as your father's widow I promise to make myself respected."

He bowed low, and with such deference that the blush stole softly up into her cheek. Then he stepped back, and with the action a heavy pall of reserve fell between them.

VII

THE TWO PARCELS

It was a shock to Stanhope to encounter Jack Hollister again when he went upstairs. He had forgotten Jack; forgotten even what Jack had told him. But at the sight of his face it all came back, and had Jack himself been less intent upon his own thoughts and purposes, he must have noticed the change which this sudden remembrance caused in his friend's expression.

But Jack, who had had time to think while Stanhope was having his interview with Mrs. White, had something to say and did not wait long before saying it.

"Stanhope," cried he, as soon as the latter had closed the door behind him, "having told you what I did, I must tell more. I do not want any indefiniteness to hang about this subject—as far as you and I are concerned, at least. I have never been Flo—Mrs. White's recognized lover. I have never even been particularly favored by her, but I have loved her ever since I first saw her at the Charity Ball, two years ago; and though I am a club man and the owner of fast horses, a pleasure yacht, and whatever else seems to go to make a devil-may-care sort of fellow, there has not been a day in all that time when I wouldn't have given it all up for a quiet country home with her in it. But she was not of my mind. At least, I never seemed to have any chance after your father began to pay his addresses to her, though I have thought (Stanhope, I could not look you in the face if I did not tell you the whole truth) that—that lately she was feeling a little differently from formerly, and that if I were patient and did not obtrude myself too much upon her she might come to see that youth should mate with youth, however desirable were the advantages which an older bridegroom might offer her. That was the reason I was so cut up when I found she was determined to keep her engagement, and that is why I have been so overwhelmed by the more than tragic occurrence of to-day. To see the man who has robbed you of the woman you love, cut down on the very threshold of his marriage with her, makes you feel—especially if you are that man's friend—as if you were his murderer; for—for it was only last night that I found myself wishing (it was while we were at dinner,

Stanhope, and I was laughing loud at the very moment, I remember, at that joke of your father's about Beaton) that a stroke of lightning would shatter the house over our heads, so that this day's sun would never rise for any of us."

"Jack!"

"You did not know I could carry bitterness to such a length, did you? I did not either. But jealousy makes a brute of a man almost without his knowledge, and I am sorry enough now, and ashamed enough too, and though I never felt before such an irresistible longing to be with her and to comfort her and to be all the world to her, in short, as I do at this moment, yet if by raising a finger we could have him back again, strong and hopeful and full of devotion to her as he was last night, I should not hesitate to raise that finger. Do you believe me, Stanhope?"

"Yes, yes," was the almost inarticulate reply. In what a tragedy were they involved! And how much deeper were its complications than even Jack realized!

"You have no liking for a girl, and do not know what love is," the latter now went on, over-anxious perhaps to clear himself entirely in his friend's eyes, "so you cannot realize, of course, how a fellow can lose his head even over a woman who does not give him one ray of hope to live on. But your day may come, and then you will understand it and not blame me so much."

Stanhope, who had been mechanically pacing to and fro through the room while his friend was talking, stopped, with his back to that friend, and remarked quietly:

"I do not blame you. If I do not understand love, I understand men; and you are a very good sort of man, if you do have your bitter moments and jealous impulses."

Jack, greatly relieved, stepped forward to the other's side. "Then, you don't mean to let this thing come between us?" he cried.

Stanhope, turning slowly, held out his hand for answer

Jack grasped it, and the eyes of the two men met. If Jealousy made a third in their party, his face was veiled in mist, and neither saw him, which was another of the tragic mysteries of that tragic day.

Jack left soon after this, and Mrs. Hastings came. The latter was one of those women who invade any house they enter; and from the moment her large and important person crossed the threshold, quietude and peace seemed to vanish, and grief itself to take on a garb of affectation, which robbed it of all hallowing influences, and made the house almost untenable to Stanhope. He, therefore, kept his room as much as possible during the evening; but in the morning, being assured that the lady had driven out to make such purchases as were necessary for her daughter's mourning, he descended to his father's study and sent for Felix and Peter. The doubts which had surrounded his father's death with horror still clung to him, and he was determined to settle, if possible, what had occurred in that short hour before the marriage, to change his father's appearance from one of joyful expectation to that of secret but scarcely concealed despair.

The two men came in together, one by the front hall and one by the back. At the sight of their young master, standing in the room where they had so often received the orders of his father, they simultaneously bowed their heads. Felix was an old man, and Peter was a young one; but both were honest, and both had held the deceased statesman in great respect. Stanhope had perfect confidence in them.

"Felix," said he to the older man, "it has devolved upon me to take charge of my father's affairs. They were very numerous, as you know, and very complicated. Among other things, I am assured that some letters were brought him yesterday before the ceremony, which it is my duty to answer. I do not find them on his desk, or in the pockets of the coat he wore; yet you brought him some mail, did you not, you or Peter?"

"Only what came while you were at breakfast," returned Felix. "You remember, sir, that you were present, and stood in the window while he read his letters."

With a shock Stanhope did remember. He had seen his father receive three letters and read three letters, and he had also seen that nothing in these letters had affected his father in the least degree. "Those are not the ones. I mean," he remarked.

"But no other mail came after that, till some time after ten," quickly declared Peter. "And there was nothing in that mail but papers, for I brought it up myself. I think that is the very pile, sir, just as I laid it down," and he pointed to three or four unopened pamphlets and a New York *Observer* that were lying in a heap near the back of the large table, called, by courtesy, Mr. White's desk.

Stanhope was not satisfied.

"Did no private messenger come to the door? Or did not my father have a caller at that early hour, who might have brought him a letter?"

Both men shook their heads.

ANNA KATHARINE GREEN

"We were very busy, the both of us," asserted Felix. "There was many a ring at the bell, and a lot of things to look after; but I don't remember any messenger for Mr. White, or any caller except one, a Mr. Townsend whom he would not see."

Stanhope knew Mr. Townsend; he was one of those politicians who would not hesitate to stop a man on his way to the altar, if he thought he could call his attention to a particular friend, just then in need of an office.

"I am sure," Stanhope persisted, "that some letter reached him in some way, just before he went to church—an important letter which I ought to find."

The two men looked at each other. "We don't know anything about it," averred Felix.

"Mr. White wrote some letters," here ventured Peter, scarcely knowing whether this piece of information would be of any importance to his young master or not. "It was while he was waiting for the carriage. He sent for me to mail them, sir."

"Yes, yes," interposed Stanhope; "I know he wrote letters, and that you mailed them, but it is not of these I wanted to hear. Where is Josephine? Let her come. She may have taken one in while you were both busy; she does sometimes, I believe."

Josephine was summoned, and Stanhope put the same questions to her. Had she carried Mr. White any letter the morning before, or had she introduced any visitor into his study? The girl flushed—she was of a timid nature, and stood in great awe of the handsome young master.

"No, sir," said she. "There was a gentleman who called, but I did not take him up-stairs, because Mr. White said he did not know him, and could not at that time see anybody."

"A gentleman?"

"Yes, sir."

"Did he give his name?"

"Yes, sir, but I don't remember it. It was something like Stewart, but not that exactly. He carried a small paper parcel."

"Did he leave the parcel?"

"Oh, no, sir: that is, I suppose not. He was gone when I went down with Mr. White's message. I suppose one or other of the men told him it was Mr. White's wedding morning."

But Felix and Peter, at whom she glanced at this moment, shook their heads. They had not seen any such person. Did she leave him standing in the hall?

"Yes," she anxiously replied. "Was not that right? He looked like a gentleman."

Stanhope, who failed to see how this person's errand could have any connection with the matter he was secretly sifting, but who nevertheless felt bound to probe to the bottom anything which came up, asked at what time this man called.

The answer came that it could not have been far from ten, as it was just half-past when she went out on an errand for Mr. White a little while after.

Stanhope, who had not heard of this errand before, felt a sudden embarrassment. He realized that he ought to inquire into it, and at the same time he equally realized that too great a display of curiosity as to Mr. White's movements immediately preceding the shooting could not but arouse the very suspicion he was the most anxious to avoid. In the struggle his interest overcame his discretion, and he inquired with what calmness he could, what was the nature of the errand upon which she had been sent by his father.

The reply was simple. She had been given a small package to carry to the Westminster Hotel.

This was startling. The man who had wished to see Mr. White a little while before had held a package in his hand; and a half-hour later this girl had been sent by his father with a package to a hotel downtown. Were they the same package? He could not forbear to ask her.

Her eyes opened at the suggestion. Did the young master forget that the man had not left his package? But she replied simply that they were not at all alike in size or appearance. The one she had carried was small and wrapped in white paper; the one which the man had held in his hand was a brown parcel and much larger.

Was Stanhope making a fool of himself? He began to think so, and presently dismissed the servants. But when they were gone, his mind returned again and again to those two packages, and he found himself wondering again and again what his father had sent to the Westminster Hotel, and what was the errand of the man who carried the brown-paper parcel. Suddenly he rose to his feet. In the waste-paper basket, under the table before him, was a piece of brown wrapping-paper, and a fine green cord—the former smooth and still showing by its folds both the size and shape of the box around which it had been bound; the latter with its knot cut, but of the length exactly to fit the parcel contained by the paper. They lay on the top, and *under them were the letters received by his father while at the breakfast-table the morning before.*

Stanhope, seizing them, surveyed the paper with interest, and was startled to detect, written upon it in characterless writing, not only his father's name, but the simple and significant word *Personal*, which when placed on letter or package testifies to its importance either to the sender or to the recipient.

Taking the measure of the parcel with his eye, and then thrusting both paper and cord into a cupboard, he rang again for Josephine.

This time she came in a flutter of excitement annoying, if not alarming, for Stanhope to see. But he affected to notice nothing, and asked her, with just a faint apology for his curiosity, whether she had observed closely enough the parcel carried by the man whom she had let into the house the morning before, to be able to tell its exact size, and whether it was a sealed package or one done up with a string.

Josephine had not the discretion of either Peter or Felix, who would neither of them have betrayed surprise even if they had felt it: so she showed her astonishment that he should still harp on this subject, even while she answered that she had not noticed the parcel particularly, but she thought it had looked like a book, and did remember that it was tied with a green string, though why she had noted this she did not know, unless it was that green was her favorite color and always caught her eye.

Stanhope, with an impulse he afterward decried, opened the cupboard above him and took out the paper and string.

"Are you sure," said he, showing them, "that the man you let in did not see my father, and leave with him the parcel you observed in his hand?"

With a stare totally unfeigned this time, she contemplated string and paper gravely for a moment, then replied:

"Some one—it could not have been the cook—must have taken it from him while I came up-stairs. You must ask Peter and Felix again, for I don't know any more about it than I have told you." And she looked very deprecating and sincere.

Stanhope was not a good actor. He was of too candid a nature to be apt at subterfuge, and it would have been better, perhaps, if he had left these inquiries to Jack. But he was committed to them now, and he was going on, perhaps to make matters worse, when there came a low knock at the door, and Mrs. White, the young widow, entered the room.

In her hand was a small white parcel, at the sight of which Josephine started perceptibly.

VIII

The White Parcel

S tanhope did not notice this parcel until after Josephine had gone. He was so intent upon regaining the self-possession of which the unexpected and not altogether welcome entrance of his father's widow had robbed him, that he had but little thought to spare for any such small details. But when his inner calmness was restored, and he turned to face the drooping figure awaiting him near the doorway, and saw that her whole attention was fixed upon a small white package which she held doubtfully in her hand, he remembered the look with which Josephine had gone out of the room, and said to himself before Mrs. White had spoken, "This is the parcel Josephine carried to the Westminster!" adding in secret amaze the inner questions, "How came it here? And why do we see it again in the hands of Mrs. White?"

It was the young widow's errand to answer these questions.

"See," she cried, trembling visibly as she laid the parcel on the table beside them, "what has just been sent me from the Westminster Hotel. It was left there for me yesterday, and the proprietor, hearing of our trouble, has just returned it. It was directed to him on the outside, but on the inside—look!" She pointed to the box from which she had suddenly torn the wrapper, and he saw there written in his father's well-known hand:

Mrs. Samuel White,
Westminster Hotel.

"From your father," she whispered. "Sent before we were married; sent in that hour in which you saw such a change take place in him. I dare not open it."

Stanhope felt an equal shrinking, but what he said was:

"How came it to be sent to the Westminster Hotel? I thought you intended to go South."

"We did, but we had planned to stop at the Westminster till I was thoroughly rested."

Stanhope's face lightened.

"Then he still intended to go there when he sent this. Open it, Mrs. White; it may end our doubts forever."

But she only drew back still further. "I cannot," she protested; "the presence of death is upon it. Open it for me, Mr. White. I have no power to do it myself."

Without another word he took the box in his hand, and tearing off the inner cover revealed a small velvet casket whose worn edges betrayed at once the fact that it was no longer new. At the sight an exclamation escaped Stanhope, and something like a flush mounted to his brow.

"I have seen this before," he exclaimed in a low voice; and he laid it reverently down with the added exclamation: "It used to hold jewels that were my mother's."

The young woman before him uttered a sudden cry. "Your mother's?" she repeated in awe-struck tones, shrinking from it with dilating eyes. "Oh, why should he send them to me?"

"The case—I speak of the case," he declared; "the jewels that it contains may be new."

"I—I cannot touch it," she faltered. "I would rather never see what it holds. It was meant as an—"

But he had already touched the spring which held down the lid of the case before him, and the brooch and ear-rings thus disclosed were of so old-fashioned a make that she had no need to lift her eyes to his to be assured that not only the case but the jewels themselves were those he had been accustomed to see in his childhood.

"I do not understand it," she declared, somewhat proudly, her dark eyes flashing with a new expression not far removed from defiance; "he had already given me jewels—diamonds—which I must have had on at the very moment he was writing my name upon these. Did he think—"

"This will tell you what he thought," interrupted Stanhope, passing her a little note which he had found wedged into the open lid of the casket.

He had feared she would make an objection to reading these words of her dead bridegroom, but she did not; the defiance of the moment giving her the courage she had lacked before. As her eye passed over the few words contained in the note thus given her, he could hardly restrain his own anxiety as to their purport; but when the last word had been read she raised her head, and he saw, for the first time since that fatal shot was heard, the glisten of tears on her lashes. He felt such a revulsion of hope that he staggered, and with difficulty heard her as she cried:

"I was not worthy to be his wife. Read, Mr. White, read; for after this we can never doubt again that his death was accidental."

But Stanhope was now the more agitated of the two, and several minutes passed before his eye could make out the words which his father had written. When he did,—this was what he read:

To My Dearly Loved Flora:

"These jewels, which were once worn by Stanhope's mother, I present to you on this day of our marriage, not because of their value or inherent beauty, but because I know of no other token that would express so deeply both the admiration and the respect which I feel for the woman I have chosen to take that place in my heart occupied till now by the wife of my youth. May you wear them once a year upon this day, if only to show that you appreciate the feeling which influenced me in this the dearest gift which I could make you."

"It was a strange thing to do," came from Flora's lips, when she perceived that Stanhope had finished the lines. "But it lifts a heavy weight from my heart, and makes it possible for me to weep. I can never wear them, though," she declared, as Stanhope mechanically lifted the casket to look again at the gems which brought back to him such a rush of memories. "You had better put them away yourself. They belong to you by right, and it is fitter that they should remain in your possession than in mine."

For answer he closed the casket and thrust it into the pocket of his vest. "I thank you," said he. "My mother's memory is very dear to me. She was a noble woman."

Flora, whose aspect had undergone a great change in the last few moments, surveyed him for an instant with rapidly filling but very earnest eyes.

"Will you not be happier now?" she asked.

The reply he made was sudden as the resolve from which it evidently sprung.

"Yes. I will take this letter, which you have just been good enough to show me, as proof positive that we misunderstood my father's emotions and the cause of his sudden end. So far from anticipating death, it was life he was looking forward to, and a life with *you*."

The word seemed both to hurt and to relieve her, but she tried not to show the conflict of her feelings as she moved slowly back toward the door. "We shall not meet again," she suggested, "till after the funeral," and waited just an instant, to see if he had anything to say to her before she went. But he gave no sign of an intention, much less of a wish, to speak; and she, with a faint sigh, too faint to be heard by him even if he had been listening for it, turned away and disappeared quietly from the room.

IX

The Brown Parcel

M r. Hollister, sir!"
Stanhope rose; he was glad to see his friend.

"Why, how different you look!" was Jack's exclamation as he strode into the room. "Has anything happened? Have you satisfied yourself that your fears were unfounded?"

His own manner had shown a certain feverish anxiety when he entered, but it had suddenly changed when he noted Stanhope's relieved expression. Stanhope's reply tended to still further reassure him.

"Yes; I cannot confide in you, Jack, any more than I could yesterday, but the grief I now feel is simple and unclouded. I mourn a father lost, but not a father desperate."

"Then I can give you this letter without dread," declared Jack, reaching out a small note which he had just taken from his pocket. "One of the letters which your father mailed yesterday is accounted for: it was written to *me*."

"To *you!*"

"Yes; for the purpose of enclosing these few lines to you. He seemed to have some premonition of his doom—though not in the way you feared," Jack hastily added, catching Stanhope's startled look. "A good many people feel so when they are about starting on a journey. I shouldn't let that influence me. Good heaven! Stanhope, what is it now?" he impulsively asked, as he beheld his friend staring with rapidly changing face at the words his father had written him.

"I do not know—I do not understand," exclaimed Stanhope, somewhat incoherently. He was dazed; there was no meaning for him at the moment in the words he was endeavoring to read.

Jack, with a sense of renewed trouble, took the paper from his friend and read:—.

"It is my first, foremost, and lasting desire, that you should
marry (if you ever marry) a girl by the name of Natalie
Yelverton. She is the daughter of Stephen Yelverton, of
whom you will probably hear shortly after my death. Why

I demand this, and why it is the only and best thing for you to do, do not seek to inquire. That I wish it, and forbid every other marriage on your part, is sufficient to prove that only in this union lies your happiness and the honor of our name.

Your affectionate father,
Samuel White

"The deuce!"

In that somewhat trivial exclamation spoke the Jack of former times, the Jack whom we have not yet met. "Natalie Yelverton! Who is she, Stanhope?"

"I do not know," was his quiet but prompt reply. "I have never seen her, never ever heard of her before."

"The deuce!" again broke from his companion's lips. He seemed almost as confounded as his friend.

But Stanhope was more than confounded; he was stricken, and that by more than one fear, more than one disappointment.

"I am overcome by this," he exclaimed at last. "I wish I had not seen it till after the funeral. I wish—God forgive me—it had never come to my hand. Why should I marry this stranger? But that is what he tells me I should not inquire. Jack, were not my troubles great enough before?"

Jack, to whom this arbitrary disposal of a man's right to choose his own wife as his own heart dictated was at this period of his career especially odious, immediately broke out in a tirade which it was fortunate that Stanhope was too much engrossed in his own emotions to hear. The last words only struck the dulled ears of his companion. They were these:

"You are under no legal obligation to do it, and I should first make sure that Natalie Yelverton was the girl I wanted to marry."

To this assertion, Stanhope evidently felt himself called upon to reply.

"I shall never marry, if I must marry a girl who goes by the name of Natalie."

His look more than his words seemed to strike Jack.

"You don't mean," he began, "that there is some one—"

"Isn't there always some one?" smiled Stanhope, bitterly. And he walked away from Jack in a vain effort to regain his self-command sufficiently to answer the questions which he felt that this indiscreet admission was likely to bring upon him.

But if Jack was light of manner, he was not indelicate, and one look at his friend's face had convinced him that the best use he could make of his friendship just then was to curb his lawful curiosity. He therefore remained silent and dubious, looking very much as if he would like to curse somebody if he could only be quite sure who that especial somebody was.

Stanhope, who had not expected this reticence, showed himself particularly grateful for it. Coming back to Jack, he seized him by the hand.

"You are a good fellow," said he, "and a true friend; we won't say anything more about this, and do you try if you can to forget it. My father had his reasons, no doubt, and—" He stopped, and a flush, deep and red mounted up his forehead. Some new fear, new shame, had evidently struck his mind, and for a moment robbed him of the last remains of his self-possession; but he speedily conquered himself. "And we should respect them," finished he. "I shall never hear any word against my father's good judgment."

"Of course not, of course not," stammered Jack. "He was one of our great men. No one thinks of disputing it."

"I have but one final question to ask. What did you mean when you said that my father seemed to have some premonition of his doom?"

"Why, only this. He said in the few lines he wrote me, that being on the point of a journey over a road not unused to accidents, he requested that in case any disaster terminated his life, I would be good enough to hand you the enclosed. He said nothing about what I should do with it if nothing occurred to him, which, now I come to think of it, seems strange."

The pallor in Stanhope's face deepened. "We will not speculate," said he. "The cross of my life has been given me to bear, and I must bear it. Not a word more, Jack."

But, when Jack was gone, many and perplexing were the surmises in which Stanhope indulged. That his father expected to be dead when Jack received this letter, he no longer doubted. That the cause of this dread expectation—an expectation which in this case could have had birth only in an intention—sprang from some sudden knowledge of the state of his young wife's affections, seemed equally evident. For what else but jealousy—a hideous, even if a misplaced jealousy, of his own son—could have prompted the look which that son had surprised on his face at the ceremony, and next these words—this mandate from the tomb—by which he was to be withheld from any marriage save one so problematical as to be scarcely taken into account?

That his father had spared his young bride's honor, first by marrying her and then by directing to her words of the most confiding affection, only pointed these conclusions in Stanhope's mind. For he knew his fathers nature, and knew it to be too essentially chivalrous for him to think of casting a shadow over a woman's reputation; and, even had he possessed real cause for jealousy, it would have been contrary to his instincts to have revenged himself upon her, save as he may have thought himself to have done so by the restrictions he had placed upon his son.

What thoughts! What horrors! It made Stanhope writhe in shame, grief, and repulsion, only to consider from what an abyss of desperation and outraged feeling the determination to make those restrictions must have sprung. For his father had loved him always and loved him well, and never would have blasted a life, from which he had always avowed himself to hope so much, by any such arbitrary commands if he had not been maddened by pain and resentment. That his father had hurt him deeper than he knew, and in other ways than he knew, did not take from the sting of Stanhope's reflections. Nor did any curiosity as to who this Natalie Yelverton could be, come at this time to alleviate the intolerable emotions under which he labored. For with him then, as later, was present the conviction that this was but a name, and only a name, and that as he would never meet one bearing it, he would never be at liberty to marry any one. A cruel outlook for a young man, gifted as Stanhope was not only with domestic tastes, but with every grace and virtue calculated to please women and insure happiness in marriage.

To rouse himself from thoughts fast growing too desperate to be endured, Stanhope finally left his room and went below to his father's study. A duty had presented itself to him there—the verification of a theory he had formed in reference to the package marked "Personal."

Josephine had said it looked like a book, but he did not believe it to have been a book. On the contrary, he was convinced that it had held the pistol which had taken his father's life.

Satisfied as he was now that his father had wished to throw a mystery about his death, or at least to avoid the suspicion of suicide, Stanhope refrained from looking for this box in any near or conspicuous place. It was in the recesses of cupboards that he sought it, and at the back of high shelves. And it was in one of these latter places that he finally found it, and with it the proof that his theory had been correct, for it exactly fitted the creases in the piece of brown paper which he had taken from the waste-paper basket the day before, as well as the piece of green cord with which that paper had been bound.

It was a new box, and on the bottom of it was pasted a label bearing the name of the firm from which it had been purchased.

The mystery of the brown-paper package had been solved, but not the mystery as to how his father had been able to send for and receive a pistol at such short notice.

X

A Change of Feeling

It was a most imposing ceremonial. Flora may feel honored, my dear, at being the widow of a man at whose funeral so many public men were to be seen. If the President himself did not come, it was because—"

The closing of the front door cut off the rest of the sentence. Mrs. Hastings had left the house of mourning with these words of satisfied vanity hovering on her lips.

Stanhope, who had just issued from his room on the third floor, felt his spirits darken and his heart grow cold as these words floated up the stair. If the mother was of this worldly mind, what might he not expect the daughter to be? And that daughter was his father's widow, a future member of his family, and at present his one greatest care.

He had not seen her to speak to since they stood together at the grave, nor did he find himself, in the dread quietude which now settled upon the house, desiring to do so, though she was at this moment the only person from whom he could hope to receive comfort or sympathy. Yet that it was his duty to see her and tell her of the intentions he had formed in regard to the future, there could be no doubt; and that he shrank from this duty and hesitated to perform it was mainly due perhaps to his dread of reawakening in her breast those doubts which had been happily laid to rest by that last gift she had received from her husband.

But the interview could not be shunned, if the relations between them were to be restored to their proper basis and he be made a true man again in his own eyes; so when the evening lights had been lit, he sent Felix to her room with the request that she would grant him a few minutes' conversation.

Her answer was such as to make all further doubt impossible; and just at the twilight-hour, when the feelings are keenest, and the heart and soul most attuned to vivid impressions, he found himself again crossing the threshold from which he had retired a few days before in such a confusion of mingled emotions.

The room, unlike the time to which I refer, was brilliantly illuminated, so that her slim figure, clad in its close black robes, stood out in bold relief from the pale yellow of the surrounding walls and furniture. She was waiting to receive him in the centre of the room, and there was a dignity in the pose of her form and the carriage of her small and exquisitely shaped head, which contrasted dangerously with the pleading softness in her eyes and the tremulous movements of her lip.

"It is very good of you to wish to see me," she said; and, though the words were commonplace, the music of the tone in which they were spoken made of them a worthy greeting, and one which many a man of prouder nature than Stanhope possessed would have sacrificed many of his lesser hopes to receive.

But Stanhope did not even notice it—he was too much occupied in weighing the words he had come to say; and she, observing his abstraction, dropped the hand she had hesitatingly put forth, while a subtle change took place in her countenance which added to her dignity while not taking from her fascination.

"I am come," he began with the usual lack of tact observable even in the best-intentioned men at such moments, "to say good-by to you. I think of leaving town early to-morrow morning."

She was startled, but she had received a certain cue to his feelings in the abstracted formality of his first greeting, and she hid her emotions admirably.

"It is soon, is it not?" she objected. "I should have thought the business connected with the administration of your father's estate would detain you here for a short time at least."

"I shall return," said Stanhope, slowly, "very soon in a few days, perhaps."

He did not say that his plan was to separate himself from her, but she knew that this was in his thoughts as well as if he had spoken.

So with tremulous tones, and a gentleness which robbed her words of any harsh suggestion, she said:

"When you come back, you will wish to find this house empty for your occupancy."

But he would not listen to this. "The house is yours," he declared. "I have already intimated that I desire it to be a part of the dower which will rightfully fall to you as my father's widow."

"I know," she admitted, still with that tremor in her tones. "But—but supposing I refused to accept it; supposing I refused to accept anything; would it—" (she found it very difficult to proceed, as for all the pleading of her eyes he gave her no help by any softening in his relentlessly cold face) "would it restore me your respect; make you think me—"

"Mrs. White," was the hasty interruption with which he sought to stave off suggestions that he feared, "you value my opinion beyond its real worth. I must beg that you do not do anything for the sake of what I may think. Your position as the widow of my father places you above any criticism of mine."

"You mean—" the passion in her burst with an uncontrollable force to light; she could no more restrain it than a seething crater can keep back the lava when its time has come to overflow—"you mean it places me beyond your sympathy, your compassion, and your love."

The word was said, and the silence which it made was overpowering to them both. And yet I think they both breathed more freely after it— she because of the great relief there is in speaking aloud what has been so long imprisoned in the breast, and he because of the opportunity which it gave him for making those explanations which the situation so forcibly demanded.

"And if it were so," was his gentle reply, "it would be well and not ill for us; for love, saving such as every man is bound to feel for his relatives and friends, is henceforth denied to me. I am no longer the master of my fate in this regard."

"No longer master of your fate?" She was frightened and could only repeat the phrase, "No longer master of your fate?"

For the first time her beauty and the feeling which illumined it seemed to affect him. A shadow crossed his brow as he put his hand into his pocket and drew out his father's letter. How could he soften the blow he was about to deal her? How could he right himself without wounding her irremediably?

Unconsciously she helped him.

"Your father's writing!" she exclaimed. "What are you about to tell me now? What new trouble is this?"

For reply he put the letter in her hand.

"I do not know," said he, "what false impressions my father may have received. But these are his last commands, written, as we have reason to know, but a few hours before his death."

She looked at the unfolded letter in her hand and she looked at him, and an expression entreating as that of a child crossed for a moment her haughty features. Then she seemed to gain control over herself, and, motioning him back, she unfolded the letter and bent her proud head to peruse it.

She had turned away as she did this; only the curve of her cheek and the line of her throbbing throat were visible to him. But these were eloquent, too eloquent for him to observe unmoved; and in a moment he found himself looking away from her slight, swaying figure, in a suspense he had supposed himself incapable of feeling when he entered the room.

The rustling of the paper as she crushed his father's letter in her hands caused him to turn about again. She was facing him, and the pallor of her cheeks made the brightness of her eyes seem almost unearthly.

"Natalie Yelverton!" she cried. "Who is Natalie Yelverton?"

"I do not know."

"You do not know?" Her surprise brought the color back to her cheeks.

"I have never heard the name before," he protested.

She started, and the letter fell from her hands.

"A stranger," she murmured, "an unknown woman!" And her eyes, fixed upon his, deepened in intensity till they seemed to tear the very secret from his soul. But suddenly a change took place in them. The rigidity left her form, and she quivered as she cried in a low and deprecating tone, "It is despotism and unwarranted. You will never feel yourself bound by commands to which no reason is attached. It would be cruel. Your father himself would not wish it *now*."

But the cold sternness which immediately chilled his features answered for him before the words left his lips.

"I can never go contrary to my father's wishes. I should find no happiness in doing so, and could therefore give none. The future of my life is sealed; do not seek to change it." And she, looking at him, knew that words from her would be but wasted breath, and that her doom as well as his own had been pronounced in these last words of her buried husband.

It was a wretched moment to them both, but mainly so to her—ah, infinitely more so to her; for in the light which her present misery threw upon the past, a change seemed to pass over the relations which she had held with this man, and what had seemed so sure to her at the time took on a cloud of doubt, and she found herself for the first time since she saw Stanhope, and seeing him loved him, asking herself if he suffered as she did, and if the feelings which she had adjudged to him had been true feelings or only the reflection of her own. There was madness in the question, but she felt bound to face it; for if he had not loved her—and what had he ever said or done to lead her to think he did?—then had she been most blamable and most unworthy, and there was justice in her doom if not in his, a justice which it would be for her to acknowledge and accept.

That she was a woman who, without great beauty, had always been surrounded by suitors did not at this moment seem any excuse to her. Stanhope was not like other men—had never seemed to her like other men; why, then, had she attributed to him their weakness, when it was his strength that she admired, and the immovable virtues of his mind? Her infatuation, and the blindness which it had caused her, came upon her with crushing force, as she stood there before him with that letter lying between them on the floor. Yet even then she could not bring herself to believe she had been entirely mistaken in his feelings, and that there had been no foundation for the dreams which had disturbed her courtship with another. It was possible he had not loved her much; had not loved her as she had him, wildly, unreasonably, daringly, in the face of duty and obligation, or he would not have bid her go on with her marriage with another, and would not be standing now in a cloud of dark and dismal thought, which seemed to shut her out instead of enclosing her within it. But surely he had loved her some; surely the words which had revealed her feelings on the eve of her marriage had not come with a perfect shock of enlightenment to him, or—or—how could he have commanded himself so well! How could he have refrained from expressing his displeasure and his disgust! She was in a chaos of distress, of shame, of self-execration; but surely, surely, there was some tenderness in his thoughts, some excuse for her extravagance, in that subtle interchange of feeling which is born of mutual sympathy and understanding.

Yet—yet—the abstraction in his face did not show it; the despair, the anguish, only too visible there, were not connected with her, or why this sense of utter and impassable distance between them? There were other griefs in his soul than any she knew, other losses and other disappointments; and as this conviction grew, and she noted more and more how they absorbed him, a change took place in her own feelings, and with it a change in her countenance, which, if he could have observed it, would have proved to him that this woman, slightly despised as she may have been, had, under all her worldliness, indiscretions, and erratic impulses, the angelic nature which is ever content to give more than it receives, and to forget its own selfish emotions in its sympathies for another.

ANNA KATHARINE GREEN

Stooping to the floor, she raised the fallen letter, finding it impossible to suppress a pang as she did so, that he, so chivalrous and courtly in his manner, could be so absorbed in his own thoughts as not even to note this action. Holding it toward him, she softly remarked:

"*This* must not lie between us." Then, as he roused to take the paper, she gently added: "That I have made a great mistake is very evident. That you are the one to suffer for it causes me deeper grief than you will ever realize. I am not all selfishness; and if, by ending my own life here and now, I could undo this wrong which you have received, gladly would I thus follow the husband I have so wilfully failed to appreciate."

He raised his hand in protest, but did not attempt to speak, and she was glad he did not.

"Of this and of the past I can say no more. You can never forgive my imprudence, as I can never forget the shame which the memory of it now causes me. Let us then waste no words upon it; but, Stanhope"— and here her voice sank till it was little more than a musical breath—"if I mistook my relation to you once, let me prove to you that I do not do so any longer. Let me be the friend which my connection with you warrants. I am too young to take the place of her whose name I have usurped, but if sympathy and an appreciation of your griefs—" She paused, and a tear stole down her cheek. It takes a bitter wrench to tear love out of the heart which has never known but the one passion.

Stanhope, hearing her voice break, opened his lips mechanically.

"You are very good," he began; but the next moment, catching a full view of her face, he corrected both his words and tones. "You are more than good," said he, and for the first time since he had known her felt the warmth of a genuine admiration kindle his sympathies in her regard.

She shook her head. "I should like to be," said she, "but my life has been given to frivolities, and goodness seldom springs from such soil. It would help me to become good," she slowly added, "if you would confide in me. Is she any one I know?"

Nothing could have been gentler than her manner, or more truly sweet than her tone, yet he started keenly.

"*She?*" he repeated with tremulous emphasis.

"The woman that you love, Stanhope."

He looked at her in astonishment, almost in anger; but the determination which had given her courage to push the conversation to this length did not forsake her.

"I know that you must love some one, or your sorrow would not have so keen an edge. It is not from curiosity I speak about her, but because I see that you must talk of her to some one, or go mad. Shall I be the one, Stanhope, or shall it be another? I shall not complain if it is, but—" Oh, the sadness of her smile! It smote him through his own great griefs; it made him feel that if he took a confidant on earth, it could only be this woman.

Walking to the end of the room, he came back and stood calmly before her.

"I do love a young girl," said he, "deeply and with all my heart. I loved her before I returned from Europe," he added, dropping his eyes and his tones.

She understood him, and a deep flush flew over her neck and brow. That was before he had seen *her*.

"You never spoke of it," she murmured.

"No: one does not speak of a dream,"

"And was it that—only that?"

"It might have been more; it should have been more but for this." He tapped his breast where his father's letter lay.

"Tell me about it," she breathed.

He led her to a sofa; he seated her, but did not seat himself. If that was a dream, what was this? To talk of *her*, and to this woman! He was astounded at himself, yet he went on. Something in the frank, earnest gaze of the young widow made it seem the only natural thing to do.

"I saw her a year ago in the country. She is not any one you know, and her name is not Natalie Yelverton."

"A young girl?"

"Very young."

"Fair?"

"Whiter than a snowflake, and as exquisitely delicate."

Flora, who was a dark beauty, smiled as one smiles to cover up a wound.

"I know she is not as cold," she said, and let her gaze linger for one long moment on the brown hair and dark eyes of the man before her. "Her fairness drew you," she declared

Stanhope shook his head. "*She* drew me," he corrected. "Not," he added, after a moment's pause, "by any effort on her part, for she is a child; but her charm is irresistible—it made a home for her in my heart at once."

"Happy child!" trembled on Flora's lips, but did not fall from them.

"It was when I was down in Bay Ridge," suddenly cried Stanhope, leaving her side, and beginning in his nervous excitement to pace the floor. "I went there a year ago—you may not have heard of it—for a few weeks' study, before going to Europe, and it was in one of the rural lanes there that I first saw her. She was standing in the shadow of a great tree, and she had in her arms a pet bird of plumage so black that her own fairness struck me at the time as something startling. The white dress she wore added to the effect, so simple was it, and yet so picturesque; but the next moment I saw nothing but her face, which, if not beautiful, wore such a touching expression that I have never been able to lose it from my memory. No other face"—he stopped, but Flora's smile encouraged him, and he went on—"has ever succeeded in driving it from my mind. It became the poetry of my life, and I would have married her, but—"

"But what?" breathed Flora.

"She was barely seventeen, and I dared not take such a child at a disadvantage."

Flora looked up, astonished. He, the son of the great statesman, with wealth, position, and luxury in his gift, take any girl at a disadvantage by winning her early affections! She smiled and suggested quietly:

"It could not have failed to have been a great match for her, even if she had been the daughter of one of our city princes."

But Stanhope answered gravely, "It is not a great match that we desire for those we love, but a happy one. I wished to be sure of satisfying her womanhood as well as pleasing her childish fancy."

Flora gave him another glance which took in his superb figure and noble countenance, glowing now with true passion tempered by an infinite tenderness, and wondered still more. Did he not know of his personal advantages? Did he dream that any other man could ever draw a woman's eyes away from him, if once he looked at her like that? But she said simply:

"Has she a mother—a father—and does she live there still?"

"No, no. But I would have found her; in a few weeks I should have found her. It was the understanding with the teacher at whose school she was, that when she had completed her eighteenth year I should be told where to look for her. Her birthday is in November—I know the date by heart—but I cannot seek her now. All such hopes are at an end for me; but the dream will never die."

Flora drew a deep breath. Was it joy or sorrow which made her breast heave? She did not know; her life was in a turmoil, and for the moment she was only conscious of one thing—a determination to be a friend to this man.

"And will she remember *you?* Have you to mourn for her grief as well as for your own?"

"That I do not know. She was so young, and I never told her—"

"You saw her more than once, then?"

"Many times, but always when her teacher was present. I wanted to make sure there was substance for my dream to rest on; that the child had a soul as lovely as her face."

"And you found it so?"

"Flora, there was a poor cripple in that school—a girl with a face saddened by illness and the lack of love till it was plain almost to repulsiveness. Mary—that was my little one's name—took that poor cripple to her heart, cared for her, dressed her, and taught her to smile. If the day was bright, they went out together, and the walk was never so long as to weary the lame one. If the day was dark, they sat and painted, or played at games such as the less gifted one could understand. Mary loved tennis, but she never played it when Sophy was present, nor would she dance if Sophy had to sit still and be unamused. I myself have seen her draw back out of sight and leave Sophy in the front, when a ride was proposed, and there were not seats enough for all."

"You do well to love her," sighed Flora. "We of the world can appreciate such natures, if we cannot imitate them."

But Stanhope did not hear. He was absorbed in his memories; and Flora's cheek grew white and her heart cold as she realized that, for all notice he would take of her now, she might weep and wring her hands in all the passion of her shame and loss. "He would not even turn toward me if I should cry out," she thought.

And perhaps she was right; love may love unselfishness while being itself selfish. Stanhope had forgotten Flora for the moment, and when he did remember her it was only to say:

"I might not feel it all so much, if I were sure she was in good hands; but I am not sure of it. There was something in her life that was not happy. Bright and quaint as she ever was, there were moments when a look of positive care would come into her face. What occasioned it I never knew; but it troubles me now, because all means of aiding her are taken from me.

"Stanhope"—Flora had leaped to her feet, with face aglow and a new earnestness in her eyes—"what was her name? Do tell me."

"It was Mary—Mary Evans." He was looking at *her* now.

"And her home, the place she came from?"

"Philadelphia, I believe."

"You believe! Did not you know?"

"Her teacher told me that her father's letters were oftenest mailed from there."

"Well?"

"But her father was a rover, and I do not think that Mary had any settled home."

"But you can find out, you say, where she is now?"

"Through her teacher—yes."

"Then do so, Stanhope; for if you cannot be her friend, I can. And such a friend! O Stanhope, trust me.

He was moved, deeply moved, by this unexpected, this angelic generosity. She had so forgotten herself that it was time he remembered her. Gazing earnestly in her face, he lifted her hand to his lips and gently kissed it.

"I will do what you ask," said he; and with that bond between them he left the room.

XI

A New Interest

W hat is this?"
        Jack had entered Stanhope's room rather unceremoniously, and found him stooping over an open trunk.

"I am going away. I was going to-morrow morning, but I shall wait a day or two longer now. I hope you have nothing to say to detain me. Till I have breathed another atmosphere, I shall not be fit to do anything in this."

Jack lowered his tones. "I went to the place you spoke of this afternoon, and found a man there who remembered selling this pistol very well." And Jack laid on the table before him a small package. "It was on last Tuesday afternoon."

"Tuesday?" Mr. White's death had occurred on Wednesday. "Did my father then buy it himself?"

"No. The clerk I talked with described the man who bought it, as a large and splendidly built man, with a face much pock-marked."

Stanhope, in sudden excitement, rang the bell and sent for Josephine. Had the man who had brought the pistol to the house been fine-looking and pock-marked? A few questions put to this girl elicited the fact that he had.

This discovery gave a new turn to their thoughts. The pistol had not been sent for on the impulse of the moment, but bought the day before by one who was evidently only Mr. White's messenger. Any conclusion could be drawn from this; and Stanhope, who had hoped for some new and favorable light from this inquiry, felt, on the contrary, that it had only brought fresh shadows to obscure an already impenetrable mystery.

"I shall never know the truth," thought he. Yet he urged Jack to make what efforts he could to find the pock-marked man, and secretly vowed within himself never to let the matter rest till he had followed to the utmost each and every clue which might be given him in explanation of his father's death.

Jack did not remain long that evening. The abstraction in his companion's manner was even beyond his large patience to endure; so, after a few hurried questions as to the place Stanhope intended to visit, he made his adieux, and proceeded to go down-stairs.

To his surprise, possibly to his chagrin, Stanhope followed him. When he reached the lower hall his head involuntarily turned toward the open drawing-room door, and then as resolutely turned from it. Stanhope, coming up behind him, glanced through this open door, and, seeing Flora's slim and elegant figure disappearing through the portieres that screened off the library, he stepped up to Jack, who, with flushed face, was putting on his overcoat, and earnestly whispered:

"If, in the years to come, you can win the heart of the woman in there, you will gain for yourself a treasure of whose worth you yourself know but little."

Jack, who was trembling with an emotion he sought to subdue, turned suddenly and surveyed his friend long and incredulously.

"Is that your opinion of Flora Hastings?" he asked.

"No," answered Stanhope, with the shadow of a smile; "but that is my opinion of Flora White. Sorrow has given her a heart. I hope it may be your fate to win that heart for your own."

Jack, in a burst of deep feeling, wrung his friend's hand, and hastily left the house. Stanhope, with the shadows settling darker and darker upon him, went slowly back up-stairs.

The next morning he went directly to Bay Ridge. He took the little ferry-boat that sailed from the Wall Street slip, and landed on the shore road leading to Fort Hamilton. It was a glorious fall day, and many delightful memories rushed upon him, as he trod the grassy slopes and threaded the picturesque lanes of this quaint and delightful quarter. But not till he was seated in the commodious and old-fashioned parlor where but a year before he had more than once encountered the dear young face he loved, did he realize how sharp memory could be when unallied with hope. Not in all the world around him was there any spot so dear to him as this, for here, in the midst of the every-day and the commonplace, had blossomed the very flower of existence, lending a charm to the plain and ordinary which is not to be found in scenes of barren beauty and soulless splendor.

Over a certain mantelpiece in a rather dim end of the room there hung a large painting, which, if he had been asked to describe the appearance of the room, would have been the only object in it he could have described. It was a copy, well executed, of Kemble's Hamlet, and the dark beauty of this princely figure with its waving plumes had a marked effect upon his imagination, linked as it was with one of his sweetest memories. He was looking at this picture and thinking of the day when he saw her sitting beneath it, an incarnation of living brightness, as it was an incarnation of mysterious gloom, when the door behind him opened and Miss Gracia entered.

With the first view of her face, he felt his already too heavy spirits sink still further. It was a good face and a kind one, with attractive little puckers in it, which spoke of deep experiences made light by great innate humor; but it was also a concerned, if not frightened face, and she hesitated as she advanced, and seemed not to know where to find the courage to return his stately greeting.

"You have come," she faltered, "for the address which I promised you a year ago?"

He bowed again; he had no words as yet at his command.

"I cannot give it to you, Mr. White," she declared. "We have lost sight of Mary; she has not answered our letters now for three months."

"Oh," he burst out, without restraint, "why did you not tell me of this? I might have found her—might have saved her. She may be ill or—dead."

"I am to blame," she acknowledged, "but I kept hoping every day to hear from her. She had promised never to let a week go by without writing to me, and at first she kept her word. But lately there has been no sign from her, and our own letters, sent punctually, have many of them been returned."

"Where did you send them? From what place did she write last?"

"From Philadelphia; I have the address here, but she is no longer to be found at this street and number. I have friends in Philadelphia, and they inquired for me. They were told—excuse me, sir; I presume you wish to know the exact truth—that no such young lady had ever lived in that house."

"Let me see the number," said he.

Miss Gracia handed him the card she held, and he looked at it long and earnestly. But it told him nothing, and he placed it in his breast-pocket with a shaking hand. "I am much obliged to you," he assured her, "for all the care and interest you have shown this young girl, and for the sympathy you now evince in my disappointment. She is the dearest object in life to me, as you must have seen, and though my circumstances have so changed since I saw you last, that I can no longer consider the possibility of making her my wife, yet is her welfare most precious to me."

"The loss of your father"—ventured Miss Gracia.

"Has made changes," interpolated Stanhope, gravely. "I confide this to you for the reason that I once told you of other and very different intentions on my part. Mary is lost to us, and neither of us may ever see her again; but there must be no misapprehension between us as to my feelings in her regard. I love and honor her, Miss Gracia, as few men love and honor the women of their choice; but I may not marry her. You will credit me with good reasons, Miss Gracia."

She bowed, stammered, and tried to show both her sympathy and her confidence. But she was grievously disappointed and secretly much shocked, and found it very hard to imagine any good reason for this change in his determination.

He saw what was in her mind and sighed, but did not attempt to offer any further explanations. Not till he rose to go did he recur to the subject again, then he said: "There is one thing I should like to be sure of before I leave you—that she, Miss Evans, did not know of the state of my feelings toward her. You promised to be silent. Did you keep that promise?"

"Implicitly."

His face showed relief.

"You have my gratitude," he replied. "It would have been too painful to face her disappointment as well as my own."

The direct gaze of Miss Gracia wavered as she bowed in answer to his good-by. It returned again, however, to his countenance as on the threshold of the door he stopped to ask where Sophy was, and if she would not be able to give tidings of her friend.

"Sophy is with me still, Mr. White, but she is not the Sophy she was when Mary stood at her side. The poor cripple has written as faithfully as I have, but the answers to her letters stopped at the same time as my own. It has broken her heart, and she looks like a nipped flower. Would you like to see her?"

Stanhope hesitated, then declined. He felt that he lacked the necessary courage for the ordeal.

"I will send her to-day a box of the choicest flowers I can find. Tell her they are from one of Mary's friends, who mourns her loss equally with herself."

The kind-hearted preceptress bowed again, this time with real feeling. But after he was gone she asked herself over and over what it was that so imperatively stood in the way of his affections. Alas, the answer always was, that he had come into a fortune and found the poor girl too obscure to share its benefits with him. Could she but have known the truth and done him the justice he deserved!

On his way home Stanhope debated with himself in regard to his future movements. He had determined to take up his abode at the club, but meanwhile he must have the change he considered necessary to a proper restoration of his equanimity. Where should he go? He had told Jack he should disappear into New England, but now he felt an impetus toward Philadelphia. While weighing the question, he let his eyes fall on the evening paper which he had bought in the ferry-house. His father's name was before him, linked with many expressions of mingled praise and regret. Such articles were common in the papers at this time, but he could not read them. The doubts of his father's last feeling toward himself beclouded his mind and made all such allusions to the dead statesman a positive pain. He therefore dropped his eye from the column, with that old expression of inner uneasiness: "Shall I ever know the truth? Will there ever be a solution to the enigma as to whether my father's death was accidental or the result of a profound if mistaken jealousy of me his son?" There was no answer, and yet, as his eye fell upon the following paragraph, he had a feeling as if some new thread, intangible and vague, had been put into his hands.

The Mysterious Disappearance of a Strangely Marked Man

"Thomas Dalton, living at number 6 Markham Place, has been missing from his home since the 20th inst. He is a man of about fifty-two years of age, and has one strong distinguishing mark. Upon the palm of his left hand are to be seen two scars crossing each other diagonally. Any tidings of the whereabouts of this man will be received with gratitude by his daughter at the above address."

Such a scar had disfigured his father's left hand. It was the sole blemish in an otherwise perfect physique. How strange the coincidence, and how confusing the thoughts to which it gave rise! The date of this Dalton's disappearance too, was it not that of his father's death? Yes; but should that excite him? There could be no connection between this man from Markham Place and his noble father; and yet this one fact of their being both marked by similar and most certainly remarkable scars did most assuredly link them together in his thoughts in a way to rouse deepest interest.

This was all the more pronounced from the fact that his father would never talk about this scar. When he as a very little boy had asked about it, the shadow which crossed his father's usually clear brow had been so dark and forbidding that it was in itself a rebuke which he had never dared to incur again. And his mother must have met with just such a repulse herself, for when a little while later he summoned up courage to ask her if she knew what had hurt his father's hand so badly, she had answered that she did not, and that he was never to speak of it again, either to her or to any one, for such things should be sacred in a son's eyes and not a matter of idle curiosity. And he never had mentioned it since, but he often had thought of it, and now was destined to think of it again, and that, too, with a burning curiosity which would not be appeased.

Re-reading the paragraph which had just made this revolution in his thoughts, he noted that the name of the man was Thomas Dalton, and that the number of the tenement from which he had disappeared was 6; and when it came time for him to step from the ferry-boat, he found himself walking up Broadway to the City Hall, instead of taking the cars which would carry him directly home. He had made up his mind to go to Markham Place and learn for himself what sort of a man this was who had a scar upon his left hand exactly like that of his father.

XII

No. 6 Markham Place

The sun had set before Stanhope had left the ferry-house, and it was dusk before he reached the City Hall. The sight of the twinkling lights which now started up on every side gave him his first intimation of this, and made him pause and ask if it would not be better for him to delay this adventure till he could have daylight upon it. The quarter in which this place lay was entirely unknown to him, and from the looks given him by the man who had just directed him thither, he judged that the place did not have the best of reputations, and that if he did make up his mind to venture into it at so late an hour, he had better make some arrangements for leaving behind him the few valuables that he carried on his person.

This was not pleasant in the prospect, but his interest was too great now for retreat; so, after a short consultation with a policeman, who, while not saying much against Markham Place itself, still advised him not to be too eager in the display of his watch-chain in the streets leading to it, he crossed over to the Astor House and gave up a certain pocket-book which he carried, into the charge of the clerk there. Then he started out again, this time direct to the little street. It was quite dark when he reached it, and the sights he saw on his way there, and the noises he had heard, unconsciously influenced his mind, and prepared him for a scene of great poverty and distress. But when he had taken a few steps past the corner, he was agreeably surprised to find the place comparatively neat and quiet. A small drug-store, well lighted for this quarter, illuminated one end of the street; and, beyond, a solitary gas lamp flickering in the cool wind took from the gloom of the remoter regions and enabled him to see that the buildings on each side were of the better class of tenement houses from which all evidences of respectability had not quite departed. A sound of loud singing, in which a Sunday-school air mingled with a popular street ballad, was the sole sound disturbing the place, and altogether it was with a feeling of relief that he entered the drug-store for information as to where No. 6 was.

The lank, pale-eyed young man who answered the question contented himself with the word "Opposite;" and Stanhope felt his courage still further increase as he noted that his errand created neither surprise nor dismay in the mind of this man. Stepping out, he crossed the street to the house which had been pointed out to him, and as he did so felt a sudden weird sensation as he noted the red glare that crimsoned its threshold. It came, of course, from the druggist's window behind him, but it lay so directly before the door that it made him feel that he would have to step through blood to enter. But, as he approached, his own figure cut off the light and the red spot disappeared, but he had an unpleasant realization that now it was shining on his back and pointing him out perhaps as a victim on the threshold of this unknown house.

A ring at the bell brought a lame old woman to the door. She looked surprised at his figure and elegance, but, when he mentioned the name of Dalton, her expression suddenly changed and became both knowing and obsequious. Motioning him in, she led him along a narrow hall to a glazed door screened by an inner curtain.

Stopping in front of this, she gave him a quick nod and senile smile. "This is where he lived," said she. "But he is gone. Went out one day and never came back. His daughter don't know what to do."

As she said this, he thought he heard a cry. Looking about, he interrogated the old woman with his eyes. She had heard the sound too, for she glanced toward the door before which he was standing.

"Miss Dalton is afraid of strangers," said she.

"Was that his daughter?" he asked, moved, he hardly knew why.

"I suppose so; there's nobody else on this hall."

"Is she—young?"

The woman leered and he looked at her. Then she seemed to grow ashamed and spoke up respectfully enough:

"Yes, very young."

He turned again toward the door.

"I do not like to trouble her," said he. "Is there any one else in the house who knew the father? Any man?" She fumbled with her pocket, glancing at him askance.

"My husband has a ready tongue," said she.

He had by this time drawn back from the door into a short cross hall directly opposite.

"Let me see him, then," was his answer.

She courtesied and limped on before him down this very hall.

"He is sometimes gruff," she whispered, looking back over her shoulder, "but you mustn't mind that. For a quid of tobacco he will talk all night, and tell you no nonsense either. Have you any tobacco about you?"

"No," he answered, "but I have what will buy some." And he slipped a quarter into her hand.

She laughed a low, happy laugh, and hugged the quarter to her breast as if it had opened before her a region of delight.

"We both use it," she chattered, and limped forward to a door which she opened and entered.

As he turned to follow her, something made him look back. Was he dreaming, or had he been suddenly translated into a state of existence where spirits visit us unawares? *She* was there, his darling, his Mary, standing in the open doorway he had just left, with her arms held out, and her face swimming in tears. A vision! But no, those tears are real. It is she herself; he has found her again, and found her *here!*

In a confusion of feeling he did not seek to analyze, he forgot his errand, forgot the old woman motioning and chattering in the room at his side, and darted back to where that young girl stood.

"Mary!" he cried; and in that one word, with its tone of infinite protection and longing, his heart told its whole tale.

She heard it, and a smile of infinite sweetness crossed her face, to which the year which had elapsed since they had last met had added the grace of womanhood.

"Oh!" she murmured, shrinking back into the room from which she had just emerged. "Has God sent me a friend? I need one so much."

He stepped after her, but did not close the door behind him.

"I came in search of Thomas Dalton, who has disappeared," he declared. "That I find *you*—"

"Thomas Dalton, as you call him, is my father," she stammered. "I do not know why—I do not understand this or many other things that are peculiar in our lives; but he wished to be called Dalton while living here, and so he was called Dalton."

Stanhope felt an inward recoil. Was this child of snow and light the daughter of an adventurer? The school in which he had first found her was too respectable for him to harbor such an idea; and yet—

She seemed to read his thoughts.

"My father is a gentleman," she declared, "and a man of learning and skill; but he is eccentric, very eccentric, and this puzzles me, as perhaps it does you."

The sweet dignity which informed her winsome and touching features as she uttered these words moved Stanhope to the depths of his soul. Could he have followed his impulse, he would have caught her up and carried her out of this doubtful place, into the light and love of his own home and heart. But a gulf had been dug between them, and he must remember that she stood beyond his reach. So, while he smiled, it was with brotherly interest and not a lover's passion.

"You shall tell me your troubles, and we will find a way out of your difficulties," said he. "Have you no idea where your father has gone?"

"None whatever," said she.

He glanced about the strange and oddly furnished room, the influence of which he had already felt in an added sense of the spectral nature of the whole scene, but of whose details he had as yet taken no note, and found that, whatever cause might lie at the base of Mr. Dalton's or Evans's eccentricities, it was not the usual one of abject poverty. Though there were no signs of luxury present, there was comfort in the air; and on the solitary shelf which ran about the whole four walls, he saw many books, of whose value he was convinced at a glance.

"I have never heard you say whether you had other relatives than your father," he ventured.

"No," she replied, watching him anxiously as his eyes travelled from the dark ceiling to the bare floor, and thence to the table loaded with strange and uncanny looking articles, over whose use and purpose she had herself so often wondered when she had seen her father working with and upon them. "We are all alone in the world. I have never heard him speak of a sister, a niece, or a nephew. The only friends I have ever had were those I made in school. I am very lonely."

"Miss Evans"—he dared not call her Mary, and the new name of Miss Dalton would not spring to his lips—"do you mean to say that you live in these rooms alone, since your father went away?"

"Yes," with a slight shudder. "How can I help it? He left me here, and here must I stay. If he had let me keep my friends— But I must not talk about my father. He is always good to me; so good, he makes me forget where I am when he is here with me. It is only in his absence I grieve. For why should he leave me without a word? He must have known how helpless I would be. Do you think—" she faltered and surveyed him with wild eyes—"that anything serious could have happened to him?"

He faltered in his turn. There was a question he wanted very much to put to her, and hardly knew how to do it without hurting her sensibilities. "What kind of a looking man is your father?" he asked at last.

"Oh, good looking; that is, to me."

"A large man?"

"Oh, no, rather small; not as tall as you are."

"Was he spare in figure—what is called wiry by some?"

"I don't know; perhaps."

"The paper speaks of a scar on his hand: was that the only distinguishing mark that he bore?"

"What do you mean? I do not know how to answer you?"

"Has he ever had the small-pox? Was he pockmarked, in short?"

"Oh, no; what made you think so? My father had a student's face; very fine when he was not worried." Stanhope felt the snapping of a supposed clue. Then this man was not the one who had bought the pistol for his father. His face showed that a change had taken place in his thoughts, but she was too inexperienced to note it. He soon recovered himself, however.

"He had cares, then," he went on. "Did they seem to be greater just before he disappeared?"

Her eyes fell, and the tear which had been trembling on her eye-lash rolled slowly down her cheek.

"Yes, yes," said she. "I cannot tell you, for he has always bidden me never to talk about him; but I am sure he had some dreadful fright. His face—" She checked herself, but the quick shudder of her delicate frame conveyed her terror at the memory.

Stanhope's interest in this matter had reached the point of pain. For her own sake as well as his own, he felt the necessity of pushing his inquiries to the last verge of propriety. He accordingly did not accept the suggestion of her reticence, but said entreatingly, "If you wish your father to be found, you must not keep anything back, Miss Evans."

"I know," said she, "but—" Her indecision was painful. But suddenly she rose above it. "I must confide in you," she declared. "He could not have meant for me to keep silence when his welfare, perhaps his very life, is involved. And you will respect what I say; you will not tell the police or—or—" She stopped and pointed down the hall before her. "Those people are listening," she whispered.

"Then speak lower," he enjoined; "I do not like to close the door. That woman has a malicious look, and you are too unprotected to be at the mercy of her comments."

"True," said she, her innocent face aflush. "If I could but go back to Miss Gracia! But that would displease father. Though he did not say so, I know he expects to find me here when he comes back—if he ever does come back."

Stanhope had his own plans in her regard, but he thought it better not to urge them just yet.

"You have not told me," he suggested, facing about so as to keep the hall before him under his eye—

"What frightened my father? I do not know myself, but—" Her tones were very low now, and she leaned toward him till her breath almost touched his cheek. "He was sitting there," pointing to the old green chair in front of the table before them, "when I suddenly heard him jump up. I was in the further room; but at the sound he made I hurried in, when I saw him standing just about where you are now, trembling like an aspen. I had seen him look frightened before, but never as he did then, and it so frightened me that I could not for the moment find words to ask him what was the matter. When I did it was too late. With a look I shall never forget, he had flung down a key which he had dragged out from one of his pockets, and gone—gone out of the door, gone out of the house; and when I ran to the front after him, he was already out of sight in the crowd that pours by the mouth of the place all day. That is how he disappeared. Isn't it strange, and isn't it dreadful?"

"I do not understand it," returned Stanhope, looking with a degree of awe at the old green chair. "Did he go out bareheaded and without means? Do you know if he had any money in his purse?"

"He always had money," she murmured earnestly; "there is never any lack of that. Indeed," she went on, glancing oddly behind her at an old chest that darkened one corner of the room, "I—" But she did not go on with this. Instead of it, she answered his other question. "He was not bareheaded, for he caught up his hat as he passed around the table. It was always kept lying here, just within reach of his hand. He never allowed me to move it or to take it away. He was very particular about this table; everything was kept just so."

Stanhope glanced again at the odd appliances grouped methodically upon it.

"Your father was interested in electrical matters," he asserted.

"Is that it?" she asked. "I knew that a bell sometimes rang. But come here!"

She flitted like a wraith across the floor. She laid her hand on a long curtain hanging in a place so dark he had not hitherto observed it, and, drawing it back, pointed to some object within.

"Is that electrical, too?" she asked, with something like suppressed fear in her tones.

Bending forward, he looked at the apparatus which she had disclosed, and vaguely nodded. "I judge so," said he, "but—"

"Don't touch it!" she almost screamed, putting out her hand to draw him back. The action loosened the curtain, which again fell into its place, instantly hiding the object of her terror. "I beg your pardon," she entreated, "I did not mean to be rude, but my father—"

"Is anything the matter?" came in piping tones from behind them. " I thought I heard some one cry out."

They both turned. The lame old woman stood in the doorway.

"You did," remarked Stanhope, with quick presence of mind. "Miss Dalton " (he forced himself to say the name) "was showing me her father's machine, and something connected with it hurt her. Miss Dalton and I are old friends."

"So I see; and it's very pleasant for her. I hope you can comfort her a bit." And with a great display of good-nature, that yet was not without its modicum of sincerity, she ambled away and disappeared in her own room again.

Mary drew a deep breath, and glanced up again at Stanhope.

"I am glad she did not see the machine. Father once became very angry because she came in while the curtain was drawn. He has never shown it to anybody, and has often set me as a guard over it when persons came into the room. How I summoned courage to show it to you, I do not know. It usually inspires me with terror, and I even dread to step into this part of the room."

Stanhope would have liked to see it again, but did not dare to propose it. "Living with your father alone has made you nervous," he smiled, losing himself again in the contemplation of her face, which now took on an abstracted air that made her seem more of a dream-maiden than ever.

"Perhaps," she vaguely murmured. Some struggle was evidently going on in her mind.

He, willing to wait for the words that would reveal what that something was, let his eyes remain upon her face, though conscious that in doing this he was but making harder his task of resistance. While he is thus engaged, and she stands silent, let us describe her face, since it was a rare one to be seen there, or indeed in any place.

The brow was lovely, dazzlingly white as I have already said, but with no hint of sickliness in its snowy expanse. Above it, and on either side, a cloud of golden hair undulated in airy curls that were like a net of sunshine.

Underneath, her eyes made a soft light, and created that expression of childlike entreaty which was corrected by the spirited outline of a nose that was just aquiline enough to give a high-bred look to her features, and lift her from the ranks of merely pretty women into those of positive beauty. Had her mouth been ordinary, all this might have been wasted; but around those two red lips, with their bewitching upward curves, lay all the sweetness of a naturally arch and lovable nature, and this, added to the soft contour of cheek and chin not too round for intellectual expression, made of this young girl's countenance a winsome whole that few men could see unmoved, and none without an added respect for the womanhood that could produce so tender an example of mingled charm and dignity. She was dressed, as she always was, in a gown that attracted no attention to itself, and yet which gave a most picturesque aspect to her form, which was slight almost to the verge of delicacy.

"I wonder"—She was speaking now, and he bent all his attention to hear what she would say—"why you asked if my father had a face disfigured by small-pox. Do you know any such man?"

She looked up as she asked this last question, and he felt his cheeks slightly crimson. Had he forgotten the errand which had led him to this house, in the interest which had arisen in her behalf?

"Let me inquire, first, if you do?" was his somewhat guarded reply

"No; but such a person came to this room immediately after my father went out. I thought you might have heard of it, and so connected him in some way with my father."

She was still looking at him, so he did not allow the sudden shock which these words gave him to appear in his face. He could not control his tones so perfectly, however, and his voice shook slightly as he replied:

"You may be right; I had heard of a pock-marked man. What was the appearance of this one, and what did he want in this room?"

"He said he wanted my father, and asked if he were in. In appearance he was very tall and very large, and had eyes that made one feel small and helpless. I did not like his looks."

"Did he leave when you told him your father had gone out?"

"Yes, but not without casting a long, slow look around the room. I did not know then what I had to fear: but since—"

"Excuse me, you must not think me persistent, but was it immediately after your father went out so suddenly, that this man came in?"

"Immediately. I found him here when I came back from the street door."

"Found him here!"

"Mrs. Bowne was with him—the woman who just came in."

"Then he was in the house when your father ran out. Perhaps—" But he did not finish. Why rouse new fears or new suspicions in this young girl's breast? "Did he make any remark when he was going? Ask where your father had gone, or say that he would be here again?"

"No; he only cast that peculiar look around him, and then one other long look at me. Why he smiled when he took his eyes away, I cannot imagine, for it was not a good smile. And he stopped again in going out, and looked back and smiled again, but not at me; and though I did not dream then that my father would not return before the day was over, I was frightened at this man and did not feel easy over his visit. Since—"

But again he interrupted her at that same word. "You shall not stay here," he cried. "It would be monstrous in me to leave you where such fears can assail you. Get together what things you need—"

But she shook her head violently. "I *must* stay," she persisted, looking, however, on the sudden, very pale and worn. "There is a reason why I dare not leave these rooms. Would it be safe to push the door to a little?" she queried, with her lips close to his ear. "I want to show you something it would be dangerous for any one else to know about."

He glanced at her and then across the hall. All was silent in that direction, but the door of the janitor's room was open like their own. Leaning forward, he gave the latter a light push, and it swung to, almost to the point of closing.

"Now, what is it?" he asked.

She seemed to hesitate. "I am not old enough or wise enough for such responsibilities," she objected. "If my father is living, I may be betraying him; but that mysterious man, and the look he gave about the room, may have some connection with my father's disappearance, for he has been in the house again, and— Take this!" she cried, with sudden resolution, putting in his hand a key and pointing hastily across the room, but not to where the curtain hung above the machine she had before disclosed, but to the old chest which he had observed in his first survey of the room. "Unlock that trunk, quick; I have no confidence in the Bownes. See what is in it and come back to me. I will keep guard while you are about it." And she took up her station at the crack made by the nearly closed door.

Startled, and totally unable to guess what he was about to discover, he crossed the room and hastily inserted the key in the large and old-fashioned lock of the huge chest before him. It turned without an effort, and, upon lifting the lid, he saw—to his astonishment, no doubt, for he had expected something sinister—a collection of old clothes neatly spread out till they covered the entire surface of the space before him. But before he could utter a word she had sent him a loud whisper over her shoulder.

"Throw those out and look beneath. One glance will do."

He did as he was bid, and this time was not disappointed in what he found. The trunk was full of money, actual hard cash to a large amount. There was gold and silver, and bank-notes and coupons, all laid in with exactness on a square of heavy cloth, and so unprotected that he flung back in haste the clothing he had taken from above them, lest the walls around him should take note of this ready fortune and whisper the secret abroad.

"I see," was his comment, as he handed back to Mary the key. "You dare not leave this chest behind you. Never mind, we will take it with us."

She did not seem to hear; she was intent upon explaining her own attitude in regard to this money.

"I did not know there was money in this chest," said she, "till I opened it two days after my father went away. This was the key he threw me. Does not the fact of his giving it up to me look as if he expected to stay away? He had never let me take so much as a peep into the trunk before."

Stanhope thought it looked as if the man had gone to his death, but he did not say so. On the contrary, he assured her that her father might only have meant to provide her with the means of satisfying her necessities in case he was detained away for some time; a supposition at which she grasped so eagerly, transparent as the reasoning was, that he could not but see how much this young girl loved and depended upon her father, notwithstanding the mystery that surrounded him.

"Yes, yes," she agreed, "that would be like him. He was always careful of me, and ever anxious that I should be comfortable. But I never knew we had so much money. But that pock-marked man may, and if he should come again—"

"He would find you and the chest both vanished," finished Stanhope. "I am going to send for a coach at once."

"And if my father should return?"

"He will be told where to find you. I am going to take you to Mrs. White. She is a good woman, and will welcome you kindly."

What was the matter? Was the sweet child going to faint, now that the strain was gone and relief promised? He reached out his arm toward her, but she drew back.

"Mrs. White?" she gasped. "Your wife?"

The room reeled about him. On the instant he understood why Miss Gracia had looked at him that morning with such disturbed eyes. Mary loved him, and she was now a woman with a woman's heart, which he felt he was destined to break.

XIII

There's Many a Slip

N ot at all," remarked Stanhope, when he could recover himself. "I have no wife; I alluded to my father's young widow. She is but little older than yourself."

It was a bitter trial to his self-restraint to see the color come back to her cheek, and the life to her eye. But the influence of his father's wishes was strong upon him, and he did not falter.

"She can do for you," he proceeded, "what I never can. Will you consent, then, to go to her?"

"If you say it is right," replied Mary, but with something of the sparkle gone from her glance.

He turned and opened wide the door he had so nearly closed.

"I will explain matters to the janitor, while you pack the chest," said he. "Do you owe anything for rent? If so, it had better be paid."

"They owe me," said she. "Mrs. Bowne begged me so hard to advance her a quarter's rent, that I did so yesterday."

"It is just as well. You will want to leave your father's books and apparatus here for a while untouched. Can the janitor be trusted with the key?"

"I think Mrs. Bowne will meddle."

"Well, that cannot be helped. You cannot remain here to watch senseless machinery."

She smiled with naive happiness. It was pleasant to be commanded by one in whom she so trusted. Yet her conscience hurt her a little, and it was with lagging steps that she finally crossed the floor and vanished into the further room.

As she disappeared Stanhope turned to seek the janitor; but, before he had reached the door, some influence made him pause and listen. He had heard something, what he hardly knew; and that something was not the light step of Mary moving about in the adjoining room, nor was it the low grumble of Mr. and Mrs. Bowne talking together in their apartment down the hall. But, whatever it was, it ceased when he stopped to listen; and he was about to move forward again, when the noise recurred, and this time he recognized it for what it was—a stealthy and hesitating step. Some one was in the main hall. Some one was approaching upon him from the front door, and, though the distance was short, the caution of the intruder was making it long. Who was this intruder, and why should any one come creeping into the house in this manner at so early an hour? Instinctively he thought of the pock-marked man, and dimly wondered if in another moment he would discern, gliding across the open doorway, the person of the one being who possibly could explain the real cause of his father's death.

This person, whoever it was, was now very near; for, by holding his own breath, Stanhope could distinguish that of the intruder. He, however, did not show himself, and Stanhope, seeing no reason for prolonging his suspense, walked rapidly to the door and looked out.

A shrinking form met his eyes, but it was not that of any pock-marked man. On the contrary, the face, which shone dimly upon him from beneath the broad-brimmed hat which so heavily shielded it, was pale and smooth, with delicate, quivering lips and a keen glance. The eyebrows he especially noted, as they were large and overhanging, and gave a decided individuality to the face, while the lock of hair lying on the collar of the loose cloak in which the stranger was wrapped struck Stanhope as being too brown for the countenance, which had a look of age not yet observable in the figure.

Who was it? A visitor, or Mr. Dalton himself? Stanhope was inclined to think it was the latter; and, bowing with great respect, he was about to utter his excuses, when the old man drew himself up and asked, with sudden sharp suspicion, in which there was an odd note of personal relief:

"And who are you, sir? And what are you doing in my room? Is not my daughter here?"

"If you are Mr. Dalton, yes. That is, she is in her own room. I was but waiting here for her to collect such articles together as she thought necessary for a short visit to a lady friend. Not knowing you were about to return so soon, she thought it better to go where she could be protected by one of her own sex. She will not wish to go now."

The old man's suspicion, which had been pronounced enough before, not only deepened at these words, but changed in character. Motioning Stanhope into the room, he stepped in after him and closed the door, giving as he did so a quick and comprehensive look about, which, as Stanhope noticed, took in the chest and the falling curtain as the chief objects of interest.

"And how do you come to take an interest in this matter?" he asked, after a sufficiently significant survey of the fine form and uncommonly attractive countenance of the young man before him.

"Miss Dalton is an old friend of mine. I made her acquaintance—" He paused; he had called her Dalton, but he could not go on without showing that he knew this to be an assumed name. It was not to be helped, however, so he continued after the momentary break— "when she was a scholar in Bay Ridge. I did not come here to see her, because I did not know she lived in this place. I had other business in this house, and, happening to see her face, naturally sought to renew her acquaintance. Conversation brought out her difficulties, and I was but acting the part of a gentleman in endeavoring to alleviate them."

There was, as I have before said, a candor in Stanhope's expression that carried conviction with it to the most doubting minds. In the old man's keen eyes, as he listened to this explanation, many significant glances glittered and passed, but amongst them doubt of this young man's good intentions had no longer a place.

As he finished, Mr. Dalton moved abruptly.

"I am obliged to you for your interest," said he; "but as you see yourself, she no longer needs your assistance. I will therefore excuse you. My daughter can receive no visitors *here*."

Stanhope bowed and took up his hat. "Please make my apologies to Miss Evans," he prayed, and instantly flushed at his mistake, which had almost the appearance of an insult. "Pardon me," he hastily stammered forth, "it is the name I knew her by in Bay Ridge. I meant no disrespect by its use, I assure you."

The old man, whose mind seemed to have taken another turn, waved his left hand slightly; and Stanhope, who had been watching for a movement of this kind, felt a sudden sick sense of familiarity as he caught sight of the two deep scars which crossed the half-open palm.

"She *is* Miss Evans," said her father, coldly. "That I preferred her to be called Dalton while we remained in this quarter, is but a proof of my care. She is destined for other circles, and, if you are the gentleman you appear, you will forget that she has ever borne but the one name."

"She shall always be Miss Evans to me," declared Stanhope.

But the old man was not easily satisfied. He did not look pleased at this and shifted about uneasily.

"I have not asked your name," said he, "because our acquaintanceship will probably not continue. But I should like to know if you live in this city."

"I do, sir."

The old man bowed. "I regret it; but, since it is so, let me ask if you feel sufficient kindness toward us to promise me that if by chance you and my daughter meet hereafter, it will be as strangers?"

It was a request which would have been staggering under ordinary circumstances, but, coming as it did after an interview which had aroused all the tenderest emotions of his heart, it took all Stanhope's strength of mind to sustain and meet it with proper composure. The father saw the agitation he had caused, and in his turn showed some emotion; but there was no sign of relenting in his manner, and his attitude of waiting for the young man's expected response remained unchanged.

Stanhope, who could not answer instantly, thought of the young girl's look when he had mentioned some one she had thought to be his wife, and felt that upon the decision of this moment rested her happiness as well as his own. If he could not marry her—and that was settled—how could they bear to meet again in any other light than that of strangers. By his own suffering, and the cost which he felt himself paying at this very moment for the intense happiness of the last half hour, he knew that separation, utter and complete, between them was the only thing to be desired. And yet how could he say the word that would cause it? How drop a curtain upon the past which would mean the shutting off of any future for them?

The old man, watching him, began to tremble.

"My daughter is liable to enter at any moment," he intimated.

The hint was enough. Crushing back every suggestion of his heart, the young man faced the elder with truth in his eyes.

"I will do what you say, if you will allow me to explain to Miss Evans that I take my permanent leave of her at your request."

"It is not necessary," the other began, but he did not finish. The door into the other room had opened, and a loud cry of "Father!" told that what they had both feared had happened. Mary was in the room.

Stanhope, with a quick look in her face, which he meant to be the last, waited till she had sprung into her father's arms. Then he said:

"Your father's return has made any interference on my part unnecessary, Miss Evans. I will therefore bid you adieu. When I am gone ask your father why I am thus abrupt, and why, if we meet again, it must be as strangers."

He bowed, and would have gone, but that just then the old man's voice rose in such a cry of mingled anger and terror that he instinctively paused.

"Advertised for me? Unhappy girl, what have you done? In what words did you advertise? Speak, speak!"

She was so frightened that she did not notice that her happiness was slipping from her. Her eyes were on her father, and her lips were vainly trying to form some words in reply.

"Speak, speak!" the father urged. "Would you kill me with suspense? By what name did you advertise for me, Evans or Dalton?"

"Dalton, Dalton," she stammered forth. "Oh, do not look at me like that. I did not know I was doing wrong; I feared you might be dead—"

"Hush! and tell me the very words you used. I want to hear nothing else. The words, the words!

But, thus conjured, her memory failed her; she could not think of anything, much less of the words required of her—her mind was a blank. Turning in her misery, she encountered Stanhope's pitying countenance. Instantly she threw out one arm in his direction.

"Ask him," she entreated. "He must have read the advertisement and may remember."

Stanhope had the paper in his pocket which contained it. Drawing it forth, he advanced and placed it in the hand held out to receive it. As he did so, he was astonished to see that a change had already taken place in the old man's manner. Although still eager, he was no longer angry. Instead, there was something like a gleam of satisfaction in his eye as he bent over to read the few closely printed sentences. Not till he reached the last paragraph did he manifest any emotion, and this was only perceptible to Stanhope, who was watching him and could not but notice the sudden convulsive closing of the other's left hand, as he read of the two crossed scars. Mary's father had mastered even this feeling, however, when he spoke again to his panting and anxious daughter.

"Well, well, it is not so bad," he remarked. "No great harm can come from this, and perhaps it may lead to something good. Have you had any visitors, my child—any one inquiring for me?"

"One," said she; and Stanhope, who felt that he was now expected to go, could not summon up the courage to do so without putting in a word calculated to solve some of his own doubts.

"It was a pock-marked man," cried he, "who entered this room and looked very boldly about him. It was on account of this fact, sir, and the fears he aroused in Miss Evans, that I presumed to offer her the refuge of a friend's house. She was afraid he would come again."

The old man, who had been seized with a vertigo, reeled and glanced hurriedly toward the door.

"When was this?" he asked, not of Stanhope, but of his daughter. "Not to-day?"

"No, no," she responded. "But he was here yesterday; I saw him in the hall; he was going up the main stairs. I think he has hired a room overhead."

Instantly a frenzy of fear seemed to seize the old man. "Why did you not say so?" he asked. "Don't you know that he is my enemy? Ten minutes have been lost; ten minutes in which we might have been working. Was that a step?" he gasped, looking toward the door and trembling anew. "You must excuse me," he pleaded, catching Stanhope's eye, whose presence he had evidently forgotten. "I have cause to fear the man of whom my daughter speaks, and— Do you think anybody heard me come into the house?" he suddenly inquired.

"I should think the Bownes might," Stanhope cautiously ventured. "Their door is open, and we have not been speaking very low."

"The Bownes are venial; they will take money. Here are five dollars, ten dollars, twenty—anything to make them hold their tongues. As for you, sir, you said just now that you proposed to take my daughter to a place of refuge. The idea was a good one, which I do not now feel like rejecting. If, therefore, you still find yourself in a position to carry out this plan, I will bid my daughter continue her packing. For neither she nor I can stay here to-night."

More disconcerted than when he was asked to break off all acquaintanceship with her, Stanhope bowed an acceptance that he had not the courage to put into words. Mr. Evans, as if satisfied, drew his daughter toward the threshold of the inner room.

"We will not keep you long waiting," said he. "If you will remain as a watch here, she shall be ready in five minutes to go with you."

"Very well," answered Stanhope, feeling that these sudden transitions were robbing him of all his self-control. "But I shall need a carriage; Miss Evans will have a trunk—"

"I will see to all," cried the old man. "Wait, that is all,—wait."

Mary, who was looking back over her shoulder, gave Stanhope one beaming smile and disappeared.

The old man followed her, and just as Stanhope was wondering what would be done with the money hidden in the chest, Mary's father hastily returned, and, going directly to the chest, threw out the clothes that were in it, and then, stooping over the money, drew up into view what looked like a canvas bag, and without a word or a look in Stanhope's direction hastily carried it into the other room.

"I see," commented Stanhope to himself. "That square of cloth was arranged with strings, so that by a single movement of the hand it becomes a bag with the money inside it. Such devices proclaim the inventive mind of an adventurer. Mary is pure as a snow-flower; but the father, for all his finely cut face, has his reasons for fearing the man he calls his enemy."

Such reflections did not tend to increase Stanhope's equanimity. Indeed, he felt himself placed by this new move in anything but a desirable position. To take charge of this young girl while she was in the unprotected position in which he had found her, was but the common duty of a gentleman; but to take her away with him, now that he knew her proper guardian to be living, involved him in difficulties from which he shrank as much on her account as his own. That Mr. Evans had shown him this trust without so much as asking his name, had likewise its influence upon him. From doubt of this eccentric old man's good character and record, he had reached a disbelief in his love and proper consideration for his child. No father who realized what a treasure he possessed in the devotion of such a daughter, would so blindly risk her welfare; and yet such is the inconsistency of human nature, at the very moment Stanhope was thus judging the situation, his heart was beating fast with the anticipation of introducing this young beauty to his father's widow and seeing her in the home which he had hitherto called his own.

His eye, falling on the table, encountered at this juncture the two or three bills which Mr. Evans had offered as hush money for the Bownes. Why were they lying there? Were they for him to use, or did Mr. Evans expect to pick them up again before leaving? The affair was rapidly growing complicated, and he began to long for more light upon it. Had Mr. Evans returned at this moment, Stanhope would have demanded an explanation of his position, before going any further. But Mr. Evans did not return just then, and Stanhope was left a little longer to his thoughts.

He was sufficiently agitated by them at last to become restless. Taking out his watch, he was surprised to see that it was after nine o'clock. As he had not eaten since noon, this in itself accounted somewhat for his sinking spirits. But it was not of this he was thinking now. He was wondering, vaguely, if they had been gone a long time or if it only seemed so. If he had been asked, he would have said that it appeared to him to be a full half hour since the old man glanced back with the assurance that they would not keep him waiting long; and yet it might have been only five minutes, so slowly goes the time when one is desperately impatient. Determining to know whether he was the victim simply of his own hurry, he kept his watch open in his hand. As he watched the revolving hands, he listened. There was no noise in the adjoining apartment; he could not even hear the light fall of Mary's foot. Had they gone into the room beyond? As he asked himself this question, he determined to wait five minutes more, and then to make some move toward ending this suspense. But before the five minutes had passed, his impatience had reached its limit, and, going to the door of communication, he first knocked and then entered.

No one was in the room he thus invaded, but there was an open door at the other end, to which he hastily passed, calling out the name of Miss Dalton.

The silence that answered him assured him that it would be useless to continue his search, and when, after a quick glance through the doorway, he saw that it communicated directly with the rear hall of the house, and thus in all probability with some back exit leading into the adjacent street, he understood that the two had flown, and that he, Stanhope White, need trouble himself no more about what words he should employ in introducing her to the care of Flora, since in all probability the dream of his life was over and he should never see again either the doubtful father or the bewitching child.

　　　　　　　　　　ANNA KATHARINE GREEN

PART III

A HEART'S CONFLICT

XIV

A Doubtful Couple

C ould Stanhope have followed the dictates of his feelings, he would have left Markham Place immediately after the discovery of Mr. Evans and Mary's flight. But consideration for Mary's future welfare and honor would not allow him to do this without some attempt at an explanation with the Bownes, who he had no doubt were aware of the father's return, and would be in the highest degree puzzled at the sudden departure which had followed it. Then there was the money which had been left lying on the table! He understood now why the father had flung it there, and chafed at the duty it involved, even while preparing himself to perform it.

Putting the bills into his pocket, he crossed the hall to the janitor's room. The door, as he supposed, was still open, and at sight of him, the lame woman came pattering forward, with the ready smile he had already taught himself to distrust. In the farther corner of the room he could just descry the bowed figure of a white-haired man, seated on a cobbler's bench and industriously engaged in mending an old shoe. This was doubtless Mr. Bowne; but, if so, he did not trouble himself to look up at Stanhope's entrance, being in haste to finish his work before the candle, stuck in an old tin cup by his side, should have quite sputtered itself out.

"Is there anything you want?" queried the old woman, with a shrewd pucker of her hanging lower lip. "Miss Dalton is a very nice young lady—"

"Miss Dalton is no longer here," returned Stanhope. "She felt the need of proper protection and has gone where she can have it. That she went without seeing you was due to her father's hurry. You know that her father came back an hour or so ago, did you not?"

"Why, no! Did he, really? And where has he been gone all this while?"

"That's no business of yours," came in gruff tones from the other end of the room. "Women should use their tongues for saying their prayers, and not for asking questions about their neighbors."

"Hear the man!" she cried, with an unexpectedly proud look toward his broad, stooping back, to which his two elbows flying industriously out and in gave just then a grotesque appearance. "Isn't he a good one? Always thinking of his duty, except when he has the tobacco in his mouth," she added, with the slyest of looks, making small her two twinkling eyes.

"I gave you money," retorted Stanhope, sternly. "If you want more you must do something to earn it."

"Oh!" she protested, with what would have been a demure look in a younger and more attractive woman—"it's work you want done. Well, here are two hands that don't stop at much that's honest."

"No, that they don't!" came in muffled tones from between the two waxed ends that the shoemaker was now holding in his mouth.

"Don't you mind him," pleaded she, eager for Stanhope's good opinion, but still indulgent toward her spouse. "He's put out because I'm not holding the candle for him. He'd be more put out if I didn't earn an extra penny when I could. So what do you want, sir? Some news about—"

"I am afraid your husband is right," broke in Stanhope, in sudden disgust. "You want to be talking, and I want you to keep silent. It's the only thing I have money for—silence, silence."

"Oh!" said she, dropping her eyes and stealing a look behind her.

"And what kind of a man are you who want to buy the truth?" demanded the shoemaker, still without turning his head. "We don't sell that kind of ware. If she says we do, she goes out. I won't have no bargaining here for the likes of what you can't eat or wear, or make yourself comfortable with. If silence could be bought in this room, I'd have bought it long ago. But it ain't on sale, I tell you, it ain't on sale."

"That's because there's never been enough money in this room to buy it," she quavered, with a high laugh in which there was no anger if there was no merriment. "No, my good man; if a poor wife cannot have the preevilege of talking now and then, when all the sounds she ever hears for her amusement is the pound, pound of the hammer on the lap-stone, then I think it's high time she did go out. But talking with one's man and talking with the neighbors are two different things, ain't it, sir? and it's the talking in the halls and on the street that you don't want, isn't it, sir?—what they mean by gossip, eh?"

"Yes."

"A woman what talks in, will talk out," came again from between those two flying wax-ends.

"When they are given this to keep silent?" asked Stanhope, hastily leaving the old woman and thrusting a five-dollar bill over the shoemaker's shoulder where he sat at his work.

There was a silence, during which the two wax-ends remained stretched out at their full length, then they came together again.

"You must like her a heap!" observed the cobbler.

Stanhope, greatly disconcerted, drew back the banknote which had not even been touched by the old man.

"It is of the father I was speaking," he remarked. "He wishes nothing said about his return, or the rather sudden way in which he left again. If you feel that this money will pay you and your wife for this little show of neighborliness, why, I will leave it, and another like it at the end of another month. But I do not want to buy any one's *truth*, and, if just so much talking must be done, let it be true talk. Only, why the talking?"

"Just so, just so," twittered the old woman, coming up behind them. "When a gentleman's so reasonable, William, why don't you do yourself the credit of listening to him? I don't want to talk about *them*. If the old gentleman came home, it's his own business; and if he went away again, it's his own business. Give me the pretty green bill, sir; I'll earn it."

Stanhope waited for the cobbler to speak, but he only grunted very gruffly, and drew fresh wax down the length of his thread. Stanhope gave her the bill.

"You will find their rooms left very much as they were," said he. "As Miss Dalton paid you for a quarter's rent in advance yesterday, you can lock their doors with a good conscience. Remember that one or both of them are liable, at any time, to send for their furniture and belongings."

"If you can trust us in one thing, you can in another," grumbled the shoemaker, as hoarsely as before.

"Shu!" cried his more interested mate. "He can trust us in everything, and that you know, William. Why be you ever making difficulties? Are five-dollar bills so common with you?"

"No, and that is why I'm so afraid of them," declared the shoemaker, flinging his shoe down and hastily turning. "But have your own way, old woman. If you can tie up your tongue, I'm sure I can mine; only don't bring that pock—"

Clash! clatter! bang! The old woman had upset a small pine table at her side, and the odd blue pieces of what looked like a broken cup and saucer were sliding over the floor. The noise startled the cobbler and made him forget what he was saying, while the apologies with which she filled the air made any recurrence to the theme impossible. Amid it all Stanhope started for the door. He was weary of his task, and thought only of escape.

But at the threshold a sudden memory made him stop short.

"In talking of this one thing I have forgotten another equally important," said he. "There is a person in this house whom I want to see. I do not remember his name, but he is a large and heavy man, with a face deeply pock-marked."

The cobbler, who was standing over the fallen table doubtfully scratching his gray head, looked up for a moment as Stanhope spoke and seemed inclined to speak, but his wife was too voluble for him.

"There is no such person here," she cried. "No such person at all!"

A hoarse "Humph!" followed by a few muttered words that were totally unintelligible, sprang from the old man's lips; then he turned his back and went and sat down on his bench again.

"But there has been such a person here within a few days," urged Stanhope. "He had a room up-stairs. Am I not right, Mr. Bowne?"

The cobbler, who had taken up his shoe again, showed by a certain stir in his broad shoulders that he heard this question, but his wife did not allow him to answer.

"Such a person looked at rooms," she declared, "but he didn't take them. He said they were too dingy. Dingy!" she repeated with fluent sarcasm.

But Stanhope was in no mood for nonsense.

"What was his name?" he asked, abruptly stopping her.

Another stir in the cobbler's shoulders, but she went on boldly:

"I don't know, sir; how should I know the name of a man who only *looks* at rooms?"

Stanhope glanced from her to the old man, who was again to all appearance reabsorbed in his work, and quietly waited. The old woman began picking up the broken pieces of china.

"I owe that man something," he observed.

Neither seemed to hear him.

"If you think he will be here again," suggested Stanhope—

"He said the rooms were *dingy*," the lame woman repeated, giving him a look that baffled him. "When a man says that, he don't mean to come back."

"I see," said Stanhope, "you are beginning to practice silence upon me."

A laugh, loud and vulgarly humorous, broke from the seemingly abstracted cobbler. Stanhope was so astonished he stumbled back, grinding under his heel a piece of broken china. The laugh as suddenly ceased, though the two broad shoulders were still shaking.

"There's my good man coming round," cried the old woman, complacently. "It takes him a long time, but he's mighty pleasant when he wishes to be, sir—mighty pleasant."

But Stanhope, who saw nothing promising in old Bowne's pleasantry or in Mrs. Bowne's garrulity on every topic but that upon which he wished to gain some knowledge, did not wait to make further acquaintance with this worthy couple. Giving them an added hint of the extra five that awaited them if they did their duty by the Daltons, he took his leave; and just as some shrill half-worn-out clock overhead struck the hour of ten, he left this house in which he had had a succession of such puzzling adventures.

XV

A Surprise

There are events that seem to draw a dividing line across our lives. As Stanhope took his way home that night, he felt as if such a separation had taken place in his life, making a distinct past to which any future which might come to him would hold but little relation.

He had taken a carriage at the first livery stable he came to; otherwise he might not have arrived home till midnight, being but little conscious of his own movements or of what surrounded him. He had a vague desire to be out of the whirl of the streets and in the rest and quiet of his own room; but beyond this he was conscious of but one thing, the necessity of work, of much work, of work so persistent and engrossing in its demands, that he would have no time to give thought to the sweet face smiling backward upon him from each and every quarter toward which he chanced to turn.

"Dreams that are dead should be buried," he had decided in his own mind; and tried to plan what course he should pursue in the way of study, or what effort he could make at securing political prominence, such as had beguiled his father's attention in his latter years. But the dream was too fresh and too persistent for him to get much further than a dull determination to do something at once, as opposite as possible to all love-making and the poetic reveries to which love-making or the hopes of love irresistibly give rise.

While yet in this mood he reached the house he still called home. But as he alighted from the coach and saw that the gas was still burning in Mrs. White's boudoir, a softer feeling returned, and a strong desire for a woman's sympathetic comprehension of his troubles came in a rush over him. This feeling increased as he went upstairs, and by the time he had reached the top of the first flight, he determined that, if the boudoir door was open, he would stop and tell Flora all the experiences of this fateful day.

And the door was open, invitingly open, just as if she expected him to stop. But when he reached it and was near enough to catch sight of the hem of a black dress sweeping across the floor, it gradually closed as if pushed by a careful hand, and he heard the young widow's laugh rise gently, but with a tone of pleasure in its cadence, that struck him with momentary astonishment, perhaps because mirth of any kind had so completely vanished from his life that even the slightest manifestation of it, so near him, seemed incongruous.

"So she, too, shuts the door upon me," mused he, as be went on quickly up-stairs. "Well, it is best. Has she not suffered enough, that I should wish to send her to bed with an aching heart?"

He was not sufficient master of his reasoning faculties to perceive that, if Flora was crossing the room as he passed her door, it could not have been her hand which had so deftly closed it.

Whether he slept that night or not I do not know; but when the breakfast-bell rang the next morning, he was ready for the meal and made his appearance in the dining-room shortly after Mrs. White.

She was expecting him and stood near the door as he came in, with a soft brightness in her proud face which had not been there on the morning before. As he entered, she looked up, and, welcoming him, waved her hand quietly toward a certain window at the rear of the room. Naturally he immediately looked that way, when he saw a young lady standing there, with light fluffy hair and a contour of cheek and chin that made the blood stop coursing through his heart.

"My new companion," explained Flora. And advancing to the young girl, she drew her kindly forward. "Allow me the honor of introducing to you Mr. White," said she to the stranger, as politely as if she were addressing her social equal. "Mr. White, this is Miss— What has happened? What is the matter?"

"Nothing," he protested, straightening himself up by an abrupt effort of will. The surprise of yesterday was nothing to that of this moment. To hide his emotions, he bowed with the utmost ceremony to the young girl quietly, almost naively awaiting his recognition, and said markedly, "I did not hear the name."

Mrs. White immediately resumed her society manner. "It is Dalton," said she; "Miss Mary Dalton—a protégée of Mrs. Delapaine."

He felt the room whirling about him. To steady his mind he allowed himself to contemplate for a moment this young girl, whom he had seen so lately and under circumstances so different, that it made him question his own sanity to behold her standing here under the protection of his father's widow and amid the glamour of the rich surroundings of colored glass and tapestried hangings with which the room was furnished. She was gazing intently at him; but the arch look of her eye explained nothing, and her lips, just quivering with a half smile, told of present happiness and future hope, but said nought to explain the inexplicable present.

"I am happy to meet Miss Dalton," he finally declared with what command he could, and turned away. The rising of the dead, even if it be only a dead dream, frightens the soul from its composure. And this resuscitation, however occasioned, meant a renewal of the conflict which had so wearied him. "I am not well this morning," he explained to Mrs. White, who was surveying him in some astonishment. "Do you think your young friend will excuse me?"

"Oh, do not go without your breakfast," pleaded the young widow, anxiously. "Take a cup of coffee, at least You need not converse," she obligingly whispered. "I will do that for you." And turning with a marked interest in her manner to the young stranger, whose beauty and ingenuous manner had doubtless been a surprise to her, she drew her toward the table, remarking gravely:

"Mr. White has had much to try him during these last few days of affliction. You will excuse him, will you not, if he takes merely a cup of coffee with us?"

Mary, who had no air of the ordinary "companion," answered with a smile that made words unnecessary; and Stanhope, who could not help watching her, though every moment added to his perplexity and inner disturbance, saw that, although she made no attempt at shyness, or even strangeness, she tried to remember—if he could not—the injunction so lately uttered by her father, that they were to meet as strangers, if by any chance they came together again.

The meal thus partaken had all the elements of a nightmare to Stanhope, especially after it became apparent that Mrs. White had failed to identify Mary with the one of his early love. Though he was relieved from talking by the friendly chatter of the two ladies, the questions that would arise in his perturbed mind made the short half hour seem an eternity, and the ceaseless passing of articles for which he had no appetite tedious beyond endurance. At last, in the desperation of the moment, he spoke.

Looking full at Mary, who neither sought nor shrank from his gaze, he asked with due politeness if she was a resident of the city.

With a demure dip of the dimples that had not been perceptible in the interview of the day before, she answered that she had lived mostly in Philadelphia, but that New York was not entirely strange to her; that she had spent some months in it with her father, though never in so pleasant a part of the city as this.

Her ease, her grace, her naturalness and quiet adaptation to the requirements of her surroundings, deepened his astonishment and increased his mental perplexity. Where had she acquired her knowledge of life, and what was the reading of this riddle? Her father had said she was destined for other circles than those in which he had surprised her. Was this the circle? Impossible. Yet mere coincidence could not account for her presence in this house, or for the pleasure which Mrs. White showed in her society. Thomas Dalton was at the bottom of this; but how? The query kept Stanhope silent.

Mrs. White, who evidently thought his reticence necessitated an extra effort on her part, remarked at this juncture that Mrs. Delapaine was not always so discriminating. "I happened to remark to her a day or two since," she observed, "that I would give the world for a sister, or at least a companion, who could be with me constantly, and she said, 'I know just the young lady for you.' But I never dreamed that this young lady would be one who would fill the place so perfectly as Miss Dalton will certainly do;" and the look she gave Mary was as unaffected in its admiration as it was unsuspicious of the remarkable bond which held the whole three of them in a Gordian knot. "She only came last night, but already I feel as if I had a friend," concluded Flora.

Stanhope, with a muttered excuse, rose hurriedly. If he was to preserve the attitude of preoccupation and somewhat dignified reserve which he had assumed, he must leave before the conversation proceeded further. But as he bent with some final explanation before Mrs. White, he caught Mary's eye, and beholding there for the first time a look of timid entreaty, he did not leave the room as he intended, but sauntered up to the mantelpiece, from which he took the morning-paper. As he opened it, the ladies themselves rose, and Flora, having some message to give the butler, stepped for the moment into the adjoining pantry. While she was gone, Mary went to the fireplace, and, throwing him a glance as she passed him, said in low but distinct tones:

"I was brought here by my father. I do not understand it any more than you do. My business is to ride with Mrs. White and to read to her. Do not betray me, for my father's sake."

The words had evidently been conned by her as she sat at the table, but the blush by which her appeal was emphasized was unstudied and full of the emotion that her words lacked. He heard the latter, but was moved by the former.

"Will you have the paper?" said he, with double meaning. "You will find it unlike most of the name, to be trusted."

She smiled, and reached out her hand. As he put the paper in it, he thought of the intentions of the night before, when work seemed to be the only duty that lay before him.

"I am caught in a net," was his inward conclusion. And for one wild minute he allowed his eyes to run over the golden head, and the piquant face now brimming with a happiness concerning which he dared not question himself. Then he bowed with kindly deference, in which there was no hint of secret understanding, and quietly left the room.

The little hand which Mary instinctively raised to her beating heart, as the door closed, showed what this meeting had been to her.

XVI

THE WAY OF A MAN

Man proposes and God disposes. When Stanhope left the dining-room on the memorable morning of Mary's appearance there, he had done so with the fixed determination of packing up his bag and starting at once for Washington. But with the very first letter he opened on regaining his room, he found so many duties devolving upon him in connection with his late father's affairs, that he was forced to give up this project and remain where he was. This meant the fulfilling of a paramount duty, but it also meant an encounter with personal difficulties of which he scarcely dared to foresee the certain end.

Without any effort of his own he had learned during the morning several facts concerning Mary. First, that she had arrived in a carriage the night before, and but a few minutes before he himself had returned; a fact which meant that she must have been driven, without any great delay, direct from Markham Place. Her trunk had not arrived with her, but was brought by an express wagon shortly after breakfast. That it was a new trunk and not at all heavy, he himself had an opportunity to notice. Of the father no whisper came to him.

Business carried Stanhope out at noon, and when six o'clock came he went resolutely to the club. It was not without a struggle, however, that he remained there till midnight. A thousand influences seemed drawing him home, a thousand impulses urging him to humor his wishes just for this one night, if only to see how so young and inexperienced a girl would comport herself in the elegant boudoir of his father's wealthy young widow.

But his nature was a strong one, for all its infinite tenderness, and he remained firm at the reading-table to which he had confined himself since the early evening, While that fair young face floated in a halo of poetry before his inner vision, he knew it would be but madness to subject himself to its influence; for the one sight he had caught of it in the morning, contrasted though it was by Flora's refined loveliness, had made his present ordeal harder and the future loneliness of his life more difficult than ever to contemplate. That there was a mystery in her presence in his home, was in itself alluring; and he felt that he had won the most triumphant of victories over himself, when, in the midst of a short conversation with the mayor, he took the determination not only to treat Miss Dalton according to her father's wishes, but to so ignore all his past relations with her as to make no effort, secretly or otherwise, to lift the veil of mystery at present shrouding her.

That this meant the ignoring of the one clue which might lead to an explanation of his father's death, he recognized as well then as he did later. But when a man is caught by a tongue of flame, he runs; nor does he see any way of escape save by flight.

Jack was at the club, and was all eagerness to accompany him back to the house in Fifth Avenue; but Stanhope was inexorable, as I have said, and held his ground both against his friend's entreaties and his own secret wishes. When the clock struck twelve, he rose. "Now I am ready," said he. Jack shrugged his shoulders. For the first time in their long acquaintanceship, he had failed to understand his friend.

It was the beginning of a long and difficult struggle. He could not leave the house in which his temptation lay, because of the affairs which relentlessly tied him to his father's desk; and, being in the house, he could not fail to encounter the two ladies once if not several times a day. But what he could help was a tête-à-tête with Mary, and this he studiously guarded himself against; taking refuge in the work which now really overwhelmed him, and relying upon Flora's knowledge of his secret position toward all women, to help him out, with that sympathetic tact which had been born in her by sorrow.

"*She* will not expect me to make myself especially agreeable to ladies," thought he, and continued to ignore their gentle claims; grinding his own heart under foot, and, in time, that of the two women also, though both were too proud to acknowledge this, either to themselves or to each other.

His curiosity—he would have called it by another name had he felt free to marry Mary—as to how her simple dress and piquant though not perfectly polished manner would fit the superb surroundings of wealth and luxury into which she had so abruptly stepped, had soon been satisfied. He had never sat with her in Mrs. White's exquisitely appointed boudoir, for discretion bade him to enter no room from which he could not readily escape. But he had met her more than once on the broad staircases and in the spacious drawing-room, and always with that sense, which could not have sprung altogether from the glamour of a hidden passion, that her quaint but picturesque figure,

ANNA KATHARINE GREEN

with its archly poised head and dimpled smile, lent to, rather than suffered from, the splendor of the luxurious furnishings about her. Side by side with Flora, her appearance was doubly attractive, and the two ladies were seldom apart now; for the young widow, sickened of her former associates, to whom she had been bound mainly by interests which had sunk to their proper level since love had unlocked the heart of her womanhood, found in the fresh, uncontaminated soul and well-trained mind of this exquisite stranger, a satisfying charm that went far, in those first days of their acquaintanceship, toward lifting her out of the depression caused by the hidden grief, above which she was so bravely trying to rise.

But love, when it is real, and daily fed by the sight, if not the sympathy, of its object, cannot forever hide either its triumph or its corresponding despair. As the weeks rolled on, Stanhope could not but see that a change was taking place both in Mary and in Flora. Though the routine of their daily life went on as usual, there was apparent in the manner of both a failing interest in all that they undertook, which astonished him in Flora, and alarmed him in Mary. That this effect was bound to follow his treatment of the latter, he should have known, and did perhaps. Yet the fore-knowledge we may have of consequences is not as poignant in its effects as the recognition of consequences when they arrive; and nothing in all the past weeks of incessant question and trouble brought him such pain as the sight of this unfortunate child's rapidly failing gayety and growing unrest.

That *she* was ignorant of what excused him in Flora's eyes, made his position the most difficult of any he had yet encountered, and he was one day turning over in his mind how he could let her know, without too great a shock to her delicacy, that his future, and therefore his present, was no longer under his own proper control, when he ran across Flora returning alone from a shopping excursion.

"Ah, Stanhope!" was her glad exclamation, "this is the first time I have seen you alone in weeks. Why are you so chary of your company? Do you not think it would make your duties easier if you allowed yourself such mild doses of social pleasure as you would find just now in my boudoir? Miss Dalton must think it strange that you never spend an evening at home. Have you so foresworn the company of women that you cannot even indulge in their friendship?"

They were standing in the front hall, he with hat in hand, ready for his daily departure to the club. As she said this he replaced his hat on the hat-rack, though why he did this he did not know, for he certainly did not intend to renounce his intention of going out.

"I thought," he remarked, with one of the rare smiles Flora could never see unmoved, "that Miss Dalton's position was such as to preclude her from making any such demands."

Flora laughed as she drew him into the parlor. "Do you suppose," she asked, "that I regard this beautiful young girl, who has every virtue and charm which I find lacking in myself, as a mere paid companion? She is my friend, Stanhope, and as such I instinctively consider her, whenever any contingency arises which calls for such thought. Do you not think her worthy of it, or have you not noticed her enough?"

Feeling like a victim suddenly seized by an inquisitor, he gave the young widow a penetrating look, in the hope of seeing whether she was inflicting this torture upon him from knowledge of his secret, or in the mere wantonness of an idle mood. From the sweet and steadfast composure with which she bore his gaze he judged that her curiosity was real, and yet his natural discretion told him to be upon his guard.

"I have noticed Miss Dalton," was his quiet reply, "and think her a very attractive young woman. But social pleasures just now are not at my command, and you must excuse me if I do not do justice to the demands they might otherwise make upon me. It is not from any churlishness, I assure you, and of this you must make Miss Dalton aware."

His voice told more of his inner depression than he realized. Flora paused as she was on the point of replying, and completely changed both her bearing and her manner of address. "There is something which I had hoped you would tell me before this," said she. Then, as he was silent, she went on softly: "Have you found any clue to the young girl you—" Her entreating eyes finished the sentence. She was a martyr to her determination to be of help to him at that moment, but he did not know it.

"Do not ask me," he cried, letting something of his inward despair flash out in response to the soft call of her womanly sympathy. "I have to crush that weakness out of my life. Do not make it harder for me by alluding to what I must totally and forever forget."

She, quivering a little at an outburst for which she was not prepared, stepped back and cast a disheartened glance up and down the long vista of magnificent objects which lent coldness to this now but little used room. How dreary to her at that instant seemed life, the world, and even this very abode of luxury, to attain which six months ago she had bartered her maiden independence.

"I beg your pardon," she entreated. "I spoke solely from an instinct of friendship. I will not offend again." And her head fell forward, though she quickly raised it again.

"And I spoke," echoed he, grieved that he had made her grieve, "from the depths of a perplexing grief of which I see you have received no hint. Do not lay up my impatience against me. You know that I would far rather hurt myself than one so kind and noble as yourself."

But this gentleness on his part was harder for her to face than his impatience. She had thought herself rid of any lingering passion for him, but this instant of mingled pain and delight undeceived her. "These are words," she declared, "which sound rather strange in my ears. I may grow to deserve them, if—" But here they were interrupted by Felix, who had a message to deliver. Glad to be relieved from an interview she felt too weak to support, Flora apologized for leaving him, and hastily went to the door. In another moment he heard her step on the stair, and, sighing heavily, turned to take one quick walk up and down the room before venturing out into the open street, when right before him, rising from a half-hidden divan in the darkest corner of the room, he beheld the slight form and pale face of her who was always dominating his thoughts.

The shock was too much for him. Starting back he threw up his right hand, uttering the one word, "Mary!"

She stood before him, fixed and immobile.

"I heard what you said," she whispered. "I could not help it. I was ashamed to rise and go away."

He felt that the crisis in his life had come. He must explain himself or forever do injury to this young and innocent girl.

"You heard words, then," he assured her, "which must have satisfied you that I bear in my heart a deep and lasting sorrow. Do you know what I meant when I said that I must crush a certain weakness out of my life? I meant my love for you."

"Ah!" sprang tremblingly from her lips.

"It is my doom, my despair, my one glory and my ever-recurring misery," he went on, with the passion of a strong nature suddenly let loose. "From the first moment I saw you, my darling, until now, I have loved you with the one passion of my life. But it is my fate never to know the joys of marriage. I adore you, but—"

"I am not worthy to be your wife."

It was said humbly, but with profound sorrow. He flushed as the low words left her lips, and passionately seizing her hand, protested that to him she was the one perfect flower of womankind.

"Then why—" she began, but broke off the sentence, as if alarmed at her temerity, saying only in a half-apologetic way, "I see; it is my father."

For a moment he was silent; that father might have stood in the way, if other things had been right, but he was not the stumbling-block just now. And so he hastened to tell her."

"No," he declared, "it is *my* father." And stopped, naturally, to see how this affected her.

But the troubled eyes that flashed upward to his showed nothing in their depths but astonishment.

"But he is dead!"

"Yes." In what words should he explain to her?

She evidently did not expect him to explain.

"I understand," said she, with a proud humility making beautiful her face, "the son of Samuel White cannot very well marry the daughter of—" She could not speak the name. Instead of doing so she turned and said gently: "I must leave you, Mr. White."

He sprang and caught her back by the hand.

"No," he prayed; "not yet; not till you have heard the reasons why I cannot marry where I would. It is not because you are the daughter of Mr. Dalton, but because you are not the daughter of another man. My father fixed my choice before he died. It was done without consulting me, but I cannot ignore his wishes in so important a matter. If I am ever married, it must be to a woman I have never yet seen. But I do not intend to marry. Now do you understand my behavior, dear Mary?"

She shook her head. She looked remote as a statue, which you might touch, but from which you could never get any response. Only there burned in her eyes a bright light under which he thought, he hoped, he saw a tender appreciation of his grief, which her lips were too proud to betray.

Abashed, and deeply moved, he bowed his forehead above her cold hand, and let one bitter sob escape him.

"You do not know what my father was to me," he protested, "or you would see why his wishes are my law."

"This is no place for me," was her sole rejoinder.

ANNA KATHARINE GREEN

"It was not because of his wealth," stammered Stanhope, feeling that his explanation was no explanation in her true eyes. "Had he been a poor man I should have obeyed him just as implicitly. There were reasons—" But he could not speak to her of them.

She, with a slight drooping of her head, had listened to these broken utterances, without a word. But when he stopped so suddenly, she gently drew away her hand and quietly remarked:

"You are very kind to tell me all this, but the one fact you stated first was enough. You are bound to another. Oh, why did I not know this in the beginning!"

She had forgotten herself, and the stream thus suddenly let loose would have its way. Clasping her two hands over her heaving heart, she let the great tears fill her eyes and fall slowly down her cheeks, while he, overcome and swept away by a passion whose only check was a ghostly hand, caught her to his bosom, crying and pleading in her ear:

"You love me then? The pain is not all mine, Mary, Mary?"

"I love you; the pain is not all yours. But I shall never permit myself to say so again. I am going away, going—"

He put her back and looked at her. "Where?" he demanded.

Her great eyes, wider than ever now with the large tears that filled them, took on a strange look of utter helplessness. "I do not know," she replied. "I have no home; I expected to stay here."

He felt overwhelmed. What had he done? What was he doing? Robbing this poor child of her only protection, her only place of refuge.

"Your father!" he found himself whispering.

"Is—I do not know where. He has left that—that place you know of. I am all alone. But it makes no difference," she hastened to declare. "I will make friends. I cannot stay here, but some other house will open to me. Mrs. White—"

But he broke in vehemently: "If either of us leave this house, it shall be I. You shall not go out homeless and friendless. Do not think of it again; promise that you will not think of it again."

"You are the master here; how can *you* leave?"

"I am not the master; the house belongs to Mrs. White."

"Ah!" she murmured, "and she *knows*."

"Knows that I love *you*? No. I have never told her that you are Mary Evans."

"I am glad," she murmured. "Ah! do I not hear her coming? Let me go."

"In a moment, in an instant. Only promise me you will not leave here."

"I cannot promise, but I will give you warning— Ah!"

She turned to fly—it was too late. The door opened, and Flora reappeared in the room.

XVII

WARNING

Recalled from the world of emotion in which they had been lost, by the look of amazement with which Flora regarded them, Stanhope and Mary came forward. "I have been obliged," explained the former, with a candor born of the moment's emergency, "to excuse myself to Miss Dalton for the seeming disrespect of our conversation in her regard. Unfortunately for us, she was within hearing of what we said. But you see she has forgiven me."

Flora did see, and could scarcely hide either her surprise or her displeasure. But she was mistress of her emotions under all ordinary occasions, and this she considered at the moment an ordinary occasion. So, with the tact of a trained woman of the world, she helped the inexperienced girl to a semblance of her own composure by her ready smile and instant acceptance of the explanation offered her. All this may have deceived Mary, but could not deceive Stanhope.

He, however, was in no mood for further conversation upon any topic; and after a few formal words, uttered in his most reserved and courtly manner, he excused himself from their presence and left both the room and the house.

He was no sooner gone than Flora turned upon Mary. The anger with which she had recognized the fact that her young companion was in a state of marked agitation when surprised by her entrance, had vanished, but the curiosity aroused by this discovery naturally remained. If this pretty young stranger had presumed to lose her heart to one so totally removed from her as Stanhope, it would be well for her to be warned of the sorrows which such presumption must entail. That the emotion she had also observed in his face meant more than his possible recognition of this same fact, had not as yet struck her. How could it, with her knowledge of him, and her lack of knowledge of the true identity of the young girl she had taken under her protection?

"Mr. White is a young man in a thousand," was the somewhat careless remark with which she opened the conversation.

"He is very handsome," was the feeble response with which poor Mary sought to imitate the seeming indifference of the other.

"I know of no finer man," remarked Flora, with amiable decision. Then, suddenly, without giving the poor child a chance to withdraw her eyes, she asked, with an arch lightness that hid depths of feeling, which, perhaps, were still unknown to her younger companion: "Have you ever been in love, pretty one?"

Mary, confused, startled, and not a little pained, blushed deeply, but did not answer. Flora at once felt conscience-stricken, and, flinging her arms around her companion's neck, kissed her warmly, while saying:

"It would not be such a surprising thing if you had. When I was eighteen I thought I had been in love several times.

"I have been brought up in a different school," murmured Mary, with the dignity of one who strives to hide a grievous hurt.

"You are right," quoth the other, "and I am to blame, especially as I know what love is, and feel perhaps even more than you do how holy and regenerating a true passion is."

Mary did not answer. The flood was rising high in her breast, and she felt like one stranded on a desolate coast.

"Is it so serious?" persisted Flora, with real sympathy now. "I did not dream—you must forgive me—I thought you might have had some fancy; but eighteen is so young for a real feeling."

"I have no mother," came from Mary's white and quivering lips. Then, as if fearing she had admitted something by this touching suggestion, she drooped her head, and added with gentle deprecation: "Why need we talk on this matter? We have never done so before."

Flora, whose heart was of gold, if some dross yet remained in it, hesitated before she answered this appeal. Though still suffering from the pang of seeing another woman stirred by the presence of one she had come to associate with an especial love and renunciation, she had no wish to hurt this woman, only to warn her. When quite sure of this, she suffered herself to speak and say:

"For the very reason, dear, that you have no mother. I am not so very much older than you are, but I have seen much more of the world, and know what we women have to expect. Those who love the deepest are most prone to disappointment. Even the most beautiful are sometimes the sufferers. I pity women who love."

"Then pity me," whispered Mary.

Flora, turning pale, took her companion's hand in her warm grasp. "Is it—is it—"

"Do not," entreated Mary, shrinking back, and trembling between her desire for sympathy and guidance, and the fear, which was more dominant still, of compromising her lover's dignity by revealing what he had not thought best to impart.

"I will not, only— There is the bell; we will have to fly from here. Come to my boudoir at ten to-night, and I will tell you a story of some one you know. It may prove how I love you and confide in you, for no one knows this story but myself and he who is the hero of it."

And without waiting for an answer, she drew Mary down the length of the rich and highly ornamented room, into the library beyond, from which in another moment they reissued to greet a couple of callers who had come to make a fashionable visit of condolence.

XVIII

WOMAN AND WOMAN

M r. and Mrs. Hastings dined with Flora that night, greatly to the latter's chagrin, and the distress of poor Mary. For Mrs. Hastings, for all her flippancy, had an uncomfortably penetrating eye, which was made all the more aggressive to a sensitive nature by a habit she had of putting up her eye-glass before she ventured a remark upon one's paleness or the lack of vivacity she observed in one's manner.

Mary, who had been informed of this lady's intended presence, and who dreaded it almost to the point of pleading illness to avoid the meeting, had done her best, in the state of agitation following the events of the day, both to look well, and to maintain a show of her accustomed spirits. With what might have passed for pride or pique had there been any expectations of Stanhope's presence, she had dressed herself in a new and most becoming gown, looking, as she entered the room, so lovely and interesting, that Mrs. Hastings, who often played, to her own great inward satisfaction, the rôle of patroness, advanced and touched the pretty girl lightly on either cheek, with her delicately rouged lips, saying somewhat too impulsively:

"How very charming we are to-night, Miss Dalton! Is all this display of taste for me alone? I cannot believe it; no, I cannot believe it." And her laugh, while fashionably proper, had a false note in its cadence, that made each tone pierce the victim of her mirth, like the barbed point of an arrow.

Flora, who knew, or thought she knew, just what feelings were agitating the breast beating under the simple white folds that had so attracted Mrs. Hastings's attention, strove to divert that lady's eye from her innocent victim. But Mrs. Hastings, when once bent upon playing the affable, was not easily turned from her prey. She liked Mary, and it amused her to admire charms so opposed to her own. So, before seating herself at the table toward which she was urged by her daughter, she remarked to the poor girl, after a prolonged stare at her pale face:

"But you look tired, my dear, and your eyes are quite heavy. That won't do. With your style you should cultivate vivacity. Merry looks and smiles would give you color and brilliancy. With such adjuncts you would be just irresistible; would she not, Flora? And then—" Mrs. Hastings had the grace to whisper now, though her whispers, like her glance, had a peculiarly penetrating quality—"we should have five at the table instead of four, which would certainly add to the cheerfulness of the party."

She may have meant to hurt—some people like to hurt the canary bird they fondle—or she may have meant only to show her cleverness; but from whatever motive she spoke, the effect upon Mary was like a whipcord descending upon a smarting wound. Drawing back, she turned as if to fly; but Flora's ready arm was there, and Flora's ready words in her ear, and she came back to herself with a spirited lift of her head that made Mrs. Hastings laugh again in her too pointed admiration.

"Oh, I see, a dangerous topic," she murmured to Flora, and allowed herself at last to be seated before an array of dainties which Flora fondly hoped would serve to beguile her, for the moment at least, from any further conversation of the kind in which she had just indulged. That her suggestions, or the intimations she had been pleased to make in her surprise at Mary's beauty, were of that light kind which springs from the impulse of the moment, was sufficiently evident to Flora, who knew her mother well enough to know that no one would be more shocked or displeased than she, had she thought that her suggestions would be followed by any such consequences as she had mentioned. But to Mary, who had turned as yet but one page in the book of the world's hypocrisy, the words so frivolously dropped were weighted with deepest meanings; and she felt more than ever, as she seated herself in turn at this ample board, that this house was no place for her, and that soon, if not on this very night, she must leave its doors for some spot where she could draw her breath without shame or the fear of prying eyes.

This thought and this intention, had there been no deeper trouble weighing on her mind, would have been enough to distract her attention and make her a poor companion for a social meal. But Flora, who was none too light-hearted herself, exerted herself doubly, choosing her topics and enlarging upon them in such an animated way, that Mary was soon startled out of her preoccupation, and became, possibly from the very fever of her thoughts, at once brilliant and entertaining.

Mrs. Hastings, noting the change, nodded appreciatively, and, notwithstanding the warning pressure of Flora's foot on her own, could not refrain from saying with a frankness most offensive: "There, what did I tell you! Is not animation becoming to Miss Dalton?" But the worst of ordeals has its end, and the meal was finally over. As Mary, accepting the release which she saw in Flora's eye, moved to leave the room, Mr. Hastings, who seldom spoke in the presence of his voluble wife and daughter, bent and offered her his arm and gallantly escorted her to the door. As she went out, he gave her a fatherly nod and smile, and she thought she heard him mutter in the depths of his long gray beard:

"Come to me, if you want a friend, my dear. Women are poor friends to women."

Flora, whose eyes glittered dangerously, looked at her mother and observed gravely:

"Had Miss Dalton been the daughter of Mr. Edward Dalton of Thirty-fourth Street, instead of being just the poor girl she is, with nothing but her innate refinement and extreme beauty to recommend her to our admiration, do you think you would have ventured to suggest to her how she could make herself agreeable to a young gentleman who was not even present?"

Mrs. Hastings, who was not easily abashed, laughed lightly:

"I do not think I should have been tempted. Edward Dalton's daughter is as plain as two sticks."

"I know, but—"

"Don't be serious, Flora. It becomes you more than it does the young doll face that has just gone out; but even in you, sobriety is only admissible when there are strangers around and the topic turns upon your late husband. I hate solemnity when it is out of place. This young girl is pretty, and I forgot myself. That she could ever seriously think of a young man so far above her, I did not, of course, imagine; but women put no restraint upon their fancies nowadays. Does Mr. White show any appreciation for her distinguished preference?"

Flora, who had her own emotions to conceal, shook her head indifferently.

"Do not ask me," she objected. "If remaining away from dinner every night in the week shows appreciation, we both have it most fully." And her laugh, truer than her mother's in tone, but falser just now to the inward sensations which prompted it, rang out in a way she hoped would end the discussion.

But Mrs. Hastings had one more remark to make, and she made it.

"If I had a 'companion' whose face and air were so out of the ordinary that she could make a picture of herself without the aid of a bow or a jewel, I should be suspicious of the young man who could sit with her every evening at table and did not. I should think he had reasons for staying away, which one, situated as you are, had better inquire into. Either he is courting some one else, or his admiration in this quarter is greater than you imagine, and may result in a secret marriage."

Flora, who felt that she so thoroughly understood Stanhope that she could afford to laugh at this suggestion, uttered some light rejoinder and turned the conversation. But she could not forget what had been said so easily, and before the evening was over she found herself in a fever of impatience for the coming interview with Mary, which should allay her doubts or confirm them.

For the belief which she cherished of Stanhope's true-heartedness was as the breath of life to Flora; and, if that should be taken away, existence would become simply intolerable to her, and goodness seem no longer anything but a name.

It was therefore with a sensation of relief that she beheld her mother grow weary and finally depart; and when the musical clock on her boudoir mantel struck ten, it was with a feeling of greater excitement than she knew that she rose to welcome Mary, whose footstep she heard descending the stair.

But the footsteps were not Mary's, nor, though Flora waited impatiently for several minutes, did she receive any intimation of her young companion's approach or of any intention on her part of keeping the engagement Flora had made for her.

This irritated Flora and rather added to her doubts both of Mary and of Stanhope. The emotion which she had observed in *his* face as she opened the parlor door upon them that afternoon, and which at the time she had supposed to be a mere reflex of Mary's, now recurred to her memory in an exaggerated light, born of her own agitated feeling. Why had he been so moved, if he were as indifferent as he seemed to this young stranger? Her feeling would have had to be strong indeed to have awakened any in him. Could not she, Flora, remember a time when she herself was nigh perishing with shame and longing before him, and he scarcely knew it, or, at the best, barely showed that he recognized it? There was some mystery here, which, as her mother had said, it behooved her, as the nominal protector of this young girl, to know; and if Mary in her shamefacedness would not come to her, then must she go to Mary—otherwise neither of them would sleep or know a moment's rest that night.

Moved by this impulse, which proves conclusively that Flora was still human, for all the generous instincts which we have observed growing in her, she left her boudoir and went up-stairs. Pausing at Mary's door, she knocked, and receiving no reply softly opened it and as softly entered. Mary was not in the room; but there was a light burning in the adjacent dressing-room, and toward this she stepped.

Her footfall may have been noiseless, for she wore the most delicate of satin shoes, or Mary may have been too engrossed in thought to hear, for she neither moved nor turned her head as the other advanced, but remained seated before a small table, staring with what seemed to be a fixed gaze at what Flora no sooner saw herself, than she stopped astounded and stared too, like a woman in a dream.

It was money, piles of money, more money than Flora, who now had thousands at her command, had ever seen before outside of a bank. Money! real, living, active money! And this young girl was but her paid companion, though she had called her friend, and felt, or had felt, toward her as such. What did it mean? How had she come by so much money, and why was she thus surveying it with an intent and immovable gaze? The open bag which lay at her side showed where these accumulated bills and coins had been stored, but it gave no solution to questions which would have staggered much stronger minds than that of Flora.

A sigh issuing from the young girl's lips broke the spell in which both seemed wrapped. Flora started forward, and Mary looked up. Their regards met across that array of bonds and greenbacks. It was, perhaps, natural that Flora's face should turn cold, and Mary's warm; that one should draw her head back with dignity, and the other droop it forward in something which, if not shame, was near enough to it to wear its guise.

"I beg your pardon," said Flora, coldly. "I knocked, but you did not hear me."

"No," answered Mary, "I was thinking. This money, which you are looking at with such astonishment, is so much more than I thought, that it frightens me. I did not know I was so rich." And with a trembling hand she lifted the bag and began putting back into it the various packages of money before her.

Flora surveyed her in a whirl of doubt and wonder.

"Then this money is yours?" she asked, in a tone that betrayed a certain incredulity.

"Yes," was the simple reply. "My father told me to put it in some bank, but I dreaded the remark it would occasion and so delayed doing so. You never thought for an instant that it was not mine, did you?"

The frank, uplifted eyes, in which appeal struggled with pride, caused the blood to rise to Flora's cheek, but did not perfectly satisfy her. Ignoring the question, but softening her tone, she said in reply:

"You say it is a great deal of money, and so it is, as far as I can judge from the denomination of such bills as I see. Is it because you love money so well, that you wish to add to your store such wages as your services earn from me?"

"No, no." Mary had risen, feeling in an instant how incongruous her position must seem to the other. "I have no need of wages; I did not come here for wages. I only came because—" Why did she blush so deeply? It seemed as if her shame would devour her before the other's searching eyes—"because my father brought me. I do not understand my position any better than you do. I have all this money, because my father gave it to me; but why, with it, I should be compelled to accept a situation which—" Her voice trailed off into a faint murmur, and her eyes, which had shone with candor, drooped heavily. "Do not think evil of me, Mrs. White," was the gentle entreaty with which she sought to recover herself. "You have shown me much kindness; show me a little more."

But Flora was not yet ready to listen to mere appeal.

"I have shown you kindness because I liked you, because I trusted you, because I thought you an honorable and open-hearted young girl; but the possession of this money, which is not only a strange thing in itself, but which is wholly out of keeping with your position in my family, certainly bespeaks a mystery in your life which should be explained. That you do not understand it yourself makes it all the more formidable. Do you think that Mrs. Delapaine shares your ignorance?"

"I do not know Mrs. Delapaine."

"Do not know Mrs. Delapaine! Why, she always acts as if she knew you."

"That is her kindness. I never saw her till I met her here in your parlor."

Flora was shocked. "Outrageous" was on her lips, but she restrained herself. "I shall see Mrs. Delapaine tomorrow," came forth instead. "Perhaps she will explain if you cannot."

Mary was silent; this was part of the martyrdom of the situation to her. Her father had told her nothing, yet expected her to comport herself in this new home with honor and dignity. Stanhope had betrayed to her his love, together with the impossibility of satisfying it, yet had not said, "You may make a confidante of Mrs. White." And so she felt helpless, having been trained from her earliest childhood to risk nothing in the way of explanation, lest she should betray those she loved.

Flora, as was natural, misconstrued this silence. "Mrs. Delapaine must have known your father well," she urged, "or her conduct is incomprehensible."

"I have never spoken to her about him," responded Mary, "but she may have known him, of course."

"Was—is your father a man of great wealth, that he can afford to give into your keeping such a fortune?"

"I do not know. He had money; but I think he must have given me nearly all of it."

The obvious questions of "Why? What did he expect?" sprang instinctively to Flora's lips, but were smothered by the thought, "It is a plot. He knows she is pretty, and men susceptible. He sent her here to win a husband."

Mary, who may have had some sympathetic insight into what was passing in the other's mind, bent over the money before her in a wild effort to hide her heaving breast and burning cheek. "You must not," she pleaded, "do injustice to my father, whatever you may do to me. He is a good man—"

"First let us put away this money," broke in Flora, "then we will talk;" being anxious, I think, to recover her own balance of judgment before proceeding with a conversation so much more exacting than even the one she had anticipated.

Mary, with ready consent, stooped for the bag, and between them it was refilled and carefully put away on one side. Then they sat down.

"Now, dear," suggested Flora, but not as she would have uttered it ten hours ago.

It was an invitation to Mary to be frank, but that was just what Mary shrank from. Yet her nature was wholly without guile, and she hated mystery as a child hates darkness. She therefore did not speak, but sat trembling, wishing that the other would leave her, or that the night would be suddenly turned into day, so that she might leave the house where love had turned to despair, and friendship become only suspicion.

Flora, who meant to be considerate, watched the young girl with sufficiently kind eyes, as she thus sat silent before her, and not till the silence became too oppressive did she venture to observe:

"The clue to all this mystery lies undoubtedly with your father. I do not blame you. Cannot you ask him to come here to-morrow and take in charge this money which seems to oppress you?"

"I shall not be here to-morrow," was all poor Mary could say.

Flora's kind heart was touched.

"Are you going to leave me?" she asked.

Mary's quivering lip steadied itself. "Could you expect me to remain after you have begun to question me and I have failed to answer? I am a child in many things, but not in pride, and, as I hope, in dignity. I cannot answer all your questions; so I must sever the bond that makes them only natural and perhaps proper. If I could, I would go to-night."

Flora, who had not looked for so much spirit where hitherto she had found mainly softness and humility, felt herself for the moment thrown off her guard. If only there had not been hiding in the background of her thoughts the suspicion of a secret attraction between this young girl and Stanhope, she would have thrown all other doubts to the winds and taken this beautiful and winsome being to her heart. But that thought colored all the rest and made any yielding on her part, for the moment, impossible. So, while she shook her head in deprecation of Mary's wish for a sudden departure, she could not restrain herself from saying:

"You must not go till you have heard the story that I promised you. It may divert you from the anxieties of the moment, and send both our minds into another channel. Will you listen while I tell you about—"

"If you are going to tell me anything about Mr. White," faltered Mary, "I must beg you to spare me. I—"

"I did not mention any names," quoth Flora.

Mary, abashed, maddened almost by the miseries and disappointments of the day, threw up her arms with a sob and turned quickly away. "I—I have betrayed myself," she acknowledged, "but it does not matter. Nothing matters now but that I am still here."

"Pardon me," objected Flora, "but it does matter. It matters to me. If you have become interested in Mr. White, I may be in a measure responsible for it. I should have told you before that he is, in a manner, engaged; that his affections are not free; that any girl would be doing herself a wrong who allowed herself to dream of a possible connection with him. But I thought" (she blushed while she talked; all this seemed even to herself such a mockery coming from her lips) "that you would see so little of him that it would be but pure impertinence on my part to suggest carefulness in such a matter. But it seems that I did wrong, and so it is I who am to blame rather than you. For Stanhope White is a very handsome man, and one that any woman might be excused for admiring."

"You tell me just what I have told myself. I know I cannot marry him. But it is hard to have to say so to another. The money that you have seen may stand me in good stead in one regard. It may lessen in your eyes a presumption which otherwise might have been deemed by you too great for sympathy."

The straight line of Flora's dark brows knit suddenly. "What must be regarded as a large sum for one who occupies the position of a companion would not probably support the horses Mr. White thinks necessary for his pleasure," she remarked.

Mary recalled the look with which Stanhope had regarded this money as it lay in her father's chest, and felt herself doubt this statement; but another arrow had been lodged in her breast, and her tender nature suffered from the repeated pang.

"But money, however much or however little, has nothing to do with this matter," continued Flora. "He is not free, or was not when last I talked to him. You heard that talk, and you know by it that he is not only bound to one woman, but that he loves another; and that this other is one whom he knew before ever you came here."

"I know," murmured Mary.

Flora's jealousy, kept down with steady courage till this moment, flamed up at these two whispered words beyond her power to conceal it.

"You know!" echoed she. "He told *you!*"

Mary, conscious of her indiscretion, paled and faltered. Flora, forgetting her sympathy, forgetting everything but that this dainty, childish stranger, whom she had supposed he scarcely had fully seen, had won from him a confidence only due, as she thought, to herself, flashed with a passion that made her for the instant overbearing and severe.

"Then you have had tête-à-tête conversations," cried she. "While I thought it my duty to apologize to you for his preoccupation and failure in polite attentions, you were having private meetings—"

"One," interpolated Mary. "You interrupted it."

Flora was silenced, but she looked unconvinced. Not suspecting the truth, she could see nothing but a marked inconsistency in the whole affair, which both baffled and perplexed her.

"There must have been much said in your short interview," was her comment, made after a minute of inward struggle and perturbation.

"Enough," was Mary's quiet response, "to assure me that I would be wronging myself as well as you to stay here beyond the morning. You see I am not happy. Is not that a proof of what he must have said to me?"

The wan smile with which this sentence was uttered would have appealed to Flora if the words had not. But those words, revealing, as they did, the poor child's hopelessness, were in themselves such a relief to the aching terror in Flora's heart, that the change they caused in her was marvelous, even in her own eyes.

"You darling! You poor darling!" burst impetuously from her lips, in the gush of this new sensation, and for the first time she seemed to experience a fellow-feeling for this young girl, caught, like herself, in a mesh it had been rapture to enter and torment to escape from.

But Mary, who, perhaps, saw in the other's relief and corresponding burst of sympathy a hint of deeper feelings than she had previously suspected, drew back and would not accept the embrace which Flora now gladly offered her.

"I have not explained myself," she protested. "Till that is done I can accept no one's kisses." And with a gesture that proved her no longer a child, she showed so plainly her desire to be alone, that Flora saw she had been dismissed, and discreetly withdrew.

XIX

In the Drawing-Room

Flora slept poorly that night, yet she rose early. The unrest of an uncompleted task was upon her, and when she heard Mary's footfall pass her door, she started in morbid excitement and hastened to follow her. But before she could leave her room she heard another step that held her back. It was that of Stanhope. He also had risen early, and was on his way down-stairs. "They will meet," thought she, and felt the blood recede from her heart and then rush back again, making her dizzy with the tumult. "Shall I go, or shall I leave them to themselves?" queried she, with her hand on the knob of the door. Consideration for them said, "Linger!" Self-interest and secret jealousy argued for interference. Self-interest and secret jealousy had their way. Opening the door, she passed hurriedly to the top of the stairs, and saw, first, Felix coming rapidly up; and, secondly, the figures of Stanhope and Mary standing in the lower hall.

"Breakfast is served," announced the butler, and rapidly ran down again.

Flora followed slowly after. As she descended step by step, she surveyed with eager eyes the forms of the two young people who were still conversing near the vestibule. Mary wore her hat and coat, and stood as if she had been stopped by Stanhope just as she was going out.

"Why, Mary," Flora thought best to cry, "are you going out before breakfast? Do not do that, I beg of you."

Her voice made them both start. Stanhope turned and stepped quickly to the foot of the stair.

"Come into the parlor," he entreated, holding out his hand to Flora. "I have something to say to you; it is of more importance than breakfast." He smiled, seeing her hesitate.

Flora, who could not have smiled herself at that instant, even if her life had depended upon it, bowed and turned in the direction he indicated. She was vaguely conscious that Mary was following them, but she said nothing to thwart this. Her day—if she had ever had a day—was over, and so was that, she thought, of the poor, sweet, gentle unknown for whom Stanhope had once struggled, and despaired. When the parlor door was shut, she turned round.

"You have something to tell me, you say."

Stanhope nodded very gravely, and she perceived now how far he was from complacence, or even from resignation. "Miss Dalton tells me that some misunderstanding has arisen between you two that necessitates her instant departure. Is this so, Mrs. White, or has she been led by her sensitiveness to exaggerate the situation?"

"I cannot answer," rejoined Flora. "If Miss Dalton feels that she must go, I have not the courage to delay her. Miss Dalton is so much the mistress of her own movements that it would be presumption on my part to detain her in a house of which she has grown weary."

"She means," observed Mary, with the spirit which is born of despair, "that, knowing I have money, she cannot see the propriety of my remaining any longer in a situation which should be filled by some poor girl. And I agree with her; therefore I go."

"She has hundreds, if not thousands of dollars in that bag," asserted Flora. "I should not consider it safe, if I were Miss Dalton, to go into the streets with such an amount in my keeping."

Hundreds—thousands! It was an astonishing statement to make, but Stanhope seemed not to feel so much astonishment as concern, which struck Flora as being most singular.

"Have you so much money with you as that?" he asked, approaching Mary and touching the small bag she carried.

"I have much; how much I do not know. But you see the bag is shabby. No one would think of snatching it away from my arm."

"Nevertheless I shall not allow you to carry it. Money so available as this should be in a bank."

"So my father told me, but I have put off obeying him. I had a dread of the questions that would be asked. Not but that the money came honestly," she added, with a proud look at Flora; "but even honest people may shrink from questions which will force them to reveal the eccentricities of those they love."

"Miss Dalton has a father who believes in keeping his ready cash near him," observed Stanhope, following his darling's eyes. "I myself have seen in his rooms much more money, doubtless, than his daughter now carries."

"You!" Flora was overwhelmed for the moment. "Then *you* knew that Miss Dalton was not what she seemed. You knew that I was taking one sort of person into my house when I thought I was taking another."

"I knew you were taking a companion; not such a one as is usually meant by the term, but one who could be a friend; whom you could love—"

"And that you—"

"Could love also. *Flora, this is Mary Evans.*"

A cry, a wild, dazed look, and Flora was herself again. "She is Mary Evans, and I have grieved her, injured her sensibilities, and doubted her! Will you forgive me?" Seizing Mary by the hand, she looked humbly in her face. "I think it was the jealousy I felt in behalf of her he called Mary Evans, that made me so inconsiderate of you. He had acknowledged to me that he loved a young girl of this name, and it robbed me of all self-control to see evidences of his being moved by another Mary. If you had told me—"

"Could I tell you that?"

"Or if *he* had," Flora went on, "all would have been different, as all will be different now. For I have promised to care for this young girl, have I not, Stanhope? And care for her I shall, even against her own will."

"I will stay to breakfast," murmured Mary, "but I must go before another meal. Not because of anything between you and me," she added, throwing herself into Flora's arms, "but because of what is between him and me. Do you not see I cannot stay? that it would be both indelicate and painful for me to do so? Say nothing, then, but let me go. So will you show me the truest friendship."

Stanhope, who seemed to divine if he did not hear what the young girl was saying, made haste to interrupt Flora's answer.

"If Miss Dalton insists upon going, let her do so; but you must go with her and see that she procures for herself a suitable and proper home. I would wish, however (and I hope my wishes will be of some value in her eyes), that she would remain here, at least for the present. For my presence will not long incommode her, as I shall take my father's desk away with me to-day."

"I will remain a week," decided Mary.

"Then off with hat and coat," cried Flora, to whom new life had come. "Give me the money, the precious money, and follow me as soon as you will, or as late as you will, to the breakfast-room." And she glided off, trampling, in this one moment, upon the last sparks of that feeling which her womanhood had no longer the least excuse for cherishing.

Stanhope and Mary, thus left alone, hesitated, and looked wildly at each other.

"Let us follow her at once," urged Mary. "I dare not hear you speak; I will not."

"O God, that I had something to say! That I might clasp you to my heart and call you mine!"

"And if I were Stanhope White, I should," came in deep tones from between the library curtains; and Flora, coming gravely back, stood calmly before them. "I have been thinking in the one minute that has passed since I fled from here, and the result of that moment's thought is this. What we owe to the dead should not stand in the way of what we owe to the living. Stanhope, your father has bidden you, in words of which I realize the force, to marry, if you marry, a woman called Natalie Yelverton. But you do not know such a woman, and do not even know that any such woman exists. Will you then destroy your own happiness, and wreck that of this innocent and inoffensive girl, by a blind obedience to commands your father himself may now deplore? You will make a mistake if you do, Stanhope White, and I, your father's widow, tell you so."

"You may be right," acquiesced Stanhope, shaken more by the look he saw in Mary's half-averted face than by the words he heard.

"I am right," persisted Flora. "Something within tells me so. If you had but yourself to think of, it would be different; but you have Mary, a girl"—Flora spoke very gently and with tender persuasiveness—"who is without a home, without proper protectors, and who, if forsaken by you, must drop from the circle which she is so fitted to adorn, and cumbered by memories and unsustained by hope, enter into some humbler sphere which it will be a daily pain for us all to consider. She has not even the advantage of having an ordinary past behind her. She has answered to two different names, and, though this may not mean much, it cannot but prove a stumbling-block in her way toward future recognition."

"It is true, O God, it is true."

"Are your father's wishes to be weighed against such considerations?"

"No, no."

"Then take this friend of mine to your heart. A man must be the judge of his own duty, and not follow the unjust dictates of a father who was unacquainted with his obligations."

And satisfied that the rest could be left to Mary, Flora withdrew for a second time from the room, and this time did not return.

XX

STANHOPE AND MARY

In her my better angel has spoken," declared Stanhope, as the hangings fell upon Mrs. White's retreating form. "Would you have me ignore her words, Mary? Darling, say that you forgive my hesitation and my doubts. Say that you will be my wife."

"And Natalie Yelverton?"

"May appear if she will. I do not know her."

"If you do not know her, why did your father wish you to marry her?"

A hard question; but Stanhope made an effort to reply. "He did not give his reasons. He said it would be for my honor and welfare; but why, he did not explain."

"Will it be for your honor and welfare to marry me?"

"I think so."

"Would to God that I agreed with you, Mr. White, but there are shadows over my life."

"I know it, but—"

"Shadows that I have never been able to drive away, and possibly never may. Are you willing to bear their probable falling upon your good name, your spotless reputation?"

Searching questions indeed! She saw him grow pale under them.

"Is there evil—forgive me, Mary, but there must be no misunderstanding on this subject—is there evil at the bottom of your father's eccentricities? Have we to fear dishonor from his oddities?"

"My father has been my teacher, and almost my sole companion. If you can judge of the tree by its fruit, then you can judge of my father's mind by what he has instilled into mine. He has never taught me evil, and he has always been good to me to the point of indulgence."

This, to a lover's heart, was for the moment good reasoning. Drawing her to his breast, he cried fervently: "He has made of you an angel, and for this I can pardon him everything. If he has causes for terror, perhaps we can make him forget them; at all events, he may tell me—"

"I do not think you will ever see him again," interposed Mary.

"Not if you become my wife?"

"Not in any event. He took a long farewell, or so he warned me, when he left me at this door. That is another grief I have to deplore. I do not know where my father is."

"It is strange; it is very strange," mused Stanhope. "He must have meant—"

"I will tell you what he meant, otherwise I should seem in my own eyes to stand in a false light. He meant to—to give his sanction to our union. I could never have told you this if you had not asked me distinctly to be your wife. But now you must know everything that I know myself."

"He meant to give his sanction to our marriage?"

"Yes."

Stanhope looked amazed, and Mary thought a trifle displeased.

"How did he know—" he began, but changed it to "Why did he give me the slip, then, bringing you alone to this house and leaving me to wait for your return in that room of his downtown?"

"That is one of the mysteries," she replied. "Ah, I feared you would be displeased! But I could not keep back the truth."

"Tell me what you do understand," urged Stanhope. "He must have given you some excuse for hurrying you away without me. What did he say?"

This from the man who had once vowed within himself never to question her on this subject.

"He told me to come with him at once. That the gentleman would follow as soon as he had attended to some matters he had intrusted to him; and took me out immediately by the back entrance."

"And where did you find a carriage?"

"There was one waiting for us."

"Waiting for you? Then he had planned to leave when he came to the house."

"It seems so, does it not?"

"It was so; but he could not have meant to have brought you here then. When did he ask you what my name was, and where I lived?"

"He did not ask me."

"Did not ask you! How, then, did he know? He did not seem to know when we were in the room together."

She looked distressed, but had no explanations to offer. "I only know," said she, at last, "that we drove immediately uptown; that he was very sad and very loving; that he held my hand, and now and then drew me to his breast with kisses, and that once I felt his tears. But he did not say anything till we arrived in the avenue, then—"

"Go on, my darling."

"He whispered very close and very earnestly into my ear: 'I am going to take you to a house where you will find a young lady and a gentleman. The young lady is a widow, and the gentleman is a bachelor. If you please the young lady, and—and—'" Mary's voice sank to a breath, and her confusion was extreme— "'and marry the gentleman, you will make your old father's last days happy. Do you hear, my child?'"

The amazement, the distrust even, in Stanhope's face became apparent. Happily she did not see them; shame had made her drop her head, as the embarrassment of repeating such words had made her lower her voice.

"And you?" he urged, "what did you say in reply?"

"Must I tell that?" she pleaded. "Oh, what could I say but, 'Where is Mr. White? I thought you were going to take me to a friend of Mr. White's.' I did not know that he was doing this, and whom could I think of on that night but you?"

Stanhope leaned forward and kissed her. She was blameless and uncalculating, if the father was not; and it troubled him to see her distress. "You must never think of any one but me," he declared.

She smiled, but it was with a wan sadness that recalled the old days in Bay Ridge. "I never shall," she answered firmly.

He stooped to kiss her again, but she drew back and shook her head. "Hear it all," she entreated.

"I am only too anxious," he answered. "What did your father say to that? Did he tell you he was bringing you to the house of Mr. White?"

"Yes, after a moment. First, he asked if you were Mr. White, and was very still after I told him that you were. I think he was surprised. As we drove up to the house he gave me the money you heard Mrs. White speak of, and I put it in my bag; then he told me that he was going to give me a long good-by; that my future was provided for, and that he could now leave me without fear or anxiety; that he was going he could not tell me where, but not so far that he should not be able to keep watch over my future and know of my success; that I was to be happy and to love him, but never to ask where he was, or to seek to find him, or to even talk about him to others, till he chose to come forward himself. Then the carriage stopped; and I was so full of emotions, and the dread I felt of entering a strange house without you to accompany and sustain me, that I could find no words with which to answer him, and with difficulty caught his final injunction."

"Which was—?"

"To use the name of Dalton; that Mrs. White expected me under that name and would not understand my use of another; and when I suggested that you might object, he answered in the gayest tone he had yet used, that Mr. White had promised to meet me as a stranger, and that strangers were not in the habit of choosing the names by which the persons they met should be accosted. And so I entered as Miss Dalton, to find that you had no intention of disobeying my father's injunction or of meeting me in any other way than that of a stranger."

The lifted eyes, the quivering mouth, the pose, half of personal independence, half of womanly longing, gave to her presence at that moment an alluring aspect which Stanhope was but little prepared to resist. Though he was anything but pleased at the mystifying circumstances which surrounded her entrance into this house, and though he doubted the father that brought her there, and doubted the coincidence which had made it *his* house instead of that of some other wealthy bachelor, he could not but be influenced by the ingenuousness she had displayed, and moved by the touching evidences of her shame, as she thus cleared her soul of what she considered as so many shadows. Leaning toward her with tenderness, he took her two hands in his and surveyed her long and earnestly. Ah, how bewitching was this face to him, with its halo of curls, and the eyes whose gaze he could never sustain unmoved. If there was poetry in the world for him, it was here. If there was hope, inspiration, the power to do and to be, it lay in the love of this pure being, whose presence made his happiness, and whose absence—no, he could not think of absence now. He had felt the touch of her lips, and his fate was sealed. As he recognized this, he smiled and strained her to his breast.

"I love you, darling; I ask you again if you will be my wife."

But she, though dizzy with a joy that suffused her whole being, did not at once breathe that fond "yes" which his ear was straining to hear. On the contrary, she drew back and shook her head, finally finding strength to say:

"I cannot answer you to-day. If in the week I have promised to stay here, your purpose remains unchanged, then I will pledge you my word. But if you falter, if one thought or one doubt comes to disturb your peace or make you regret your warmth, then do not try to hold me; for I had rather bear a broken heart to the grave than see in my husband's eyes a fear of the past or a dread of the future. Your life is clear, but mine—"

He was about to interrupt her and cry, "My life is not clear!" when the door opened and Felix's voice was heard in the hall, repeating for the second time:

"The breakfast is served, Mr. White."

And the impulse passed—not to come again that day.

XXI

Mrs. Delapaine

That afternoon Flora, dressed in her heaviest weeds, called upon Mrs. Delapaine. For though the young widow was satisfied with Mary, and felt that Stanhope was doing well in marrying her, she was still woman enough to think it the part of wisdom to solve the mystery of Mary's connection with this lady; that is, if it could be done with discretion. And Flora had no doubt of her discretion, any more than she had of her motive.

Fortunately for her patience, Mrs. Delapaine was at home, and, when she saw Flora, grew quite warm in her greeting. For she was a close friend of the family, and thought that Flora's position as widowed bride was a very unfortunate one.

"My dear, how kind of you," was the kind exclamation with which she seated herself at her side.

Flora, who had come from the florist's, put a large bunch of chrysanthemums in the elderly lady's hand. "I was buying roses for Miss Dalton," said she, "when I happened to remember your fondness for these flowers."

"My dear child!"

"Mary is going to a little musicale this evening. Mrs. Ashton was good enough to invite her, and I do not see why she should remain shut up at home, because I am. Do you not think I did right?"

"Certainly; that is, is she going alone?"

"Oh, no; Mrs. Talcott is to call for her."

"Oh, Mrs. Talcott!"

"She has taken quite a fancy to Miss Dalton. She says that with a little manipulation she could be made the belle of the season."

"Indeed! I did not know Mrs. Talcott had so much taste."

"Or so little respect for the *convenances*, perhaps? But Mrs. Talcott does not know the terms upon which Miss Dalton entered my house. She thinks her some early friend of mine. No one knows, Mrs. Delapaine, but my mother, and yourself who found her for me. Therefore she has been received with great warmth upon all sides. Is that a deception on my part? Should I have introduced her as a '*companion*'—a girl as beautiful as Miss Dalton, and one toward whom I feel so many instincts of friendship?"

"Mrs. White, you embarrass me," responded the frank, honest-hearted woman she addressed, with a slightly puzzled air. "There are times when one's duty is not quite clear; and rules, correct enough in general, seem to call for exceptions. Miss Dalton—" She did not know herself how to proceed. Flora watched her carefully through her veil, which had fallen partly over her eyes.

"I think," Mrs. Delapaine remarked at last, "that I should make an exception in this case. Do you pay Miss Dalton a salary, or rather is it your intention to do so?"

Flora had reached the point she wished, and glowed with inward satisfaction.

"No," she said; "Miss Dalton does not need money. But this you must know better than I, for it was you who introduced her to my notice."

The other looked down, but it was in a meditative way that told little of her thoughts or feelings.

"I should say, then, that you were entirely exonerated in introducing her to the world as your friend. Does Mr. White know that she has money?"

This unexpected introduction of Stanhope's name called up the color to Flora's cheek so vividly that it was fortunate that her veil had fallen partly over it.

"Stanhope?" she repeated. "Oh, no—yes, I mean. He made the discovery to-day."

Mrs. Delapaine, who had a vein of humor in her staid, matter-of-fact character, smiled as she looked up.

"And will dine at home to-night, is it not so?"

Flora, taken aback at a suggestion which seemed to show a closer knowledge of what went on in her house than she had supposed possible in the few visits that lady had made there, faltered for an instant before saying: "How came you to associate his name with hers? Do you not think it sounds very suggestive?"

"Any too suggestive?"

There was inquiry in Mrs. Delapaine's tone, and a decided curiosity in her whole manner, that aroused Flora. If Mrs. Delapaine could ask questions, so could she; a privilege she was determined to use, and that immediately.

ANNA KATHARINE GREEN

"I will answer that," she returned in her most playful manner, "when you tell me why you recommended her to me as a paid companion when you knew that she had money."

"I did not know she had money."

"No? Yet you did not seem surprised when I told you that she had."

Mrs. Delapaine laughed good-humoredly, but rather enigmatically too.

"I think," said she, "that you had better answer my question now."

Flora was baffled. She was too much mistress of herself, however, to show it, unless the way she threw her veil back hinted at a nervousness not betrayed by her easy smile.

"If you mean," she remarked lightly, "that I ought to tell you whether Stanhope has shown any interest in Miss Dalton, I shall have to reply that he has. But there is no engagement, nor has he seen fit to make his intentions public. You will, therefore, respect our secret, which I should not feel justified in confiding to any one but you."

"That is right, and you may trust me. I thought he could not be blind to so much piquancy and grace."

A wound may heal, but it is a long time before it loses its sensitiveness. Flora felt an inward pang at this remark, which seemed to put her own attractions so completely on one side; but her face lost none of its sweetness, nor did her steady gaze falter or grow bedimmed.

"Miss Dalton is a lovely girl," she admitted cordially, "and it will be a great pleasure to me to welcome her into the family. Where did you meet her first, and how long have you known her?"

It was Mrs. Delapaine's turn to hesitate and look a trifle confused. But Flora appeared not to notice this, and even showed her carelessness to such an extent as to take a flower from her companion's hand and affect to enjoy its perfume.

"I shall have to answer that question, as you did one of mine," laughed Mrs. Delapaine. "Why do you ask?"

"Oh, from idle curiosity, I suppose. Everything concerning Miss Dalton is naturally of interest to me now."

"Well, then, I am going to astonish you. The time and manner of my meeting with Miss Dalton is so unimportant that I do not think I shall gratify your idle curiosity. What do you think of that, my dear? That I am a flippant and disagreeable old woman."

"No, but that"—Flora rose at this point, driven to her feet by a sudden change of mood—"that there is some mystery connected with Miss Dalton, which you do not feel inclined to disclose."

"And if there were, dear Flora?"

"Should Stanhope marry her?"

The quizzical, good-natured face of the kindly old lady took on a more serious expression under Flora's searching eyes.

"I think he should," said she. "I decidedly think he should."

It was a relief, but yet not a victory. Flora had secured an opinion, but not a spark of enlightenment, and her pride could not but feel it. Mrs. Delapaine noted her discomfiture and gently patted the little hand that lay outside her muff.

"Do not quarrel with an old woman's whims. Were I as young as you, I should doubtless have entered into this subject with more eagerness, and been ready, perhaps, to ask and answer all the questions that so prolific a topic might suggest. But I have outlived the age of gossip, and dislike, above all things, to talk upon a person's antecedents or personal affairs. Yet, lest you should think I am keeping back something that might reflect upon Miss Dalton, I will say this, that what I know of her tends to make her a fit rather than an unfit choice for Stanhope, and that, in the event of their mutual liking becoming an engagement, I shall be the first to congratulate him. And I know what he is, Flora, for I was his mother's friend, and have been his these many years now."

There was no more to be said. Flora had failed to satisfy her curiosity, but had won what was perhaps more desirable. Showing her satisfaction, she took a warm leave, and in a few minutes more was rapidly rolling down the avenue with the roses for Mary.

XXII

A Crisis

Three days passed. Cheerfulness, joy, and hope had taken the place of gloom, reserve, and despondency in the stately house on Fifth Avenue, and even the servants felt the difference, and cast significant glances at each other. Stanhope remained home to dinner, and the dimples which had nearly vanished from Mary's cheek began to exert again their witchery, to the delight of Stanhope and the sympathetic enjoyment of Flora. Her conversation, too, which had been hitherto repressed, sparkled now with many quaint conceits as natural to Mary in her merry moods as was the serious earnestness of her language in the more sober moments of her life. She had begun to hope. The ground was growing firm under her feet, and her young spirits could not but respond to the promise of the future.

Yet the eye which sparkled now more often than it drooped had not lost its keenness or forgotten to watch the face of Stanhope for any change in its new expression of glad content. Though her feet felt firm, her heart still queried; and every night, when she laid her head upon her pillow, she could not help whispering to herself;

"One day more, and no doubt has come to him yet."

But doubts are so insidious, and their first growth so easy to conceal, that Stanhope was well on toward a certain dissatisfaction with himself before her loving heart, or even his own judgment, suspected it. He knew, of course, that he was restless, and longed for the week to end; but he thought it was because he disliked all suspense, and wished his future to be definitely settled for him. Yet as the day drew near he found himself recoiling from its responsibilities; and when he asked himself why, it was the image of his father that started up in his fancy to answer him, saying in the words of that fatal letter which had been burned, but whose language floated ever before his eyes:

"It is my first, foremost, and lasting desire that you should marry (if you ever marry) a girl by the name of Natalie Yelverton. She is the daughter of Stephen Yelverton, of whom you will probably hear shortly after my death. Why I demand this, and why it is the only and best thing for you to do, do not seek to inquire. That I wish it, and forbid every other marriage on your part, is sufficient to prove that in this union alone lie your happiness and the honor of our name."

Strong and uncompromising words! and, coming from such a man, not to be deliberately disobeyed without peril, or, at least, loss of peace, to a sensitive-hearted son! Yet was he doing this with every glance of love he gave to the sweet young girl who had stolen his heart; and no matter what arguments Flora in her sympathy, and he in his fondness, might urge in Mary's behalf, he could not deny to himself that he was taking a great risk in thus going contrary to wishes uttered so peremptorily.

One thought, one alone, still kept the balance even. It was the old one which had helped him to his first resolve, and lately, with Flora's change of manner, had helped to weaken it, that his father, strong and sensible man though he was, had been influenced to his display of tyranny by a mistaken jealousy; so that in slighting these commands he would do that father no wrong, since the motive for making them had been founded on a misconception. The failure of a Natalie Yelverton to appear, seemed to favor this idea; yet such was Stanhope's sensitiveness in regard to the whole matter, that he could not but feel that way down in his cup of joy lay dregs the bitterness of which he might be called upon to taste at any moment. How fixed was this dread, and with what shrinking he recoiled from it, he was soon destined to know, and Mary with him. It happened thus, and made a change in the pure delight of those three days.

They were coming out of church—it was on a Sunday morning—and Flora, who had many friends, had stopped for a moment's conversation in the vestibule. Stanhope and Mary were thus left for a moment alone, when they too were approached by a party of people, among whom Mary recognized a gentleman who sometimes came to the house. Feeling a certain diffidence at being associated just at this time with Mr. White, she stepped back as these persons came up, but did not withdraw so far that she could not hear Stanhope's voice as he answered this gentleman's greeting. Introductions followed, and she was just anticipating a beck from Stanhope, when she observed him give a sudden start and turn so pale that her own heart leaped in dismay.

When she had regained her self-command she saw that he was looking at the young lady before whom he was standing, with a gaze that was almost haggard.

"Yelverton, did you say?" he asked, turning quickly toward her introducer.

"Oh, no," that person laughed, "but something very much like it. Silverton, my dear Mr. White; Miss Antoinette Silverton from St. Louis."

The relief that instantaneously flashed over Stanhope's face went to Mary's heart. If he thus feared the entrance into his life of the unknown woman bequeathed to him by his father, what sort of comfort could she anticipate for herself, across whose life at any hour the shadow of this woman might fall? Though he seemed to realize at once what he had done, and strove by every effort within his power to hide the betrayal he had inadvertently made, neither he nor she could be blind to the significance of what had occurred. Nothing was said, however, till they reached home, and Flora, who had felt the cloud which had fallen upon them, was the first to speak.

"What is the matter?" she queried, leading the way into her boudoir. "What has happened?"

"Nothing and everything," answered Mary, after waiting a moment for Stanhope to speak. "Mr. White met a young lady whom he took for Miss Yelverton."

"He did?" Flora looked almost as much moved as he had done. "Where was it? In church?"

"It was a mistake," Stanhope now remarked. "Her name was not Yelverton, but Silverton. But I thought it was Yelverton, and could not restrain a movement of surprise. Mary saw me."

The look that Flora cast toward the young girl showed that she understood.

"Well," said she, determined that no weight should be given to the occurrence by any action of hers, "why should all this make two such trusting lovers unhappy? If it had been Miss Yelverton, we might all have felt it for the moment, perhaps; but it was not and—"

"It will be Miss Yelverton some day," murmured Mary.

"After you are married, perhaps," rejoined Flora.

"We shall never be married," persisted Mary.

Stanhope in his dismay took the young girl by the hands. "Mary!" he cried, "Mary! Will you let so small a thing as this separate us?"

Mary looked around; Flora had slipped from the room and they were left alone.

"Stanhope," she replied, letting her full misery show at last in her upturned face, "it is not a small thing. You have shown me in a moment what you dread, and what consequently I must daily fear if I ever become your wife. Some tie, unknown to yourself perhaps, binds you to this woman; and while this remains, and you feel the straining of the cord, I cannot but consider myself an interloper, no matter with what fervency you love or however desirous you may be of ignoring the duty imposed upon you by your father."

"You an interloper—you, who are the very breath of life to me?"

"Yet whose presence cannot make you forget that there is another woman who has claims upon you."

"It was the surprise! I shall not sin thus again, my Mary."

"Perhaps not; but the shrinking and the fear will remain, and that would be still worse for our happiness."

"O Mary! Mary!" He wanted to say that he was not sure there was any Natalie Yelverton; that the injunctions of his father may have been simply meant to prevent him from marrying at all, but that would involve explanations he could never enter into with this frank and unsuspicious young girl. So he resorted to entreaty, though knowing, with the inconsistency of a struggling soul, that her words were but the echo of the secret thoughts constantly disturbing his own peace.

"Can you, do you love me so little," he queried, "that you will forsake me for any cause? What can life be to either of us now without the other? How could I be true to another woman, with you living and breathing in the world?"

She drooped her head, but had no answer.

"Darling, darling, I may not feel quite free or quite light-hearted; but would I be freer if left to give my faith to this stranger? I am tied now, dear, with closer bonds than any woven by my father's injunctions. Will you tear them apart, then, when I say they should remain firm?"

He was trying to convince himself as well as her. Did she know it? The quivering of her lips seemed to show that she did, but yet she said nothing.

Wild with his own struggle, and loving her as he had never loved her before, he took her head between his hands and passionately raised it toward his.

"Love like ours," he cried, "is not for a day or a year. You cannot forget me, Mary."

Her tears welled up and welled over, and she trembled under his clasp; but her lips did not part, and he saw she was as unconvinced as ever. At the sight, his doubts and fears, the sense of his duty, and, indeed, every consideration save that of love, vanished into nothing.

ANNA KATHARINE GREEN

Raining kisses on her brow, her lips, her eyes, he strained her to his heart and asked again:

"Now can you leave me?"

She tried to smile, but she did not have the power; he kissed her again.

"Now?"

She raised one hand; it seemed to plead for mercy. But passion has no mercy. "You are mine now," he whispered, "and I will hear of nothing more that can disturb our love."

But still she did not speak. In a spasm of fear he leaned down and looked earnestly in her face. It was pale as death, for all the love-light upon it.

"Mary?" he cried in agony; "speak to me; say that you hear me!"

But her lips remained closed, and her form, where it rested against his arm, grew suddenly heavy. She had fainted in his arms.

XXIII

Mary's Decision

For two days Mary was really ill; but on the third she was well enough to sit up and face the question that was before her. It was not an easy task, nor was there any help for her in the ease and luxury by which she was surrounded. As she looked about her, her eyes fell upon a jar of superb roses that had been placed on the little table at her side; and, as she noted Stanhope's taste in their selection, she realized what courage it would take for her to renounce the paradise she saw before her in his love. Under the roses lay a little box inscribed with her name. Instinctively she leaned to take it, and it required a superhuman effort on her part not to do so, for she guessed what was contained in the dainty white case, and dared not look upon the little circlet which summoned her to joy when her rightful course lay in the way of sorrow and renunciation.

For she knew that, however fierce a struggle she might wage in the interim, fate and her conscience would lead her from this house on the morrow; and the fight she was having, and which was making her cheeks wan and her eyes dull, was not whether she should go or stay, but whether she should go without again seeing Stanhope.

Love, longing, and the instincts of youth urged her to look upon him once again and win his sympathy for, if not his acquiescence in, the sacrifice she was about to make. But wisdom, and the fear of yielding where firmness was required, told her not to risk herself again within his presence; for she was no stronger now than she had been two days before, and might fail as signally now as then in preserving her composure and carrying out her purpose. But, ah, to go without a last good-by, a final pressure of the hand to assure her that he forgave!

The prospect, which had been bitter enough in the week past, was doubly so now. For then it had seemed sufficient to her to seek another home; but now she knew that she must withdraw herself entirely from his knowledge or her sacrifice would be incomplete. And where would she go, where could she go, that he would not find and follow her? But one place rose before her eyes, and that was so wretched and distasteful that she knew not how to contemplate it. Markham Place, before she had known Fifth Avenue, was miserable enough; but now that she had tasted of life's real joys, how could she return to the dreary purlieus she had left and make a home for herself in scenes so uncongenial? Yet in what other spot was she known? To what other refuge could she fly and retain any hope that she would ever see her father again? Where his apparatus was, where lay hidden the machine that he loved, there would she go; and if he had remembered his promise, and still remained where he could keep a watch over her movements, would he not know that she had failed to win the home he had chosen for her, and hasten to her again with his protection? Surely, surely. But, oh, the grief, the recoil, the heart-sickness which over-flooded her at the prospect. Poor child, had she but thought of Mrs. Delapaine!

Her money had been safely lodged in a bank, so she had not that to worry her. But her dresses, and the various belongings which she had accumulated in her month's stay in this home of profusion and luxury, these she did not know what to do with if she was to preserve any secrecy in her departure. At last she decided to pack them all in her trunk and leave them behind her. Had she not come to the house empty-handed, and should she not go away as she had come? It was the easiest plan she could adopt, and white silk dresses and delicate lace furnishings would not be wanted in the home to which she was now going.

The good-by letters which she felt it was necessary to leave for Stanhope and Flora were her next task. These naturally took her some time, and cost her many tears and heart-burnings. When they were finished she felt exhausted and lay down, and it was while she was so doing that Flora came in for a little rest and chat.

"Ah, Mary," said she, "you do not look as well as you did this morning. You have been fretting. If this keeps up I shall send Stanhope to you. He has begun to be very impatient, I assure you."

"Don't, don't!" The poor child was so frightened she could hardly speak. "I shall be better to-morrow. Indeed, I promise you that I will be better to-morrow."

Flora smiled, though in her heart she felt like anything but merriment.

"I did not mean for him to come in here," she assured her. "It is but a step to my boudoir, and he is so anxious, dear."

"I cannot," whispered Mary; "I have not the strength. His flowers have overpowered me. How, then, could I bear his presence?"

Flora's eyes flew to the roses, which were beginning to droop a little.

"They, too, need a change," said she, and bent toward them to rearrange a spray that had nearly fallen from the jar. Instantly her eyes fell on the little box that lay beneath. "Ah, what is this?" she cried. "Have you seen it, Mary? See! a tiny white casket with something in it that is very precious."

But Mary's face was turned away.

"I have not seen it," said she.

"Then look at it now."

The box was thrust into her hand, and she could not prevent her fingers from closing over it. "I think I know what it is," she murmured, and laid it under her cheek, where it rested on the pillow.

Flora looked disappointed, but said nothing.

"Do you know, Mary," she finally asked, "how fortunate you are?"

The fingers clutching the little box tightened.

"To be the chosen wife of Stanhope White is a lot that many women will envy you. Do you not think you should accept it more joyfully?"

"But I have not accepted it."

"I will not listen to that."

"I should not accept it."

"Yet you will."

The tone was so positive that Mary was startled.

"Do you think I have so little courage?" she faltered. "I think the woman who could wear Stanhope's ring upon her finger, and does not, is mad. And so will you think, too, when you are quite well."

Mary rose on her elbow and eagerly surveyed her friend. "Ah, if you were only my conscience!" she cried.

"I am; I am determined to be. I do not mean that you two shall lose your happiness for a mere dream of duty. Life is full enough of actual necessities without fashioning one out of material so flimsy as this. You shall accept Stanhope; and to-morrow I expect to see you wear his ring."

A smile broke out on Mary's lips as she sank back. "Then leave me, dear," she entreated, "to prepare myself for so great an honor. If—if Mr. White is lonesome or anxious, tell him I am doing well. I do not wish him to be unhappy. Say to him that you left me with a smile upon my lips."

Flora, who was watching her with troubled eyes, felt her heart swell. Leaning down, she kissed Mary fondly, and Mary's arms closed round her neck. As Flora felt the pressure of the little box against her cheek,

ANNA KATHARINE GREEN

she confided to herself, "If I had not yielded to my unhappy love for Stanhope, this poor child would not be hesitating thus to take her own." And choked with remorse, Flora was more determined than ever that no cruel jealousy of the father should draw the dividing line between these two she best loved.

As she left the room, Mary followed her with her eyes. The love in them Flora did not soon forget, even when it became a painful memory.

When the door had closed, Mary rose up and began to pack. She had expected to put off her departure till the next day; but the resolution in Flora's manner determined her to go before their wills could come again into collision. That she would have an opportunity to leave sometime during the evening, she did not doubt. Flora was engaged to dine with her mother, and Stanhope would be sure to go to the club; when they were gone, she had but to send for a carriage. Surely flight under such circumstances would be feasible enough, if only her strength would hold out. And her strength seemed likely to do so, for fever supplied the necessary lack of power and carried her on without herself realizing from what resources she drew. At five o'clock her packing was finished, and she sat in her ordinary dress at the fireside, waiting for the departure of Stanhope and Flora from the house.

XXIV

Stanhope's Decision

Meanwhile, in the library below, Stanhope and Flora were having a very serious conversation. She had told him of her interview with Mary, and they had both come to the conclusion that the latter's manner showed a secret intention to withstand the temptation of an immediate engagement. That Mary meditated flight, neither dreamed, not realizing, perhaps, the strength of purpose which often underlies a childlike manner.

Stanhope, who had felt himself forced to acknowledge that Mary was not without some justification for her doubts, was trying to summon up courage to broach a theme he had hoped and intended should be forever closed between himself and Flora; and the latter, seeing that he had something trying to say, waited with gentle patience for his words. They came at last and were these:

"Flora,"—he called her Flora now—"I had never meant to allude again to the circumstances of my father's death; but the position in which I find myself seems to force the subject again to my lips. If I thought, or rather if I knew, that the letter he wrote me was written under a misconception, and with the simple intention of preventing a union which could never have been seriously contemplated by either of us, I would dismiss all compunction at going against his wishes, and take Mary to my heart with such singleness of purpose that she could never again doubt me or dream that my happiness would be better served by her refusal than by her consent to marry me."

"Now you are wise."

Flora spoke hoarsely, for she keenly felt the allusion in Stanhope's words, little as it was meant to hurt her. But she kept her ground bravely and smiled as she spoke.

"But I am unnerved by the fear," Stanhope proceeded, "that these commands of my father were based on other and better grounds. If there should really be a Natalie Yelverton, whom for some reason it was to my honor to marry, how I should feel if, by failing in my duty, I imperilled my father's memory or did injustice to an innocent girl depending on me!"

"We have talked this all over before," ventured poor Flora. "You must have a motive for saying it again."

"I have. Flora, we thought we knew why my father fired that fatal shot; but may we not have been mistaken in our conclusions? The man who bought the pistol for my father was a large, splendidly formed man, with a countenance heavily marked by the small-pox. In the house where Mary lived before coming here, there was seen but a short time ago such a man as this. Were he the same—"

"But why should he be? Pock-marked men are not so scarce."

"I know, but I have an intuition that he is the very man." Stanhope did not like to tell her his real reasons for this.

Flora hung her head. She dreaded to have this matter probed into; dreaded to have her own old wounds reopened.

"I wonder, then, that you have not sought him out."

"I tried to do so, and failed. But I am going to try again. I am going back to the house where he was seen. I do not suppose he is there now, but I may succeed in gaining some information that will help me to find him."

"And if you do?"

"I may be able to learn from him whether or not I need fear the appearance of a Natalie Yelverton in my future life."

"From *him!*"

"I know it sounds unreasonable. And yet where else can I go, from whom else can I hope to receive even a glimmer of light?"

"That is true."

"It is a forlorn hope, but it is a hope, and so before I see Mary again I am going to make the effort to satisfy myself on this point."

"Then you are going down there to-night?"

"Yes."

"I wish you all success, but—"

"What, Flora?"

"If you succeed—if you find out that your father took his own life intentionally, it seems to me now as if it would kill me."

Stanhope felt a movement of dismay. He had forgotten how this would affect Flora.

"Forgive me," he pleaded; "I had not thought of that. I have grown so selfish. What am I to do, Flora?"

"Can you ask? You must not think of me, Stanhope. Only think of her."

"But—"

"Only of her. And now you must excuse me; it is time I went to Twenty-sixth Street. If when I return I find you here I shall expect to learn what you have discovered downtown. Good-by, Stanhope, and remember you are to think only of her."

A few minutes after this her carriage rolled away, and some little while later Stanhope ordered his own horses and went out to his dinner at the club. When both were gone, a door above opened and Mary came stealing out upon the landing.

The order which she gave to the driver of the coach that carried her away that night was Markham Place. Had she ridden down the avenue as far as Thirty-fourth Street, she might have heard the same command given in another voice:

"To Markham Place."

PART IV

STEPHEN HUSE

XXV

A Strange Occupant

When Mary reached the head of Markham Place she alighted from the coach, paid the driver, and told him to wait where he was for ten minutes, and if she did not return by that time, to drive away. Then she turned toward her old home.

One glance and she stood stupefied. What had happened? Had she mistaken the house? A sign was hanging up over her father's window, and business of some kind (it was too dark for her to see what) was being done in her own rooms.

Summoning up her courage, and remembering that but a few weeks had elapsed since she trod these pavements with confidence, she took a few steps toward Number Six and looked up. The sign, upon which the lights of the drug-store shone brilliantly, read thus:

STEPHEN HUSE
ELECTROPLATING

A sudden sense of her utter homelessness overcame her. Not only the unknown name staring her in the face, but the changed aspect of the place, which had been adapted to the needs of this newcomer, made it seem like some strange and unaccustomed spot with which she had no memories, and to which she could lay no claims. Not till her discomfiture gave way to her natural indignation at the advantage which had been taken of her by the Bownes, did she find strength to proceed; and not until she had proceeded and stood immediately before the house, did she observe that the business of the day was not yet over in the electroplater's rooms, that his light was still burning, and that she could thus see through the curiously clouded window-panes into the room which had once been so religiously shut from every peering eye.

The change in all the appointments, which had followed its being turned from a mere domicile into a shop, distracted her gaze, at first, from certain small details which afterward fixed all her attention; for as soon as her eye could pass beyond the queer wheel in the window, the vat, the whirling electro-machine, and other singular and unaccustomed objects which occupied the space nearest to her, she perceived, with an emotion for which she was scarcely prepared, that there still remained in odd corners of the room, and against the farther walls, articles which had been her father's, and were so still, indeed. Among them was the chest, empty, she knew, of money, but sacred to her from the romantic associations which centred about it, and, better still, the long, gray worsted curtain, falling, just as it did of old, from ceiling to floor, though whether or not it still covered the apparatus once hidden behind it, there was nothing to inform her.

An old man with high shoulders stood with his back toward her, wrapping up some small, bright objects in bits of tissue paper; but as she continued to look, half-fascinated, at a scene which to her was at once both strange and yet so oddly familiar, the old man turned and came toward the window. One glance she caught of a peculiar but not unkindly countenance framed in short wisps of gray hair, then darkness fell between them; the old electroplater had drawn down the shade.

"The rooms are mine; I have paid for them for two months yet," thought Mary, and instinctively moved toward the door. She had forgotten the carriage; forgotten that her ten minutes were nearly up, and that if she wished to seek another refuge she must return at once. As she paused in the doorway she did not notice that the red rays from the opposite window lay on her skirts like blood.

A strange man answered her summons. This made her feel more of an interloper than before. He was older than the electroplater, and much more feeble and bent; but he had a humorous twinkle in his eye, and as soon as he saw her face and noted her lady-like manner, he drew back with as much respect as it was in him to show, and bowing awkwardly, but with evident sincerity, asked her whom she wanted to see.

"The housekeeper," she said, "Mrs. Bowne."

"I take care of the place," he cried. "The Bownes are gone; sent away, I think, miss, for taking of money they shouldn't."

Mary looked blank. "Oh, where shall I go?" she impetuously cried out. "These rooms here at the right belonged to me, but there's a stranger in them. The Bownes relet them; or did you?"

"I let them, miss. I thought I had the right. The former tenant ran away, they said. Excuse me; were you the young lady who lived in there with her father?"

"Yes," she answered, choking down her growing terror and dismay. "And I paid for the rooms a whole quarter in advance, just before I left. I expected that the rooms would be locked; they were full of our furniture and my father's books, and—"

"I'm very sorry," protested the man. "The Bownes said nothing about the rooms having been paid for. If you gave them the money, I think they must have carried it off. Birds of prey, miss—nothing but birds of prey."

"Is there no woman here?" faltered the poor child. "Have you no wife?"

"Oh, miss, ugly men are the ones that get wives; and I—well, I'm not handsome, but—"

The laugh and chuckle with which he finished were meant good-naturedly, but they jarred upon her. Turning toward the door, she was about to escape when she thought of her father's model.

"There was," said she, "in the room when we went away, a machine which my father was making, and of which he thought a great deal. Do you know if it is safe?"

"Surely, miss, there was something behind a curtain that neither of us dared to touch. If you mean that, I think it is there still, a-blinking in the dark. Machine do you call it? Well, well, well! It's for no honest work, if you do give it a decent name."

"It is a model; it is worth money; I shall come back for it to-morrow." And this time she ran quite out of the house.

Why did she come immediately back again with frightened eyes and an agitated air? In the street, rolling rapidly toward the house, she had seen a carriage. It was not the one in which she had ridden to the place, nor was it such a coach as was usually to be seen in these humble quarters. It was a gentleman's turn-out, and the step of the horses was familiar to her.

"Oh, where shall I go?" she exclaimed, feeling her resistance melting away within her, and realizing that if she saw Stanhope now she must yield to his entreaties, possibly to his own undoing. "Is there no place where I can hide?"

The housekeeper, who was on his way back to his own quarters, paused and looked helplessly toward her. At the same moment she heard the carriage stop, fortunately not at the curb-stone in front, but on the opposite side of the way, probably before the drug-store.

"He is coming; he will find me in another minute," she panted, turning to fly she knew not where. But just then a door—the door to her father's old room—opened, and the old man she had seen through the window crossed the threshold and stared in astonishment at her.

At sight of him, she rushed impetuously forward with outstretched and appealing hands. "There is some one coming," she cried. But the old man seemed to comprehend her fears, without words.

"Come in here," said he, in a tone both harsh and strange; and, seizing her by the arm, he drew her into the shop, just as the ring at the front door announced that Stanhope had arrived.

XXVI

The Electroplater

L ittle as we may enjoy it, we shall now be obliged to return and explain somewhat more fully concerning Stephen Huse and his entrance upon this scene.

He was first seen in Markham Place two days after the disappearance of Thomas Dalton and his daughter from their rooms in No. 6. He came in at the east end and stood looking up and down the street with the uncertain air of one who sees it for the first time; then he crossed to the drug-store, before which he hesitated, as was said by one woman who was watching him, like a man who has been sent for something and who has forgotten what it is. At last he went in, and for a few moments contented himself with peering into the rather shabby showcase and casting his eye over the directory hanging by a chain in one corner. The clerk, who was in the habit of seeing many such men in his store, did not notice him at first; but at last, perceiving that the man was old and that there seemed to be something the matter with his hands, he asked in his gruff good-nature, if he could not help him to find the name he wanted.

The old man, who looked like an artisan out of work, was startled by the sudden voice, and hastily dropped the book. Then he turned and surveyed the clerk with a singularly direct gaze which was almost challenging in its character.

Astonished at this, the clerk returned his look with one that was as searching if not as intelligent.

"Queer customer," thought he, struck by some peculiar incongruity in the face and figure before him. "What is it that makes him look so odd?" and decided that it was the total lack of eyebrows in the face before him; then changed his mind and concluded that it was the contrast between the nose, which was as perfect as a gentleman's, and the complexion, which was as hardy and seared as a workman's; and then changed his mind again, and said to himself, "It isn't any of these things: it's his eyes, that seem to know everything; or it is his mouth, which quivers like a woman's, and yet seems to have a man's determination in it too."

"I reckon you'll know me when you see me again," mumbled the stranger, in a harsh and guttural tone that completed the sense of incongruity which his appearance had made, and turned back toward the directory. "I was trying," he went on, in a voice somewhat faint and hesitating for a man who was evidently still capable of a great deal of hard work, "to find a person by the name of Dalton; Thomas Dalton, I think he calls himself."

"Thomas Dalton! why, he lived over there," rejoined the clerk, nodding toward the other side of the street, "there where you see the sign up of 'To Let.'"

The stranger, who seemed somewhat taken aback by this information, stared for a moment, then moved quickly forward and peered through the window at the place indicated.

"In that house?" he queried, staring at No. 6 somewhat blankly. "Are those rooms to let?" he asked.

"So it seems."

"Then he is not there now?"

"No; cut; run; vamoosed. First the father walked out and was not seen again, and then the daughter. Queer doings, eh? Did you know them?"

The old man shook his head, looking thoughtfully at the window opposite.

"I'm hunting for a shop," said he. "I'm an electroplater. Is that a printing establishment on the corner?"

"Yes."

"That would give me power," he decided, "at a slight cost. I think I will look at those rooms."

"You don't seem to be in a condition for work just now," remarked the clerk, glancing at the old man's hands, which were both done up in white linen.

"No," said he, "but that'll pass. I burnt myself with sulphuric acid; I will be all right in a week."

"Both hands, eh?"

"Both hands. Gross carelessness. I'm paying for it now."

"Now, see here! Here's a salve that will do the business in three days. Most wonderful in its action. I put it up myself and—"

"Yes, yes, that's all right; but I don't want any man's compound. Drugs are all poison, I say, and when I come to them—"

"Wait, are you sure you don't know the Daltons?" called out the clerk, for the stranger seemed leaving.

"Not if there's a daughter. The man I know was never married. He is a pattern-maker by trade, and I thought he might help me to find the shop I wanted."

"Oh, another man," cried the clerk, and went back to his prescription counter.

The stranger, blinking at him for a moment in a doubtful sort of way, smiled as he noticed the indifferent look which slowly settled upon the other's face, and, mumbling something to himself, passed quietly out. Pausing on the pavement in front, he smiled again, possibly because the quick and furtive backward look which he gave failed to detect any change in that same clerk's look or expression.

Crossing carefully to No. 6, he rang the bell and then stepped back to cast another look up at the large brick building adjoining. Truly nothing could be more convenient for his purposes. The engine that ran the presses was in that very part of the building that jutted against the tenement before which he was standing, and if a shaft were run through the party-wall he could have the power he wanted by night as well as by day. This was great luck for him and made his countenance brighten perceptibly.

A man, older than himself and much more feeble in appearance, came to the door. Was his presence unexpected, or did he look as odd to the stranger as that stranger had looked to the drug-clerk? I cannot say; but the stranger started when he saw him and seemed inclined to draw back, but next moment stepped forward and uttered his errand.

"I want the housekeeper," he said, glancing up and down the dark passageway before him.

"And who told you that I wasn't that very man?" rejoined the other. "Do I smell new? I've been here only a day, but I'm boss here for all that."

"Oh!" exclaimed the other with what seemed like relief; "then you have the letting of these rooms here on the ground floor?"

"To be sure."

"Well, I'm on the hunt for rooms and think I'll have a look at them."

"All right, comrade; but there's things in 'em. Former tenants skipped, leaving a lot of trash behind."

"Humph! didn't pay their rent, eh?"

"Don't know; the man who was here didn't have much to say about it. Guess you've hit it, though, for the sign was put up before I came; and Mr. Zink—he's the man who owns the house, you know—says I'm to let the rooms with the understanding that the things are to stay in 'em for a month, or till old man Dalton comes back to claim 'em."

"I'm afraid they'll be in my way," mused the stranger, "but I'll look at the rooms. If I can make a shop out of this first one, I don't mind much about the rest. Do you think I can make it into a shop?"

"What kind? We get more for shops. What's your business?" And he looked hard at the stranger's swathed hands.—.

"I'm an electroplater. I want a shop where I can get power easy. Now, that printing establishment next door was what turned me in here."

"I see. Well, if you are not too particular, I guess we can come to terms; only it will have to be money down if we go into any kind of changes for you. Mr. Zink don't believe much in experiments."

"I'll pay money down if the place suits me," answered the man, in an easier tone than he had before used. "But you must be square, for I know as well as you what rooms in this quarter are worth."

They had by this time reached the door of the front room, which the old man first unlocked and then pushed back.

"There!" said he, "it's just as those folks left it." The stranger, entering, gave one hasty look before him, which a nice observer would have noticed flew first to the curtain behind which had stood the table supporting Thomas Dalton's model. But old Curtis, as the new janitor was called, was not a nice observer, and only perceived that the would-be tenant did not seem to be displeased with what he saw, though to his eyes the place looked most gloomy, cold, and uninviting.

"I could do my buffing here," mused the old electroplater, walking slowly to the window and measuring the room and its availability with a seemingly practiced eye. "Yonder I could place my vat, and up here I could rig a shelf that would hold my machine nicely. The belt would run down here, and against this opposite wall I could store away my orders till I was ready to deliver them. All I should want would be to have a shaft run through the wall into the next building; and as for these things of Mr. Dalton's, if I could push them a little to one side I could get along for a while without much difficulty. Ah, what have we got strung up here?"

It was the curtain he alluded to, and as he spoke he tried to push it aside with his right elbow. "A place for hanging clothes, eh?"

There was eagerness in the tone that belied the studied carelessness of his manner; but the housekeeper did not observe this, and twitched the curtain aside with his high and mirthless laugh, saying:

"Perhaps as you're a mechanic you can tell what it is for. Do you see that machine? Well, that's the one thing the Bownes, who had my place here, you know, spoke to me about. They said it had the devil in it, and warned me not to touch it."

The stranger, whose eyes gleamed brightly as he gazed at the unfinished model thus revealed to him, did not answer for a moment. He seemed to be engaged in running over each part and portion of the same with first an inquiring and then a gloating eye, an expression which had hardly left his face when the janitor dropped the curtain.

"What do you think it is?" asked the latter.

The stranger shrugged his high shoulders and tried to assume an indifferent air. "Some nonsensical invention," he rejoined, and turned again to his survey of the rooms.

The result was that the electroplater took the rooms, and in a few days settled himself in them and opened business. He had found no difficulty in getting a countershaft run through the party-wall, and as soon as his hands had recovered their power to work, his spare and awkward form could be seen day after day bending over the whirring wheel that had been placed in the window. His orders, which at first were few, soon increased; and the industry, which was a new one in the neighborhood, gave quite a look of life to that end of the place.

His window, which at first had been spotless, grew gradually misty with the flying particles from his wheels, and his utensils, which had been uncommonly bright when he came there, soon began to show use, somewhat as his hands did. Promptly at eight o'clock the belts were thrown off the buffing wheel and the curtains drawn down; but the whir and hum went on, sometimes into the night and sometimes almost till morning.

After the first two weeks he attracted little attention, and after three his figure had become so well known in the place that the little children called him Daddy Huse, though it was noticeable then, as always, that they never crowded around him when he went out, or raised their voices in loud calls or laughter when his slight but nervous figure, with its awkward shoulders, shuffled by them in the early twilight.

He was not sociable, and by and by every one learned it; but he was not unkindly, nor was he exactly morose. He was simply always thinking, and this, in such a quarter, does not lead to much neighborly gossip. So he was eventually dropped even by the housekeeper, much to his own relief, no doubt, and to the advantage of his work. Yet no one considered him a mystery, because no one saw what he did when the shades were drawn down at night far below the window-frame.

But we must see what he did then, and judge from it, if possible, what lay under the idiosyncrasies of the workman.

First, there was the sudden change which his whole person took on when this shutting out of every possibly peering eye took place. The roughness, the humbleness of the artisan seemed to fall from him, and an intellectual light to suddenly dawn upon his strange face, intensifying its incongruity of expression; while something not so easy to understand came with it, altering his whole manner and making the room thereafter seem, not so much the workshop of the artisan, as the secret cell of a philosopher.

He was a great buyer of newspapers, which he kept stacked on a table and read in the early evening. But what was strange, and to an onlooker would have been incomprehensible, was the fact, that it was not the editorial pages that he read, or even the news columns, but those short paragraphs given to social events, and such personal items as related to persons moving in a society of which he surely could not have had even a glimpse. These he would devour, not looking less like a philosopher because his mind was for the moment fixed on trivialities; and when by any chance he chose to vary his entertainment, it was to the marriage list he turned, and sometimes to the notices of deaths.

But this was not the only strange thing he did. When his reading was done, and the frugal meal which he cooked for himself on his own stove had been eaten, and a short walk taken, he was wont to return again to work, like a man who neither wishes nor requires rest. But his work at night was not the work of the daytime, any more than his appearance while engaged upon it was the same which characterized him at the buffing wheel or over the vat containing the plating solution.

And what was this work? Had Mary Dalton possessed the power of clairvoyance, and could she from the luxurious home in Fifth Avenue have been able to see into the sombre den where her father's books and mechanical apparatus still remained, she would have been startled, no doubt, to behold the hand of this strange-looking man laid upon objects that were at once her terror and her pride. Yet this she would have seen. For Stephen Huse, fascinated, perhaps, by the unfinished model he had found hidden behind the folds of the woolen curtain, had not only so far ignored the advice of the timid housekeeper as to touch and examine it, but had even gone so far as to bring it from its place and practically to go to work upon it.

That he had at once solved the purpose of the machine, and knew to a dot the mind of its inventor, was evident from the precision of his efforts to perfect it, and from the ease with which he had discovered the hidden cupboard in which had been stored away certain articles necessary to its completion. That, notwithstanding, he worked in fear and terror, either from a sense of guilt or a dread of detection, was equally evident; or why did he give those sudden starts when an unexpected noise disturbed the silence, or cast those sly and inquiring glances from time to time at the curtained window or the muslin-covered door?

He was not a sociable man, as I have said, but he talked to this machine at times as we talk to a friend, or rather as we talk to an enemy, with long-drawn whispers and shrinking looks, as though some secret were between them that it would terrify the walls to hear. On the night it was finished, for it came to its completion very soon, this talk was broken by long and exultant surveys of the hideous thing, which, now that it was done, seemed to bear a strong resemblance to the interior of the electroplating machine standing in full sight against the opposite wall; and yet it was not an electroplating machine, or there would have been no reason for the mingled dread and fascination with which he eyed it, or for those deep and awful looks which from time to time shifted across his face as his two stained and badly scarred hands stole first toward one shining copper knob glittering from the revolving armature, and then to its fellow glowering on the other end; but not to both at once; oh, no! not by any dreadful chance to both at once, for he had managed to measure the terrible force generated in the weird, clumsy contrivance, although he had not the more accurate dynamometer of the present day to aid him. The results satisfied him, judging by the long-drawn sigh of relief that ended his experiments.

He had pulled out the table upon which the machine had rested when it was in hiding behind its shrouding curtain, and the belt, borrowed from the other machine, now connected this new invention with the countershaft. But there seemed to be no work for the whirling armature, and after a short minute of fearful scrutiny and alternate exultation and shrinking terror, he threw off the belt with one wild jerk, and thrust the table back again out of sight.

But he did not go to his rest. All that night he paced the floor, shuddering as he passed the fallen curtain, and only recovering his courage as he came into that part of the room devoted to his daily toil. The dream of days had been realized, but the horror which came with it was not to be appeased by aught but the refreshing gleam of morning sunshine.

He had been in this room about three weeks when this eventful night occurred; and it was, I think, about two days later that he had the dangerous fright of which I must speak before I recur to Mary.

XXVII

DALTON'S INVENTION

It was high noon on a certain day shortly after the events I have just mentioned, and Stephen Huse, who had a large order to fill before seven o'clock that night, was busily engaged at the buffing-wheel. As this stood directly in the window, his back was to the rest of the room; and though at night he was never easy except when facing the door upon whose muslin-covered glass the silhouette of every passing figure was plainly thrown, in the daylight, and while absorbed in his work, he seemed to be well-nigh oblivious to everything but the whirring wheel and the especial duty of the hour. On this day he felt especially unconcerned; and, had the buzz of the wheel been less emphatic, one might even have heard the snatch of a song on his lips, and when he turned, as he did now and then, to lay down one polished object and take up another, there was a gleam of cheer in his aged face, caught, perhaps, from some passing hope, or as if the mere act of working had the power to still the feverish thoughts of night and calm the fears which were so apparent in every move he made after the shades were drawn in his shop and he fell again under the shadow of that unholy machine to which he devoted so many midnight hours.

He had passed to his table and back again, and was just settling himself anew to work, when a voice spoke suddenly in the room behind him which at once stopped his fingers and caused the blood to freeze about his heart.

It was a rich voice, a mellow voice, but it meant death to Stephen Huse. Falling back from his wheel, like a man who feels the clutch of fingers round his throat from behind, he listened for one wild moment for a renewal of those tones, asking himself if his hour had come, and repeating again and again to himself: "I will not have it. I am mistaken; it is not he. I am not ready; nothing is ready—not even my mind. I have imagined the voice; it is not he."

But he had imagined nothing. Again the rich voice spoke, and this time Stephen Huse's whole body cringed and surged forward on his wheel, though still he did not turn his head.

The event, though anticipated long, was so sudden, it robbed him of his self-possession. It made him deaf, blind, senseless almost. Though he had imagined it often, though he had gone over and over the scene of this meeting a thousand times in his dreams, now that it had come he was no more ready for it than a child for the thunder crash. He had imagined it, but never without the shadow of a warning, never without his mind being in some state of preparation for it, *never with the belt off the machine glowering behind the woolen curtain*.

He had fallen forward, I say, but an accidental touch of the wheel burned into his hand and started him upright again and turned his thoughts in another direction. "Remember that you are Stephen Huse," that wheel seemed to say. "While you are the electroplater nothing can hurt you." And so impressed was he by this thought, that in an instant almost, certainly before his agitation had been seen by those behind, he was enabled to press once more the metal he was polishing against the buffing-wheel, and so continue work with a certain automaton-like motion, though his whole being was concentrated into hearing what was said and done by the person or persons who had entered the room at his back.

It was the voice alone which he had heard at first, but presently, as his self-possession increased, he was able to distinguish the words which were being uttered by the intruders. That they were not meant for him gave him his first sense of relief, and that they were meant for the owner's agent, of whose presence behind him he was also conscious, completed the satisfaction of the moment, and gave him time to settle his shoulders into that high and awkward line which so altered his whole appearance, and to adopt that air of complete absorption in his work which he felt to be his only safeguard.

Meantime the stranger continued talking. The words were commonplace enough, but they were full of meaning to Stephen Huse.

"Ah, I see! I see! You have turned the room into a shop. A good idea enough, but it looks as if you did not expect the former tenant to return."

"A bird in the hand," quavered old Father Curtis, "is worth two in the bush. This man pays fair rent, which is good for us; and lets the other man's chest and things stay here, which is not bad for him."

"So, so! His chest, eh? And his books too, I suppose."

Stephen Huse, whose face had blanched at mention of the books, bent still further over his wheel, pressing the article he held so closely against it that his whole frame quivered.

"Yes, these are his books," piped the housekeeper, shuffling over the floor after the other, whose step Huse could feel in his throbbing breast, though his ear could not hear it. "Cheerful reading, eh? I looked at 'em once, but have let the dust lie on 'em ever since. Too deep for me, and too mortuary, eh? I had that word out of the papers and pride myself a bit upon it. Don't it fit, sir?"

The other, who was a tall, large man whose presence seemed to fill the room, making the man beside him and the man at his toil in the distant window seem like shadows beside his commanding personality, made some slight response and drew down a book that leaned toward him from the long row before which he was standing.

"*Gun-shot Wounds!*" he exclaimed, reading off the title in a singularly deep and mellow voice. "So Thomas Dalton dipped a little into surgery, it seems."

The words were to himself, but to one accustomed to watch the electroplater at his work, it would have been apparent that they went further and pierced deeper than the speaker intended, or at the present moment was to all appearance aware.

"I have known Dalton a long time," was his next remark, "but I did not imagine that his knowledge was so varied. Note what a man reads, and you learn the man, they say. Let us note what this man reads, and perhaps we shall be able to learn the secret of his disappearance."

Taking down another book, he glanced it over. "Ho, ho! 'Care of the Drowning, and What to do in Cases of Sudden Asphyxia.' Very good! And here's a treatise on poisons, and more than one pamphlet on 'Singular Cases of Men who have been Restored to Life after a Period of Seeming Death.' Curious! one would think he had a mania on the subject of death!"

"Mortuary literature, I called it," chuckled old Curtis. "Wasn't I right?"

The stranger, lifting his head, ran his eye along the shelf above him and smiled with a curious, deep, and unfathomable satisfaction that was not without its element of sarcasm. "Electricity! Magnetism! Patent Office Reports! and a whole row of works on the various sciences. I think I know the man now, and can guess what errand it was that took him away."

Turning about, he glanced toward the window, and the light thus falling on his face showed it to be deeply pockmarked. "I should like to speak to this Huse," said he, and took a step forward.

At the move, Stephen, who had not turned his head an inch since the man came into the room, stiffened and drew back again, as if something from the flying wheel had struck him in the face. But he bent forward again almost immediately; and to the janitor, who was just going out of the door, his shoulders had never looked higher, nor his whole form more awkward or ungainly.

Meantime the stranger continued to advance in a leisurely manner down the room. His step, which was naturally slow, paused and hesitated just now longer than usual, so that many minutes seemed to pass to the agonized man at the window before a smart click was heard which proved that the intruder had stopped at the table to handle some of the many objects that were lying upon it.

It was a slight sound, and seemingly unimportant, but as it struck upon the ear of Stephen Huse it appeared to work a change in his inmost being. His cheeks, which had merely been pale, turned suddenly blue, and had the wheel whirling before his eyes been able to speak, it would have told of the birth of some awful purpose, that, rising like a ghost from his soul, now stared out of those fixed and horrible orbs bent unblinkingly forward.

But the wheel had no voice, and to the stranger sauntering carelessly onward, there was nothing in the bent figure, rising dimly before him, to attract his attention, much less to arouse his fear or awake his apprehension.

The electroplating machine was busily at work, and a whole row of variously shaped objects hung in the solution. As the stranger approached the vat, his feet involuntarily paused again, and his ever-ready hand went out, when suddenly from the seemingly unconcerned man in the window, a voice came, so shrill, so high-pitched, and so charged with some heavily suppressed feeling, that, had the stranger been of a more highly organized temperament, he must have paused and asked himself what secret terror or mad desire could be working in the heart of the man that could emit such sounds.

"You had better be careful," this singular voice cried. "Strangers had better not potter about too much where electroplating is going on."

"Might get a shock?" laughed the man, looking into the vat with growing curiosity.

"Might get a shock," repeated Huse, still without turning his head.

"Well, all the shock that little thing could give me," chuckled the other, throwing back his splendid shoulders and cying the brushes resting on the commutator, with sarcastic good-nature, "would affect me just about as much as a mosquito-bite, I should say."

"Perhaps; but all the same, I say, keep away," cried the other. And, without looking at his visitor, he left his wheel, and with a face whose expression was happily hidden in the darkness of the shop, he suddenly took the belt from the electroplating machine and carried it quickly over to where the curtain hid Dalton's invention.

"Can't trust me, eh?" signified the stranger, with careless good-humor. "One would think you knew me. I remember that my mother used to say, when I was a small shaver, that I would play with the lightning if I had a chance."

Stephen Huse trembled like a man in an ague, but he said nothing. He was fitting the belt to the new invention.

"Ah, and what have you there?" asked the stranger, coming so near that his steadfast and powerful frame touched the weak and trembling arm of the workman.

"It's without a name yet. I call it an electro-dynamic engine," explained the other, with shrill curtness; and with one awful side look at the unconscious giant, he went back to the window, where he took up a fresh object and held it madly against the buffing-wheel.

"An electro-dynamic engine. And what is that?" inquired the other, leaning over the mysterious machine the armature of which was now whirling with dangerous speed.

Stephen Huse, with his face bent over his work, did not answer. He was listening with suppressed breath for something more than speech, and had the darkly blurred window before him been a mirror, it would have shown a face horribly distorted by some inward struggle.

"I've heard the word," continued the stranger, touching first one part and then another of the curious machine before him, "but my scientific knowledge is not great enough to tell me what it means. Have these knobs I see here any use?"

An odd sound came from the man at the wheel; he seemed to be choking. Did the fear that this intruder, evidently known and greatly feared by him, would grasp those two knobs and so meet from the interrupted current an instant and terrible death, paralyze his speech and make him incapable of action, *or did he wish him to stumble upon the doom lying hidden before him*, and, having some conscience left, shrink in dreadful terror from his own inward expectancy? His silence, his fixed, awful, watchful, listening silence, does not tell; and yet when with a short laugh the careless stranger comes finally from the thing, the sudden mad desperation with which Stephen Huse flings up the window and takes in the wholesome autumn air would have revealed something of his feelings, had not the stranger's mind been wholly fixed upon a purpose of his own which he was now determined to put into execution.

As Huse drew back and fell mechanically again to work, the other came up behind him and touched him on the shoulder.

"Pardon me," said he, "I have business with you."

The electroplater stopped an instant, shook his head, and mumbled something about having more business now than he could attend to.

But the stranger was not a man to accept a rebuff. Laughing as only he could laugh, he stood his ground with imperturbable good-nature till Stephen Huse felt himself forced to say:

"And what do you want done? We do nothing but electroplating here. If you have any of that to be done you'll have to have the work ground and polished elsewhere."

"Thank you, but I am not interested in electroplating; yet my work is paying work, and one that you can do at small cost. I want a chance at an interview with Thomas Dalton, the man whose rooms you are occupying, you know."

The high shoulders of Huse grew higher, and he pressed the corundum he was holding so hard against the wheel that the particles flew off in all directions, making the speaker draw back a step.

"What have I to do with that?" asked Huse, glancing at a small clock hanging up before him on the window frame.

"Everything, I think. You know that the man disappeared suddenly, do you not?"

"I know," returned the other, in apparent exasperation, possibly assumed to cover up his growing terror, "that I have all his gimcracks to look after."

"That's what I have observed, and that's why I say I have business with you." How mellifluous were his tones, and how his large person seemed to overshadow the smaller man before him.

"If Dalton is not dead, and I do not think he is, he will be back here some day to steal away these things. He may come openly, but I am more inclined to think he will come secretly, and that no one will know it but you. Now, if he does—"

There was a pause, and in it a bill was softly pushed under Huse's hand. It was a large one, but the scarred fingers did not close readily upon it, and the stranger went on to say:

"I like Dalton; we were old comrades, and, though I've risen in the world and he has gone down, I cannot forget that I owe him a debt I shall never be happy till I pay. Will you help me to meet my obligations by letting me know—well, we will say by telegraph—if he returns to this place?"

"You want to do him a harm," grumbled the other, fingering the bill slightly.

The smile of the other was large and indulgent. Stephen Huse did not see it, but he may have felt it, for his whole form seemed to contract for an instant.

"And what makes you think that?" asked the other, eying those scarred fingers, now trembling over that bill, with the look of a tempter who expects success. "Have I not said I liked him, and that I only want to see him in order to pay back an old debt?"

"Yes; but this?" He held up the bill, but still did not turn his head.

"Oh, I've no lack of money; don't let that trouble you."

Stephen Huse laid down the bill and went on with his work.

"I'll telegraph," he muttered.

The stranger smiled blandly, and with that large indulgence which very powerful men bestow upon the puppets which answer to their will; and leaning forward he whispered: "You will oblige me. A quick word, mind you, and to this address. Dalton himself will thank you, if you can bring about a meeting between us without his knowledge."

"Very well," again muttered the other over the whirring wheel.

"Good! I'll trust you, then. Any favor I can show *you*?"

"I must get this work off," grumbled the electroplater. "If you'll be so good as to give me more room—"

"Ah, I see; I'm in your way. Well, well; now we understand each other, I'll be off. We do understand each other, eh?"

If he meant to irritate the electroplater into turning around, he failed. Stephen Huse, laying down the piece from which he had almost buffed the nickel coating, put the bill into his pocket, and hung up the card he had received in a rack over his head, but deigned neither to utter a word, nor to bestow a glance upon the good-humored but resolute man behind him. The latter laughed as if he had met a queer customer, and presently drew off, going near again to Dalton's machine, which was still whirling upon its rude framework.

As he paused there, fascinated and vaguely curious, Huse had a return of his former excitement; but it did not show itself as before, and ere many minutes the stranger walked away and left the room, and very soon the house.

As he passed the window, Huse started back and turned about to take down a fresh piece of work from the bench, so that if the stranger had desired to see his face, he was baffled in the attempt. By the time he was ready to turn back again, the stranger was out of sight, which was fortunate for Huse, for the intense emotions he had suppressed till now were having their way outward, and the gleam in his eye had a wildness in it which would have attracted the attention even of an uninterested person. And so would his action, had it been seen; for no sooner had he made sure that his enemy was gone, than he dragged the bill which had been given him from its hiding-place, and, crushing and tearing it with his hands, he threw it into a pile of refuse where he trod it down with his feet. Then he walked slowly over to Dalton's invention and took off the belt which had set it whirling. "Not to-day," he muttered, and gave one fearful look at the slowly slacking armature; "will it be to-morrow, and when it comes will it be murder, or will it be—" The word did not pass his lips. The emotions of the past few minutes had been too severe for his enfeebled frame, and he sank in a faint upon the floor.

When he came to himself the noonday sun had faded from the street, and the room showed its loss by the increasing gloom of its corners. But one object shone brightly, and that was the stranger's card hanging up on the distant window-frame. It was a large but neatly engraved bit of pasteboard, and bore upon its face these words:

Col. Robert Deering
Brevoort House

XXVIII

Fresh Surprises

Mary's first feeling, upon entering her father's old room, was one of perfect safety; her next, a most unreasonable fear lest Stanhope should not be particular enough in his inquiries, and so go away without finding her—so contradictory are the emotions that sway the human heart. For the first few minutes, then, she kept her eyes on the muslin-covered door in the wild hope of seeing the shadow of her lover's form as he passed up-stairs or into the janitor's room opposite; and not till the sudden closing of the front door, and the return of the janitor alone, told her that Stanhope had indeed left the house without an attempt, as she thought, to penetrate into her hiding-place, did she turn with a sigh to the strange man who had offered her the refuge of his shop.

The first look she cast at his face gave her a shock, the next made her tremble from head to foot; and, though she was listening with a despairing heart for the sound of departing carriage-wheels, she could not prevent her eyes from travelling with eager, almost frightened scrutiny, from the locks of thin gray hair floating above the worn forehead of the electroplater to the dark and disfigured hands, idly fingering some polished articles he had been engaged in putting away when he heard her appeal for assistance.

The old man, whose eyes had fallen to the floor, did not help her with a word or look, and so a minute passed in silence that was uninterrupted by any sound from within or without; then the electroplater suddenly raised his eyes, and fixing them upon her, he said tenderly:

"Mary?"

With a cry of "Father! father!" she leaped into his arms, and the two faces met.

There were tears on her cheek of his shedding as well as of her own when she finally drew back, and with wondering and curious eyes surveyed him again from crown to chin.

"What does it mean?" was her first question. "Are you the man who does the business here? You are my father, and yet you are so changed that nothing but your voice crying my name convinced me it was you."

"Thank God for that!" was his heartfelt reply; then, seeing her eyes travel involuntarily toward the window, he inquired, "From whom are you trying to escape?"

"Stanhope White," she faltered. "He loves me, but I cannot marry him. Oh, what should I have done if I had not found you here to-night!"

The old man, across whose features an indefinable air of refinement had passed with her recognition of their relationship, looked startled at this speech, and would have questioned her; but she, as if anxious to avoid this, laid one finger on his hair and suggestively remarked:

"This was always brown before."

His chin fell and his lip trembled. It is a sad thing to have to blush before one's child.

"I know," said he. "I colored it. I have colored it for years, that the change, when I chose to make it, might be more marked."

"And your face, father dear? It is not the same face. What have you done to make it so brown and strange?"

"Do you not see, my darling?"

"You have lost your eyebrows! O father, why did you shave your eyebrows?"

"I did not, Mary. I pulled the hairs out, one by one."

"Father!"

"I was in danger, Mary, and a man will do much when his life is at stake."

His trembling tones, his whole anxious, troubled visage, made her for an instant forget that the carriage over the way had not yet started. Staring upward into his face, which was not yet a familiar one to her, she faltered: "Is it the pock-marked man you fear? Is it to escape him, that you have changed your personality and become a workman?"

Her father nodded, but with a furtive look about him that called up a long past to her troubled mind, and made her realize for the first time that his fear of this man dated back to her childhood, and that this change in his outward appearance and attitude toward men and things was the culmination of a hundred efforts on his part to elude a fate continually dogging him.

"I do not understand," she timidly intimated. "Could you not have appealed to the police? Are they not bound to protect all honest persons? Must a man suffer as you have done, and at last lose his very position amongst his fellows, just to escape an enemy?"

"You do not know my enemy," he retorted. "He is no common man; neither can the police help me"

"Father!" Her whole soul was in her accents now. "Is there any reason why you cannot go to the police?"

He trembled, dropped his head, but said nothing.

"You have always been so good," she continued. "I have honored you; I honor you yet. But I know, I see, there must be some good cause why you must fight this struggle alone. Would it not be better for you to tell me the truth, so that I might help you intelligently, instead of blundering as I have done sometimes in the past?"

"I cannot tell you; there is no need," was the shrill and almost wild reply. "Enough that I fear this man and have spent years in trying to escape him, by frequently changing my abiding-place, and sometimes, as you know, my name. But he is not to be thrown off the scent by any such means; and when I heard that he had been *here*, I saw that my old schemes were worthless, and that if I wished to escape his pursuit I must do it by some daring move so utterly out of keeping with all my former actions that he would be blinded to my identity and his suspicions even be kept down. There was but one way to do this—to first lose my old self, and then to come out boldly before the world in a character so open to inspection, he would not even think of challenging it. That this meant separation from you made it all the better; for your fate must be different from my fate, and your future unclouded by anything that may happen to me." Mary, with her ear turned again toward the street, sighed softly, but did not yet seek to contradict her father. Instead, she gently answered:

"But why come back here, where he has known you to be, and where he is liable to come himself at any time?"

"Because that is the very thing Thomas Dalton would not do. Because the very bravado of the thing is its best safeguard. Because, thanks to an old artist friend of mine, I have been able to disguise myself so well, or rather to so alter the very expression of my natural face, that my neighbors fail to know me, and my child even looks upon me with doubtful eyes every time I stop speaking and stand silent before her."

"But—but the business? How do you know the business? You do carry on electroplating here, do you not?"

"Faithfully, and they say well. It did not take a long apprenticeship. I have always been handy at mechanics. Then it is to the interest of the parties from whom I hold a plating license, to help me with any information they can give. It is really very simple."

"I suppose so," was her rather absent reply, as her eyes went wandering toward the curtain behind which the model had always stood. "Is the machine still there?" she whispered.

He turned pale, and caught her back by the arm, for she seemed about to rise. "Yes!" he answered, choking over the word.

"I am glad of that," she answered softly. "You would have felt badly to have been separated from *that*."

He looked at her with a deep and penetrating gaze. Did she suspect its awful secret? Did she know that with this machine in the room he was in hourly consort with death? Her meek, upward glance, so full of pain, but so devoid of suspicion, assured him that her soul was clear on this point; and, drawing a deep breath of relief, he ventured in another moment to observe:

"Another reason why these rooms were the only place for me;" and stooped to kiss her forehead, perhaps to hide from her the trembling of his lips.

"But your hands! O father, your hands! What has happened to your hands?"

"Dearest, there was a scar to hide."

"And so you burned them both! Oh, dreadful, dreadful! You fill me with terror, father."

His gloomy brow showed that he was not without terror himself. "I hate suffering," he acknowledged bitterly; "but life, Mary, life! What were I without life? I could not follow your career—a career which I mean shall be as great, lordly, and noble as yourself. That is why I shrink so from death. I love you, I have always loved you. You are the light of my eyes—"

"I know it, father, I know it; and I grieve to disappoint you—"

"You are so beautiful, Mary. Do you know how beautiful you are?"

"My beauty will avail me little if—"

"I do not doubt you feel at home in the splendid mansion where you live. You did not have to learn to be a lady, did you?"

"I had much to learn, but—"

"Was it a surprise to Mr. White when he saw you in his house that morning?"

"Oh! yes, yes—"

"And did he at once show his pleasure? Tell me, dear, tell your old father. How long a time elapsed before he offered himself to you?"

"Very soon, father; too soon—"

"You love him, do you not, Mary?"

Her hands went up in one wild gesture, and she burst into tears. "I love him so well," she sobbed, "that I will never marry him."

Her father, not at all taken aback at what he doubtless considered a mere girlish whim, smiled softly to himself as he patted her on the shoulder.

"You will marry him in a month," he affirmed. "If only I felt as sure of my future as I do of yours."

"I will never marry him. If I were determined before, I am more than determined now. What you have told me to-night has put an end to any wavering I may have had before. He, the noble, the irreproachable, marry a girl whose whole heart should be with her unhappy father? Besides, he should not marry me. He is bound, or ought to be, to another woman, and—"

"What?" The old man, Thomas Dalton—or, should we say, Stephen Huse—showed trouble and anxiety now. "He is married to some one else?"

"No; not married."

"Engaged, then?"

"No; not engaged, but bound by his father's wishes. Mr. White ordered him, on his dying day, to marry a girl—"

"Well, well?"

"He has not yet seen, but whom he is likely to see any day."

The wrath which suddenly appeared upon the unaccustomed features before her astonished and alarmed her.

"How dare he do it?" cried he, hotly. "How dare he interfere with your happiness and his?" Striding off, he mumbled to himself and struggled for self-control in the darker recesses of the room, while Mary, released for a moment from the constraint of his presence, dashed to the window and pulled aside the shade that covered it.

The carriage with which half her thoughts and half her heart lay, still stood before the opposite drug-store.

Her father, seeing her at the window, gave a cry and drew her quickly back.

"Do not make the task before me any harder," he protested. "Have you forgotten that I am still Stephen Huse, and that I am not in the habit of having fashionable visitors?"

She glanced down at her dress, which was simple for Fifth Avenue, but rich indeed for Markham Place, and drew meekly back. "Forgive me," she pleaded, "but while he stays so near I am but half alive. Do you think he is waiting for me? If so, he will have to wait long, for I have found my father."

"Does he love you enough to wait?"

"Yes, yes."

"And yet expects to marry another woman?"

"Not if I will marry *him*."

"Ah!" The old man looked relieved.

"Father, father, do not weaken me. It has been such a struggle for me to come to this decision. I had to fly away. He is so far above all other men. I worship him, but I will not injure his career. Will you not help me to be strong? For your own sake, father, and for the right which you have loved since I have known you if not before?"

"And if I do, where will you go? Can you stay here?"

She had not thought but that she could, but now she saw it would be impossible.

"No, but you will find me a place. It is not as if we had no money."

"And it is not as if you had no beauty. Where can I, a poor artisan, take you, a reigning belle, without arousing gossip or awakening suspicion? You will have to go back to Mrs. White or lose your future, Mary. I know no other course unless you have some friend—"

"My friends are all his friends," she put in.

"Go back with your lover. It will be to a happy fate."

Mary felt a sudden discouragement. With her father and her own inward predilections against her, how could she hope to hold her ground? Yet she made one more effort.

"And what if Natalie Yelverton comes to mar it?"

"Natalie Yelverton!" The old man's jaw had fallen, and he looked amazed.

"That is the name of the woman his father commanded him to marry."

"Oh!" And the old man wheeled about and began fingering the work which he had finished during the day, but no more thinking of it than she. "I said," he spoke up at last, with his back still to her, "that you would be married in a month. I now say that you will be married in a week. You have your money, Mary?"

He had turned about as he said this, and she noted, with a wild beating of her heart, that there was a resolute look in his eye such as she had never seen there before.

"It is in a bank," she faltered.

"Hold on to it, Mary, till you are married. There is nothing like money for people who have no firmness of ground under their feet. I wear mine now in a huge belt about my waist. But if I am ever found dead do not seek to claim it; for Stephen Huse is nothing to the future wife of Stanhope White, and Thomas Dalton will never be seen again."

"And—and—"

"Shall I call a carriage, dear, or will you go out and join Mr. White in his?"

"I will do neither"—she was in a state of desperation now—"unless you can swear to me that there is nothing in your life which if known would shame Stanhope White from marrying me."

Was he desperate too? The excitement which sparkled in every feature of his strange face, once so handsome and now so marred and transformed, roused her alarm, but did not awake her suspicion.

"And, if I can, will you do as I desire and marry him before the week is out?"

"If he wishes it." She had forgotten her rival—forgotten the Natalie Yelverton who still stood between them.

"Then listen, child. As God sees me, I swear to you that if Stanhope White could look into my life he would see much that is unhappy, but nothing that should separate you and him."

"O father!" The relief she showed was instantaneous and unquestioning. "Then there is nothing wicked, nothing disgraceful in the past that oppresses you? Thank God! Thank God!" and she clasped his knees in her new joy, and kissed both of his scarred hands in an outburst of delight that was marred by no doubt.

But he, who had looked almost majestic the moment before, shrank imperceptibly from this touch of his innocent daughter, and hoarsely repeating, "I have said," he put her gently back, and continued with quiet persistence: "And now will you take an oath, in your turn, to do what you have promised?"

But, at this return to a subject from which she shrank, she grew pale again and seemed to be afraid and faltered. "I dare not," fell from her lips. "There seems to be something wrong about it Do not ask me to swear."

With a smile he caught her laughingly to his breast. Either some lie he had told or the unwonted determination he was showing seemed to intoxicate him.

"You need not swear," he assured her. "With love upon my side, I have no need of oaths. You will marry him. And now, three kisses for a bridal blessing! Oh, I shall die of content the day I know you to be married to him."

Visions of joy, visions of future peace would float before her in spite of herself.

"And what excuse shall I give for returning, after saying I should never be seen by them any more?"

"If he asks for one, he does not love you. But he will not ask; not after he has seen your face."

"Father, you have conquered. If I appear weak, it is because I have had no help from you."

"That is right! Blame me, blame your old father for your happiness; for you are happy, Mary, as never in your life before. But it makes me young to see it; makes me forget we may never meet again. Ah, little one, little one, some day you may blame your father, indeed, but never for forcing you into a promise without which you had been lost."

"And you?"

"Oh, I may live on for years now, darling. The man I feared was in this very shop two days ago and did not recognize me."

"Father!"

"And I like my work; it keeps me from thinking. You may leave me with a good heart, Mary."

But she could not do this so readily as he seemed to imagine; for underneath all his forced and rather feverish cheerfulness she detected the irrepressible grief of a father parting with the one darling of his heart. In vain he chided her; in vain he told her that the time was short, and that her lover would be gone if she delayed; her arms would cling about him, and her tears wet his cheek, till at last he grew desperate— perhaps with the struggle of suppressing his own swelling emotions— and, putting her gently aside, said firmly:

"We must say good-by, darling, and at once. If you are happy, I shall know it; if you are prosperous and good, the fame of it will come to me. Rest in that thought, and may the God in heaven bless you."

"And must I never see you again? May I not write, or hear in any way from you?"

"No; a watchful eye will be upon you as upon me. I dare not trust to any communication."

"But if you should want *me?*"

"I will send you *this*." Hastily drawing a piece of paper toward him, he scribbled a cabalistic sign in one corner. "When you see this at the head of the personal column in the Herald, you will know that you are wanted *here*. Otherwise, let Markham Place be as a spot forgotten. And now one last kiss, for the horses opposite are growing impatient."

She lifted her face to his, and a last embrace took place between them. Then she ran hurriedly out. But at the front door her courage failed her. What if Stanhope were not waiting for her outside? Should she go on and humiliate herself by seeking him? Glancing back, she saw that her father had left the door of the shop open, and she was almost tempted to return. But she knew that this could lead to no good result. So, suppressing every fear and suggestion of timidity, she opened the door and looked anxiously forth. The glare of the drug-store was immediately before her, and in the opposite doorway, with their faces turned toward each other, and not toward herself, she saw two men. One was Stanhope, and the other— As she caught sight of this other, natural instinct made her close the door behind her, and crush her own figure into as dark a corner as she could find; for it was her father's enemy she perceived, the pock-marked man of whom she had so much reason to be afraid.

They had just issued from the store, and as she watched them, with a growing terror paralyzing all her limbs, she saw them cross the pavement together, and, as she thought, turn themselves toward the spot where she stood so poorly concealed. But no, it was not upon her their thoughts were fixed, possibly not upon her father, for just as she was about to sink to the ground in her irrepressible dismay, they stopped, and the carriage, which was still in waiting, drove up, and they both got in, and the door closed upon them, and the carriage rolled away.

When all was again quiet in the street, and she had come quite to herself, she heard a voice whisper in her ear:

"Go, my daughter, for the janitor. He will find you a carriage. You must be at home before Mr. White; so tell the driver to go quickly."

XXIX

Attack and Defence

When on this eventful night Stanhope White rang the bell at No. 6 Markham Place, it was not, as we know, to seek Mary Dalton. His errand was one of inquiry, and the object of it, to learn the whereabouts of the one man who could throw light upon the mystery of his father's death.

When, therefore, he was met at the door by old Curtis instead of the chattering Mrs. Bowne, and recognized, as he speedily did, the utter futility of expecting information from this quarter, he felt that the last avenue had been closed to any further enlightenment on the one topic most affecting his future happiness. He was, therefore, proportionally startled when, upon crossing to his carriage on the other side of the street, he perceived, standing in the well-lighted drug-store, a large, powerfully built man, with a face which would have been handsome if it had not been so deeply pock-marked.

Was it, could it be, the man he was seeking? He had an intuitive sense that it was; and, moved by the impulse of the moment, he passed the carriage and entered the drug-store, Colonel Peering—for it was he—turned as Stanhope's handsome figure darkened the doorway, and their two eyes met in one quick glance, which certainly had more in it than usually marks the first meeting of two total strangers. Then the older man drew back, and, taking Stanhope in with that air of superiority which sat so easily upon him, proceeded to light the cigar which he had just bought.

Stanhope, with his heart beating fast, walked directly toward him.

"I beg your pardon," said he, "but, if I am not mistaken, you are the man for whom I have been searching for some weeks."

The colonel, who had perhaps had his moment of preparation, and yet who may not have expected this direct address, surveyed the candid and strangely attractive face of the young man before him, and dropped his eyes for just one significant instant. Then he spoke, easily, and with that geniality of tone whose usual effect was to make an instantaneous friend of the person addressed, but which, in Stanhope's ear, sounded like a warning.

"I am Colonel Deering. If that is the name of the man you are looking for, he can always be found at the Brevoort House."

"And *I* am Stanhope White."

If the other had not known who his interlocutor was, he might have given some tokens of an uneasy surprise. But he did know, and so only bowed with great good-humor and a polished courtesy which rather disconcerted Stanhope, proving as it did that the man was a gentleman in manner if not in heart.

"I am happy to make your acquaintance. Your father's name was of course well known to me. I am honored to meet his son."

"You knew my father?"

The colonel, lifting his cigar, took one long whiff. "Pardon me," said he, "who did not know your father?"

Stanhope felt his face turn white. Glancing about, he discovered that they were comparatively alone, the clerk having withdrawn behind the prescription counter when he saw that they were bent upon conversation and not upon business.

"But you knew him intimately? You were at the house the morning he—died?"

The other, straightening himself, looked coldly at the young man, then took another whiff at his cigar. "I presume I am not the only man who entered your house on that day. Why do you make particular mention of me?"

Stanhope, who was almost the equal of the other in height if not in breadth, and who had a pure purpose to sustain him, met the stern and repellent look which accompanied these words, with one as unswerving though it was much more excited.

"Because," said he, leaning forward and speaking very slowly, "you were the one who brought him the pistol by the unlucky shot of which he came to his death."

"Ah, you know that." It was calmly, almost respectfully said, yet the colonel was taken aback and not a little disconcerted. Stanhope recognized this. It gave him his first distinct doubt of the man, and made him wish that Jack were present to aid him with his judgment at this important moment of his life.

"You acknowledge, then, that it was so?" urged he "You bought the pistol in Nassau Street and brought it to my father on his wedding morning?"

"Certainly; why should I not?"

"Did he ask you to do it?"

The answer to this did not come so readily; but it came, and with it a return of the colonel's usual suavity.

"No; I doubt if he knew that I was in town. I wished to make him a present, and I chose the one which would be most likely to recall the old days when we were comrades. That the result would be so immediately disastrous, was certainly as painful to me as it was to you, and I here express my sorrow for the grievous accident which terminated so useful a life. It will not bring your father back, but it will partially relieve my mind."

"You have been long in relieving it," rejoined Stanhope, not at all deceived by the other's broad, free manner, as to the agitation by which he was moved.

"I acknowledge it, and, had I not been forced by you to speak upon this subject, I should never have sought to do so. I did not see what good it was likely to do you to know that your father suffered from my too earnest friendship for him."

"Colonel Deering"—Stanhope's voice shook, though he endeavored to steady it—"I want to have a long talk with you. There are reasons why I should know the whole story of my father's unhappy end. Will you come to the club with me? There we can have a room alone, and I can put the questions I dare not utter here."

"But I have already told you all that I have to say," protested the other, in quiet surprise. "You charge me with having left a pistol at your house on the morning of your father's marriage, and I reply that the charge is true, and this pistol was a gift in memory of old experiences, What more can I have to add to that?"

"Much. You saw my father—"

The ashes, which had looked firm on the end of the colonel's cigar, suddenly dropped, besprinkling his well-brushed coat. It was a slight evidence of perturbation, but it was unmistakable in a man of his nice habits. And so Stanhope felt, though he did not know the man.

"So you have become acquainted with that fact also," interrupted the colonel, shaking his coat free with a careful hand. "You must have looked into the subject closely; which, of course, is not strange under the circumstances."

"You can help me. You are the man I want," whispered Stanhope, in natural excitement. "Will you come to the club?"

The colonel, who was a slow man, glanced across the way, and took a minute to consider. He had come to the place that night in an idle mood, and with just a vague intention of calling again on Stephen Huse, at a time when the electroplater would not have his business to distract him from a conversation which might be mildly interesting to a visitor who was fond of odd characters and unaccustomed scenes. But it was not this which made him pause, but a deeper and much more important reason. To go with Stanhope White meant an immediate disclosure of facts which he had hoped to keep forever secret, while to refuse the natural request of this young man would be to hamper himself with the aroused curiosity of one who would never let him go till some sort of explanation had passed between them. So when his mind had taken in all the situation, and he had reached his decision, he turned back to Stanhope, almost as a father might to his son, and saying, "It is the least I can do for you," led the way himself to the carriage which he had had full opportunity of knowing belonged to the man beside him.

During the ride to the club-house, they were both more or less silent: Stanhope, from a secret doubt of the other's purposes; and the Colonel, from the necessity which he felt of consulting his own position and calculating upon the bearing which the admissions he had just made were likely to have upon his future course in this matter. But as soon as the lights of the club-house began to shine upon their faces, both roused, and Stanhope spoke.

"I have a friend," said he, "whom I desire to have with me at this interview. His name is John Hollister, and you can feel yourself as free to speak before him as before myself."

"If you wish auditors, I of course have nothing to say against it," was the quiet reply; "but I would advise you not to force a third party upon the scene unless it is absolutely necessary. The less such matters are aired abroad, the better, I should say."

Stanhope, who felt himself in deep water, did not know whether to be swayed by this advice or to follow his own instincts. He concluded to compromise matters.

"We will begin the conversation alone," said he; "but if at any juncture I feel the necessity of my friend's presence, I reserve to myself the privilege of calling him."

"As you will," acquiesced the other, following Stanhope into the club-house, where their two fine forms and uncommon faces attracted much attention as they passed up the staircase and along the halls to the rooms reserved for private interviews.

As they paused before an empty one, Stanhope beckoned to a steward whom he saw passing.

"Is Mr. Hollister still here?" he asked.

"I think so."

"Will you ask him if he will be so good as to come to the adjoining room? I wish to see him before I go and would like to have him hold himself in readiness."

The man bowed, "I will tell him, sir," and hastened on.

Stanhope turned to the colonel, and together they entered the room before them.

It was sumptuously furnished, and among its appointments was a large mirror, in which, as they advanced, both their figures were fully reflected. Involuntarily the eyes of each sought the countenance of the other, and thus the colonel became aware of a trepidation in Stanhope's manner which the latter might have been able to conceal from a direct gaze, while Stanhope had the opportunity of seeing that his companion was much paler than he had been at the beginning of their encounter in the drug store. The smile that struggled to the faces of both as their glances thus met in the mirror, deceived neither, and it was with a profound sense of the importance of the moment that both finally turned and faced each other.

"Colonel Deering," began Stanhope, without any attempt at preliminaries, "you have admitted that you saw my father on the morning of his death."

The colonel bowed. "I am not alone in that," said he; "there must have been many hundreds in the church when he was married."

"But you saw him alone in his study, and under circumstances which must have led to conversation?"

"Certainly: a short conversation."

"Colonel, you are a stranger to me, but I shall have to trust you with my most weighty secret. The world, our friends, society in general, think that my father shot himself accidentally; but we—his wife and myself— fear that he drew the trigger intentionally, driven by some secret grief or trouble to which we have no clue."

"Your secret shall be respected," replied the colonel, "but why burden *me* with it? That I should have been the unhappy cause of his possessing a pistol at such a time is surely enough sorrow for one man to carry, without the knowledge that this pistol had proved a temptation in his hands."

"Yes, if nothing were to be gained by the knowledge. But, sir, my whole future happiness hangs upon the information which I hope to gain from you as to the state of my father's mind on that fatal morning. If the shot was unintentional, or if it was occasioned by a disappointment or a fear wholly disconnected with yourself, then I shall feel free to follow the dictates of my heart and marry the woman whom Providence has seemed to point out to me as my future wife. But if his trouble came from you or through you, then there may be such secrets involved in this matter as would make the action which I contemplate a most undesirable one, both for myself and the innocent girl whom I love."

"I do not understand you," quoth the colonel, drawing back with a decidedly repellent action as Stanhope pressed toward him in his earnestness. "What makes you think that I am connected with any trouble your father may have had on that day?"

"This. Before you came to the house, or rather I should say before the hour in which you acknowledged that you saw him—"

"I have not spoken of any hour."

"We know that it was about ten o'clock—he was cheerful, happy, joyous, as a successful man and a prospective bridegroom should be. Afterward—or I should still say when I saw him next, which was when I joined him in the carriage—he was pale, silent, and strangely depressed. Why, then, should I not consider that your visit had something to do with this change? It was the only one he received."

The colonel, who was walking up and down in the small space toward which Stanhope's eagerness had pushed him, wheeled about and looked at the young man's anxious face with a deep and growing intentness which seemed to take in the whole character and promise of the noble fellow.

"You were justified in considering this," he finally rejoined, with a quick change back to his former cordial manner. "But you will have to look further than the interview between your father and myself, for the cause which drove so great a man to the act of which you suspect him. My errand was the simple one of which I have spoken, and the conversation to which it led was the short, bluff, hearty one suitable to a meeting between old comrades."

"*Are you sure*, colonel?"

The older man, with years of self-reliance and easy supremacy behind him, was not one to be easily moved by any man's attack, from whatever position he chose to occupy; but at Stanhope's repetition of these words, and the look, deprecating but firm, with which it was accompanied, a slow but unmistakable color began to show itself through the pallor of his scarred face. Angry with himself at this revelation of feeling under eyes whose candor alone may have produced it, he turned instantly pale again; but the revelation had been made and he could not recall it.

"I do not like to ask if you doubt my word, Mr. White, but you have forced me to do so. For this lack of confidence in me you must have good reasons, or you are not the gentleman you appear."

Stanhope, without replying, crossed to the opposite wall and gave one smart tap upon it. "We will have my friend here," said he, "before we proceed any further."

Colonel Deering was glad of the reprieve, for he wished to re-collect his thoughts and steady himself for the coming conflict. Stanhope, on the contrary, was on fire to continue the conversation, and could hardly wait for the appearance of Jack. When, therefore, the slim, elegant figure of his friend appeared in the doorway, he did not wait to answer the languid inquiry and polite surprise visible in that easy-going but far from shallow person's handsome face, but dashed at once into the subject occupying him.

"Jack, I want your attention. Colonel Deering has asked me why I persist in thinking he knows more of my father's final hours than he is disposed to tell, and I am going to answer him. As I shall say nothing I am not prepared to stand to, I think it best there should be a witness present, and there is nobody who could better occupy that position than yourself."

Jack, who at the first glance had noted the pitted face and towering figure of the stranger, knew without further explanation with whom he had been brought in contact, and, though he gave no evidence of it, his faculties at once roused themselves to the occasion. That the colonel showed plainly enough, by his careless and condescending bow, that he placed the young man thus introduced to his notice, among the ornamental but otherwise useless appendages to society, gave an added zest to the moment, and made it all the more easy for Jack to sustain the manner he had thought best to assume.

"I will be a witness, certainly," he drawled, seating himself carelessly in the most comfortable corner of the large *fauteuil*. "Anything to oblige you. You have something to say to this gentleman, you inform me?"

Stanhope, who knew his friend well, turned from him without speaking, to give his long-delayed reply to the colonel.

"I persist," said he, "in intimating that you either told my father something which at once robbed his life of value, or recalled by your presence some fact in the past of so significant a nature that it daunted one who was never daunted before by grief or disappointment. Your interview with my father was one of unusual significance, because he not only showed great feeling after it, and, indeed, made those instant preparations for death which were only too speedily followed by death itself, but because your presence is one which seems to inspire apprehension even in the breasts of those usually brave and fearless. I know another man who shrinks so much from meeting you that he fled his house at your arrival and has not been seen there since."

"Ah!" came from the stranger's lips, with a peculiar smile. "You are well informed, indeed. I begin to think you know as much of my affairs as I have long known of yours."

"I know nothing of your affairs. Would I did! But I do know Thomas Dalton. Now, why do you persecute him, and why did you visit my father on the morning of his marriage, with a pistol in your hand for a gift?"

Straight home went the question, but the colonel had prepared himself for a keen attack and barely quivered by a hair's-breadth.

"You associate," said he, "two names as wide apart as the poles."

"Not so wide apart," urged Stanhope, "that there was not one thing in common between their owners."

"And what was that?"

Stanhope held up his left hand with its palm turned toward the speaker. Tracing upon it a cross with his right forefinger, he said:

"You were an old comrade of my father; were you an old comrade of Thomas Dalton, too?"

This time the colonel's nerves yielded to the attack. He shuddered and gave the young man a look which seemed to bid him "Beware!"

"That," he retorted, "has nothing to do with the subject at present before us. If you, Samuel White's son, choose to press me, against my will, to re-open a past which now that your father is dead it would be more fitting on your part to leave buried in his grave, I must reply to your questions so far as he is concerned; but I am not bound to give you any information in connection with my relations to Thomas Dalton."

"Then we will let that matter rest. I have seen enough this last minute to convince me that we shall have all the tragedy we desire if we unlock the secret of your comradeship with my father. It must date back some thirty years; for never in my life, and I am twenty-five, has your face been seen in our home."

"Your arithmetic is correct, Mr. White. It is twenty-seven years since my hand last touched your father's."

"Did you not touch it in the bluff, hearty greeting which you have just told me you gave him on the morning of his marriage—and his death?"

It was a rapier thrust for which the colonel, with all his studied coolness, was unprepared. His chin fell, and the determination of the man, for the first time perhaps in years, faltered. Stanhope at once pressed his advantage.

"You call the connection between my father and yourself by the name of comradeship. It is a friendly term; but was your feeling for my father one of friendship, or was it, as would appear by the gift you so unfortunately associated with his marriage-day, that of enmity and revenge?"

The colonel had turned his back upon Stanhope as the latter began his sentence; but, at the completion of it, he faced back, and never in jovial meeting or daily association with his friends had he looked more suave or more quietly possessed of his most potent and irresistible qualities. But as he was about to speak, and perhaps assert his profound esteem and admiration for the dead statesman, a quiet, almost languid hand was laid on Stanhope's arm, and Jack Hollister's indifferent voice was heard saying:

"I think you had better leave the rest of this conversation to me. The place is too public for raised voices, and the topic you have chosen seems to make you forget yourselves."

"But—"

The hand that was laid on Stanhope's arm looked very white and slender, but the fingers were made of steel and made themselves felt at this moment quite sharply. Stanhope immediately paused, and Jack's smooth and delicate voice went on.

"The colonel may not wish to answer your last question. If he does not, I would not press him. What good can it do you to know whether his feeling was one of kindness or dislike toward a man who is now buried? That he saw your father so soon before his death is an interesting fact, of course; and if he will tell us just how soon that was, or how long, I think we can let all other questions go for to-night; do not you, Stanhope?"

The flush on Stanhope's face and the nervous working of his muscles showed that these words had provoked a keen struggle within him. But the eye of Jack was fixed upon him; and while that eye, and Jack's whole attitude indeed, seemed to provoke nothing but disdain in the mind of the quietly watching colonel, it told Stanhope something which kept down his impatience from too visible an outbreak, and finally forced him to say:

"As you will, Jack. You are in cool blood, and I am worked up past all discretion, possibly. If the colonel will answer this last demand—"

"Which is to say when he left Mr. White's house on the morning of his visit there," put in Jack, unconcernedly enough, and yet with the persistence which demands reply.

"I will waive all others," continued Stanhope, "for to-night."

"You are very good," replied the colonel, "but you have answered that question yourself. You said that it was about ten when I entered Mr. White's house."

"And about ten when you left?" drawled Jack.

"Of course, as I stayed but a few moments."

The bow Jack made contained both thanks and an apology.

"I regret," said he, "that I have had to intrude my voice into this conversation. We can now allow Colonel Deering to depart, can we not, Stanhope?"

"Certainly, if he will hold himself in readiness to see me again. There is much I want to know—"

"Of course, of course, but— Colonel, I have no doubt my friend knows where you can be found?"

"He has my card."

"Then that is certainly sufficient. A gentleman who has given his card always holds himself ready to receive visitors."

"I am at home at the Brevoort House," observed Colonel Deering, bowing calmly to Stanhope.

"I will see you there to-morrow," was the latter's quick answer.

Jack, glancing at the colonel's imperturbable face, as that gentleman acknowledged this response and backed courteously from the room, wondered quietly to himself if the latter would be on hand to receive this especial guest on the morrow.

As the door shut, Stanhope sprang toward his friend. "Why did you stop me in my inquiries?" he cried. "Why didn't you let him answer my question as to whether he was my father's friend or not?"

"Because he already had answered it."

"Already! How? I did not hear—"

"No, nor I either, but I saw. His back was to you, but not to me; and as you spoke, pressing this inquiry point-blank upon him, such a gleam of malignity and deadly hatred sprang into his face, that I knew it was your father's enemy who stood before us, and—"

"And what—"

"I did not choose to have him go on and perhaps incriminate himself; for—"

"Jack! Jack! what do you mean? You look as excited as myself. Incriminate himself? How could he incriminate himself?"

"Easily, my poor Stanhope, for—do not look at the door, for you shall not pass it till he is safely out of the house—I believe as well as I can believe anything which I have not seen myself, that the man who has just gone out of the room, not only carried into your house the pistol which took your father's life, but shot it. In short, that the death which we both deplore was a murder, and that this Colonel Deering was the murderer."

XXX

A Midnight Conference

It was with considerable trepidation that Mary drove up to the house from which she had fled such a few hours before. Nothing but the hope that she had come back in time not only to forestall Stanhope's return, but that of Mrs. White also, gave her courage to mount the steps and ring the bell whose sound she had supposed herself to have heard for the last time. Felix's face, as he opened the door, gave her her first sense of relief. As it had looked when she went out, so it looked at her return, neither event having seemed to have aroused in this incomparable servant either curiosity or question.

Returning his wonted bow with a kind little nod, she asked if Mrs. White had yet come in. The answer set her heart at rest.

"No, Miss Dalton, but we expect her any moment. She said she would be home at half-past ten."

It was then just twenty-five minutes past; and as Mary ran up-stairs, it was with decided relief that she heard the carriage roll away which had brought her to the house.

Slipping softly into Mrs. White's boudoir, she passed hurriedly to the desk, upon which she had left two letters of farewell addressed to Flora and to Stanhope.

Though the gas was turned down, there was enough light given out by the fire on the hearth for her to see that they were still there, and to all appearance had neither been seen nor handled. With a heart full of thankfulness she put them into her pocket and went immediately to her own room, where everything looked so natural and so inviting that she burst into uncontrollable tears as she closed the door behind her, realizing that she had reached home and that the wearisome struggle of the last few days could never by any chance be renewed, since she had given her promise to her father to marry Stanhope immediately if he should so choose it. That he would choose it, the little box distorting one of the envelopes hiding in her pocket quietly assured her; and almost before she had rid herself of her hat and cloak she had pulled the box from its hiding-place and was trying on the gleaming jewel upon which she had not dared to bestow a single glance before.

"I will wear it at the breakfast table," she decided, but paused dismayed as the doubt swept through her that Stanhope might not be at the breakfast table; that he was with the unknown persecutor of her father, whose business with him she could not understand, and which might be most serious, and that till she heard her lover's step upon the stairs she could not be even sure that he was safe.

To listen for his step, then, became her first duty; and, as the fire was still blazing in the grate, she sat down, just as she was, before it, a prey to anxieties which were but the culminating misery of a long and wretched day.

The return of Mrs. White caused the first break in the heavy silence which had seemed to settle over the house. As she heard the sound of this lady's voice and the rustle of skirts in the hall below, she felt a sense of companionship which robbed the hour of some of its brooding quiet; but this slight bustle was soon over, and presently all was still again in the great house. Had Mary known that in the room below another watcher was waiting for his step with equal interest, though with less fear, she might have been tempted to have joined her apprehension to Flora's curiosity, and so have passed two less lonesome hours. But she knew no more than Flora of the reasons which the other had for anxiety; and so these two sat on, each by her own firelight, till eleven and even twelve o'clock sounded, before the tension of their feelings was relieved by the unmistakable click of Stanhope's key in the front door lock.

Flora, whose mind was fixed upon learning the result of his visit to Markham Place, went boldly to the door of her room with the intention of asking him a few hurried questions before he passed upstairs. But she did not pursue this intention. Some one was with him, and, though she thought she knew the step, natural caution made her shrink from showing herself.

Mary, who on the contrary was mainly intent upon his safety, was entirely satisfied with his presence in the house, and not till she heard the sound of accompanying steps did she rise from her seat or give any tokens of increased agitation. Then, indeed, she did start and rush forward almost to the door that separated them, for she thought it was the pock-marked man who had ventured into the house; and the terror with which she had been brought to-consider him influenced her to such a degree that she could hardly restrain her feelings or prevent herself from calling out to Stanhope to beware.

But just as she hesitated at the door a voice spoke in the hall beyond, and she heard the word "Jack;" and, realizing at once her folly, she drew back, and for the rest of the night was a happy woman, revelling in the sweetest of dreams.

Would she have slept so easily or dreamed so lightly of the coming days, had she known the nature of the errand which had brought Jack to the house at this midnight hour?

In the bachelor apartment in front the two young men, sitting on opposite sides of a small table, talked earnestly together. The first surprise caused by Jack's astounding statement had passed, and Stanhope was ready to weigh with careful consideration the reasons which the former was ready to offer for the belief which he had so boldly expressed of Colonel Deering's guilt.

The first and most startling one was a fact which had been known to Jack for a couple of weeks or more, but which he now communicated to Stanhope for the first time. This was, that, contrary to the opinion of the family and the knowledge of all concerned, Mr. White had not been alone at the time of his death, but had had with him, or, if not with him, so near him as to make of that person an undoubted witness, a tall, finely formed man, answering precisely to the appearance of Colonel Deering.

This revelation, which fell with astonishing force upon Stanhope, had come to Jack, not from the servants or from any one who had seen him in the house, but from a young lady living on the opposite side of the avenue. During a visit which he had paid this lady a few evenings before, she had inquired who was the large and elegant man who had been calling upon the Whites at the time the new-made bridegroom had shot himself; and when Jack looked astonished and expressed his ignorance of anybody having been present except the family, she declared that she had certainly seen such a person come from the house just a few moments before the alarm spread through the street of Mr. White's death, and, upon being pressed to be more explicit, explained that she had been standing in the second-story window, looking out for the departure of the bride and groom, and that seeing this stranger come down the steps, was so attracted by the unusual size and grace of his person, that when she heard, as she did a few minutes later, of the dreadful tragedy which had just taken place in the house she had felt curious to know who the distinguished stranger was who had been calling upon them at so memorable a moment.

That it was, or might have been, the same man who brought the pistol to the house some hours before, had immediately struck the mind of Jack; but, having no means of establishing the fact, he had refrained from disturbing Stanhope's scarcely regained equanimity by relating a circumstance which could not but rouse his intense interest without affording anything to satisfy it. When, however, he saw Colonel Deering at the club, and noted not only his person, but the look of implacable hate which had, for a moment, distorted his features at the mention of Mr. White's name, Jack had had no difficulty, with this surmise for a start, in formulating the theory of murder which had given Stanhope such a shock.

"For," he now continued with that strict and steadfast earnestness which he invariably brought to bear upon business matters, "there are various small but undeniable evidences which point in this same direction; and, if we are fortunate, we shall, in all probability, find others, as we bore into the subject under the new light afforded us by this evening's experiences. Have you ever thought, Stanhope, that we had no good reason, no *very* good reason, for charging your father with suicide? A man on his wedding-day would require some mighty cause to induce him to end so prosperous a career. No petty jealousy would be sufficient, whatever we may have feared in the first shock of our horror. With such gifts as he possessed, he could not have felt any petty jealousy even of a younger lover of his wife. Only the deepest and most maddening of disappointments would have driven him to such an act, and such he never suffered from any source with which we are acquainted. His death was then accidental, unless this man had something to do with it. And this man had; or why was he in the house so long on that day, without the knowledge of any one but your father, and why did he leave it in so surreptitious a manner, if he were guiltless of the shot which so suddenly took your father's life?"

Stanhope, who had turned his face away, that he might not betray his lack of agreement with all of Jack's premises, looked back again in keen surprise at this conclusion of his friend's argument.

"I do not follow you," he declared. "How long was this man in the house? A half hour? He could not have been longer, for my father himself did not return from his wedding till nearly two o'clock, and the shot took place at half past."

"Did any one let him in at two?"

"I do not know; do you?"

"I know what the servants say."

"And what is that?"

"That none of them opened the door to any stranger after Josephine let in the man with the brown parcel."

"But that man was Colonel Deering, and the time of his entrance was ten. Do you mean to say that he stayed in this house, unseen by any of us, from ten till half-past two, or till he was seen going out of the front door by Miss Morton?"

"I do."

"But my father was married during that time; and, if I am not mistaken, the door of his study stood wide open while he was gone."

"I know; but there are other rooms than the study."

"What rooms?"

"Your father's bedroom, for one."

"Yes, but—"

"Colonel Deering could easily while away a few hours there, with a half-dozen cigars or so to keep him company. When one has a revenge to carry out, or an enmity to satisfy, an hour or two of waiting does not count. The colonel has a large stock of patience and drew upon it, that is all."

"But you must have proof that he stayed there to venture such a surmise at this time. Have you? Is there any evidence to show that what you state is true?"

"Stanhope, when at your request I went into your father's rooms, immediately after the departure of the jury, I noted two things. One was the presence of tobacco smoke in his bedroom, and the other a collection of cigar ashes and stumps on one of the window-ledges. The smoke had a peculiar scent of its own, which many might not have noticed. But I have acute senses, and, though I thought it was your father's cigar which I smelt, I remembered the effect it had upon me; and when I recognized the scent again, as I did just now when I was introduced into the presence of Colonel Deering, I naturally recurred to the discovery of that day, and connected him with the faint perfume I had noticed in your father's room. If this man uses a particular brand, I shall consider it settled that he smoked the cigars whose ends I found lying there in a pile of ashes."

"My father never smoked more than one cigar at a time, especially in the morning. I cannot conceive of an occasion upon which he would be tempted to smoke a half dozen, and the maids we employ in this house are too well trained to leave cigar-ashes lying on a window-ledge."

"Very good. Now for my theory of murder. This man, as you have seen, is of a cool, persistent, implacable nature, gaining his purposes by the force of mass and not by any display of effort. He settles upon a thing or an idea, and his weight makes him a winner. He does not bluster or fume or threaten; he simply persists. A tremendous personality, which I advise any man not to antagonize.

"He hated your father—why, we have not as yet the least means of knowing. As you have never encountered him in your life before, the cause of this hatred dates back probably beyond your birth, and, as you have intimated, to those days when your father dug gold in the Far West. That he should have cherished this hatred so many years, and finally have satisfied it when they were both on the verge of old age, may be from the force of circumstances, and may be from the inherent nature of the man himself, who is as slow, I should say, as he is sure. When we first heard of him he was buying a pistol, and on the next day—the day, as he must have known, of his intended victim's union with a young and beautiful woman—he calls with it at the house, in time, he may have thought, to prevent this marriage. The cause of the early disagreement between himself and your father may have been a woman—who knows?—and it may have been a part of his plan to trip up your father on the verge of his happiness. However that may be, he came to the house at ten, and probably, knowing the risks he ran of a refusal if he gave his own name, or perhaps merely wishing to get rid of the girl who came to the door, he called himself by some fictitious name, and, when Josephine had disappeared by the back staircase, quietly slipped up the front way and entered your father's presence unannounced.

"That he had some previous knowledge of the house and your father's habits I expect hereafter to discover, and, had Josephine gone up the front stairs, he would probably have stolen up the back. That he went up somehow, and that he saw your father and spoke to him he has virtually admitted; but even if he had not done this we should have been sure that he found his way to the study, from the fact that the package did, and that there was nobody besides himself to carry it there.

"What happened on his entrance we can only imagine. He says that he gave your father a bluff and hearty greeting; but this we have reason to doubt, both from his manner to-night and from the fact that no one in the house heard their voices or even suspected your father of having a visitor in his study. Yet they talked, and the pistol which the colonel had brought with him was exhibited and possibly handled, for the wrappings of the box were found in your father's basket, and the box itself, on a high shelf in the same room.

"Why it was not used then and there, it will be for us henceforth to determine. All we know now is that the interview was serious enough to completely change your father's aspect, and yet not so serious as to alter his plans or to keep him from going to the church to be married. As soon as he could rid himself of the presence of his guest (and in another moment I will tell you how I think this was done), he went on with his preparations; and when Felix came into the room, as you remember he did about this time with the mail, he found your father at his table writing the letters which a few minutes later he gave to Peter to mail. One of those letters was addressed to me, and it enclosed the peculiar, and, if you choose to consider it so, ominous letter to you. From that letter and the intimation it appears to contain of anticipated disaster, you may argue that he dreaded immediate death from the hands of his late visitor. This may be so; but I choose rather to believe that he did not realize, unless it was in a general way, how dangerous were the intentions of the man who was at that very moment, possibly, within ten feet of him. Or why, having once separated himself from the colonel, did he not take measures against that person's doing him any further harm?"

"You have thought it all out, Jack, and must answer your own questions. If Colonel Deering was in my father's bedroom all the time you say, and if my father had those reasons for dread which we believe to have been shown by the agitation which he displayed after their interview, why did he not summon assistance and have the man taken away while we were gone to the church?"

"I am ready to answer, but I first want to ask you a question. At what time in the morning did your father dress for the marriage ceremony?"

"I do not know; but I presume, early. He was a man who always anticipated such matters."

"Do you think it possible that he was ready by the time this man intruded upon him?"

"Yes, it is possible; but only Josephine can speak positively on the subject. She will remember, I am sure, just how her master was dressed at the time."

"Then we will ask Josephine to-morrow. Meanwhile you can answer this. When you went for your father to accompany you to the carriage, did you see him go into his bedroom before starting?"

"No; he merely jumped up from the table where he was sitting, and, catching up his gloves and handkerchief, followed me without a word to the lower hall. It was not till we were in the carriage that I noticed how pale he was."

"Of course you do not remember whether the bedroom door was open or shut when you went into the study?"

"No."

"We will take for granted, then, that it was shut; and now I will answer your question. The reason that your father left the colonel shut up in his bedroom and went to church and was married, and came back unsuspiciously to this room and the death which lurked within it, was because he did not know that his deadly enemy was there, because he thought he had left the room and the house; whereas the colonel had done neither, having taken advantage of your father's abstraction, perhaps, to step through the bedroom door instead of the one next to it, by which trick he gained a refuge from which he was able to shoot your father four hours after, upon sight."

"Jack! Jack! we were in the room ten seconds afterward, and there was no colonel there, nor any signs of his having been there."

"Yet he was seen coming out of the house by a lady opposite. Stanhope, you were longer than ten seconds in getting to your father's side. Mrs. White was in her boudoir putting on her bonnet; you were in this room, a whole flight and a long hall from the scene where this shot took place. In case you both rushed immediately—and no one does rush in the first instant of terror—you could not have got there under sixty seconds, at least; time enough for a cool man to drop his pistol and slide from bedroom to study, and so out by the way of the rear door to the back stairs. If the front study door was open you might have seen this hurried exit as you came down the hall; but it was closed, I understand, as was the bedroom door when you went in."

"True, true! and the servants, as chance would have it, were all in front. There was no one on the back stairs, and no one in the rear halls below. He had a clear sweep before him, and probably went out at the front while we were all huddled in our dismay round the study door."

"Stanhope, your father died beside the bag which he was supposed to have been packing when the fatal shot went off. Was Colonel Deering near enough to him at that moment to fire the shot, which any one versed in those matters must have seen went off close to your father's head? I have evidence that he may have been, and positive proof that at

ANNA KATHARINE GREEN

some time during his stay in the room he leaned directly over this bag. I have spoken of the ashes and stumps I found on the window-ledge, but this was not the only discovery I made that morning. In the bag, and scattered over the articles lying nearest to the top, were more ashes; and as these could only have fallen from the cigar of a man leaning across it, I drew the conclusion that the near shot from which your father died was not delivered by himself, but by the man who smoked the cigars whose remains were found so plentifully scattered through the room. You may wonder that I did not speak of this discovery when I made it; but then I supposed your father to have been the smoker, and so considered the matter too trivial for discussion."

"Jack, you are very convincing; but have you thought of one thing? If the pistol was presented to my father in his study at ten o'clock, how came it in the colonel's hands four hours afterward in the bedroom?"

"It may never have been presented to your father. The colonel may have been the one who undid the package and hid the box in the cupboard and threw the wrappings into the waste-paper basket. He had time enough to do all this, and more, while you were all at church. But, if this seems strained to you, what evidence have we that your father did not repudiate the gift when he saw what it was, and that the colonel walked off with it, leaving your father to dispose of box and wrapper as he thought fit?"

"None, Jack, none; and you have well nigh convinced me of Colonel Deering's guilt. His look, his bearing, the quickly suppressed but unmistakable signs of agitation on his part under the cross-examination I gave him, all tend to strengthen your theory in my mind. Oh, if it is true—"

"Wait, Stanhope. Remember, it is only a theory I have advanced, and as such it must stand every test. If your father smoked those cigars himself, or if he is found to have gone into his bedroom after the end of his interview with the colonel, then we shall have to reconsider our premises."

"I cannot; I never shall be able to. From this moment onward the colonel is to me the murderer of my father."

"And to me; but—"

"But what?"

"Where did your father keep the jewels which you tell me he sent out of the house that morning by Josephine?"

"In his study; in the safe there."

"Then he did not have to leave the room to procure *them*. Well, your belief, and even my belief, must not lead us into any follies. The colonel will have time to think to-night, and by to-morrow he will be armed at all points. Let us be wary, then, in our attack, for to lose a point now may lead to final failure."

"I know it, I feel it. I even dread that he may use these precious hours in effecting his escape. Why did you hold me back, Jack? I might at least have had the satisfaction of accusing him to the face."

"And been called a fool for your pains? No, Stanhope; we will have the law back of us when we accuse him of a crime."

"But will we find him? Won't he fly now that he sees himself suspected?"

"He may try to do so, but I doubt it. He is too marked a man to hope to elude the police."

"But—"

"And he is under police surveillance. Do you think I would let him go unwatched after such a suspicion as I speak of had taken hold of me? A word telegraphed to the superintendent of police did that piece of business for me; and in the morning, when we have fixed up the two or three points to which I have alluded, you shall yourself go with me to Mulberry Street, where, if we are considered to have a case, a warrant of arrest will be made out, which will effectually dampen the spirits of our dangerous friend."

Stanhope, who was trembling with excitement, looked anxiously at the clock. It was after four.

"How the hours creep!" he cried. Suddenly he turned upon his friend with a changed expression. "Do you think, Jack, that the Natalie Yelverton to which my father assigned me in his last letter has any connection with the old grudge to which he has fallen a victim?"

"I don't know; she may have," stammered Jack. "But no, no; she must be young, and this grudge is very old. Yet—yet, I do not wonder you are alarmed. *She may be the daughter of this very man*."

Stanhope, who had sprung to his feet in his sudden dismay, sank slowly back again.

"God grant it," he whispered, "for then I need not marry her; "and for the next few minutes his thoughts were lost with Mary, while those of Jack stole tenderly to Flora sleeping in happy unconsciousness of the fresh phase which her bridal tragedy had just taken on.

XXXI

A Decided Move

As soon as the hour warranted it, Stanhope and Jack went below. Finding Felix in the dining-room, they asked him the two questions that were burning on their tongues. First, if Mr. White had dressed himself early on the occasion of his marriage, and, secondly, if he had been seen smoking at any time during that morning. The answers were as expected. Mr. White had dressed very early, and had not been seen smoking at all that day.

Josephine was interviewed next, and she told them much the same thing, adding, in response to a question interpolated by Jack, that Mr. White's handkerchief and gloves were lying on his table when she first went in to speak to him, as well as when she went in for the box he had desired her to carry to the Westminster Hotel.

"Was everything else the same? Did he look the same and speak the same?"

"Yes, only he was standing up the second time. He had the package in his hand and seemed in a hurry. I noticed nothing more."

"Did you notice if the bedroom door was open?"

"No, sir."

"Josephine, you are a careful girl about your work. Did you notice when you came to tidy up the room, after my father's death, a heap of cigar stumps and ashes on one of the window-ledges?"

"Yes, sir, and I wondered at it; for Mr. White never smoked in his bedroom, and never, to my knowledge, left ashes lying around in that way before."

"Were those ashes there when you went in after breakfast to make up the bed?"

"No, sir; oh, no!"

"You are sure of that?"

"Can you ask, sir?"

"Inquire whether she found the missing sixth stump on the floor," whispered Jack to his friend. "We must account for the cigar Colonel Deering was smoking at the time of the shooting."

Stanhope at once turned to Josephine.

"When you cleaned up the ashes from the window-ledge, did you find on the floor, or anywhere in the room, the end of another cigar?"

"No, sir; but before that time, when I went downstairs with the other girls, very soon after Mr. White's death, I saw such a stump lying on the back staircase, and thought it very strange; for Mr. White never went out there, nor yourself either, and the strangers had not yet come in."

"Ah!" sprang in satisfied exclamation from both her eager listeners. Unconsciously to herself, she had sounded Colonel Deering's doom in those few short words.

The breakfast to which the household soon sat down was not without its element of excitement to all concerned. To say nothing of the great and important matter just then agitating the minds of both Jack and Stanhope, it was the first time the former had seen Flora at her own table, and also the first time Stanhope and Mary had met since the latter's sickness. That Mary herself had much to move her no one can deny, and even Flora was not without her anxieties.

Mary had meant to wear her lover's ring to breakfast, and had even started with it on her finger; but, when she heard Jack's voice in the dining-room, she had slipped it off, conscious that her courage was not sufficient to meet any stranger's inquiring gaze. But the light of the diamonds was in her eyes, and Stanhope did not need the sight of his jewels to know that his cause was won, and that Mary would offer no further demurs to their marriage. This was a delight that yet was not without its pain, adding, as it did, a further complication to the situation. Not knowing what the poor child had been through since he last saw her, he saw in her compliance the triumph of love over discretion, and adored her for it even while he asked if it would not have been better if discretion had held its own for a little while longer or at least till it was evident that this new horror which had risen in his life was free from any connection with the hated name of Natalie Yelverton.

That he should hesitate in his intentions toward Mary now that she had overcome her scruples and showed him her pure heart filled only with love, would be, he thought, a most unworthy act; and when, the meal being over, they all drifted into the library, it was to her side that he at once stepped.

"Where is the ring," he whispered, "the sign of our engagement?"

The eyes that stole to his made him forget everything, in a trice, but the witchery of the moment.

"You shall put it on to-night," she murmured; and though the morning was dark, and the skies without and the atmosphere within were gray and dull, the brightness and the perfume of paradise seemed, at these words, to sweep through the dismal room, making these two young hearts to thrill as if neither sorrow nor fear outlay the charmed gates that for a moment enclosed them from all the world.

The voice of Jack excusing himself to Flora woke them from their happy dream, and a few minutes later Stanhope found himself walking down the avenue with his friend, intent upon pursuing the serious business entailed upon him by the discoveries which they had just made in reference to his father's death.

That he should leave the house without answering the appeal in Flora's eye, was part of the plan he had entered into with Jack; they both considering it wisest not to take the young widow into their confidence till they had laid their suspicions before the police.

Their interview with the superintendent can best be told by its results. On this same day, at noon, the bellboy at the Brevoort House carried up to Colonel Deering Stanhope White's card; but, when the colonel descended, he found three men awaiting him in the small room chosen by Stanhope for this interview. One was Jack, to whom the colonel required no introduction; the other, a large, quiet and powerful looking man, of proportions similar to his own, whose name was not mentioned to him, though he looked directly at him the moment he entered the room.

"Colonel Deering," began Jack, in a tone so different from the drawl of the evening before that it seemed to give a shock to his auditor, "you were told that we should be here to-day, and you see we have kept our word. Is there anything you would like to say on your own behalf before we proceed with the questions you undoubtedly expect?"

"I should like to know who this third gentleman is," was the instant retort. "I said I would see Mr. White, but I did not say I would see all his friends."

"Let me tell him," said the stranger, moving forward with a quiet air of being master of the situation, that should have warned the other of his identity before he spoke. "Colonel Deering, I am a police officer, and my business here is to show you this warrant of arrest, in which you are charged with the murder of Samuel White, hitherto supposed to have died by an accidental shot from his own hand."

The emotions of such a man as Colonel Deering are tremendous when once roused, but so is the will, and this will had been in full exercise when he entered upon this interview. He therefore showed that this blow had taken him between the eyes, by the barest quiver of his powerful frame, betraying so much nerve, indeed, that Stanhope thought he must have been prepared for the attack, by his own fears and the knowledge of having been watched through the night. But this was not so. The accusation was wholly unexpected by him, and so was the arrest; and this he soon made apparent to the officer, as, without a word of reply, he stood for a moment with his eyes on the floor, subduing his anger, possibly his terror, to the point of being able to speak without a change in his usual tone.

"I regret," began Stanhope; but at this word, uttered by the son of the man of whose death he had just been accused, Colonel Deering drew back, and lifting his eyes, which at the moment seemed to emit blood-red sparks of suppressed menace or hatred, he said:

"If you will give me fifteen minutes in which to think over the position in which I am placed by this absurd charge, I will excuse you from any regrets you may be upon the point of expressing." Then, as he saw Stanhope's startled look, he added, turning to the officer: "I will make you no trouble. You will take this"—and he drew from his pocket a small revolver, which he handed over as he spoke—"and, if you see me attempt to escape, you will know what to do with it; only do not speak, for my thoughts come slowly and will not bear interruption."

The officer, who had met all kinds of men in his life, and who thought he understood this one, glanced at Stanhope, and then folded his arms with the pistol held at cock in his right hand. "We have fifteen minutes to spare," he observed. "If you wish to avail yourself of them in this way, I see no objection to your doing so. But I should think you would prefer to use them in settling up your affairs for departure."

The colonel, who had seated himself beside a small table, frowned at this suggestion, but answered nothing. He had already fallen into thought, and the tick of the clock on the mantel was now the only sound disturbing the quiet of the room.

As that tick went on, and the commanding head of the colonel fell forward into his two hands, Jack and Stanhope stole awed looks at each other and then at the quiet and imperturbable figure of the officer standing with unmoved patience at the other end of the room. Did they feel the oppression exercised by the tremendous personality of the accused man, or did they expect from this deathly quiet some result which would be as startling as the delay?

If they did, they were soon disappointed, for when twelve heavy, oppressive minutes had slipped laggingly away, the colonel's bowed head slowly rose, and they saw on his scarred and severe features a resolution to make no scene, possibly to attempt no denial.

"You have my thanks," were his first words, as he rose and stood before them in all the dignity of perfect selfpossession. "That I should be accused of a crime, was a surprise, needing some time for my comprehension; but you must have your reasons for it, or such a man as Stanhope White would not lend his presence to this outrage. I shall, therefore, go with you without hesitation or demur, confident that my innocence will assert itself as soon as I am examined."

"You are wise," remarked the officer; and at once took his prisoner in charge.

XXXII

A Soul's Struggle

It was about three o'clock when Stephen Huse left his buffing-wheel to attend to some matters at the other end of his shop. He had been thinking of Mary, and his face, as he wandered back through the unsympathetic surroundings of his work-room, wore a wistful look that for the moment robbed it of the ruggedness which had been apparent in it since he changed his employment. He loved the child but little less than he loved his life. Perhaps he loved her more; but he did not yet realize this, for she had never been threatened with danger, and his life had, and his chief consciousness was with the latter fact and the untold shrinking which had accompanied it.

The day was dull, as I have elsewhere said, and in the shop, which was always dark except at the end where the window was, the shadows were as thick as those of a winter's twilight. He may have felt their gloom, or he may merely have missed the necessary light to find the object he required; for his brow knit as he paused near the long table in front of the door, and his mouth, which had once been beautiful, compressed itself into a troubled line that made his face seem like the image of some bitter thought. But in an instant, and with a flash like that of a darting sunbeam, his whole countenance changed, and he stood suddenly transformed.

On the table, among a heap of rusty tools and battered books, lay an exquisite white rose. It was so fresh he should have smelt its perfume before he sighted its beauty; but it was the glistening whiteness of its dewy petals that first attracted his attention, and made his old heart leap and his eye moisten as he lifted the sweet blossom and laid it tenderly against his cheek.

"It is from Mary," fell in quiet conviction from his lips. "She has sent me this as a token of her welfare and happiness." And he kissed it again and again, as he rapidly considered in his mind which of the many customers who had visited him that day had been her probable messenger.

He finally fixed upon a certain coachman who had brought him some bits of harness to replate; but he did not long busy himself with conjectures as to how the rose came there, for the sweet certainty which it brought of the success of his schemes in Mary's regard so filled him with delight that his mind had no room for any other consideration. Carrying the blossom over to the window he laid it down and endeavored to go on with his work; but he found this difficult, and never perhaps, in the whole course of his experience as an electroplater, did he feel the hours drag so slowly as they did that afternoon.

He wished the day over, that the time might come for reading the evening papers. For he was sure that if Mary had really engaged herself to Mr. White, she would remember that he could only learn of it through the papers, and so see that some announcement of the fact should be made in them. When the hour did come, and he hurried to the corner for the papers he desired, he was astonished to perceive half a dozen other persons crowding eagerly about the news-stand. Evidently some occurrence of importance had taken place on that day; but as no event disconnected with Mary could affect him, he did not even ask what was the cause of the excitement which he saw, but seized the first paper that came to his hand and dashed with it back to his retreat.

It was a cold night, and his fire had burnt low; so he threw the paper on the table while he refilled his stove. Some minutes consequently elapsed before he turned to it again; but, when he did, this is what he saw printed in large characters at the head of one of the columns.

"Arrest of Colonel Deering for the murder of Samuel White, whose death has hitherto been supposed to be the result of accident."

Surely, surely, his eyesight was playing him false, and he beheld some fanciful phrases born of his own overheated imagination, and not a plain statement of facts, such as one is accustomed to meet with in the practical sheet before him. But when he had stepped nearer, and read not only these words but others, explaining this arrest and detailing the evidence which justified it, he broke forth into such a peal of laughter, that any passerby hearing it would surely have paused to ask what could be the occasion of so terrible a burst of emotion from a quarter usually given up to the practical details of daily work.

But, happily for him, there was no one at this moment in the halls or on the sidewalk in front of the house, nor was there an echo powerful enough to carry his tones to the ears of Mary or the conscience of Stanhope. So the sound of this awful mirth passed unheeded; and, when quiet came again, there was no one to note the intense and contradictory emotions which now swept across this most mysterious man's face, as he bent above the columns which followed these startling headlines.

He had already seen that the charge had been preferred by Stanhope, and that there was conclusive evidence that the accused was on the spot when the shot was fired; but as he read of the self-possession of the prisoner, who denied his guilt, but admitted that there was a long and standing grievance between himself and the dead statesman, his passion found vent again, and he threw up his arms with an exultant gesture, crying:

"Caught! caught like a badger in the toils! His recklessness has undone him, and I am free!" And plunged back again to the paper with an avidity which almost tore the sheet to pieces in his hands.

The next line that he read was this:

"*The police confident of the fact of murder, and the prisoner non-committal.* Since Colonel Deering's incarceration, he has been known to make but one request, and that was for the immediate recovery of one Thomas Dalton, who, as our readers will remember, disappeared from his home, at No. 6 Markham Place, some four weeks since, and who, this man says, is necessary to him as a witness."

"Ah!" burst from the reader's lips as he crushed the paper violently together. "Does he seek to drag me down with him in his fall? He cannot do it! Thomas Dalton is gone; wiped out from the face of existence! Even his daughter does not know where he is; and if God does, God will keep still. For my turn has come at last; or why these deadly coincidences pointing so unmistakably to the guilt of my bitter enemy?"

He read on. The reasons for the suspicion of Deering were given at some length; and as coil after coil of the evidence which had been collected against him lay unfolded before the astonished gaze of Mary's father, the satisfaction grew in his heart, and short, sharp exclamations fell from his lips, ending with a triumphant exclamation in which he seemed to sum up all his own joy and his enemy's defeat.

"Deering is lost, and I am free!" And the glance with which this was said travelled, as of old, to the death-dealing machine behind the curtain, but was no longer furtive or terror-stricken, but exultant, and so daring it almost reached the point of contempt.

But gradually, as he proceeded in his task and finished the columns devoted to this theme, the joy which had buoyed him up and made him young again faded from his countenance, till he grew more old and haggard than he had been before he commenced to read. The paper fell from his hands, and he sank into an attitude so fixed that it was evident he had been seized by a great horror which was slowly paralyzing him. Presently, however, another change came, and he leaped sharply to his feet and began pacing with rapid strides through the room, that, with its various machines and appliances for honorable toil, looked as far removed from the passionate struggle at present agitating this man's soul, as was his workman's garb from the intellectual aspect of his countenance.

The silence, which he for the most part maintained, gave way now and then to a cry, of which he seemed unconscious; and finally his emotions vented themselves in words, and such disjointed sentences as these issued from his lips in alternate whisper and shriek, as he was overcome by fear or reawakened to resolve.

"Why this recoil from accepting the release offered me? Why concern myself with a man whose death is my only salvation? If I keep still, his doom is certain; nothing can help him. The past and the present are both against him. The deeper they probe into his life the more reasons will they find for condemning him. That he should have remained on the spot so long is fatal to his cause. Not even his superhuman coolness and indomitable will can extricate him from the net into which he has so deliberately walked. He has destroyed a great man and must suffer the consequences. That he did not destroy him in just the way they think, is no reason why I should interfere. I have schemed, worked, hoped, prayed for this release for years, and now it has come! Why should I not rejoice over it? I do rejoice—I do! I do! I breathe a new life. Fear and shame have vanished; and when conviction has come, and this man is swept out of my life, I will be free to turn gentleman again and live with my lovely Mary."

"*Will I?*" The question rose in a shriek, like the burst of a flame lit unexpectedly in the gloom. "*Will* I?" He thought of her beauty, thought of her purity, thought of the marriage of which the white rose, even then shining in the dim recess of the window, was a symbol; and, as he thought, the gleam of awakened passion passed out of his face, till it was gray and wan as ashes that are ready to be blown away in powder.

"I have but to keep still and let justice take its course," wailed up from his breast after another moment of heavy silence. "I shall not have to do anything. It is only the other day that I stood here while he toyed with death, and then I made no sign. Why can I not do it again? It should be easy—easier than it was then; for I shall not have to be the witness of his doom. But it hurts me—hurts me in my heart of hearts. *Has* God found me? And is it His finger that is laid upon my heart?"

It was God who had found him, and His finger pressed heavily where it lay; and, though the weary sufferer struggled hard against it, it slowly caused the deep resolve of years to fade away till he stood once more a despairing, broken-spirited being in the solemn stillness of this incongruous room. But, though his spirit was broken, there was a light on his brow, which, while it was not that of happiness, had birth in a source that would have seemed to Mary's eyes much more precious and holy.

Yet the cause of truth and justice was not quite won, as was shown by the few additional words which fell spasmodically from his lips.

"It is such a complete release; it has not even left me a cause for fear. Even if Deering is tempted to talk and tell the whole story of our fatal connection, he can do me no harm, for I am Stephen Huse; and Stephen Huse and the horrors of that old camp in California are as wide apart as the poles. It is Providence who has done all this for me, and shall I fly in the face of Providence for the sake of such a man and such a foe? Mary would say yes; but Mary is an angel, and I am but a weary, worn-out old man."

But the spell was working, and the moment came when doubt seemed to vanish entirely from his mind and leave him with but one idea—the necessity for action.

Thereafter he was very still. He looked around him at his books, his mechanical appliances, the dread machine, and the tokens of the daily toil in which he had lately been engaged; but it was as a man in a dream, who has no especial interest in what he looks upon. Finally he took down his coat and hat and put them on in an abstracted way, like one under the sway of some dominating idea. When he was quite ready for the street, he glanced about him again, and, seeing the white rose shining on the window-ledge, crossed over to where it was, took it and hid it in the breast pocket of his coat. Then he reached up and put out the light, and, going quietly to the door, opened it and went softly out.

He had aged ten years since he came into the room one short hour before.

XXXIII

Stephen Huse

L ate in the evening an old man in the garb of a workingman came to the corner of—Street and Fifth Avenue. He had entered the avenue by the way of—Street, and, as he stepped into the broader thoroughfare, any one watching him might have observed that he stopped and looked somewhat dismayed as his eyes fell upon the crowd that still hung about the steps of the White mansion. But his hesitation, if it was such, did not last long, and soon he was seen pressing boldly through the throng till he reached the front of this very house.

There he paused, for a policeman was before him, and not till he had given some hurried explanations was he allowed to pass. But once allowed to mount the steps he had no further difficulty, though the policeman had warned him that he would not be allowed to enter, as Mr. White had sent out word that he would receive no more visitors.

He persisted, however, in ringing the bell; and, when Felix came, he made haste to tell him that it was not Mr. White that he wished to see, but the young lady who was at present living in the house.

Felix, who was discretion itself, looked at the old man and felt awe-struck. There was something in his face out of keeping with his general appearance; something that commanded respect and insured the honest purpose of his errand. Beckoning him in, Felix led the way to a tiny reception-room in the rear, and was about to leave him, when the old man took a card from his pocket and begged him to carry it to the young lady. It was a business card, on the face of which was an indefinable scrawl, which would have reminded a scholar of one of the Hebrew characters; but it said nothing to Felix, even if he took note of it, which I doubt, he being one of those invaluable servants whose curiosity is limited to the line of their duty.

Mary, who was in the library near by, gave an irrepressible start when she saw this card. Her father here! The surprising, the astounding news which she had just heard, of the pock-marked man's connection with Mr. White's death, had prepared her for the relief which her father must feel at this sudden removal of his enemy from his path; but she had not expected it to lead him here, especially in the character of Huse.

But she was glad he had come, for the diamond was sparkling on her finger, and she longed to make him a partaker in her joy.

She was dressed as he had never seen her, and under the excitement of her feelings was a radiant vision as she came into his presence. It seemed to impress him, but only for a moment, and before her smile had reached its fullness, it faded under the shadow of his heavy, hopeless aspect.

"What has happened?" she asked, coming very near to him and speaking cautiously, though the room they were in was quite secluded. "Are you still afraid of the man who has been found to be so very wicked? I thought you would be relieved by his arrest."

"Mary,"—he spoke thickly, and yet with a certain fervency, like a man who felt himself in peril and depended upon her for escape—"shall I risk my life to save a man who knows no gratitude? Colonel Deering did not shoot Samuel White with his own hand. Shall I make this known, when the end will be his release and my death?"

Mary, to whom this question came with paralyzing effect, staggered as this new flood of agony swept down upon her bright and budding hopes.

"Oh, why ask me?" she cried. "I am your daughter: can *I* condemn you to death? And yet if he is innocent—"

"You would not love me if I kept still?"

Her eyes, dilated with her sudden misery, flashed imploringly to his face.

"Truth is more than life," she whispered. "You would never be happy if you let your enemy perish under a false accusation."

"Do you believe that? Do you feel that? Is there enough goodness left in me for remorse?"

"Father, you are wholly good, or I could not love you so dearly. Have you not taught me truth and honor from the time I was a child till now? If you had not prized those qualities, you would have let me grow up without such teaching. Why do you ask, then, if you have any goodness in you?"

"Because I have been thinking evil; because, in my terror of this man, I have let myself be moved by wicked impulses; because, even now that I have confessed to you that his hand is innocent of blood, I yet shrink from making the fact known."

"But are you sure, quite sure, he had nothing to do with Mr. White's death?"

"He did not shoot him."

"He was in the house."

"He did not shoot him."

"How do you know that, father?"

"I do know it."

"And can you make others know it?"

"I can."

"By your word?"

"By my testimony, yes."

"Then you have no choice, father."

"I knew my angel would say so."

"Father, is there nothing Stanhope can do to make this duty less hard?"

"I do not know."

"Shall we try him? He is in a room near by. Shall I call him?"

"And tell him that I am your father? No, Mary. Your father is gone, lost, dead. *I* am Stephen Huse the electroplater; and if I escape at all it will be because no one will think of confounding me with the man once known as Thomas Dalton."

"Then I must be wary, too, and perhaps you will escape. This Deering cannot be so vindictive as to persecute one who has preserved his very life?"

"You do not know him, Mary; I have nothing to hope from him. It is the police who must save me—if I am saved."

"And the police will. Why, of course, the police will see that you come to no harm. Why are you afraid at all if you have their protection?"

"Because they are not omnipresent. Because I cannot explain to them my need for protection."

"Then what do you hope?"

"There is but one thing I can hope—to obtain Colonel Deering's release without his knowing it. If that can be done, I may continue to succeed in hiding from him my identity."

"That duty shall be Stanhope's to perform. He is so good, father. If he only knew—"

"I will see your lover, but you must let me see him alone. I cannot trust your discretion or your fortitude."

"Then let me go for him before any one else comes to take up his time. O father, father, when will we see the end of our troubles?"

"When I am dead," was his bitter reply; but happily she did not hear him, being too engrossed with the duty before her to catch the faint whisper in which he spoke.

"Shall I tell him that a strange man wants to see him, or shall I give him your name, and say that you live in the rooms where he once saw me?"

"The latter, darling. I do not think he will recognize me. Do I look like the man he once had a short conversation with?"

"Not at all. You are strange to me, and must be a stranger to him."

"Then call him, darling, and God bless my angel child!"

She would have lingered for a final embrace, but he would not let her.

"Go," he cried, "go, while my determination lasts."

At Stanhope's entrance, the aged figure rose and took upon itself a semblance of dignity.

"Mr. White, I suppose," said he, trembling slightly, but meeting the young man's eyes with quiet resolve.

"I am Mr. White. You have business with me?"

"Yes, sir, important business. I read the papers tonight, and saw that a man had been arrested on suspicion of murdering your father."

"Yes; do you know anything about him? Have you evidence to give in this matter? You are an electroplater, I believe, living in a house I know something about in Markham Place. Did you ever see Colonel Deering there?"

"Yes, sir; he was in my place a short time ago. But that is not what I want to talk about. I have another thing to say; I—"

He talked so low, Stanhope unconsciously moved a step nearer to him.

"Go on," urged he; "there is no one here to be afraid of."

The old man made an effort. "Colonel Deering did not shoot your father," he declared.

"How! What! You tell me that? How do you know?"

"I saw him when he came out of this house on that fatal morning, and he was well around the corner on his way to Sixth Avenue before the pistol went off in your father's room."

The trembling which seized Stanhope at this unexpected announcement seemed to communicate itself to his strange visitor. "I—I hope you believe me," he faltered.

"I don't know what to believe. You heard the shot? You saw the man? And where were you?"

"On— Street, in an area there. If the man—Colonel Deering you call him—had not been so tall and commanding looking, I might not have noticed him; or if the sound of a shot from this house had not followed his passing by, I might not have remembered. But, as it was, I do, sir; for the man stopped and looked up before he went on, and that attracted my attention and made me see that he was the same gentleman who came into my shop not long ago, asking for Thomas Dalton."

"Ah, there is no doubt about his identity, then. You relieve me, Mr. Huse, relieve me wonderfully. Are you prepared to tell this same story to the police?"

"Yes, sir, if it is necessary. Is it necessary, sir?"

The quaver he could not keep out of his voice attracted Stanhope's attention, and made him look at him long and earnestly.

"You look tired," he said, "and nervous. Will you allow me to send for a glass of wine?"

"No, no, sir; it is nothing. I work late and feel any extra exertion afterward. When shall I go with you to the police?"

"I would say to-night, but you do not seem in condition to stand the excitement. Shall it be to-morrow, at nine?"

"Yes, sir; any hour you please. I merely want to do my duty; I have no interest in the man."

"Nor I; but he must not suffer unjustly. I shall see the police to-night, and to-morrow will call for you at your home, for the purpose of taking you before the superintendent."

"I thank you, sir; I am not as strong as I once was. To-morrow, then." And Stephen Huse began to shuffle toward the door.

But, half way there, he paused and looked about; and when he was in the hall he gave another scrutinizing glance around him, as if he would fix in his mind the looks of all he saw. To Stanhope, who had no clue to his thoughts, this looked like an old man's curiosity; but to Mary, who glanced after him from the depths of the long drawing-room, it passed for what it was—a father's interest in all that interested the child whom he loved so dearly, and yet from whom he had felt bound to separate himself as completely as though he were, indeed, the man for whom he passed.

XXXIV

OVERTAKEN

There was no work done in the electroplater's shop that night. Even the curtain which hung before Thomas Dalton's mysterious machine remained undisturbed, though Stephen Huse's wakeful eyes turned more than once toward it as the slowly creeping hours stole by.

Now that he had had time to think, he saw that there could be but one outcome to his contemplated action. The impossibility which remained of his giving any account of himself, beyond the few weeks in which he had been a tenant at No. 6 Markham Place, must, in case he was pressed to explain himself, lead to suspicions on the part of the police which could but end in the discovery of his identity. But he gave no token of weakening in his purpose; and when, at the appointed time, Stanhope appeared, he found the old man ready to accompany him.

There was a paler shade, however, over his strange and unreadable face than there had been the day before; and Stanhope, who could not know that in spirit the aged electroplater was struggling like a condemned man on his way to the scaffold, laid much of the suppressed agitation which he saw, to the old age of the man, and was accordingly considerate.

But at the entrance to the large building in which Huse had been told he would see the superintendent of police, his young companion saw that there was another reason for the old man's dread. Pausing in the doorway, he turned an anxious eye upon Stanhope and tremulously inquired if he would be obliged to meet Colonel Deering.

Stanhope, who knew little of what was before them, answered that it was possible, whereupon the other faltered out:

"I would rather be saved from confronting him. The day he was in my shop I thought him a trifle too peremptory, and we had some words. It would not be pleasant for me to stand before him as a benefactor. I had rather he did not know to whom he owed his release."

Stanhope, who was mainly struck by the repugnance evinced in these words—a repugnance which, if the truth were told, was not unshared by himself—said nothing save in the way of a promise to keep him and the colonel apart, if possible, and thus succeeded in getting the electroplater into the building and before the superintendent.

When Mary's father found himself really committed to his task, his manner changed and his appearance became almost prepossessing. Glancing about him and observing no one in the room except the keen but kind-looking man at the desk, and his silent secretary, he lifted his head and looked like the honest man that his calling demanded, while across his troubled face a faint smile broke, which relieved it from the expression of fear with which he had entered.

Questioned, he told his story substantially as he had done the night before in Stanhope's house; and, as it was a true story, all the astute listener's keen inquiries failed to shake it. The result was a conviction, on the part of all, of the colonel's absolute innocence, whereupon the superintendent nodded with kindly approval of the old man and said quietly:

"You will be glad to hear that this evidence of yours has released an innocent man.—Sergeant, call in the colonel."

With a quick start Stephen Huse glanced at Stanhope, who hastened to interfere.

"I beg your pardon," said he, addressing the superintendent, "but Mr. Huse has a strong desire not to meet Colonel Deering. If you could excuse him before the colonel comes in, he would be greatly obliged. He does not feel the need of thanks."

"Ah, and why do you not want to meet the colonel?" asked the superintendent, turning toward Huse with one of his quick looks.

The electroplater, driven to bay, rose with some dignity to meet the occasion.

"Because," he replied, with just a show of the resentment he so deeply felt, "I do not like him. He came to my shop a week or two ago, and was so overbearing in his manners that I conceived a great dislike to him. Truth and justice compelled me to tell you what I saw on—Street, under Mr. White's window, but truth and justice do not compel me to listen to thanks from a man I abhor. May I not, then, be allowed to escape them? Need he know through whose testimony he has been released?"

The superintendent, who was accustomed to surprises, showed but little of the astonishment he felt at this display of feeling on the part of this respectable workman. But he studied the old man's face and saw, or thought he did,—truth in its peculiar outlines. He, therefore, like Stanhope, laid much of this ebullition to the old age and consequent nervousness of the man; and, while he explained to him the impossibility of keeping back his name from public knowledge, he also assured him that he need not see the colonel if he did not desire it. And, pointing toward a door at his right, he bade him go into the small room he would find there and take a rest while the necessary interview between himself and the colonel took place.

Huse, trembling as much with fear as old age, passed hurriedly to the refuge offered him. As he was about to close the door, Stanhope, who had followed him, whispered kindly in his ear:

"When he is gone I will come for you. Meantime, rest quietly here; there is no one to disturb you."

The grateful look which the electroplater cast him affected him strangely. There was a likeness in it to some look he had received before, but he could not remember from whom it had come. While he was puzzling over this the colonel came in.

The superintendent, who had regarded this man as one virtually freed from suspicion ever since he had been informed of what Mr. White had reported in regard to him the night before, bowed apologetically as he met the prisoner's eye, and shortly said:

"Colonel Deering, I have a few questions to put to you, to which you need not hesitate to give straightforward replies. By what route did you leave Mr. White's house on the fatal day you visited him?"

The colonel, who had been looking at Stanhope, whose changed aspect he could not but note, answered with his usual slow impressiveness:

"I went away by— Street. I wished to go downtown, and chose to take the Sixth Avenue cars."

"Then you passed along the side of Mr. White's house?"

"Of course."

"Where were you when the shot was fired in Mr. White's bedroom?"

The colonel, with a quick look which spoke of sudden hope and confidence, answered at once and without hesitation:

"I was under his window. I would have told you this yesterday if you had asked me with the same appearance of being ready to believe what I had to say."

"Yesterday there was no witness to confirm your words; to-day there is."

The colonel, with a keen look about him which took in all the corners of the room, bowed, with his gaze finally resting on Stanhope.

"I cannot believe," said he, "that it is to Mr. White I owe this late confirmation of a fact which overthrows the whole theory of murder."

"No; I am but a messenger," quoth Stanhope. "The witness is a man who was in—Street at the same time as yourself."

"I thought my innocence would become apparent."

"Colonel Deering"—it was the superintendent who spoke—"have you any objections now to tell us how it was that you entered Mr. White's house at ten and did not leave it till half-past two? If, as you have admitted, there was an old grudge between him and you, you certainly must have needed a strong inducement to remain so long under a roof where you could not have felt yourself welcome. In justice to yourself, then, and to Mr. White, who cannot but feel a strong interest in this subject, I ask you to explain this."

The colonel, who had grown in height and breadth ever since he saw the possibility of release before him, bowed with a grand air, and answered in tones so urbane that one was tempted to ignore the note of condescension which, unconsciously perhaps, ran through them.

"Gentlemen, I will. While there was any doubt as to whose hand held the pistol by which Mr. White met his death, I felt that silence would be my best safeguard, as the explanation I had to give was so unusual in its character. But now that you recognize that the verdict given by the coroner was a true one, and that, despite the evidence against me, and the fact of an old animosity existing between Mr. White and myself, his death was an accidental one, I am ready to tell you by what chance I was shut up in his bedroom for the space of four hours.

"My errand to the house was to give him a pistol. That this was a suggestive present, and utterly out of keeping with the festivities of the day, I do not seek to deny; but I hated the man (his son, against whom I have nothing, will excuse my frankness), and wished to give him a shock, and possibly recall memories that would serve to dampen his pleasure on this day. It was for this reason I came to New York, and it was for this reason I did not give my right name to the girl who opened the door. I wished to surprise him, and, having learned from workmen who had been in the house some particulars in regard to its inner arrangement, I was prepared to make use of whichever staircase was not taken by the person who carried up my name. She took the back stairs, so I immediately went up the front, but I did not venture to show myself till I heard her returning steps on the rear stairs. Then I pushed boldly forward and entered his presence, just as I had planned to do, unexpected and unannounced.

"You do not know what reasons I have for execrating the memory of your famous fellow-citizen, nor do I intend to tell you, for they are all buried now, and I have no quarrel with his son; but they were reasons strong enough to give me a keen pleasure in the surprise I had caused him. When he turned and met my eye, I saw that the occasion which had made our last meeting memorable had not been forgotten, and that his bridal felicity had come to a sudden end. My errand was therefore accomplished, and, leaving my wedding-gift upon his table, I paid him a hasty adieu and attempted to bow myself out. We had not spoken a word.

"But I made a mistake. I had meant to go by the rear door, and if necessary by the rear staircase; for Mr. White had risen from his desk at my entrance and now stood between me and the door by which I had come in. He was not looking at me, was indeed turned away from me, for my presence was not pleasant to him; but I was looking at him, and that is why I withdrew by the bedroom door—which, as this young man knows, is in close proximity to the other—and did not know my mistake till I had closed it upon myself and turned to go down-stairs. Then I saw where I was, and was about to start forward to rectify my mistake, when the key turned sharply in the lock and I found myself a prisoner.

"Gentlemen, it had been half a lifetime since I had had any dealings with Mr. White, and I possessed no means of knowing what sort of man he had become. I therefore took it for granted that he had locked me in from some sinister motive, and, not being the man to make a disturbance upon such a supposition, I immediately turned back into the room and settled myself to wait calmly, and without any outcry, for the release which must come sooner or later from his hand.

"I had cigars with me and I smoked, and, when the time seemed long, I rose and sauntered about the room, which contained many objects of interest to an art-lover like myself. That he would leave me there and go to the church, I thought very probable; but that hours would elapse, and neither he nor another come to my release, I had certainly not anticipated. However, my cigars and my patience both held out, and having seen by a glimpse into his travelling bag, which I found half open on the trunk, that he must come into the room again before starting upon his wedding journey, I gave myself no alarm and quietly awaited developments.

"They came about half-past two in the form of a quick step at the door and a hurried turn of the door-knob. As the step was his, and the failure to open the door an evident surprise, I saw that my first surmise in regard to his motives for locking the door were false, and that the action which led to my imprisonment had been the result of absent-mindedness or inadvertence. This conclusion was immediately verified by his expression when he finally entered, the astonishment with which he encountered my tall form awaiting him in the middle of the room being as great as when he saw me a few hours before crossing the threshold of his study.

"'Were you ignorant of the fact that you had locked me in these rooms?' I asked, advancing with as great a display of courtesy as I had before shown of animosity.

"He gave me a look which I took to mean acquiescence. I accordingly added with still more politeness:

"'Then I will at once take my departure,' and bowing low stepped past him into the study. As I turned to leave the room by the door I had before missed taking, I caught a final glimpse of him. He was standing just where I had left him, and in his hand was the pistol I had brought him as a present a few hours before. It was the last I ever saw of Mr. White.

"I went down by the rear staircase and out at the front door without meeting any one. My ways are quiet, and I presume I made but little noise. However that may be, I was not heard, or there would have been a witness in the house to prove that I departed before the pistol was fired. The shot came just as I was passing under the windows on— Street, and it startled me somewhat, so that I looked up. But I did not go back, for reasons you can readily understand; nor did I know how fatal that shot had been till the extras were called in the street, and I saw the city flags at half-mast.

"An odd and unexpected explanation, is it not, but a true one, Mr. Superintendent, as I call upon your witness, whoever he may be, to testify."

Stanhope, who had hardly drawn a full breath during this long recital, heaved a deep sigh, and walked slowly to a distant window. He believed the man, but, oh, how he hated him! He could hardly prevent his feelings from showing in his face.

The superintendent, on the other hand, felt a curious drawing toward this calm, implacable, self-poised specimen of Western manhood; and, though he could not feel sympathy with the vindictive nature of the man, he could not but give credit to his dominating spirit, which nothing could subdue and but little daunt.

He did not, however, betray his subjection to the fascination which had been exercised upon him, as he remarked with well-simulated coldness:

"That was a strange mistake of yours, to take a gentleman's richly furnished bed-chamber for the blank walls of a back hall."

But the colonel, not at all abashed, smiled with easy superiority and said:

"You forget that I backed out of his presence. If you will allow me, I can show you in an instant how it was done. You see those two doors? Well, they are situated very much like those in Mr. White's study. Now, supposing I meant to go out of one, and, having my eye on you, inadvertently passed out of the other, do you not see how unapt I would be to see into what surroundings I had stepped until I chose to turn around." And, as he was suiting the action to the word, he opened the door, and before the superintendent could stop him, had backed into the small room in which Stephen Huse had taken refuge.

A cry went up behind him from the startled electroplater, an involuntary cry which made the colonel turn about with amazement in his face.

"Ah," said he, "whom have we here?" And before Stanhope could interfere, he stalked up to the shrinking figure of the old man and looked him piercingly in the face.

"The face is familiar," said he. "Ah, I know; you are the man who lives in Thomas Dalton's old rooms," and was about to turn nonchalantly away, when Stanhope, who stood anxiously in the doorway, unfortunately remarked:

"He is the man who saw you under my father's window."

At which, with a quick impulse, the colonel turned back; and looking closer and closer at the old man, who seemed to shrivel up before him, he muttered a low exclamation, and sarcastically observed:

"I do, indeed, know this man," and returned with lifted head and a strangely satisfied mien to his former position before the superintendent.

When they all left the magistrate an hour later, Colonel Deering was seen to lean calmly down and whisper a question into the electroplater's ear. It was short, and its meaning was perfectly apparent to his shrinking listener.

"When and where shall we have our talk?"

The answer was equally short and pregnant.

"This afternoon at three, and in my shop."

PART V

COLONEL DEERING

XXXV

New Fears

S tanhope went home from this interview a very happy man. The doubt of his having been justly or unjustly the indirect cause of his father's death, as well as his later fear lest that death had been a most wilful murder on the part of this dangerous stranger from the West, had both yielded to the explanations which he had just received; and, though he could not but harbor feelings of the greatest repugnance toward the man who had thus gloried in poisoning his father's final hours, the relief to his feelings was immense, and quite altered the aspect of the future.

But it was not this which gave him the glad, free air of a new-made man, and lent to the strange and lowering day a sunny atmosphere which made his walk home a delight and a remembrance. It was a letter which he had received upon leaving the house that morning which had made this change, a letter in a strange hand and from an unknown correspondent, but which contained a piece of news that took away the last impediment to his marriage, and made the harboring of any further doubt as to his duty, uncalled for and impossible.

It came from Utica, and ran thus:—

Dear Mr. White:

"I am requested by Stephen Yelverton to inform you that his daughter, Miss Natalie Yelverton, has lately died in Liverpool, England, of a severe attack of pneumonia, which came upon her just as she was on the point of embarking for this country. He says the news will be of importance to you and begs me to acquaint you with it at once.

Hoping, etc., I am,
Yours with esteem,
Alvin G. Teare

It was a bona-fide letter, and it lifted a weight from his heart; yet he had not reached his present height of satisfaction without making one effort to insure its absolute truth. Being now assured that the communication sent by his father on the day of his marriage was the result of the interview which that father had held with Colonel Deering, he took the opportunity when parting with that gentleman to surprise the truth from him.

"Colonel Deering," he had cried, as the latter lifted his hat, on the corner of Bleecker Street and Broadway, "who was Natalie Yelverton?"

The hand which had been raised in final salutation fell suddenly.

"Do you not know?" asked the colonel, eying the young man with a strange mixture of interest and astonishment.

"No. Beyond the fact that she was the daughter of Stephen Yelverton, and that my father desired me as a final reparation to marry the girl, I know nothing. Do *you?*"

The silence and the unchanged look with which his inscrutable companion regarded him proclaimed that he did; but he said nothing, and Stanhope went boldly on.

"I received a letter this morning, saying that she was dead. Is the news true? Can I venture to marry where I will with a free heart?"

The colonel, rousing himself, bowed with deep, perhaps sarcastic, reverence.

"You take it for granted, young man, that I know more of the Yelvertons than you do. Perhaps you are right. I have no quarrel with you, as I have said before, and so will say for your relief, that Natalie Yelverton is dead, and that you may marry where you will."

It was this which had made Stanhope so joyous.

His first word when he entered the house was to Flora.

"O Flora dear," he cried, going up to her with outstretched hands, "I have just heard facts which throw quite a different light upon the causes which led to my father's death. The shock which disturbed him so, and which, perhaps, by unsteadying his hand, resulted in that accidental pulling of the trigger which we so deplore, was due entirely to the appearance of this Deering in his study and afterward in his bedroom. And, further, I have this morning received reliable information that Natalie Yelverton is dead, so that no bar now remains between me and happiness. Later I will tell you all, but now I must see Mary."

"You will find her in the library. If you are happy, she is not. Her cheeks are like chalk, and she starts at every sound, like a person in mortal terror. She will not explain herself, but something worries her almost beyond her endurance."

The answer which Stanhope made was to fly at once to the library, where he found Mary awaiting him in a state of agitation that was as mysterious as it was alarming.

"My father?" she gasped, and then paused frightened. Her fear had betrayed her into revealing her heart's deepest secret.

"Your father?" repeated Stanhope, wonderingly. "Have you heard from him?"

She paused, stammered, and then tried to relieve herself.

"Did I say *my* father?" she asked. "I mean *your* father. Did you find out if he was murdered?"

Stanhope, who was naturally unsuspicious by nature, accepted the amendment without doubt or hesitation.

"How deeply you take my interests to heart! No, Mary, he was not murdered, actually; but, indirectly, his death was due to the deadly hostility of this man. The shock of seeing an enemy, when his mind was full of sweetest hopes, unnerved him and led to the accident which terminated his life. But Colonel Deering did not shoot him."

"Was—was the testimony of the poor old man whom I introduced to you of value, then? Did it serve to release Colonel Deering?"

"Entirely; your father's humble successor has been of great benefit to us, and sometime we must make him feel it."

She was silent for a moment and seemed to be gathering up strength for her next question.

"Did—did not the colonel make some recognition of the service which had been done him?"

Stanhope shook his head, astonished at the intensity of the interest she showed.

"The colonel and this aged workman have met before, and not to their mutual good-will. We tried to keep the two from an encounter, but we did not succeed—Mary, Mary, what is the matter? You are sick, fainting!—Flora! Flora!"

"Hush, hush!" entreated Mary, starting up with renewed strength. "Do not call any one; it is you who must give help, you who must save him. I cannot keep my secret any longer. It is my *father* who is in danger. *He* is Stephen Huse, and Colonel Deering is his mortal enemy."

"Stephen Huse is your father? Ah, ah, I know now why his look was familiar. And he has disguised himself to this extent? O Mary, Mary, now I know why there has always been a look of anxious terror underlying all your joy."

She rose from his arms and stood trembling, looking about mechanically for her hat and wraps.

"We must go to him," she cried. "Whatever he says, I will not leave him alone, now that he has been seen and recognized by his enemy. He was recognized by him, was he not?"

"I fear so. I remember looks and words now that scarcely attracted my attention before. Get on your things, love, and we will go at once to Markham Place. Colonel Deering shall not injure your father while I have an arm to protect him."

XXXVI

Confronted

The day, late as it was in the fall, had in its lowering atmosphere a strange element of heat. As Stephen Huse awaited his visitor, in the centre of his shop, a low rumbling in the skies overhead explained why it had become so dark that his spare, worn form, swaying slightly under the weight of his emotions, looked like a wraith hovering in the murky dimness.

There was a whir in the room, but it did not come from the revolving buffing-wheel. That mechanism was stopped, but on the large banded table at the side of the room, Thomas Dalton's machine was in full motion.

Three o'clock had struck, and Deering's ample shadow (he was never slow in keeping appointments) was apparent upon the muslin-covered door.

"Come in," cried the trembling occupant, not waiting for the knock he had so long dreaded.

He was answered by the immediate entrance of the colonel, whose features, seen in the obscurity of this beclouded day, seemed to wear an expression peculiarly threatening and determined.

"You see I am prompt," said he. "I should not have been so particular, if you had held to your oath and not sought to escape me by every stratagem in your power."

At these words Stephen Huse—or shall we call him Thomas Dalton?—rose with unexpected spirit.

"I was on the spot, Robert Deering, fifteen years ago, when the summons came to meet you in a certain house on Amity Street. But the deception you practised upon me then exonerated me from appearing again at your beck or call. Dead men—and you sent us word that you were dying—have no further claims upon the living. Besides, you gave us distinctly to understand in this same message that we were free to go unscathed."

"Your companion did not so interpret my words. When he saw that I was still living, he took my presence as a command, and paid the forfeit he had incurred, at once and without demur, although it was his wedding-day."

"Samuel White was of more determined spirit than I, and more nice in his sense of honor. I am simply a weak and trembling old man, who loves life and means to cling to it."

"You did not so interpret my message yourself," persisted the colonel, with a total disregard of the other's final sentence; "or why did you spend all these intervening years in disgraceful subterfuges to escape the doom you have yourself acknowledged to be your rightful due?"

"Shall I tell you? Because you did not deceive me on that day of the riot. I saw you, saw you behind the partition of the room in which you had hidden yourself, and, perceiving that you were well and unhurt, realized that you had been playing with our misery as with a toy, and that in thus allowing us to leave the house alive you were but planning a fuller and more overwhelming revenge when the time should be ripe or your patience be exhausted. The devilishness of the idea turned me forever against you. To an honorable adversary, I was prepared to yield up life and all its interests; but to a demon who endeavored to plant hope in our hearts, so that our overthrow at the last might be more complete, I was ready to throw down the gauntlet of defiance. White did not see you; and as I did not think it desirable to acquaint him with a fact that would embitter his whole future life, he went on his way rejoicing, while I—Well, compliance had not saved me, but subterfuge might, so I resorted to subterfuge. The name I had changed once, I changed again, and, leaving all my old associations, carried my child into scenes which I hoped would raise a barrier around us, and win for me the oblivion that I now craved. That my success has been poor, and that you gloat over it, shows you to be the wicked and implacable man I have always considered you."

The colonel, who had folded his arms while the other was speaking, kept that brooding posture for some minutes after he was done. But there was no relenting in his countenance, that was fixed and set as a stone.

"Samuel White did not talk when he saw me," he quietly remarked at last. "The mark on your hand has suffered somewhat by the efforts you have made to destroy it; but if the least outline remains of the cross, which is at once an acknowledgment and a promise, then you are more than a coward to hesitate when I tell you that your final hour has come. Let me see your hand! No crisscross scars can hide the old outlines from my eyes." But the hand of Thomas Dalton remained shut, and the wild, haggard gleam which had been driven from his eyes by the indignation of the moment was fast glazing them again.

The colonel smiled sarcastically.

"You are mine," he declared. Then, with a certain curiosity in his voice, he added, "How came you to be in the area opposite Samuel White's window at the moment he shot himself?"

"I was hiding from you. I saw you turn the corner and slipped into the first refuge I came to."

"But why were you in the street? Did you expect any catastrophe, or think to escape your own end by being a witness of his?"

"No; I was only desirous of warning him. I had seen you the day before, in a crowd, and realized that our doom was approaching. So I hung about his house, thinking to utter a word in his ear as he came out. But I was too late; the avenger was already in his presence."

But the colonel's curiosity was not yet appeased.

"Had you not seen fit to tell what you saw then, I should now be in prison instead of here. Why did you tell? Did you think gratitude would make Robert Deering forget justice?"

"No; I have a conscience and I listened to it. It has cost me my life."

The sardonic look which responded to these words ended in an equally sardonic laugh.

"Then you have learned to love virtue during these years. I had not expected this; but it served me well in a most unexpected strait, so I cannot say that I regret it."

Dalton's lips fiercely compressed themselves. He was stung into fury.

"Do you think, that because I was once driven by hunger and desperation into the committing of a deplorable deed, I have in my breast no sense of right and justice; that I could have a daughter as pure and high-minded as an angel, without feeling some of the impulses of goodness? *You* have no crime upon your soul, and yet I would dare swear, in the presence of that God whose thunder is rumbling above us, that there is more love of goodness in my breast to-day than in yours. The heart which for twenty-five years has been the abode of naught but a horrible revenge cannot contain much virtue."

"The name which you choose to give to justice is of your own choosing, and as I have waited so many years for the penalty which you owe me for the crime you perpetrated upon the one beloved object of my life, you should rather praise my forbearance, than complain of my rigor."

"Better, far better, I had paid the penalty at once."

"So I thought then, but you had your choice and you took it. Riches had such an allurement to your eye."

"I have never been able to enjoy them."

"I did not mean that you should."

"But my daughter will. Your revenge dares not extend to her."

"Again that word revenge."

"Will you, if I follow my doom, leave my daughter to the happiness she has the right to enjoy?"

"I do not fight with women."

"She and Samuel White's son love each other. It is the one proof I have received that Providence has not entirely forgotten me."

"Is the weapon to be a pistol this time?"

Thomas Dalton fell back, a white horror settling grayly over him.

"You have had time to choose your method; I see that you have studied the subject thoroughly," observed the colonel, waving his hand significantly toward the books ranged over his head.

The taunt passed unheeded over Thomas Dalton's bowed head.

"I should like to have seen her again," came in soft murmur from his lips.

As if in answer, a quick cry rose from the dark corner behind the colonel. Mary had entered the room from her old apartment in the rear, and now stood panting and eager, with her hands held out in passionate entreaty toward her father.

"Father, father, are you well?" she cried, and passing hurriedly by the colonel, she took up her stand between them. "Any harm that is done to this old man must be first done to me, Colonel Deering. I am his child, and he has been long enough under the dominion of your hatred."

The colonel, who liked spirit in a woman, and who, whatever were his faults, was never known to be harsh or dictatorial to such of the sex as roused his admiration or moved his heart, bowed with respectful interest and gently remarked:

"I shall do no harm to your father. Whatever harm is committed upon him will proceed from himself."

"As in the case of my father," spoke up another voice in his rear.

The colonel turned sharply and confronted the severe face of Stanhope.

"Ah, a trap!" he exclaimed. Then, calmly surveying the young man, he severely remarked: "You had better ask what crime that father committed; yes, and what crime this man has committed, before you meddle further with me, and my rights as an avenger of innocent blood."

"Crime!" repeated Stanhope.

"Crime!" reiterated Mary, turning to her father with wild and entreating eyes.

"Crime," denounced the colonel, frowning heavily upon all three, like a gigantic figure of Fate.

"I have deceived you, Mary," came forth in low tones from the cowering form of Thomas Dalton. "I am not the guiltless man you think. I did commit a crime—it was in the old days before you were born—and the terror of the remembrance has been upon me ever since. I killed—"

"Let me tell the story," broke in coldly from the immovable colonel. "If you children, with whose innocence I have no quarrel, had been content to leave me undisturbed, I should not have broken the secrecy of years by telling a tale it is not for your happiness to hear. But your persistence drives me to explanations, and now they shall be as full and impartial as the justice for which I stand."

Mary, frozen to her place, stared at her father. Stanhope, drawing a step nearer, took up his stand where he could meet the colonel's eye.

XXXVII

In the Sierras

Twenty-seven years ago there was terror in a certain camp at the foot of the Sierras. Snow had fallen in the night, and the huge wall of desolate peaks rising to westward was gradually donning a garment of white, which meant death to most of the trembling wretches cowering despairingly beneath it. A gaunt spectre had come into that camp two weeks before. Its name was Starvation. No man had cozened with it then, though every man was conscious of its presence; but now it sat in their midst and was to every man as his fellow.

"There were twelve men in the party, two of whom stand before you to-day; and there was—a little child. That child, a boy of twelve, was—my son. (Hold up, Dalton! It is part of your punishment to hear this tale.) A boy of twelve in a place where strong men trembled! Bernard was his name, and he was a beautiful boy, with a stock of glee and pluck which had not yielded under repeated disasters, and which, in the face of the new danger now menacing the whole party, still kept up his spirits and unconsciously put to shame the more down-spirited men.

"I loved him—better than my life I loved him; and when I reflected that I had brought him to this place to die,—I cursed the gold fever that had maddened me, and vowed, if I ever got him away in safety, that I would shut my eyes on the glittering metal, even if I found it lying in nuggets at my feet.

"There was another fiend besides Starvation in our camp that day. It was Sickness. A week before, our guide had died, and we had not dared to whisper the name of his disease. But we fled as we saw the breath leaving his body; and, being ignorant of the road, fled into the wrong defile, and so lost six precious days in wanderings that, rightly directed, might have carried us over the mountains before the snow came on.

"This morning another man had wakened delirious; but, though a shudder had gone through the camp, the greater evil closed our eyes to the less, and whether we should attempt a passage over the mountains or wait in the hollow for the possible coming of a relief party was the one burning question of the hour.

"I was for going on, and so was White, and so was—this man; but others held back in dreadful terror of the fast-filling gorges and blinding snow-blasts. If we did not start at once we could not go at all; and the grizzly spectre, grinning upon our hesitation, would soon be the sole inhabitant of the camp.

"Some must go, even if some must stay; and as this fact became known, a movement took place in the camp, and through the gray mist of flying snowflakes you could see the silent passing to and fro of gaunt and famished men, as they separated into two parties—six going toward the mountains, and six, of which the sick man was one, remaining on the slope descending toward the fast-disappearing plains.

"My little son stood laughing, right joyfully, between the two.

"'Which party shall I join?' he cried, turning gleefully from one side to the other, as if he were engaged in a merry game. Then, as I cried his name, reprovingly, he flew like an arrow from a bow and nestled in my arms, saying, 'Did you think I would forsake you, father? I only wanted to tease, just because we may not be able to tease much longer.'

"Some food, of which there was very little, had been given us by those who had decided to stay behind and wait; and, as each man seized his portion, I noticed that the boy got less than his share. But I said nothing, for I knew that, unless chance led us into the one safe and direct pass, we would all perish before our scanty supply of bread was exhausted, so weak were we all from fasting, and so visible was the trembling in our limbs, as, one by one, we attempted to move.

"You who have never known cold or hunger, whose portion it has been to reap the golden results of your fathers' sufferings, try to picture for a moment the horrors and the desolation of the scene as we stepped into Indian file and turned our faces from our companions toward the unknown dangers before us. Death lowering in the cañon, death frowning from the peak! Yet to my fearless nature the prospect of threading these perilous defiles was less horrible than that of waiting in dreary inaction for relief which might never come; and had it not been for my little son, whose feet were obliged to take two steps to mine, I should not have bestowed a thought upon the danger before us, in the fierce satisfaction which I always felt in moving.

"We started—White, this man, Dick Hughes, two Kentucky brothers, and myself, with little Bernard bringing up the rear. But presently, as I was feeling for a place in which to plant my feet, which were strangely numb even for that icy atmosphere, I found myself blinded by something more impenetrable than the drifting snow, and, throwing out both arms, I fell forward into what seemed a bottomless pit. The sickness had seized me, and the party had to go on their way without me.

"Look at my face and guess what that sickness was. It ravened in my huge frame, and for nine days made the little hut that was put up for me an abode of demons. Then, I woke to the realization of things; and the first object that my eyes rested upon was my little son, alternately shouting and weeping in his delight at seeing my eyes without the glassy look of delirium in them.

"'O father! you know me?' he cried, and kissed my hands, and the blanket that covered me, till I could have shrieked aloud in my terror; for I knew now what ailed me, and realized the peril he was creating for himself.

"But I was too weak to shriek, and, when his transports were somewhat abated, I could only lie still and gaze at his face, and try to read in its flitting expressions what had happened in the camp during the blank of my long unconsciousness. Nothing that was good; for the white, soft skin, which had once been so beautiful, was drawn tight across his cheek-bones, and the eyes, for all their dancing mirth, had in them that hungry look which I had previously seen in the eyes of the men alone.

"'Has no relief come?' I moaned at last.

"He shook his head and cast around the little hut a cautious look which was quite new in my experience of him.

"'No,' he whispered, leaning over me till his mouth was close to my ear. 'But you need not care about that; I have food enough for *you*.' And with a sly step, the reason for which I was slow in understanding, he crept to a corner of the hut, and stooping down, with more than one startled look over his shoulder, appeared to dig away some earth from the bare soil of the floor, and lifting up what looked like a piece of bread, he smiled with such heavenly sweetness, it made the tears come to these marble eyes of mine.

"But I was hungry, and took the morsels he broke up for me, with a greedy delight, that awoke in him the wildest pleasure. With every mouthful I swallowed, he gave a low cry of intensest gratification; and when, my craving satisfied, I turned my tired head to the wall and fell asleep, the last thing I heard was the little prayer he was uttering by himself in happy thankfulness.

"The man you see before you is not the man who loved Bernard Deering; and when I woke, it was with quite a softened heart I turned to search for my little lad in the gloom of the windowless cabin. He was not in sight, and I tried to call him; but it was several minutes before he came to my side, and then it was from the outside camp where he had been with news of my probable recovery.

"'O father!' he exclaimed, as the door swung back, giving me a fleeting glimpse of miles on miles of desolate whiteness, 'there is hope for us, hope for all. A strange hunter wandered into camp this morning, and he says that there is another party coming up from the plains who have no end of provisions in their wagons.'

"'Then I must get well.' was my reply. 'They must not find a dangerous malady in camp to frighten them from giving us assistance. Did that other man die, Bernard?'

"The little fellow hung his head, then looked up brightly. 'He did not have any little son to look after him.' said he.

"'And the party which went up the mountain? Have you heard anything from them?'

"'They all came back a week ago, father. There was no finding the pass, they said; but, since their return, they have regretted that they did not go on.'

"'And why, my little son? Is it so dreadful here in camp? Are more men sick or starving?'

"'It is very dreadful, father; how dreadful you can imagine, when they are no more afraid of coming into this cabin than they are of crouching over the fires out there?'

"'And you—are you quite well, my son?'

"'Oh, yes;' but the words came with forced energy, and I saw that the relief must come soon, or my little son would not be with me long, to awaken in this hell of horrors and despair a gleam of love and promise.

"I must have gone to sleep again very soon, and in that sleep I had a dream. Let that old man there—he is younger than I by several years, but who would think it?—tell me if it is not a true one!

"In a cañon between huge rocks five men were plodding with hopeless persistence through deeper and deeper drifts of snow. Winds that seemed loosed from the bursting gates of an angry heaven hurled in their faces the stinging crystals whose mad gyrations had already bewildered their brains. Feet that failed to lift themselves, bodies that swayed and all but yielded to the driving storm, showed by their failing strength that these five men could go but little farther if the fury of the elements kept up and the stretch of towering rock did not soon offer them some refuge.

"The first man, he who led the party, was tall, robust, and determined-looking. Though he was but twenty-three, he had the self-poise and varying charm natural to the true adventurer, and, in this hour of possible defeat, held his head high and called out more than once encouraging words to his less happy companions. The next one was a slighter man, but he had nerve also, and when he fell he rose again and pushed forward with a certain dogged courage after his sturdy leader. Their hearts had been set upon finding gold, and nothing short of death was going to daunt them. The three last, who straggled helplessly in the rear, seemed to have less enthusiasm to sustain them. One by one, as I looked, I saw them falter and fall, and though roused, even held up, by the two men who went before, they would soon fall again and nestle their faces in the snow, as if seeking the grave it continually offered them. Their doom was upon them, and soon only the two leading men were to be seen struggling on, while in the desolate pathway behind three long white mounds slowly reared themselves into view where all had been level before.

"The sight of these three mounds seemed to awake in the breasts of the remaining two an increased horror, for, ere long, the first man threw up his arms in despair and rushed heedlessly forward, as if to demand from Fate a speedy release from this terrible cañon, while his companion begged for mercy with his face turned toward heaven, and stumbled, as he followed, like a man in delirium.

"I looked to see two more mounds rise in the smooth waste of that narrow pathway, when suddenly a cry broke from the foremost, and they both paused, with gestures of wild relief and delight.

"In the pitiless wall of stone towering upward on the left, a refuge had opened, and the next moment they were within the snug hollow of a narrow cave, where the winds could not reach them, and where their eyes, almost closed by the driving snow, were free to open once more to the light of day.

"There is virtue in the ravening wolf, but not in the rapacious gold-seeker. Instead of falling on their knees and thanking Heaven for their almost miraculous escape, they began to peer about among the rocks sloping down toward the entrance, and, when their glances met again, there was a hungry look on either face that did not spring from the craving of their famishing bodies. 'Gold!' came from the cracked lips of one, and 'Gold!' fell from the swollen tongue of the other.

"They had bread with them, and they ate, but their glances were ever wandering to the dark rocks above their heads and to the stony floor beneath their feet. Suddenly one of them gives a great cry and bounds to a fissure at the side of the cavern. He had espied some thing there, and when he comes back his hand is in his breast and his body is shaking with the violence of his emotions.

"'Let me see!' shouts the more powerful man. Whereupon, slowly, reluctantly, the hand comes out, and there in the palm, clenched tightly by three straining fingers, behold a nugget of gold, big enough to make both men exclaim, and then stand silent, panting, and eager.

"'We must take care of ourselves,' was the comment of one, as they both sat down again, knee to knee and shoulder to shoulder, for mutual warmth and support. 'Life begins to be worth something.'

"The other laughed, and began to portion out the bread and calculate how long it would last. Meantime, the snow still fell, closing up the entrance of the cave, inch by inch, till hardly enough light sifted through the opening to enable them to see each other's faces.

"'The flakes are growing larger and fall more slowly,' quoth he whom we have called the leader. 'It will be clear by night, and to-morrow we can turn back again. Shall we keep our discovery a secret, we two?'

"'Yes, yes,' chimed in the other. 'Have we not found treasure at the risk of our lives?'

"'The camp is a poor place,' was the next remark, 'but it is better than the mountains. If we are ever to be rich men and win our way to the front, we must keep body and soul together till relief comes. Are we to be comrades henceforth?'

"'We are to be comrades.'

"'Courage, then! And if food fails us, we will live on gold. Hurrah! hurrah!'

"It was a faint cry, for the once stalwart man was at the last ebb of his powers; and, when it was uttered, his head fell forward, and the two men huddled together and dozed, while slowly and more slowly the drifts accumulated and the winds sank, till there was silence in the air, and the storm was over.

"Three days after they showed themselves again in camp, weaker than when they left it, but with a fierce look in their gleaming eyes, that was not natural to them, but sprang from the demon who had taken up his abode in their hearts when their feet stumbled upon gold in the wild recesses of that hidden cavern.

"This was my dream, and I ask this livid, shaking old man before me, if it was not a true one?"

XXXVIII

BERNARD

A groan came in reply. It pierced Mary's heart, but it made the relentless speaker go on still more quietly and impressively, like some old-time genius delivering an oracle.

"Soon I knew whence this dream came. As I woke from this vision of human avarice, in a scene where awe and gratitude alone should have had place, I became aware that I was lying close against the wall of my cabin, and that two voices, so changed by privation that I barely recognized them, were uttering eager words in my ear. You know who the speakers were—one of them is not far from us now—and they were talking thus outside of the hut, because they feared my listening ear within. Poor fools, they little realized how wide were the chinks in those hastily constructed walls! Their talk was of gold and of the discoveries they had made in a cavern halfway up the cañon; but they might have spared themselves the chill of the night blasts, for the tale fell dully on my ears. I found the irregular breathing of my little son, lying over my feet to keep me warm, more absorbing in its interest to my troubled mind; and, listening to this broken music, I slipped off again into dreamland.

"My awakening was startling. Loud and angry voices were in the room, amongst which I heard a piteous cry—the cry of my little son.

"Leaping to my feet—I who could not turn in my bed the day before—I beheld those two demons struggling over a piece of bread which had fallen from Bernard's hand. He had been surprised while digging it up from its hiding-place in the corner; and they, mad and perishing, but with a longing to live begot by the promise of gold which their discovery had given them, had felled him, each with a cruel hand, to the ground.

"'He has stolen it!' 'He has robbed the mess, and we all starving!' shrieked the one, and yelled the other. But the little voice arose, weak and trembling, with a last effort: 'No; I saved it for my father. It was my own bread, which I did not eat.'

"God! and they had killed him! He died, in another moment, there before my eyes. No use for me to fall upon his thin and tender body and shriek to Heaven for the life which had vanished from his loving eyes.

"He was dead! And those two wretches, with the bread lying between them on the floor, saw me close those beautiful orbs, and did not kill themselves in horror of the deed which had caused me this unspeakable loss.

"Two hours later relief came, and they had bread, all the bread they could eat. But the sight of my dead darling was my sole food by day and night, and I asked for no other save the justice that was due me on his slayers.

"Our camp had now dwindled down to four men, which with the party that now joined us made up the number of twenty-three. Calling them all together, over the body of my little son, I asked for a court to be held, and punishment to be meted out to the men who had killed him. As there was every prospect of our being obliged to remain where we were for months, no one could expect me to break bread, or breathe for another day the same air, with the murderers of my boy.

"There was no sheriff amongst us, but there were twelve honest men, and, when I told them my story, they decided that the murderers must die. This was the law of the camps, and no court quarreled with it. Otherwise murder would have been rampant, and life and wealth entirely insecure.

"The sentence, when it fell, seemed to sting these men hotly. They stared at each other, and then stared at me, and then, with the realization which food had brought them of the justice of their sentence, they bowed their heads and said that it was well.

"They were handed over to me to dispose of. I did not wish this; but, as it was understood that each man was to be his own executioner, there seemed to be a bitter justice in my being made the witness of their retribution.

So when night was come and all was still in the camp, we went to the distant spot which had been chosen as the scene of this final tragedy. It was half up the very cañon which they had threaded weeks before with hearts full of desperate hope. They had no hope now, and their white, still faces showed it; but, as they approached the path which led to the El Dorado they had discovered, the cheek of one grew hot, and the hand of the other began to tremble, till the passion that was within them found vent, and they both cried out, 'A fortune for a reprieve, Deering! We know where there is wealth enough to make the whole three of us kings!'

"'So do I,' was my quiet response, and the answer seemed first to stun and then to overwhelm them. 'I do not sell the justice that is due my innocent son, for all the crowns that could be piled up in Europe!' And they said no more, and we went on our way.

"But a burning dart had cleft my breast, that sank and sank, with more and more biting venom, into my heart with every forward step we took. What reparation for my life-long loss was there in the death of these men on the brink of such wretchedness as threatened us all at this dreary time?

"None; they would be but receiving a release instead of a punishment. While I would lie groaning for the touch of my little son's hand on mine, and the whisper of his loving words in my ear, they would be lying at peace under the snow, asleep like him, and doubtless as sweetly.

"I could not bear it. Life stretched out before me a hideous blank. Why not fill it with a horrible interest, in the way of a living punishment for these two pitiless men who had struck and killed a little, innocent child? I looked at them and determined to follow the impulse which had seized me. The one man loved money because it would bring him power and position; the other, because of the ease and luxury it promised. I would let them have their will; and then, when life was buoyant, and they possessed money and influence and *children*, dash the cup from their lips and make them taste the dregs of despair, just as I had done, and was doing, and should continue to do as long as breath was left in my body.

"That they would refuse the respite offered them, I did not fear. I knew my men, and I knew the greed of gold that lies at the base of all human nature.

"So when we came to a halt at the place appointed by their judges, I did not utter the one word they expected to hear, but busied myself with building a fire. That this would arouse their wonder, I expected; but I offered them no explanation of my movements, and forced them to wait, without apology, till I was ready to face them again. Then I spoke, as a strong, determined man with justice on his side should speak:

"'You have offered to buy a respite; but the Deerings do not sell. Swear that you deserve death, and that you will embrace it when the day comes round on which I remind you of your oath, and I will let you go your ways for the space of twelve years lacking four months'—the age of my little boy.

"They were like men hurled into sudden light from the darkness and dimness of unrelieved night. They stared at me and then shouted aloud, staggering to and fro over the snow, like drunken men, till gradually they became used to the idea, and the man now before us shrieked out:

"'Twelve years! One could crowd a long lifetime of enjoyment into twelve years if one had unlimited gold!' While White, who was of a less impulsive temperament, raised his handsome head and seemed to tread the world down under his feet, as he said:

"'What do you mean, Deering? You would delay this shot twelve years, and then expect us to kill ourselves, each with his own hand, according to the sentence passed upon us this day.'

"'I mean that—a year for every year of my son's life. Do you accept?'

"'We accept.' It was the weaker man who spoke.

"'And you, White?' I urged, though I saw the hunger for life flaming in his eye.

"'Let me live to gain the place I feel myself capable of holding amongst men, and I shall be willing to die'

"'Then take this oath, Samuel White. "On the thirteenth day of July, 1863, which is just twelve years lacking four months from to-day, I, Samuel White, promise to meet Robert Deering, at whatever place he shall appoint, there to fulfil upon my own proper person the sentence of death which has this day been rightfully passed upon me."'

"It was a grim oath; but he took it, with the stars shining down upon his upturned face and lifted hands, and so did his companion. And when, the words said, I asked each of them for his pistol, and shot it between the towering walls of the cañon, there was something in the echoes that followed which seemed to give assent to the oath, and roll the words up to the mouth of that distant cavern where there awaited them the wealth to make those twelve years easy, and the end hard.

"When we again faced each other, I thrust each man's weapon into the fire. When the muzzles were red hot, I drew them forth, and holding them toward their owners, I said, 'That I may know you possess the necessary courage to fulfil this oath, take this burning steel into your grasp, and imprint, each of you, a cross upon the palm of your left hand.'

"They recoiled, but I would not listen to remonstrance or appeal; and in a few minutes they had each impressed upon their quivering palms the seal and promise of future retribution; and the tragedy of Hunter's Cañon had reached its climax.

"We went back to camp, and I nursed them in secret till their hands were healed. I said in explanation to my companions, who had heard the shots in the mountains and wondered to see the three of us return alive, that our numbers were too few for two such strong and able-bodied men to be spared; and they, drooping already at the prospect of a long winter in a none too healthy camp, acquiesced in my decision, and allowed the men to reenter their midst and take up their places again in the fast lessening circle.

"And there they remained strong and well, while the true-hearted and the brave sank one by one around us, till only we three were left. That they would fail or fall I had never feared; for I knew then, as I know now, that eternal justice would hold, and that the price I had fixed for these men to pay would be laid down before me to the last jot and tittle. And it has been, though it has taken time, much longer time than I anticipated. Samuel White paid his debt on the day of his greatest pride and felicity; and now this man, after twenty-five years of struggle and subterfuge, is about to pay *his*."

XXXIX

The End of a Long Revenge

There was silence for a moment; then the colonel, gazing at the drooping form of his victim, added in a changed voice:

"Shall I let these children see the warrant which was made out for your arrest in San Francisco, and which I have carried in my pocket for twenty-six years? I am the sheriff of Fresno County, and have the right to arrest you on the spot."

Thomas Dalton, goaded to madness, both by this tale and the effect it had evidently had upon Mary, gave one bound and threw himself upon his whirling machine.

"No, no," he cried, "I will spare them that shame!" And clutching the deathly knobs before him with his two scarred hands, he threw back his head in final appeal to Heaven.

"Father! father! what are you doing?" shrieked his child, bounding after him as she saw his face turn gray and a convulsive shudder run through his cowering frame.

But Robert Deering, who now knew the purpose of that machine, tore her away, and, holding her back with an arm of steel, watched with the calm but triumphant eyes of a Nemesis the struggling form of his ancient enemy.

But Mary was not to be stilled.

"He will die! Stanhope, he will die! There is poison, fire, death in the horrible machine. See! see! he is sinking; tear him away!"

Stanhope had been thrown into a sort of trance by the story he had just heard; but he heard this cry, and, bounding by the colonel, he was about to seize her father by the arm, when the colonel's left hand, rising slowly, pointed so significantly at the old man's face that Stanhope instinctively paused and let his own eyes rest upon it in troubled inquiry.

A strange look was on the old electroplater's upturned countenance. It was not that of death, white as he was, but of baffled intentions and disappointed hopes.

"It will not work; it is too weak!" rose in a shriek from his blue and quivering lips; and, overwhelmed by shame, he fell back, crushed and powerless, into Stanhope's arms.

The colonel, with a great laugh, loosed his grip of Mary, and strode lightly forward.

"I knew that it was child's play," he cried, and laid his own hands on the copper knobs, when—was it Providence or was it doom?—a sudden and tremendous bolt swept down from the long threatening skies, and, adding its power to that of the machine, smote that powerful frame, and in one instant laid it an inert and breathless mass at their feet.

THEY ALL FELT THE SHOCK, and it was some minutes before Stanhope could recover his powers sufficiently to realize what had occurred. But, when he did, he made but one bound to the dead man's side, and, feeling in his breast, drew forth from a secret pocket an old and discolored paper, which he hastily opened.

Giving it one look, he uttered a cry of surprise and staggered to his feet. Turning toward the old man, who was feebly bending over the fainting form of Mary, he seized him strongly by the arm.

"Are you Dalton," he cried, "or are you Yelverton? He addressed you as Dalton, but this warrant is made out against one Stephen Yelverton."

With a dazed look, Mary's father mumbled over the two names as if both were strange to him. But Stanhope, upon whom the light of new hopes seemed breaking, increased the pressure of his hand and hoarsely whispered, "If you are Yelverton, she is Natalie. Say so, and make a man of me at once!"

At which the poor, forlorn, and much taxed father roused, and giving Stanhope one intelligent look, answered mechanically, "She has been called Mary since she was three years old, but her true name is Natalie—Natalie Yelverton. Your father knew this name, and Deering knew it; but no one else, not even herself."

XL

The Bow of Promise

Flora sat in her lonely boudoir, a prey to thoughts that were almost indignant. Why had Stanhope left the house so suddenly, without giving her the fuller explanations her interest in the subject of Colonel Deering's release surely demanded? Was Mary as near to these interests as herself? Had not she, the widow of Samuel White, the first right to know why his suspected murderer had been allowed to go free?

She could not understand this treatment. Though she had overcome her passion for Stanhope, she had not lost her love for Mary, and waited with the utmost impatience for their return to the house from which they had gone so unceremoniously.

At last she heard a carriage stop in front, and, though Stanhope and Mary had left on foot, she ran to the window and looked out. A coach stood at the curbstone, and from it she was amazed to see step, first Stanhope and then a very feeble old man whom the former took tenderly by the arm and led up the steps. While she was wondering over this, Stanhope appeared again, and this time assisted from the carriage Mary, whose drooping head and listless form showed that she was in an almost helpless condition.

Flora, who at this sight had immediately rushed downstairs, was in the vestibule to meet them. Stanhope, who had now taken Mary in his arms, carried her first into the parlor and laid her on a divan. Then he turned to Flora, and, indicating the old gentleman who had feebly followed them, said with that smile which won all hearts:

"This is Mary's father, Mrs. White. As you see, he is not at all well, and I must ask you, out of the goodness of your heart, to entertain him till I can prepare proper accommodations for him. As for our little Mary, she has suffered a great shock, like the rest of us, indeed, from the thunderbolt which fell an hour ago in Markham Place."

"You have been struck?"

"No; *we* have not been struck. But—" Pausing to look at the old man standing between them, he did not finish his sentence; nor did Flora hear for some little time the explanations over which she had made herself so unhappy that afternoon.

When she did, she felt that she could not sufficiently reproach herself for the injustice of her feelings, and endeavored to make such reparation as was possible, by doing everything in her power for Mary and her father. She nursed them both through days of illness, and was rewarded at length for her efforts by seeing the light of intellect return to the pale face of the old man, and the bloom of health to the youthful cheek of Mary.

Meantime Stanhope spent many hours in contemplation upon his father's life as it was now revealed to him. Though overwhelmed by the disclosures which had been made to him of that father's early crime, he could not but admire the power of mind with which the final shock had been met and the terrible debt paid.

That in the face of immediate death, and at a moment when life was brightest, the world-renowned statesman and triumphant bridegroom could so ignore his own despair as to calmly plan such a performance of the duty before him as would insure the least suffering to those he left behind, roused the admiration of his son, as it would have awakened the gratitude of his wife had she ever known the true history of her husband's unhappy end.

That the doomed man should have pursued his intentions of marriage in face of the dread penalty before him, showed the calmness of thought he brought to bear upon the situation. To die without marrying her, however specious he might make his explanations, would, in this carping, suspicious world, not only have raised questions against her honor, but robbed her of those advantages of wealth and position it was too late now to accord to her by will. While to die from a seemingly careless shot so soon after their wedding would equally insure her the commiseration of her friends and the large dowry which he doubtless felt to be her due.

The letter which he wrote her, and the suggestive gift he sent, were but an added touch, all showing his anxiety to save her all unnecessary pain; little realizing, and in so far happy in his ignorance, that a secret lay at the bottom of his young bride's heart, which would lead, through the remorse thus engendered, to that sifting of facts from which would spring the very disclosure he was evidently so anxious to avoid.

That he should think of his only son and plan so deeply for his happiness, in the one short hour he took before his marriage, was perhaps not so strange. With the prospect of speedy death rising before him in the unlooked-for presence of his implacable enemy, his thoughts would naturally fly to Yelverton, destined like himself, no doubt, to pay at this time the debt of their mutual crime; and, thinking of him, he would also think of the daughter, and of how she was the only woman in the world who would never be able to reproach Stanhope for his father's crime.

So with the determination of a strong heart, bent upon lightening as much as he was able the possible shame and suffering hanging over the head of the one most dear to him, he had recorded his wishes and issued his commands, with all the precision and force of a great mind holding its own under the heaviest shock of fate.

That Samuel White dwelt on these wishes, and that they gave him the one gleam of light possible to him in those final hours, was soon to be made known to Stanhope from other sources. One day, as he was leaving the house, he encountered Mrs. Delapaine, and the sight of this old friend recalled to him a fact he now felt doubly anxious to have explained. This was how she, who professed not to have seen Mary till she met her in this house, came to recommend her to Mrs. White as a companion.

Mrs. Delapaine seemed to be as eager to talk to him as he to her.

"When are you going to be married, Stanhope?" she asked, as soon as they were seated together in the parlor.

"Soon," was his quick reply. "As soon, indeed, as Miss Dalton is able to stand up in this room and receive the clergyman's blessing."

"Good! She needs care, and you need repose. Will you forgive an old woman if she puts a personal inquiry? I think you will, since you must know she has a motive for it. Stanhope, are you perfectly happy in this marriage? Is there not some small inward sting connected with it, that worries and annoys you? If there is—"

"But there is not. I have my griefs, but Mary is innocent of them. In my marriage with her I hope for perfect union and perfect peace."

But Mrs. Delapaine was not satisfied. She looked at him and drew her own conclusions. "Something worries you. Is it remorse for having accused an innocent man of crime, or is it the remembrance of Colonel Deering's sudden death, coming so soon after his release, that has plowed those fresh furrows in your forehead?"

"That were enough to do it, Mrs. Delapaine. To see any man die before your eyes by a stroke of Providence is a painful sight; but when that man is connected with all there has been of disturbance and trouble in your life, the pain becomes a horror and cannot soon be forgotten."

"I realize that, and yet—and yet—your eyes do not meet mine, Stanhope! You have some secret distress which I should know; for—"

"For what, Mrs. Delapaine?"

"I am your father's deputy, and feel a responsibility for your happiness more than you will ever know."

"My father's deputy?"

"Hush! I have tried to keep my secret, but have failed. I must know if you are really happy, or I shall never be able to sleep for thinking that I should have told you of the letter I received from your father on the day he died!"

"A letter? You, too! O Mrs. Delapaine, what was in it?"

"Have you ever thought, do you still secretly think, that for any reason you should not marry Miss Dalton?"

"Not now. I did once—I did yesterday, perhaps—but not now."

"Still it would make you happier, would it not, to know she was your father's choice for you?"

"Miss Dalton?"

"Yes, or Miss Yelverton, which is her real name, I believe."

Stanhope recoiled.

"Ah, you know that! *He* wrote you that?"

"Read this letter; I have had it in my pocket a dozen times when I came to the house, but have always refrained from showing it, thinking that all was going on well enough without my interference. But, lately, something in the atmosphere of the house, something in Mary's face and your own excited manner, tells me that all is not as well as it seems, and so the letter has come out at last. Read it, Stanhope, and acquit me of all further responsibility."

Stanhope took it. He could not tell her that the trouble in the house sprang from the discovery of an honored father's early crime, and the heavy retribution which had followed it. That he and Mary must bury in their own forgiving breasts, hoping by their mutual love and sympathy to gain ultimate peace and resignation.

The letter which Stanhope read, and which was the third and last of the three written by Mr. White before he went to his wedding, ran thus:

Dear Mrs. Delapaine:

"In a short hour I am going to change my condition, and marry, as you know, a young wife. Before I do this, and so enter upon duties which may distract my mind from claims which are now paramount in my consideration, I wish to record in these few words to you, the nearest and oldest friend of the family, one desire which I cherish in regard to Stanhope's future.

"This is his marriage with a young girl he has not yet seen, and probably has not as yet heard of. Her name is Natalie Yelverton; but, for reasons I see no necessity for stating here, she is living at present, or rather her father is, under the assumed name of Dalton. I do not know her, but I do know her father, and nothing that could happen to my son would so please me as his marriage with this young woman, who I am assured is both good and beautiful. If therefore at any time you discover a way to bring these young people together, you will do what would please his mother, could she see you from above, and take from me a responsibility which I fear I am but little fitted to bear.

"She lives with her father at No. 6 Markham Place. All the rest I leave to you."

"One would think he foresaw his fate," commented Mrs. Delapaine, as Stanhope's eyes rose from the page.

"My father had the forethought of love," was the low response. "Did you seek Miss Dalton, or did she seek you?"

"Neither. I was intending to go to Markham Place the day after recommending her to Mrs. White as a companion, but was forestalled by her appearance here."

"And you knew, what I did not until very lately, that her real name was Natalie Yelverton. Strange, strange! Ah, if you had realized how essential to my happiness was this knowledge, what suffering you might have spared me!"

And he told her of the letter he had himself received from his father, in which, unhappily, the name of Dalton had been omitted.

One scene and we are done. Mary Natalie White had been for three hours a bride, and though her father, called always Mr. Dalton, had not been willing to attend the ceremony of her marriage, he was waiting in an upper room to give her the blessing she had insisted upon receiving from his hand.

Old in experience if not in years, and feeble from suffering if not from age, he stood tottering in the centre of the room, waiting for the vision of youth and promise which was to soothe him for the misery of many years. At last it came, and, as his dim eyes turned to welcome it, a smile rose to his lips which was a day-spring of hope to the young bride.

Stanhope, who was not far behind, advanced with Mary to the old man's side.

"Is she not a wonder?" he cried, lifting the veil which covered her face, with a touch as proud as it was tender.

"A wonder that I do not deserve to look upon," responded the father.

But she, with a warm glow, and a look that was almost inspired, threw her arms about his neck and softly whispered:

"I have something to tell you, father. When the minister asked so solemnly if any man could show just cause why we should not be lawfully joined together, I felt for the moment an unreasonable fear lest the imperious voice of one we knew would sound in my ears a dreadful menace. But before the instant was gone, and while I was still trembling with the thought, there came to me the sudden vision of an angel face, and on that face, which could only have been Bernard's, I saw a smile. It was our marriage blessing, father."

The old man caught her to his heart, and for a moment there was holy silence in that room.

A Note About the Author

Anna Katharine Green (1846–1935) was an American writer and prominent figure in the detective genre. Born in New York City, Green developed an affinity for literature at an early age. She studied at Ripley Female College in Vermont and was mentored by poet, Ralph Waldo Emerson. One of Green's best-known works is *The Leavenworth Case*, which was published in 1878. It was a critical and commercial success that made her one of the leading voices in literature. Over the course of her career, Green would go on to write nearly 40 books.

A Note from the Publisher

Spanning many genres, from non-fiction essays to literature classics to children's books and lyric poetry, Mint Edition books showcase the master works of our time in a modern new package. The text is freshly typeset, is clean and easy to read, and features a new note about the author in each volume. Many books also include exclusive new introductory material. Every book boasts a striking new cover, which makes it as appropriate for collecting as it is for gift giving. Mint Edition books are only printed when a reader orders them, so natural resources are not wasted. We're proud that our books are never manufactured in excess and exist only in the exact quantity they need to be read and enjoyed.

Discover more of your favorite classics with Bookfinity™.

- Track your reading with custom book lists.
- Get great book recommendations for your personalized Reader Type.
- Add reviews for your favorite books.
- AND MUCH MORE!

Visit **bookfinity.com** and take the fun Reader Type quiz to get started.

Enjoy our classic and modern companion pairings!